Benetton

Benetton

The Family, the Business and the Brand

JONATHAN MANTLE

LITTLE, BROWN AND COMPANY

A *Little, Brown* Book

First published in Great Britain in 1999 by Little, Brown and Company

Copyright © 1999 by Jonathan Mantle

A CIP catalogue record for this book is available from the British Library

ISBN 0 316 64083 2

Typeset in Dante by M Rules
Printed and bound in Great Britain by Clays Ltd, St Ives plc

Little, Brown and Company (UK)
Brettenham House
Lancaster Place
London WC2E 7EN

Contents

Contents

Acknowledgements

This book has been researched and written with the co-operation of the Benetton family and business, but is entirely independent of editorial control by Edizione and Benetton Group. The author would like to acknowledge the assistance given by the following members and associates of the family and the business, without whose time and effort this book would not have been possible: Luciano, Giuliana, Gilberto and Carlo Benetton; Carlo Gilardi; Oliviero Toscani.

Also Veronica Artuso, Emma Cole, Louise Hurren, Paola Innocente, Domenico Luciani, Seema Merchant, Laura Pollini, Elisabetta Prando, Vittoria Rubino, Federico Sartor.

The author would also like to thank the following: Jerry Bauer, Carole Blake, John Hinchliffe, Georgina Howell, Alessia Melli,

Acknowledgements

Virginia Nicholson, Caroline North, Roberta Oliva, Paolo Panizzo, Suzanne Ruggles, Nicky Samengo-Turner, Alan Samson, Linda Silverman, Edda Tasiemka, Mike Wells, Bill West, Piero Zantarello.

Alla Mia Carissima

Prologue

Thirty-eight thousand feet above the United States of America, 1998

Luciano was in the air, reading a fax. In the few minutes he took to read it and assemble his thoughts, he would have travelled from Nevada to California. Distances were time and cost to Benetton.

Elsewhere in the private jet, there were media relations people and people from the commercial department. Most of them were asleep; some of them were not even born when the business began.

Eight thousand shops. Eight billion dollars. The next move. The next press conference. The imagery . . . the United Nations . . . Toscani . . . the green hair. How much longer could he keep going?

Benetton . . . the questions . . . the answers . . . the family. Even the question no one asked out loud, but a tiny number asked in their minds. Were they not just a family, but *the* Family?

Eight thousand shops. Eight billion dollars. This was the reality. There was another time, however, when this was the dream and he was the dreamer. When the capital city of your country was another world and tomorrow was a million years away. When the land and the furniture and the china were all gone, and you bartered anything you could find.

Luciano rarely looked back, and only in a detached spirit. He could recall most things as they really happened, but he often claimed not to be able to do so, and he hardly ever spoke of them. Unlike Toscani, he did not need to reinterpret the past, endlessly, according to the needs of the present.

Toscani . . . the questions, the answers. Luciano read the fax and dictated his thoughts for the office to call the recipient with the answers. By this time they were over California. They were heading for the next press conference.

And, afterwards, in so many minds, the questions remained about the family, the business and the brand. About Luciano himself, who by this time would have flown on again, to Hawaii, Tokyo, Ho Chi Minh City, Phnom Penh, Yangon. Luciano spent most of his time in the air. It was almost as if, beneath the sophisticated exterior of the globetrotting billionaire businessman, there was still a small boy frightened of staying in one place on the ground for too long.

1   Birth of a Salesman

Badoere, northern Italy, 7 April 1944

The war had divided Italy; now it was tearing it apart. The Americans and British were advancing from the south and the Germans were retreating in the north. From the air, American B-17s and British Lancasters were reducing village, town and city to rubble. This was the Allied war in Europe, before the coining of euphemisms like 'collateral damage', when this still meant cold-blooded murder.

When the bombs reached the ground, the story ended quickly, if you were lucky, and slowly if you were unlucky, after the screams died first beneath the rubble. Elsewhere, on the ground, in this part of northern Italy, the retreating Germans were also under attack

from Italian communist partisans, for whom anyone who had sup-
ported the fascist dictator Mussolini was a further target. In between
the air raids, the land battles and the warring partisans, hunger and
sickness were everywhere.

Badoere is a fine-looking market village a few miles west of the
town of Treviso. The village has a distinctive circular market place,
also distinguished by its colonnades and the smell of cattle drop-
pings. Before the war, the market here was the commercial and
social highlight of the week. Parents promenaded with children,
and boyfriends, under strict chaperonage, strolled with girlfriends.
The stalls sold everything from meat and vegetable produce to toys
and picture postcards. A photograph of the market in its glory days
still hangs on the wall of the local baker's shop. On the morning of
7 April 1944, however, the market was long gone, the square was
empty and there were new faces in the village. Among them were
the family of Leone, Rosa, Luciano, Giuliana, Gilberto and Carlo
Benetton.

The Benettons were sheltering from the threat of bombing to
their home town of Treviso, and shared a house with a farming
family. They were welcome guests for they paid their way, came
from a farming family themselves and owned small parcels of land
in the vicinity. Each day they tried to carry on life as normal. This
morning, Leone had already hitched a lift into town early to attend
to what was left of his bicycle rental business there. Now Luciano,
his son, was getting ready to cycle to school.

'Eh, Luciano,' the farmer's wife was calling.

Luciano already had his bag on his back.

'Luciano,' the woman was calling again, 'wait, don't go.'

Luciano Benetton was eight years old. It was a twenty-mile
round trip to and from school. It was bitterly cold in winter, but his
father had made a pair of handlebar covers from rabbit fur to keep
his hands warm. There were often threats of air raids and partisan

skirmishes and German roadblocks. But school was important, and the road was flat, like so many roads in the Veneto. His father wanted him to study and become a doctor. He did not want Luciano to suffer the misfortunes that had already befallen him in business. Neither did Luciano, for that matter. Luciano adjusted the bag on his back, ignored the calls of the farmer's wife and set off on the long road into town.

Treviso, the Veneto, northern Italy, 1935

After the mountainous snowscape of the Alps, the Veneto is a densely populated, fertile river plain of farms, vineyards and factories. This is a region of villas built between 1500 and 1700 by rich Venetians as summer homes to escape the heat and pestilence of Venice, and of historic walled towns like Treviso and villages like Badoere and Ponzano. Luciano Benetton was born here in Treviso, the first of four Benetton children, and although the family was poor, they were urban poor, not rural dirt poor, and the spirit of a better life through enterprise was alive in the Benetton blood.

Leone, Luciano's father, operated a small car rental business in Treviso and harboured the ambition to relocate his family from the tiny house of his parents-in-law to a home of their own in the town. Rosa, Luciano's mother, had been born in Ontario, Canada, where her parents had emigrated from nearby Ponzano and run a store, before returning with her parents to Ponzano when she was eight.

Leone already had three little cars for hire, and he was on the way to realising his ambition for the family to be able to afford a home of their own. If he wavered in this, there was a reminder in Ponzano of the fruits of success, albeit now withered; the Villa Minelli. This was built in the sixteenth century by a family of Venetian silk and wool merchants who once commuted here to its high-ceilinged, cool rooms by canal from Venice. In the surrounding farm buildings, their servants made wine from the local vines. By the time of Luciano's birth, the Villa Minelli had already been empty for over a hundred years, its rooms shuttered like so many of its kind, and many of the canals were clogged and filled in. But it was still a powerful symbol of the magnificent rewards – and the mortality – of human endeavour.

When Luciano was one and a half years old, Leone Benetton still had the same three little cars for hire, and the family was still living in the house of his parents-in-law. Rosa was pregnant with their second child. Leone Benetton looked around him and saw that this business plan was not going to work. He had been thinking about this for some time. He came home from work one night, and said 'I'm going'.

He always meant to come back. Ethiopia, where Benetton senior went, had been invaded by Italian troops under the direction of the dictator Mussolini a year earlier. Many ordinary Italians, however, saw the opportunity to migrate to North Africa as nothing to do with support for Mussolini and everything to do with support for their families. Leone Benetton joined this exodus of young men determined to make their fortunes abroad. He sold his car hire business, travelled to Addis Ababa, and bought a truck. He trucked cement and building materials back and forth across the hot, dusty foreign country, and always on the dashboard was a photo of Rosa and Luciano. He stayed in workers' lodgings on the edge of town, ate hardly anything, reinvested everything in his new business and dreamed of the day when the name of Benetton would be known across Africa.

Then he fell ill with malaria. He spent six months in hospital until he was well enough to go back to work and went to find his truck. It was gone, stolen while he was incapacitated, and he never recovered his health or the truck or the photograph of his wife and son. In 1939, he returned home, broke and still ill, to his wife, son and baby daughter. Later, all he would tell Rosa about the theft was that the thought of the picture of her and Luciano in the hands of a stranger had been enough to break his heart.

But Leone Benetton was not about to give up. While the family remained without a home of their own, he started up in business in Treviso again, this time with a bicycle borrowed from his sister and a bicycle hire and repair business, in the Piazza San Francesco. This is one of Treviso's lesser squares, in the north-east of the town near the city wall and dominated by the tall, austere church of that name, patrolled by brown-robed friars. Within only a few months, however, in spite of the unpromising location, and with the help of business from the local garrison of the Italian army, Leone's bicycle fleet had grown from one to one hundred.

Mussolini had lured Leone and others to Africa and ruined their fortunes and their health. The fortunes of the dictator, however, were still in the ascendant and, like Hitler, he harboured ambitious commercial and cultural plans for his people. Mussolini had come to Treviso the previous year and addressed cheering crowds in the main square, the Piazza del Duomo. His plans included fashion. Mussolini had declared: 'An Italian fashion in furniture, decorations and clothing does not yet exist – to create it is possible, and it is necessary to create it.' 'Fashion assemblies' were organised, with the aim of eliminating from fascist homes the influence of French fashion, 'which exalted the woman as broomstick, the first cause of moral imbalance'.

In the same year that Leone Benetton had returned home, ill and broke, from Africa, Mussolini demonstrated his moral balance by siding with Hitler upon the outbreak of the Second World War.

Benetton

Piazza San Francesco, Treviso, 1942

For a couple of years, the war hardly impinged on the Benettons, Ponzano and Treviso at all. The bicycle business grew in the square and the family achieved their ambition to move into a home of their own. They found a place in the Piazza San Francesco, near the bicycle shop, and on hot summer evenings the family would sit outside the shop in the square and eat ice cream. Luciano was by this time seven, his sister Giuliana five, and Gilberto, the third child, was one. Leone's health was subject to lapses as his business improved, but this was the price often paid by the successful entrepreneur. He took on three staff to oversee repairs and sales. He bought some cheap property which he rented out.

However, the insecurity of the times was growing beyond the control of the family; the war was coming home. In Milan, 150 miles to the west, British bombers devastated the city and killed hundreds of civilians. This was an act for which one survivor, as yet unborn, would claim to be eternally grateful. The Toscani family, whose father Fedele was a photographer for the Milan newspaper *Il Corriere della Sera*, already consisted of father, mother and two daughters. Exhausted by war and motherhood, Signora Toscani had already had one abortion when she found herself pregnant again. This time, however, the Royal Air Force prevented her from keeping her appointment with the abortionist. Her third child, Oliviero, was thus born and would follow in his father's footsteps as a photographer. One of his most famous and controversial images would be that of a newborn baby, and it would scandalise the children of the British airmen who had bombed his home town and slaughtered so many of its inhabitants, saving his life in the process.

A year after the Benettons had moved into their own house, the dictator Mussolini was deposed by the King, imprisoned, rescued by

German special forces, and installed as a German puppet in the token republic of Salo on the shores of Lake Garda. With the advance of the Allies from the south, German reprisals against the local resistance were becoming increasingly savage and frequent. The Germans often killed ten Italians for every German killed. The corpses of civilians were strung from trees and balconies of buildings. Many of them were mined and had to be blown up in midair by Allied sappers. In the Veneto, strikers were forced back to work at gunpoint. As the Germans began to lose control, the Allied bombing raids came nearer and grew in intensity. The family stopped sitting outside in the square in the evenings. Leone's visits to hospital, where he was having treatment for kidney disease aggravated by his malaria, were also becoming longer and more frequent. The bicycle business dwindled and the square echoed to the sound of goose-steps. With the German defensive line running straight through the Veneto, Treviso was becoming a target. Eventually, having lived there for just a year and a half, the family, like hundreds of others, were forced to move out of town. In their case, they went to the market village of Badoere, where the fourth child, Carlo, was born, and from where Leone continued to travel into Treviso to work and Luciano cycled to school.

Badoere, northern Italy, 7 April 1944

'Luciano,' she was calling that morning, 'wait, don't go.'

He was determined to ignore her and started pedalling his bicycle.

'Luciano!' This time the voice was his sister's. Although she was younger than him, he could never totally ignore Giuliana. At least he would stop for a moment, before setting off again.

'You can't go today,' she was saying, 'the bombers are coming.'

'They always say that. So what's new?'

'This time it's true, I swear it. He heard it,' she gestured to the cousin of the farmer, who had just arrived and who nodded.

'They'll never touch the school,' Luciano said, but he was thinking about his father, who was already in the town. There was no way to call him back, as his sister had called him, and as his mother was now calling them all inside.

Luciano looked back at the road to Treviso. At that moment, in the distance, from the direction of the town, the first air raid sirens were beginning to wail.

Much later, after the first wave of bombers had passed overhead and the first detonations had sounded, and then the second wave had come, the sound of the bombing had gone on and on until it seemed that it would never stop. Only then did they notice that it had stopped and there was silence, except for the sobs of Rosa Benetton. Another hour passed, and then, although they did not at first believe it could be him, the door opened and Leone Benetton appeared. He embraced his weeping wife and told them what had happened. He had reached the town as the bombing began, taken shelter and somehow survived, motionless, terrified, for hours, amid the rain of high explosive and the screams of the wounded and dying. After the raid, the town was like a charnel house. The dead and dying lay beneath the rubble or had been tossed into the streets. The river over which Treviso was built was stained a dark red. Even the dead were killed again, when the churches were shattered and funeral vaults spilled open. Over 1,000 of the living inhabitants of the town died.

Later, and too late for Leone Benetton, controversy would exist over whether it was the Americans or the British who bombed Treviso on 7 April 1944. Of one thing, however, there was no doubt. The Allies bombed the wrong town. The air crews mistook Treviso for a town further north, where Mussolini was believed to be hiding. A further, doubtful distinction was that Treviso, after Naples, had just become the most heavily bombed town in the country during the Second World War.

By June, the Allies had taken Rome; in August they reached Florence and liberated the city. Liberation, for Italians, was the freedom to wander in their country's ruins. In Milan, 23 per cent of homes were rubble and a further 36 per cent badly damaged. Four hundred thousand homeless people wandered the country. Forty per cent of the country's hospitals were out of commission or totally destroyed. Sixty per cent of state roads and 20 per cent of local roads were impassable. Eight thousand bridges had been destroyed, as had 50 per cent of the railway rolling stock, 60 per cent of locomotives, 90 per cent of the passenger cars, 80 per cent of the electric lines, fifteen miles of tunnels and 70 per cent of the harbours. Industry was in near ruins and the currency in a state of collapse. The only market was the black market, and the predominant colour of clothing was black.

In the Veneto, the temperature fell to −11°C that winter and food was chronically short. Apart from barter, the only source of food was the black market. In Treviso, the rubble remained where it lay, as did the bodies of many of its citizens. In Ponzano, the Villa Minelli was packed with starving refugees. In Badoere, the Benettons struggled with the rest. Leone's health was failing further; Rosa had developed a heart condition. But Luciano went on cycling to school as he had always done, his hands protected by the rabbit fur against the cold, confident in the knowledge, as he would recall: 'We were safe in the countryside, my father was alive, and we were all right.'

Milan, northern Italy, 28 April 1945

In Milan, the deposed dictator Mussolini and his mistress Clara Petacci were shot dead and their bodies hung upside down from a

11

lamp post. In a typical Italian touch, her skirt was pinned up around her ankles to maintain public decency. Crazed with relief at the death of Il Duce, whose alliance with Hitler had brought the country so disastrously into the war, many onlookers took photographs as souvenirs: one photograph of the scene, by Fedele Toscani of *Il Corriere della Sera*, was flashed around the world. Nearly fifty years later, Toscani's son Oliviero would plan a shocking worldwide picture strategy with Luciano Benetton.

In the Veneto, the Benetton family had moved back from Badoere into the Piazza San Francesco in Treviso. A sign on the shuttered shop door encouraged customers to seek out the proprietor at the house nearby, but there were few takers. His business gone, Leone went into a steeper decline, alternating between a hospital bed, and a bed in his father's house nearby. His suffering and facial disfigurement as a result of his illness were such that he would not even allow his children to see him. When Giuliana managed to visit him on her birthday, he covered his face with a blanket so as not to shock her. He promised her a special present when he was well again.

Piazza San Francesco, Treviso, 12 July 1945

On Luciano's tenth birthday, three months earlier, his father had paid him the compliment of giving him the job of adding up the figures for the annual working men's outing, to the cost of which he and others contributed each month throughout the year. This morning, Luciano was busy with this task. He was also responsible for looking after what little remained of the bicycle business. At the other end of the room, Giuliana was knitting a sock for Carlo, the youngest. Luciano, who was an observant boy, had noticed that Giuliana never looked happier and more animated than when she was knitting, which she had learned to do from instructions in children's comics at an early age. This morning, however, she was uncharacteristically silent.

Brother and sister were alone together. Gilberto and Carlo were staying with cousins; Rosa was with their bedridden father at their grandfather's house. There was a knock at the door. Their cousin Letizia appeared. Her face told them the worst.

'I've come for his suit,' she said.

Leone Benetton died at least knowing that the war was over. He left a widow, four young children, a couple of humble rental properties, a few small plots of land and a Fiat Topolino car, hidden in a barn away from the Germans. At the age of ten, Luciano's childhood was over.

The following year, the Benettons once again moved out of town, this time to Santa Bona, on the north-west outskirts of Treviso. Rosa's heart condition had recurred and she often had to rest in bed. Luciano and his sister were terrified that she too would die, leaving them in charge of the family. This was the fear that drove Luciano to get up early before school and cycle with a heavy load of newspapers to Treviso station, where he sold them; to walk the streets after school, delivering bread and selling soap door to door; to stand in queues waiting for rationed bread, fish and salt; to scrub his younger brother Gilberto's nappies on a wooden board. This drove Giuliana to make virtually all the clothes for the family; to work a knitting machine in her spare time, although she was below the legal age, among grown women, in the tiny workshop of a neighbour; and to dream of leaving school as soon as possible, so that she could work there full time.

Their fear was doubly real, coupled with the daily insecurity of the country as a whole. In the first year after the end of the war, prices and unemployment soared and there was a revolt of former partisans. Shops were looted in Venice, and in Treviso, where work began to rebuild the town, 1,000 unemployed workers forced the prefect, a town official, to 'promise' them jobs. Across the Veneto, the diet of excessive polenta, or corn, caused diseases like pellagra, and the malnourished people of the Veneto, once so prosperous, became disparagingly known as the *polentini*.

American journalists came to report on the country after the twin devastations of German occupation and Allied liberation. Marya Mannes reported in American *Vogue*:

> The people in Italy who are really hard put are the middle class who have neither the income of the wealthy nor the amoral wits of the poor to save them from hunger. The average meal in a Roman Italian restaurant costs about 500 lire. In illegal exchange, about US $1.40 – not bad for visitors. For the Italian clerk – for any white collar worker in the middle class – 500 lire represents his entire earnings for one day on which he must support a family of at least five people.
>
> So what does he do? First, he sells all his furniture, all his china, anything that can possibly bring in money. When he has no more to sell, he and his family subsist on bread, fruit and vegetables. Even pasta – the traditional staple and standby – is too expensive to buy.

But she went on: 'There is a ferment in the Italian air that makes one believe, rightly or wrongly, that if Italy is allowed a period of peace and freedom, she may bring to Europe and to us an extraordinary, creative vitality.'

The following year, *Life* magazine reported:

> The fabled Italy of Julius Caesar, the Renaissance and the Roman Catholic Church is today on the brink of Communist revolution. On the walls of her ruins are the slogans of the party. Along

historic Roman roads march members of the Communist labor unions. Across the stately gardens of the Vatican falls the shadow of the hammer and sickle . . . Slowly, painfully, Italy is trying to rebuild itself. Against this background, the struggle between right and left for the control of Italy goes on. And the war-ploughed land is as fertile for the seeds of Communism as it was after World War I for the seeds of Fascism.

America did not want communism in Italy or anywhere else, and in the poor south of the country pursued its anti-communist strategy in ways that would yield catastrophic results. In the less poor north, and particularly in the Veneto, the most business-orientated and hard-working part of the country, the Christian Democratic Party led the organised opposition to communism, and American aid accordingly focused on the Catholic Church. In exactly the same way that communism would be depicted by Cardinal Spellman and the Catholic Church in America as a threat to the family – rather than the threat it actually posed, to the power of the Church itself – in Italy the local priest became the conduit for American aid, and he expected his flock to vote Christian Democrat in return. Christian Democrat election posters featured mothers shielding their children from the 'wolves' of communism, and snakes bearing the poison of 'free love' rearing up to destroy the family.

In this post-war maelstrom, the phrase 'the family' took on a greater multiplicity of meanings and applications than anywhere else in the world. It ranged from the two extremes, of a virtuous, hard-working model of stability, to an evil social organisation based on intimidation, violence and murder. Between these extremes, ordinary people were somehow supposed to lead their lives with some sort of normality that had in reality disappeared, along with housing, food, currency and many of their fellow citizens, beneath the rubble of their cities. No wonder they initially placed so much faith in the democratic process, a faith which was misunderstood by many foreigners, even after a prolonged stay in the country.

Two years after the end of the war, the American writer on advertising, Marshall McLuhan, noted that an American officer in Italy was perturbed by what he found here:

> The Italians can tell you the names of the ministers in the government, but not the names of their favourite products or the celebrities of their country . . . the walls of the Italian cities are plastered more with political slogans than with commercial ones. According to the opinion of this officer, there is little hope that the Italians will achieve a state of prosperity and internal calm until they start to be more interested in the respective merits of different types of cornflakes and cigarettes rather than the relative abilities of their political leaders.

The truth was that fascism and Mussolini had sheltered Italians from the cold winds of the free market. Even after the calamity of the war, many were left yearning for a return to a strong hand of government. Mussolini's empire building had, after all, enabled Leone Benetton to go abroad in search of the fortunes that eluded him at home. Mussolini's strong-arm men had protected Fiat from strikes and trade unions, and thereby enabled Leone Benetton to buy the Fiat Topolino he had hidden in the barn. Mussolini's army had provided the customers for Leone Benetton's bicycle business. Without Mussolini, Leone Benetton would not have gone to Africa and caught malaria, and Benetton would still be in the Treviso telephone listing today under car hire. Yet in spite of this, many business leaders believed that the price had literally been too great; after the catastrophe of fascism and Mussolini, central government should never again be allowed to influence business to more than a minimal extent. Thus the words of the Venetian textile tycoon, Count

Gaetano Marzotto: 'Can the state bureaucrats do something more than he who knows his own business?' he asked. 'The state should stick to administering justice . . . to law and order.'

Count Marzotto had a point. Italy's 3,000 textile businesses had employed 14 per cent of the population before the war; after the war, unlike their German and Japanese counterparts, they were largely intact. Marzotto and others wanted to exploit new export opportunities, an ambition which would be thwarted by a strongly centralised government, as was the case with the socialist government that was then paralysing Great Britain. But there was no cotton, and there were no resources as yet to awaken the forces of supply and demand in the domestic market.

Meanwhile, the 'shadow of the hammer and sickle' evoked by *Life* magazine was looming larger across the country, and in the process raising greater fears in Washington. Three years after the end of the war, in 1948, the beleaguered Christian Democrat Prime Minister, Alcide de Gasperi, faced with the threat of the communists taking power, went to Washington. He came home with a loan of US$100 million. In the south of the country, however, the American strategy to combat communism was already resulting in an unholy alliance between American aid and organised crime masquerading as the anti-communist dream ticket. Between the Christian Democrats and the communists, a third force was being transformed from a local protection racket into an unofficial power in the land – the Cosa Nostra – the Honoured Society – the Mafia. No town would come to symbolise this evil more than the town of Corleone.

Corleone, Sicily, 10 April 1948

Corleone lies at the southern extreme of Italy, in the west of Sicily. Sicily was an island of scorching sun and rock, of oppressed peasantry and squalid towns dominated by the Mafia; since the war, the condition of the people here had been even harsher, if such a thing was possible. This condition reached its apogee in one town. An Allied intelligence officer engaged in anti-Mafia operations during the war, wrote: 'In this world one occasionally stumbles upon a place which, in its physical presence and the atmosphere it distils, manages somehow to match its reputation for sinister happenings. Such a town is Corleone.'

This was a town of only 8,000 people, yet 153 murders had taken place there in the past four years. The period of mourning for a father was five years; for a brother, three years; for a son, three years. Men and women were united in one colour: black. The repatriation of Mafiosi from America, and the American crusade against communism, had spawned a new Mafia growing rich on the traffic in narcotics and given tacit American backing.

On this day in April 1948, a convention of the heads of the Mafia of all Sicily was being held in nearby Palermo. Following this, the order was given for all-out support for the Christian Democrats. Labour union leaders were already being marked down for elimination. The Sicilian communist leader, Girolamo Li Causi, had been wounded when the Mafia had opened fire on a Popular Front meeting; many years later, one of his daughter's earliest memories would be of going to school on the back of a motorcycle ridden by a man with a rifle slung across his shoulders. In Corleone, the local Christian Democrat chairman was a Mafia leader. He was also a doctor. He issued several hundred certificates of blindness for extreme myopia to the women of Corleone, who were then escorted by Mafiosi to the polling booths to make sure they voted for the right ticket. The walls of the town were plastered with election posters. One of these read: 'Long live God! Vote Christian Democrat'.

Corleone and the Mafia were about as far away from Treviso and the ethos of hard work and family as you could possibly get. Yet, for some, the name of the town – and the criminal organisation that controlled it – would, wrongly, become associated with the name of Benetton.

Santa Bona, Treviso, 1949

In Santa Bona, the Benetton family were in desperate financial straits. One by one, Rosa had sold off all the little plots of land Leone had left them, in order to buy food and clothes. The rental properties no longer provided enough income to keep them. Giuliana had achieved her ambition to leave school at the age of eleven and was knitting full time in the little garment workshop. Luciano was still at school, and still getting up before dawn to cycle each morning with thirty kilos of newspapers to sell on Treviso station. Wearing gloves made it impossible to pass the newspapers through the window of a train in return for money, and he went on to school with his hands chapped and criss-crossed with paper cuts. A schoolboy of fourteen doing the work of a man, he was always hungry, however much of the bread he was supposed to deliver each evening he managed to eat on the way. One day, his younger brother Carlo came home from school with a composition he had written: 'My father is called Luciano,' it read, 'he works hard looking after us.'

Yet still this was not enough. Years later, in Red Square, Moscow, after communism had collapsed there too, Luciano would recall these childhood times in vivid detail: the autumn mist that each year heralded the coming of another winter of struggle, with no solution in sight; the struggle to live from day to day, in failing light; the struggle of a family without a father.

This problem might have been solved and this burden lifted had his mother been able or inclined to marry again. For whatever reason she would never do so and her children would have no say in the matter. As Luciano would recall: 'I was not able to solve problems at that age.' Meanwhile, a few days later, after a sleepless night, and like his father before him, Luciano concluded that his current business plan was not going to work. Secondary school was not compulsory at this time and he had made up his mind. He came downstairs and said to Rosa: 'I'm not going back to school next year.'

'It wouldn't be right,' he went on. 'Giuliana works full time already, and she's younger than me. I'm going to try to find a full-time job.'

His mother said nothing, and put her arms around him. Then he burst into tears. At the moment of manhood, as he later recalled, he felt like a very small boy. Many years later, Luciano, the man to whom this child was father, would recall:

> What would have happened if my father was still alive? I have thought about this many times. I am convinced that things would have been very different. In those days, every family wanted a son who would be a doctor; later, it was a job in a bank. We would not be here today.

Luciano had already been working after school as a stockboy in a store in town called Alla Campana. The store sold fabrics and some clothing. Luciano left school and went to work there full time. He swept floors, carried boxes and learned the rudiments of retailing: customer handling, stock control and elementary book keeping. Like his father, he also had a weakness for snappy dressing. He saved enough money from his wages to order a suit of his own design. He was determined this should represent the height of fashion: baggy trousers and a tightly cut jacket, on the pocket of which he added a watch chain – without a watch. It took him a year to save the money for the suit. When he wore it, the girls turned and laughed at him in the street. Luciano was outwardly defiant; he was a breadwinner and entitled to dress as a man about town. Privately, he concluded that he still had a lot to learn about the fashion business.

Luciano was well built and self-possessed for his years, as well as smartly turned out. After a few years, he changed jobs. The Dellasiega brothers took him on as a sales assistant in their clothes store in the town.

Later, Luciano would say: 'The traditional shops were destined to die . . . and we killed them.' The Dellasiegas were traditional shop-keepers. Meanwhile, they saved him from selling newspapers on Treviso station, and living off the bread he was supposed to deliver in the evenings, and sweeping floors and carrying boxes, and from a destiny as a doctor, which he had never really wanted to be. They taught him everything they knew about clothing, about style, about tailoring, about cut. They encouraged him to develop his innate talents as a salesman. Luciano showed his gratitude by being a model sales assistant; he was never late for work and always polite to customers. But even though he had at last found a steady job with regular pay, he was never going to settle for a life behind the counter in compensation for the loss of his childhood, and as a business career. He and Giuliana were alike in so far as they shared a powerful preoccupation with bringing home money; but they were also very different, and in ways that they did not yet know would complement each other with extraordinary consequences. She seemed at her happiest, almost mesmerically so, merely in the act of knitting. He was as hard working as her, but he was more ambitious, as his father had been, and he wanted to create something new. During his long days at the Dellasiegas' shop, Luciano Benetton had plenty of time between being polite to customers to think about what this might be.

Clothes retailing in provincial post-war Europe was so different from today, it might have belonged to another world. Clothes were strictly

Plan begging bowl. In America, only mobsters kept their Italian names. Americans of Italian descent who wanted to make it big changed their names, as others changed theirs to the likes of Dean Martin and Tony Curtis. They became part of the America which had occupied Italy, and still occupied the dreams of Luciano Benetton and his friends in Treviso.

One of these friends was Domenico 'Nico' Luciani, an intellectual boy who was then trying to feign madness to escape being drafted into the army. Luciano, as the eldest son of a deceased father, was exempted from military service. Nico had never known riches, but his family were comfortable. Nor had he known the kind of in- security with which Luciano had to deal from day to day. He and Luciano were devotees of American culture in the form of books, movies and newspaper stories. They were also business partners. One of their ventures, with ingredients 'borrowed' from Nico's grandfather, who owned a bakery and vineyard, was to manufacture and sell grapes and sandwiches at local fairs. Nico had at first obtained the grapes, a Canadian variety particularly prized in the region, simply by taking them from his grandfather's vineyard during the day when his grandfather was not looking. The old man soon noticed something was amiss, however, and thereafter Nico was obliged to renew their supplies by climbing over the wall at night. He and Luciano eventually saved enough money to buy an old Vespa motor scooter, which they hid at the house of a girl they knew.

Another of their ventures was to build a basketball court. The land was provided free by the parish of Santa Bona. The two of them toiled for months in their spare time to dig the foundations and lay the hardcore. They bribed some roadmenders who were laying asphalt nearby to lay the surface. The parish provided the baskets in return. The local priest also gave them space for a changing room. They formed a team, with black and white shirts, and ambitiously called themselves Juventus after the great Italian football club. They competed respectably in the Treviso basketball championships. Then they decided they wanted to be able to play basketball at night, and persuaded the priest to allow a single spotlight to be mounted on the church overlooking the court. When they played into the light from the beam they could see virtually nothing, and lost the half by a huge margin; then they changed ends, and it was the turn of their opponents to be dazzled, and the balance was redressed. Years later, both Luciano and Nico wore glasses, perhaps as a result.

Luciano and Nico were addicted to sport in general and also took up swimming, sneaking away from their parents to swim in winter in the local canals, where other boys had drowned from time to time in the icy waters. They took up Greco–Roman wrestling, a highly disciplined and stylised sport which demanded a special combination of aggression and control; they were different sizes and never wrestled each other, but Luciano excelled at this, while Nico was, in his own words, 'frequently destroyed'. They also took to rowing, joining the club based on the river in the centre of town where they became part of a more cosmopolitan set who saw beyond the restrictive political values of the rural parishes. This new social life, and the Vespa scooter, were key parts of Luciano's life beyond the family for whom he was compelled to be father, son and brother all at once. He loved his family, but he needed and invented a parallel freedom from them. This urge on his part found fulfilment in endless, frequently hazardous rides on the Vespa with Nico, including once to see the Mille Miglia motor race in Padua, and in romantic excursions to Venice with his girlfriend, Miriam, and Nico and his girlfriend. Years later, Nico would claim he could not remember the name of his own girlfriend because he had never really been 'convinced' of her feelings for him. Luciano, however, although 'convinced' by Miriam would never mention her, and would probably have claimed to have forgotten her name had he been pressed on the matter.

The intellectual Nico and the entrepreneurial, inventive Luciano, just over two years his senior, were best friends. Sometimes, however, even Nico could not understand his friend: 'How can you work in a place like this?' he asked Luciano in the Dellasiegas' shop one day.

They had had this conversation many times.

'Because I have to, idiot,' Luciano replied. 'I'm a breadwinner. Anyway, I like what I'm doing,' he went on, 'it gives me time to think.'

'About what?'

'About getting rich.'

Nico always paused for a moment here.

'How are you going to do that, then?'

'I don't know,' Luciano always replied. 'But I'm working on it.'

The factors that would enable him to find the answer were slowly making themselves felt even behind the counter of the Dellasiegas' shop in Treviso. One of the things Luciano had noticed was that people had more leisure time and more money. He himself played the accordion in a band for money. More and more people were coming into the shop to buy clothes, even if they could not find what they really wanted. At the same time, freedom of choice was becoming a reality. The old social structures and barriers were breaking down; day-to-day survival was no longer the all-embracing preoccupation. Italy was recovering with a momentum that was increasingly its own. It had natural gas and textiles. Count Marzotto, who had warned against excessive government interference after the war, employed 13,500 people in his chain of mills, restaurants and model farms. Thirty-three years later, Marzotto and Benetton would battle it out for control of Italy's state-owned textile empire.

Other old businesses like Fiat, Olivetti and Pirelli were recovering their power at home and in the international markets. The self-made entrepreneur Enrico Mattei, who like Luciano Benetton had left school at fourteen, was becoming a popular hero, with his running of ENI, the state-owned oil empire with its petrol stations and motorway restaurants. 'For the first time in the economic history of Italy,' the United States embassy in Rome reported with amazement in 1954, a government-owned entity in Italy 'has found itself in the unique position of being financially solvent, capably led, and responsible to no one other than its leader.' *Fortune* magazine reported:

> There is a vast stir and bustle in Italy today. City streets are clamorous with traffic, ports crowded, factories humming, shops glistening. Italy is still undersupplied with raw materials; its teeming population is still underemployed; the standard of living, particularly in the south, is low. Yet since the end of the war industrial production has risen almost 50 per cent above prewar base, the lira is stabilized, extensive war damage has been repaired . . . Exports have changed in character too. The traditional olive oil, cheese and wines, for example, have fallen off while fashions, fabrics, finely made calculators, sewing machines and the like have risen rapidly. On many of these products 'Made in Italy' has become a stamp of excellence.

The *New York Times* began talking about 'the Italian miracle'.

This may have been an overstatement to many like Luciano who were actually there at the time, but there was no doubt that the Italian economy was beginning to grow. And yet here was Luciano Benetton, as his friend Nico never ceased to remind him, still behind the counter of a clothing store. 'I'm working on it,' Luciano would tell him. 'I'm sure it exists somewhere. I just have to put my finger on it.'

The Dellasiegas did not often hand out compliments, but they were honourable men who knew quality when they saw it, in sales assistants as well as clothes.

'You're not doing too badly, Luciano, you're not doing too badly at all,' one of the brothers told him one day, after he had been working there three years. 'You're getting to know about clothes and you're a born salesman.

'Stick with us, and we'll make it worth your while,' he added, and then frowned. 'What's that you're wearing?' he said.

'It's a bow tie,' said Luciano, 'I made it.' He raised his hand to his neck, as if to protect himself.

'You made it? Out of what?'

'Out of a piece of cloth,' Luciano replied; he was proud of his bow tie, which had red, green, yellow and blue stripes on a white background. He had borrowed the needle and thread from Giuliana.

'A piece of cloth?' Dellasiega repeated incredulously. The traditional shopkeeper looked like he was going to choke; then he went quiet. 'Actually, it's not bad,' he said. 'It's original, as ties go. But you're a salesman, not a clown. I never want to see it in this shop again.'

Luciano was twenty years old and had been behind the counter for a year when he realised he had put his finger on it. As long as he looked for the answer in existing places, he would never find it. The kind of shop and the kind of clothes he was envisioning did not exist here or anywhere else. They existed only in his imagination. At the same time, the market for them was very real.

In his imagination, the shop did not have a counter and the clothes were visible and accessible in style and price. Young people came into this shop with their own money, without their parents, and without knowing what they wanted, and they came out with clothes they had bought of their own free will; and they came back again and again. These clothes did not as yet have precise shape or form but they were comfortable and casual and colourful, and the young people who bought them were the same age as Luciano and his friends. There were thousands of these young people, millions of them, out there, and yet they did not have anywhere to shop. Luciano knew who they were; but what did they do? They went to secondary school, like Nico, and worked, like Luciano and like Giuliana, and played sports, like basketball and rowing. Luciano, who played both these sports, had also noticed that it was impossible to buy good inexpensive sports clothes in spite of the fact that there was an equally huge demand. But who would make these clothes that did not yet exist and who would sell them, and how, and where?

Luciano came home after one day and a year behind the counter and knew he had the answers. He did not go straight home, but instead went to the little garment sweatshop nearby where his sister, who was now eighteen, had worked full time for the past seven years. Seven years' hard labour, for which her employer had graciously rewarded her with a modest pay rise and the title of 'master craftswoman'. In her spare time, what little she had of this, his sister was revealing an unexpected creative streak. She designed and made brightly coloured jumpers for the family; one of Luciano's friends had particularly admired a yellow jumper she had designed and made for him. In a country where the mandatory colours of a jumper were grey, blue and burgundy, and many people still wore black, this in itself, he had realised, was a fashion statement.

He arrived early on this evening and Giuliana was still working at her machine. She was like a dynamo; her face was perfectly still, her hands and fingers flew back and forth. He waited until she had finished and greeted her as usual. They walked out of the little sweatshop and set off for home. On the way, he turned to her and said: 'Giuliana? Why are we working for other people?'

2   A Woman of Substance

Santa Bona, Treviso, 1955

'Why?' he had repeated. 'Why don't we start up on our own?'

'Because it's too risky,' she had replied.

'Why?' he persisted.

'Because we're too young,' she retorted.

'You make them, I'll sell them. Why not?'

'That's just like you,' she said. She was tired after the long day. 'You always say, "if you could make more". I make socks for the boys, and you say "Why not make two or three more pairs, and we can sell them?"'

She was quiet after this for a long time. As they reached home, she said: 'We're going to have to buy a knitting machine.'

That night, over dinner, they announced the news to the rest of the family. Rosa thought they had gone mad. Did they want to plunge the whole family back into poverty?

Luciano looked anxiously at Giuliana.

'Don't worry, Mamma,' she said, 'we won't give up our day jobs. We'll work at night and in our spare time. You know we can do it.'

Rosa had to admit that they could. She herself had been working in her spare time for years, doing embroidery on a piecework basis for a little extra cash.

'Where's the money going to come from to buy this machine?' said Gilberto.

This was a trickier question; although he was only fourteen years old, Gilberto was not only blunt, he was also the acknowledged financial brain of the family. The youngest brother, Carlo, never turned down an odd job in the neighbourhood and could also be relied upon to follow the same line: 'Yeah, where's the money going to come from?' he echoed.

Luciano tried to stay calm. He had no idea where the money would come from. 'We'll hire a machine,' he said. 'Look,' he went on, aware that his position as breadwinner gave him a precious authority at this moment, 'the important thing is that we are all agreed. Yes or no?'

They looked at each other and nodded.

'Good,' said Luciano, 'agreed, then. The money will come along, somehow.'

'We hope,' said Gilberto.

Luciano looked at his brother, whose nappies he had scrubbed, and at Carlo, who had called him 'daddy' in his school composition and who was still at school and able to enjoy being there. Sometimes it was hard being the breadwinner.

The best knitting machine cost around 300,000 lire, or US$200, a huge sum. Luciano sold his treasured accordion and raised 10 per cent of the cost. Gilberto was persuaded to sell his bicycle; apart from sport, he was happier behind a desk. They borrowed from family and friends. Slowly, they raised the money. Two months later, Luciano and Giuliana went to Treviso station. Luciano bought a newspaper from a boy with chapped and bleeding hands. On the front page was a photograph by Toscani senior. They took the train to Milan where a trade fair of knitting machines was taking place.

'I want them all,' she said.

She chose the best machine she could find and they went home on the train to wait for delivery. They went back to their day jobs; neither breathed a word to their employers. Several weeks later the machine arrived. They threw a party in its honour and jokingly christened it 'the new member of the family'. Within a few weeks they realised this was no joke and that the new machine had changed their lives. It was the first of many to do so.

Each day, after they had finished school and their various other jobs, Luciano and Gilberto set up the reels of wool ready for the machine. Each night, after a day's work in the sweatshop, Giuliana worked the machine from six o'clock until eleven; sometimes past midnight. Rosa was her first assistant, assembling and ironing the knitted jumpers, stitching them together until two or three o'clock in the morning, often working in bed to save the heating bill. Once a week, Luciano and Gilberto bicycled off to the wool distributor to pick up the next supply.

Within a few weeks, with the help of the machine and the family, Giuliana Benetton had produced her first collection. This consisted of twenty knitted jumpers made out of combed wool, in the dominant English style of the time. The roll necks and V-necks and turtle necks were also in the traditional style, but the difference lay in the colours. Giuliana, the dutiful daughter with a nun-like devotion to the knitting machine so intense that she often had to be forced to stop for food, had introduced yellows, greens and pale blues; colours that nobody had seen in these kinds of clothes before. They gave the collection the French name 'Très Jolie'; unlike the late Mussolini, and like most of their contemporaries, they had a healthy respect for Paris as the centre of world fashion. Luciano's friend Nico Luciani designed an elegant multi-coloured label bearing this name. Luciano set out to sell these on foot, by bicycle and on the ancient Vespa, to the citizens of Treviso.

He sold the first one to Mr Zuchello, a neighbouring grocer. When the customer handed over the money without so much as a hint that this was anything other than a straight commercial trans-action with no sense of doing a favour, Luciano experienced for the first time 'the same intense feeling', as he later put it, 'as a scientist whose theory has just been proved correct'. There were many other times when he failed to make a sale and returned late at night after a long ride by motor scooter back down an unlit, unmade road, to the house. But the key to the sales he did make was in the colours, and in the hunger of so many young people especially to wear them; a hunger so intense, as Luciano later put it, that it was as if they 'had been starved of colour during the war'.

Within four months of Giuliana starting to manufacture, Luciano was selling twenty Très Jolie jumpers a week. They paid back the money to friends from whom they had borrowed to buy the machine. Two months later, while Luciano still worked full time during the day for the Dellasiegas, Giuliana gave up her job at the sweatshop to work full time at home. She was making up to four-teen jumpers a day, virtually single-handed. The following year, in 1956, they bought a second machine and Giuliana took on their first employees: Diana Torresan and Carla Crosato, aged eleven and twelve respectively. Giuliana was now employing the kind of young girl she herself had once been. They bought a third machine, and the home turned into a clothing factory. The tiny bedroom Luciano shared with Carlo was also the storeroom for boxes of wool. They slept practically on top of each other amid the smell of wool and dye. Some nights, the boxes would topple over on them, and Luciano, who would one day be accused of cruelty to sheep, would dream that he was sleeping in a shepherd's hut.

'Be careful,' said Rosa, 'don't overdo it.'

They were working nearly twenty-four hours a day, running out of space, and experiencing one of the most hazardous points in any business; how to expand without jeopardising everything for which they had worked in one fatal move.

In the beginning, the Dellasiegas were sceptical when Luciano tried to persuade them to sell Très Jolie jumpers in their shop.

'Too risky,' they said.

Luciano decided on a different strategy. The Dellasiegas were conservative towards woollen jumpers in general, rather than Très Jolie in particular. That winter, and only after much effort, he managed to persuade them to market a small range of woollen jumpers by another manufacturer. When these sold quickly the Dellasiegas were amazed. Luciano seized his moment. Without inviting the representative of the other manufacturer back to accept a reorder, he persuaded the Dellasiegas this time to order a small range of Très Jolie. This time they agreed and the Très Jolie jumpers sold as quickly, in fact even more quickly, than the competition. The traditional shop of the Dellasiegas had just become the first, and least likely, retail outlet for the house of Benetton.

This first success elevated Luciano to a new plane in the eyes of his employers. Luigi Dellasiega, who had once spoken sharply to him about his home-made bow tie, repeated the all-important words of approval he had made on that occasion.

'You're not doing too badly, Luciano, you're not doing too badly at all,' he told him.

In the same year, 1957, the brothers made him an offer he thought he would never hear. 'Luciano,' they said, 'we'd like to, ah . . . place an order.'

The first 'flash' collection, Treviso, 1957

The order was for 600 jumpers. The family was thrown into shock, followed by a frenzy of activity. Luckily, they had already gone some way towards meeting the challenge of growth by renting another house nearby, where they moved the business, together with five employees. The order from the Dellasiegas justified this move. Furthermore, at least Luciano would not have to sell speculatively on a door-to-door basis. Giuliana took on another girl and they delivered the order on time.

In the years to come, they would look back on this as their first 'flash' or additional unscheduled collection, a demonstration of the ability to meet a sudden change in customer demand that would one day make them world famous. Meanwhile, they had crossed a line from being a family of amateurs to a family of professional manufacturers. Henceforth, too, they were no longer operating in frenzied isolation, but as a true part of the local community of family businesses to which many of their friends already belonged; and of the wider community of the Veneto, the latest in the business tradition into which their parents and grandparents had been born. To the present time, all their efforts had been first to survive and then to find their own identities. This was an impossible luxury until the first problem had been overcome and greater freedom of choice was available in the country as a whole. Now, they could draw a line between the years of working for other people and the first year of working for themselves.

The following year, in 1958, when Luciano finally gave up working for the Dellasiegas, the shop had an entire shelf dedicated to Très Jolie. They were still Très Jolie to everyone; only the family knew themselves as Benetton. Before he left his job in the shop to work for himself, and after Miriam had disappeared from the scene, Luciano had also met the woman he would marry. Teresa was the blonde, vivacious daughter of an engineer from Padua, who had moved to Treviso. She came into the shop one day and was instantly attracted to the tall sales assistant with the air of gravity beyond his years. She was different from most of the other girls Luciano knew, who had worked from a young age in sweatshops like Giuliana.

Giuliana herself had already been engaged, until her fiancé made the mistake of saying to her one day: 'It isn't right that you should go on working after we're married. It's me or the job . . . your choice.'

Giuliana had made her choice and found another man. She married him, and after their first child, Paola, was born, Giuliana went straight back to work. Teresa, although aware of the spell she cast over Luciano, and in spite of the fact that she herself had never had to work, was smart enough to take a position on side with his sister. Once she and Luciano were engaged, she came to work with Giuliana Benetton.

Rome, Italy, 1960

Luciano had never been to Rome before. He was taking the first vacation of his life to attend the Olympic Games. Suddenly, all roads led there. In addition to the Games, the city was popular in

American movies, featuring beautiful, fashionably dressed stars like Audrey Hepburn in *Roman Holiday*. Italian stars, cars and fashion were reaching the American mass audience. The high fashion houses, centred on Rome and Florence, specialised in expensive knitwear, sportswear and casual wear, with names like Laura Aponte, Avolio, Baldini, Falconetto, Mirsa and Paola Nucci. The streets of the capital teemed with tourists and visitors from all over the world. This was the Rome of *la dolce vita* – the good life – and it made Luciano Benetton realise how sheltered a life he had been leading.

The Rome he was encountering for the first time was the centre of the consumer revolution that was sweeping the country. The 'shadow of the hammer and sickle' reported in *Life* magazine only thirteen years earlier had been obliterated by the bright lights of free enterprise, and governments were both willing to ride the capitalist whirlwind and powerless to do otherwise. Italy was experiencing *il boom* – its economic miracle. Eighty-one out of every thousand people here now owned a television set. Eight out of a hundred owned an automobile. People were eating fewer beans and polenta and more eggs, cheese, butter and meat. There was sugar and coffee and olive oil in the kitchen. The children had raincoats to wear to school. The family, especially in the industrialised north, had discovered *il weekend*.

This was the spirit of discovery, in addition to being a tourist, in which Luciano first walked the streets of the capital. Besides the Dellasiegas, he was selling Très Jolie to shops in Treviso and Venice, but not yet here. He wanted to know what the stores looked like in a major city. Rome, like many ancient cities, is divided into quarters that have evolved naturally over generations to specialise in selling a particular item. Near the Piazza di Spagna, on the Via Gambero, Luciano came across a shop of a kind he had never seen before, except in his imagination.

This shop exclusively sold woollen garments, jumpers principally. It was filled to bursting point with them and with customers wanting to buy. These customers knew exactly what they wanted because they had come into this shop and found it. Nor were they merely Romans or even Italians. American air hostesses, British businessmen, French models and Olympic athletes from all sorts of countries were queuing at the counter. The jumpers on sale were well made and in a wide range of colours, but Luciano was gratified to discover that they were neither as well made nor in as wide a range of colours as Très Jolie. The counter, in his opinion, still placed a psychological barrier between the sales people and the customer. But Luciano had seen enough here to know that the future he had envisaged was real, here on a street in the capital. He pushed his way back through the queue of customers and emerged again onto the teeming pavement. With his back to the stream of cars, buses and motorcycles, he looked up at the shop. It was owned by a family of whom he had never heard, called Tagliacozzo. He went back to his cheap hotel, watched the rest of the Olympic Games and took the next train back to Treviso.

Ponzano, the Veneto, 1960

They had moved the factory from the house in Santa Bona to a larger, rented factory, formerly a warehouse, in their parents' home village of Ponzano. A few hundred yards away, a miserable shadow of its former splendour, stood the Villa Minelli, successively a summer palace, an orphanage, a home for refugees and by this time an agricultural machinery store.

In the 'new' factory, the knitting machines and their youthful operators clattered away with the same noise from which Luciano had escaped all too briefly and to which he returned excitedly with his new idea. Luciano and Giuliana were already planning their next move, to build on land next door a factory of their own, somehow, with money they did not yet have. Meanwhile, he wasted no time in telling her that they had to find a way of breaking into the Roman market.

She set about designing a new range based on, but calculated to improve upon, the tastes in colour and texture he had noted in the capital. The new range included a mauve pullover, made of a mixture of the softest wools, and jumpers in thirty-six different shades of lambswool; enough, surely, to arouse the palate of the most jaded shopkeeper. A few months later, armed with a suitcase full of samples, Luciano returned to Rome.

He had by this time noticed an advertisement in a trade paper, placed by a Roman called Roberto Calderoni. Calderoni was offering his services as a sales representative for a women's fashion house. Luciano had written to him, saying instead that he was looking for a representative to sell woollen jumpers. In the highly demarcated business of fashion and clothing, this was an unorthodox move on the part of Luciano. Calderoni was even more surprised when Luciano Benetton turned up on his doorstep.

Luciano was not the only employer seeking Calderoni's services, but, from the moment they met, the young man from out of town and the sophisticated city boy hit it off together. Calderoni came from one of the great Roman Jewish business families. Like Luciano, his childhood had been marked by the war; he had survived the Nazi holocaust as a child hidden in a Catholic convent. After the war he had finished his studies, worked in a textile business in Switzerland and then worked with his father. He was looking to set up on his own as a representative and agent. He was three years older than Luciano, fiercely ambitious and independent minded and, if anything, possessed of an even greater technical understanding of the business. He became the first representative, outside the family, for the Benettons and Très Jolie.

Calderoni made two crucial initial suggestions. He advised Luciano on the level at which to set his prices for the new range, far lower than the woollen garments currently available in the Roman market. He also introduced him to key retailers in the city and, in particular, to the people whose shop had inspired Luciano to return there in the first place.

The Tagliacozzo brothers, Rome, Italy, 1961

The shop on the Via Gambero, where Luciano had stood in amazement that day, was one of several owned and operated by another remarkable family. The Tagliacozzos, like Calderoni, were Roman Jews with a merchant tradition going back several generations. During the Second World War, unlike Calderoni, who had managed to hide in Rome, the parents of the present generation of the Tagliacozzo family had been deported to Auschwitz. The father had died in the holocaust while the mother had survived and emigrated to Israel. The present generation, Umberto, Sergio and Armando Tagliacozzo, had been brought up there and then returned to Rome to resume the family business.

Sergio Tagliacozzo was a highly intelligent, thoughtful man like Luciano Benetton, albeit to the point of absent-mindedness, and he cut a donnish, stocky figure in contrast to Luciano's height and sharpness of dress. His eye for quality and commerciality was second to none, and one look at the samples Luciano had brought with him to Rome was enough. Tagliacozzo placed an order for the entire range. This was Luciano and Giuliana's first sale in the capital.

Other merchant families and shop owners in the capital were initially not so enthusiastic when Luciano and Calderoni made their presentations. Soon, they too, however, were placing orders, at first in small quantities for what they anticipated would be the most sophisticated end of the market. After several reorders, each bigger than the previous one, they too became regular and major customers.

The Tagliacozzo brothers, meanwhile, became firm friends and mentors to Luciano Benetton. Luciano had already observed how they had turned around the traditional relationship between customer, retailer and supplier, where the latter had dictated, via the middleman, what the former could and could not choose to wear. Instead, the Tagliacozzos sold what their customers wanted and dictated this to the supplier. Luciano was attentive; he wanted to know more. The Tagliacozzos told him how they believed the future lay in a chain of shops producing a range of designs in many colours at affordable prices. These shops could go beyond Italy, even beyond Europe; to America and further afield.

Luciano listened to what the Tagliacozzo brothers had to say, and went back to Ponzano. The idea of a global chain of shops excited him, but as a supplier and not as a retailer. Retailers had the additional cost of running their shops, and he was a supplier, after all, who already understood what the customer wanted to buy. He had no more desire to be a retailer than the Tagliacozzos desired to be designers or manufacturers. Nevertheless, one day, perhaps, through the Tagliacozzos and others like them, the whole world would know the name of Très Jolie.

Santa Bona, Treviso, 1961

Luciano and Teresa were at Rosa's house, pacing up and down nervously, waiting for Gilberto. They were getting married that morning. The contents of the envelope Gilberto was bringing would dictate where and for how long they could afford to go on their honeymoon.

Eventually Gilberto arrived, smiling, and handed over the money. The moment the ceremony was over, they took off in a brand new Fiat 500, Luciano with his tall frame hunched over the wheel, for Spain, Gibraltar and the Pyrenees. They drove nearly 4,000 miles there and back and came home to a small rented house of their own in Santa Bona. Then they both went back to work, Luciano on the road, making sales, visiting Calderoni and making more contacts, and Teresa at the factory, working with Giuliana. The following year their first child, Mauro, was born. Like his cousin, Paola, he too spent the first few months of his childhood at the factory. He lay in a Moses basket between the knitting machines, cooed over and pampered by Diana and Carla and the other girls who operated them, and who were working even harder now that there were so many orders from the capital.

Ponzano, the Veneto, 1962

The success of the Roman range of jumpers soon outstripped that of the combined markets of Venice and Treviso and was reflected in the greater variety and sophistication of the pullovers that were coming out of the makeshift factory in Ponzano. Business would double in the two years after Luciano and Calderoni's first presentations in the capital. At the same time, although Giuliana's workers were as willing as ever, the factory was fast losing the ability to keep up with the increased volume of orders. First, they had had to meet the challenge of expanding from their own home into the rented house. Then they had moved to the converted warehouse. Now, they needed new equipment and a new factory and they did not have the money for the latter in particular.

Gilberto, by this time, had finished his year of national service and entered the business as full-time financial administrator and controller. This was payback time for the plain-speaking kid brother with the head for business. Gilberto put in place agreements whereby merchants like the Tagliacozzos and others received a discount if they paid on receipt of the merchandise. If a collection was particularly successful, and sold faster than usual, the business was paid faster than usual, and Gilberto was quick to point out the link between maximum creative effort and cashflow. At the same time, he looked for ways to keep down existing costs and to minimise the cost of new investment.

When they heard that a local stocking factory was looking to sell off its obsolete machines, Gilberto and Luciano went to investigate. They knew nothing about stocking manufacture, but they knew a technician called Vittorio Sartori. Sartori saw that these machines could be converted into knitting looms, and the Benettons bought twenty or thirty of them at a fraction of the cost of a new machine of the type sold at the Milan trade fair. After Sartori had converted them, they not only knitted woollen jumpers, but still cost much less than a new machine. Never one to rest on his laurels, Gilberto also made sure that when converted machines were no longer needed, they were sold to their competitors at a profit.

A new factory, however, was a different proposition altogether. They had already converted two existing buildings and the inherent limitations of these were affecting their ability to sustain the high volumes needed to make the narrow margins in this business. Even if they sustained these margins at their present level, they could still not hope to finance a purpose-built factory themselves, even with the help of all their friends and family. For this, they needed the services of a bank.

The latest banker was perhaps two years older than Luciano. He gave him a patronising look. 'You young people are all the same,' he said. 'You want to run before you can walk.'

This was Luciano's fourth interview with a bank manager. He had asked each of them for a loan, making a detailed presentation of sales projections, offering substantial sureties and from each of them he had received the same reply. 'You're trying to go too far, too fast,' the bank manager smiled the same patronising smile. 'You don't believe me, but it's for your own good. One day you'll thank me for it.'

Luciano had stamped home to Teresa and the baby. 'Don't worry,' she told him. 'We've come this far, and we'll go further. Forget those idiots.'

She was the only person who could make him do this: relax, and forget. Relax and forget the worries and sense of duty that had been ingrained in him since he was a boy. At the same time, this premature maturity was precisely what had attracted her to him in the first place.

A short time later, he had reason to remember with gratitude what the bank manager had said. He was in the tiny office they jokingly called the 'executive suite' at the factory in Ponzano.

'Did you hear what the banks have done?' said Gilberto.

'No,' said Luciano; nor did he want to hear.

'You haven't been reading the papers,' his brother went on. 'A man like you, claiming he's always up to date. Haven't you noticed the country is falling apart?'

'Go on, then.'

'They've called in all loans to businesses which did not provide adequate guarantees.'

The Benettons had no loans to be called in because the banks had refused them, not believing in the success of their development programme. The two brothers looked at each other and burst out laughing.

'My God,' said Luciano, 'they're all in a mess, and we don't owe a cent. We're going to be rich!'

Anyone could crow over the way natural justice had taken its turn to wipe the smile off the faces of the banks. But the cycle would soon change again. How could they exploit this opportunity?

Builders and materials suppliers were traditional borrowers, living from contract to contract on short-term loans. They were bound to be among the hardest hit. Meanwhile, Très Jolie was booming; shoppers in the big cities were showing no sign of feeling the recession. Maybe, just maybe, they could drive a hard enough bargain to build their own factory without help from outside.

He put it to the family at Rosa's house over Sunday lunch.

'Where's the money going to come from?' said Gilberto.

He always had the latest figures: 70 per cent of their revenues went on materials, wages, running the machines and rent for the existing factory. There was very little to spare. Hell would freeze over before a bank would lend them money. With virtually no spare cash, there was no safety net. With no safety net . . . Gilberto looked round the table at the others.

This time, however, the others, including Carlo, were with Luciano. 'The money will come along somehow,' Luciano said for the second time. They had already faced similar situations; this time, however, a far bigger sum was needed, and he had one child, and another on the way, and no longer an accordion to sell.

Luciano's first call was on a builder called Simonetti. He had put up factories on the industrial estates on the coast and was regarded as the best in the region. He was also suffering from the recession and Luciano knew this.

They met at one of Simonetti's building sites. Luciano described in detail the kind of building he had in mind; what it had to be able to do; how soon they needed it; how it would make Simonetti a great deal of money. How, if he could not help, there were plenty of other builders who would be only too happy to take on the job.

'Can you do it?' he asked.

He had expected the builder to leap at the chance. Instead, Simonetti said, 'What makes you so sure people are going to go on buying woolly jumpers?'

Luciano explained the psychology of consumer behaviour in a recession. While people would think twice about buying, say, a new car, they would never surrender their right to wear affordable, colourful knitwear. On the contrary, the more the socialists tried to squeeze the individuality out of them, the more explicitly people would demonstrate their determination to preserve this right by going shopping.

Simonetti did not look entirely convinced by this argument. He himself would have to put up money for the construction as the Benettons did not have the necessary capital. Two days later, however, he telephoned Luciano. Yes, he would take on the job. Luciano was still exultant a few days later, when Gilberto called him over. 'I've found two banks,' he said, with a disbelieving air, 'who will lend us some of the money.'

The banking crisis had been concentrated locally on the Veneto and Lombardy. Gilberto had decided to look further afield, to the national banks. With their modest backing and some money of their own they were able to buy the land in Ponzano. They engaged Simonetti as the builder and commissioned a well-regarded architect called Cristiano Gasparetto. Gasparetto needed a collaborator for the job and was happy to listen to the suggestions of the family on the subject. Luciano's next call was on his friend Nico Luciani.

He and Nico went back a long way. They had ridden their bicycles around the Piazza San Francesco in the early days. They had been partners in the illicit sandwich business and many other ventures. Nico had designed the Très Jolie label. He had given up a career in the navy and was studying architecture at university in Venice under the supervision of the celebrated professor Carlo Scarpa. His response took Luciano by surprise.

'No way,' he told him. 'I'm not in the business of putting up factories for the bourgeoisie to tyrannise the workers.'

Nico, it seemed, had moved to the political far left; he was also very busy at the time. Even though he had never put up a building of any kind, on this occasion he did not want to start with his former comrade, Luciano Benetton.

'However, I know someone who would,' he added, contemptuously; it was the last time they were to speak for a quarter of a century.

Tobia Scarpa, like Nico, had not yet put up a single building. In every other respect, however, his qualifications were impeccable for what Luciano had in mind. Scarpa's father and Nico's teacher, Professor Carlo Scarpa, was a noted figure in post-war intellectual circles and a disciple of the great American architect Frank Lloyd Wright. One of his favourite forms of seminar for his students at Venice University was to wait until darkness fell and then project the outlines of Lloyd Wright's buildings on the walls of Venetian palaces. Scarpa junior had inherited his father's adventurous imagination, which was shared by his wife, Afra. The Scarpas were currently employed by two big companies, designing revolutionary new types of furniture and lighting.

In Scarpa, Luciano had found his architect's collaborator. Gasparetto and Scarpa would see the project through to completion, whereupon Gasparetto would cease to have a connection with Benetton and the Scarpas would continue alone, a deep rapport having developed between them and Luciano Benetton. This was the first and perhaps the most enduring example of Luciano's uncanny ability to see in people a capability of which even they themselves were unaware, or if aware, of which they were unsure.

It was also the beginning of a brilliantly creative and turbulent friendship.

In only eight years, the family had taken Très Jolie from a collection of twenty jumpers designed and made at home and sold door-to-door by foot, bicycle or motor scooter, to a professional business manufacturing 20,000 jumpers a year and selling them through shops in Treviso, Venice and Rome. However, just as the name Très Jolie still reflected the superiority of Paris over Rome in terms of image and brand power, so Luciano was aware that Italy lagged behind the competition in terms of wool quality and manufacturing. Even the Benettons and Très Jolie would find themselves left behind if they tried to compete internationally with their current production methods, in spite of their lead in colour and design. In order to make the business as competitive abroad as it was becoming at home, Luciano had to continue the learning process that he had begun with the Dellasiegas and continued with the Tagliacozzos. In order to do this, he had had to go further afield than Rome; he had to go abroad.

This time he went north, across the Alps, Switzerland, Germany and France, to a country he had never visited before, and which he hoped would be the next stepping-stone in the process that would take them into Europe.

3   The Secret of the Itch

London Airport, England, 1962

'**E**xcuse me, sir,' the British police had a way of imbuing polite-
ness with a particular menace, 'would you please tell me
how much money you have with you?'

Luciano, who would become one of the richest men in the world,
showed him the modest contents of his wallet. The policeman at the
immigration desk nodded, but still looked doubtfully at the young
foreigner travelling alone who was not wearing a jacket or tie.

'I'm here on a research trip,' Luciano said in English. This was a
language he understood, but he would never admit to doing so, and
he would never speak it in public; it was almost as if an interpreter
gave him time to think.

Benetton

The policeman looked at him again and jerked his thumb past the immigration desk. Welcome to Great Britain, home of racism, sheep and the finest wool and manufacturing in the world.

The traditionally bad weather in Scotland gives rise both to the need for warm, hard-wearing clothing, and the rain which enables the grazing for the sheep from which this clothing is made. So important did this business become that between 1780 and 1850 entire villages there were forcibly depopulated and the Highlands 'cleared' of people so that sheep could take their place. Many of these dispossessed Scottish families migrated to America and Canada. To this day, their descendants return to Scotland and England as tourists, and after Buckingham Palace and Harrods their next port of call in London is to the Scotch House to buy Scottish knitwear.

Luciano's tour of the British Isles lasted ten days and took him to the key woollen garment manufacturers in England and Scotland: Pringle, Ballantyne, Braeman and Hogg of Hawick. These names were synonymous with quality at home and in the international markets. With Scotch whisky and life assurance, knitwear was Scotland's most successful export. Scottish jumpers were expensive, beautifully made, soft and yet hardwearing, and conservative to the point of dullness in colour and design. British parents of reasonable means bought these jumpers for their children, as their parents had done for them. They were symbolic of heritage and enduring values; their advertising evoked images of kilts and heather and wholesome outdoor activity, with a strong hint of exclusivity and social status. The range of colours was equally exclusive: grey, blue, red and camel. This reputation for quality, and not the stuffy image or limited range of colours, was what had brought Luciano here on his first visit to Britain. Here, in 'the home of wool', he particularly wanted to learn 'the secret of the itch'.

The British companies were intrigued and flattered by the visit of the trim, bespectacled, serious-mannered young foreigner, and impressed by his technical grasp of the subject. Luciano described to them the manufacturing processes they were using in Ponzano, taking care to stress the modest scale of the factory and the antiquated nature of the machinery. He told them how they had converted the stocking machines and how their main problem lay in achieving the softness in the finished garment. He remarked on the softness of the British Shetland and cashmere wool and they told him many things in return. The Scottish companies were particularly forthcoming.

The Scots themselves were indefatigable travellers in pursuit of business and in the sophisticated visitor from another northern climate they found a ready and respectful listener. Some of their techniques to soften wool and remove 'the itch' were primitive in the extreme; at Hogg of Hawick, in the Scottish borders, they immersed the raw wool in water and beat it with wooden poles. Other approaches were more sophisticated and yet simple; they stored raw wool for at least three months in a darkened room, with controlled humidity; this removed the static electricity in the wool and gave it greater softness and density. Luciano had never heard of either of these techniques before. Nearly twenty years down the track, he would return and buy a Scottish company. Meanwhile he listened carefully and made detailed notes back at his hotel. At the end of his trip, he ordered a number of British-made machines for dyeing, knitting, ironing and drying wool. Then he flew home, armed with the fruits of his latest research and relayed them to Giuliana. 'We saw that what we wanted to do had already been done in Scotland,' he would recall, 'but we wanted to do it in our own style.' They decided that the way ahead lay in combining their range of bright colours with Scottish quality, adapting the manufacturing methods where necessary. There would be softer wool, but no hand-beating with wooden poles in the revolutionary new factory that Gasparetto and Scarpa were creating on the drawing board.

Giuliana was not the only person keen to hear the news that Luciano had found the means to enable them to catch up with the international competition. Adalgerico 'Ado' Montana was a man in a similar mould to Vittorio Sartori, the technician who had helped them convert the stocking machines. Montana was a dyeing specialist, who originally came from up the coast in Trieste, near the border with Yugoslavia. His family had been dyeing wool and fabrics for three generations, and like Calderoni, the Tagliacozzos and Luciano himself, his family and fortunes had been marked by the war. Montana had come to work in Treviso where, in impoverished circumstances and a tiny workshop, he plied his art with the air of a medieval necromancer. Luciano had met him a couple of years earlier, after his first visit to Rome and before his visit to Scotland. Montana's mastery of colour, his ability to synthesise them and give life to materials, particularly to wool, hypnotised Luciano. Montana was a genius who lived from hand to mouth on what business Luciano and others could bring his way. He became one of Luciano's mentors and together they scoured books on modern artists like Kandinsky for colours which they had never seen before and which they tried to recreate. Montana hardly ever went outside his workshop. Luciano's journeys had widened his technical knowledge and given him the confidence to ask the bigger technical questions.

Fashions in colour changed fast, especially in the big cities, which were their main market. Yet all their jumpers, and everybody else's for that matter, could only be assembled after the constituent parts had been dyed individually. This meant that the process of making a finished jumper took longer, and made it difficult to react to sudden changes in fashion. Nobody, not even Pringle, or Ballantyne, or

Braeman, or Hogg of Hawick, let alone the Benettons, had found a way past this problem. The universal assumption was that to dye an entire jumper was to run the risk of shrinking it and filling it with holes.

One night, in Montana's workshop, Luciano said, 'Do you think it will ever be possible to dye an entire jumper after it has been made?'

Montana had thought for a moment and looked up from his book. 'That may well not be entirely beyond the bounds of possibility,' he said.

Rome, Italy, 1964

Piero Marchiorello was not quite as poor as Ado Montana, but he had very little money. He worked for his father in a little clothes shop in the hill town of Belluno, fifty miles north of Treviso, at the foot of the Alps. It was winter and they had come to Rome for a meeting of small retailers.

Marchiorello was thirty-five years old, and he took some time out from the trade gathering to check out the latest fashions. He found himself first in the Piazza di Spagna, then on the Via Gambero; and he was looking into the window of the shop belonging to the Tagliacozzos. On display was what looked to him like a rainbow of coloured jumpers.

Marchiorello did not know that this was what they were until he went inside and picked one up.

'Who makes this stuff?' he asked the sales assistant.

The assistant told him it was a company called Très Jolie in Treviso. Marchiorello had never heard of them. He wrote down the name and address, went back to the small retailers' convention and then took the night train to Venice. Two days after he had seen the

Luciano had looked at the model and seen not merely a factory in which people would earn money to lead their lives, but an environment. The autonomy he had given Scarpa had paid off and they had immediately accepted the design. Moreover, they decided to give it an additional, expensive feature. Plenty of factories in the Veneto had landscaping of some sort, albeit none as stylish as this, but none of them had air-conditioning. This one would have both.

The cost of the new factory had doubled in six months, but they were saved by an increase in business. Luciano had been right about the reaction of the shopper in a recession. They had doubled production to meet demand and were making 100,000 jumpers a month. Gilberto and Carlo were buying as many more machines and taking on as many extra people as they could find. The range of shops through which Très Jolie was sold now extended from Venice and Rome, to other big cities like Florence and Naples. In Treviso, meanwhile, in his workshop of many colours, Ado Montana had discovered that it was possible to dye an entire jumper.

Montana had been experimenting without success with formulae and temperatures for several months; as predicted, the jumpers either came out of the dyeing vat shrunken or filled with holes. One day, as much by trial and error as anything else, they pulled a jumper from the vat which appeared to have done neither. They examined every thread and seam and found it to be flawless. Luciano immediately ordered some dying machines and installed them at the end of the factory line. Henceforth, they would be able to dye complete jumpers as soon as they were assembled. He would remain coy about the exact combination of dye and temperature, but the result was that they were able to put finished jumpers into the shops faster than the competition.

A Scotsman had told Luciano 'the secret of the itch'. Now, the big-city shopper could change his or her taste in colour as fast and as frequently as they liked, and the increased cost of the new factory was covered by the increase in orders, thanks to the ingenuity of a dyer from Trieste called Ado Montana. The breakthrough also marked a change in the fortunes of the colouring expert; thirty years later, this impoverished one-man band would be the owner of a large company that specialised in dyeing.

Ponzano, the Veneto, 1965

The new Benetton Brothers factory opened on a spring morning with celebrations that went on into the night. The 'brothers', including Giuliana, had been working on the preparations for weeks. Five hundred invitations had gone out, including to all the employees and the inhabitants of the village. The Dellasiegas, the Scarpas, Marchiorello and Montana were there. An aeroplane had been hired to bring Calderoni, the Tagliacozzos and others from the capital. A government minister performed the official opening and asked where the owners were; surely these children could not be the proprietors of such a grown-up enterprise? A bishop gave his blessing. Giuliana, with a sober new hairstyle and new blue outfit, led the dignitaries on the guided tour. The women knitting machine operators also had new hairstyles for the occasion. Rosa glowed with pride and sighed, wishing that their father could have lived to see this day. Later, Luciano said he felt as if he was graduating from university.

If this was a rite of passage for the family, it was also a statement. They had arrived, here in the village where they had always been, but in a new sense; as a power in the neighbourhood. This was the renaissance of 'the urbanised countryside' – *la campagna urbanizzata* – that was once again seeing the rise of hundreds of small family businesses synonymous with a single area of manufacturing. Shoes were made to the south-east of here in Ascoli Piceno; textiles

to the south at Prato; ceramics at Sassuolo; and the garment manufacturers and assemblers were here in the Veneto.

Over thirty years later, hundreds of these garment assemblers
are sub-contractors working exclusively for Benetton. Others have
been absorbed into the business or eliminated by automation. Today
the Benetton Brothers factory still looks like a spaceship that has
been set down amid the vineyards, albeit in a parking lot of other,
bigger spaceships that dwarf the Scarpas' first creation. The factory
retains a timeless beauty, a testament to creativity, accentuated by
the fact that the manufacturing processes are now elsewhere and the
original building is dominated by Giuliana's design studio. The irony
is that while it possesses a timelessness of design, even on that first
day over thirty years ago, in terms of its manufacturing capability,
the brand-new factory was already obsolete.

Belluno, northern Italy, 1965

Four months later, Luciano and Teresa, who was eight months pregnant with their third child, drove north up the road from Treviso in
a truck full of knitwear. Their destination was Belluno where Piero
Marchiorello was waiting.

Belluno, far more so than Treviso, was a small town of traditional
shopkeepers. Marchiorello was determined to show off the jumpers
in waves of colour, that would have the same hunger-quenching
effect on the young people of the town as Giuliana's first designs had
done on the youth of Treviso. He and Luciano had agreed that
slightly more than half the clothes displayed should be aimed at
girls and women. Marchiorello had already taken on a pretty girl
assistant.

Marchiorello had designed a simple, brightly lit, white-walled
interior. There was still a counter between the sales assistant and the

customer; they had been unable to remove this under the terms of the lease. But the counter had been repainted and there were lots of light pine shelves onto which Luciano and Teresa were now piling red, blue, yellow, orange and green jumpers.

'I love it,' Teresa said. 'Pity it's in a dead end.'

'They'll come,' said Marchiorello. 'You'll see.'

Like the jumpers, they had given the shop a foreign name; this time, however, it was English. Swinging London was the height of fashion in clothes, the visual arts and music. The Beatles and the Rolling Stones were breaking big in Italy as they were everywhere. They called it 'My Market'.

A month later, Luciano and Teresa's third child, a daughter, Rossella, was born. The bulletins on her health were almost as frequent as the telephone calls from Marchiorello in Belluno.

'It's happening,' he told Luciano. 'they come in and stand there like they've been frozen, like they're drinking in the colours.'

As he had predicted, word had soon gone round the young people of the town that My Market was the place to be. Marchiorello and his assistant were selling twenty jumpers a day, twice as many as expected, and more than enough to cover their costs. Although the new factory was their pride and joy, the success of the little shop at the bottom of a dead end in a small town in the hills, the first exclusively to sell their range of clothes, was a source of intense satisfaction to Luciano and the Benettons. Six months after My Market opened for business, Marchiorello came to see him again.

'It's like I said,' he told him. 'If we can do it in a place like that, just imagine what we could do somewhere smart, where there are lots of people.'

This time, Luciano needed no persuading. Things were going even better than they had been six months earlier and there was a new corporate confidence in the air. During the summer they had changed the name of the business from Très Jolie to Benetton and registered the name of the company. This made no difference to the day-to-day running of the business, but it formalised the roles that the three brothers and sister had evolved between themselves. Luciano was president and commercial director; Giuliana was in charge of design; Gilberto was finance director; and Carlo was in charge of production. The volume of orders was already so much greater than the capacity of the new factory that they also started to sub-contract the assembly of some of the garments to many of the little clothing businesses in and around the area, like the workshop that had employed Giuliana in Treviso. These sub-contractors often employed fewer than fifteen people in order to save on social security costs, which inhibited the growth of many ambitious companies without access to this skill base. As long as the volume of orders continued to grow, these satellites of the spaceship in Ponzano would play a bigger and bigger role in the growth of Benetton.

Luciano had wanted to reach the point where their own name, and not that of a made-up French brand, was on their garments. With the registration of the Benetton company name this point had arrived. One of Giuliana's stylists, Franco Giacometti, designed a logo featuring a stylised knot of yarn for their labels; their first corporate advertising, in black and white by Carlo Mazzaro, also featured this design. With colour advertising, this logo was placed together with the word 'Benetton' in white on a background of green, Giuliana's favourite colour; this became their trademark.

Luciano, however, had no such intentions as yet for the shop that was carrying the new Benetton brand or for any of its successors. Marchiorello had come to him with an idea prompted by the success of My Market and not Benetton. If Marchiorello failed, the name of My Market would suffer and not that of the company. Meanwhile, Marchiorello was telling Luciano he had found what he believed was the perfect location for a second shop; the fashionable ski resort of Cortina d'Ampezzo in the Dolomites.

Cortina d'Ampezzo was only two hours north-east of there, but it was about as far removed from Ponzano, or Belluno for that matter, as a place could possibly be. Cortina was glamorous, it was blessed with ski slopes so good that it had hosted the Winter Olympics and it was a favourite haunt of the international jet set. Luciano, Teresa and the children had taken holidays there and mar-velled at the procession of names from royalty, show business and the gossip columns. Cortina was also a popular haunt of the young, whose favourite pastime when they were not on the ski slopes was to be seen in the latest clothes, which necessitated the devotion of a considerable amount of their time and energy, as well as their dis-posable income, to the act of shopping.

The Cortina business community was closely knit and suspicious of newcomers from out of town; finding a shop to rent here was more difficult and expensive than it had been in Belluno. Eventually, they found a small shop available for rent on the corner of the Corso Italia, one of the main thoroughfares after the ski slopes closed each night for promenaders and shoppers. Again, the shop would be called My Market and again the deal with Marchiorello was simple: buy exclusively from us and keep the profits. A more demanding clientele, however, called for a more sophisticated selling space. This time, Luciano told Marchiorello that they should entrust the Scarpas with the design of the shop. This decision on Luciano's part, to devolve responsibility for running the shop and at the same time keep creative control, was to lead to a formula repeated, with varia-tions, over 500 times by the end of the decade, and over 9,000 times by the year 2000.

The Scarpas leapt at the chance. They were passionate intellectu-als who liked nothing better than to sit up late after dinner with Luciano and Marchiorello, extrapolating cerebral theories on life in general from their theories on human behaviour in the retail environment. Marchiorello, the non-cerebral retailer, would soon yawn and nod off during these discussions, but Luciano was fascinated; they stretched him and satisfied his thirst for knowledge. As with Calderoni, Montana and the Tagliacozzos, they also took the place of the formal education he had never had, only in his case this education would never end.

Cortina d'Ampezzo, northern Italy, 1966

They opened the new shop on a snowy morning in January at the height of the ski season. This time, there were shelves of jumpers in all colours around the walls of the shop and no counter; a simple table stood in the middle for the cash register and where the sales assistant wrapped the purchases. There was bright lighting and loud music. The jumpers on sale were in the widest possible range of colours but only in the two smallest sizes they made; this shop was aimed exclusively at the young. The young sales assistant was under instructions to let people come in and see for themselves, to pick up the jumpers and handle them, free from the patronising and often intimidating attention of the traditional shopkeepers whose stores lined both sides of the rest of the street.

Two days later, Marchiorello called Luciano in Ponzano.

'They're queuing round the block!' he told him. 'We've sold a third of the stuff already! Come and see for yourself, and bring some more stock!'

Luciano drove north up the icy roads with Carlo, his younger brother, who was a skiing fanatic. They arrived in Cortina just as the sun was setting on the Dolomites. This was a sight they would never forget: the golden light on the peaks and slopes; the crowds of people in the snowy streets; and, outside My Market, a queue of young people trying to get in. Inside the shop, another queue of young people were pulling jumpers of all colours and styles off the shelves and handing them to the sales assistant, five or six at a time. Marchiorello had not been exaggerating; if anything, they were going to run out of stock sooner than he thought. Luciano and Carlo went back to the car, unloaded the boxes of fresh stock and made their way past the queues outside and inside the shop; and once again, as he had done with his very first sale ten years earlier, they did so with that same intense feeling, like scientists whose theory has just been proven correct.

The traditional shopkeepers of Cortina at first dismissed My Market as a passing fad, and one that would go as quickly as it came. However, as the season wore on and sales continued to boom, they were forced to admit that they were wrong. Fashions changed quickly, this was true, but most of the clothes in My Market were not fashionable in the traditional sense; they were accessible, yet different. Meanwhile, Luciano made sure that, at the extreme end of their range which was most fashionable and therefore most susceptible to sudden changes in taste, these changes could be anticipated faster than their competitors and with a wider range of colours, through the whole garment dyeing process they had perfected back at the factory.

The word 'Benetton' is Franco–Italian in origin and is one of the very few Italian names ending with the hard consonant. Luciano had noticed that the name sounded English to the English, French to the French, German to the Germans, American to the Americans, and so on. The immediate and spectacular success of the shop in Cortina now sent clothes with the Benetton name home with holidaymakers all over Italy and across the land borders into Austria, France and Switzerland. Wherever they went the name sounded at home. Even Luciano, observant and forward-thinking as he was, privately had to admit that this was a major piece of luck.

Across the country, meanwhile, people were waking up to the fact that these clothes were not only fun to wear but were also a hot commercial prospect. Calls began pouring in to Luciano's office in Ponzano from prospective store owners. Most of these were young people, like Marchiorello, but they were not known to Luciano, and they themselves had no idea of the informal commercial relationship that existed between the two shops and the company that supplied them. Luciano did not feel comfortable with the American-style franchise agreement, where the store owner simply had to find enough money and sign a written contract agreeing to pay for the use of the brand name, and then to pay royalties on sales and profits. He felt more comfortable with the less stressful, more intuitive approach, which placed a higher premium on the creative symbiosis he believed Benetton needed with its retailers. Marchiorello was one such kindred spirit who had become a friend, but even a dynamo like him could only open and manage so many shops. It was among his other friends, therefore, that Luciano also began to look for prospective store owners. While the telephone had continued to ring, he also looked at the map and began to search for a location for the next shop. It was Marchiorello again, however, who had already decided where this should be.

Padua, northern Italy, 1967

Padua, forty miles south-west of Treviso, is one of the oldest university cities in the world. Galileo and Copernicus were students there; Shakespeare sent Hamlet there for his further education. Had Luciano himself been able to go to university, he would probably have gone to Padua. Thirty thousand students did so every year from all over Europe. Like many famous university cities, Padua also had a traditional commercial community attuned to the shopping habits of its older residents which were in many ways inadequate to meet the needs of a young, increasingly fashion-conscious student population.

There were dozens of cafés, cinemas, theatres and bookstores, but still relatively few shops catering exclusively for the young consumer of limited means and unlimited appetite for what was happening now in a popular culture dominated by New York, San Francisco, London and Paris. Yet, the traditional shopkeepers of Padua did not seem to want to have anything to do with this revolution of the young and the vast new market opportunities it presented to them.

They had heard what had happened to their counterparts in Cortina. When they heard Luciano and Marchiorello were planning to open a My Market in Padua, they tried every means possible to keep them out of the central business district. Two shopkeepers who had sold Très Jolie and now sold Benetton among other brands, and whose shops were close to the proposed new My Market, came to Luciano with an ultimatum.

'If you open in Padua, we'll stop selling Benetton,' one of them told him. 'You'll be our direct competitor. You'll ruin us.'

'I don't think so,' he had replied. 'In fact, if anything, I think it will make things better for you.'

He knew he had no means of proving that this would be the case, but he also knew that they knew there was nothing they could do. Besides, the volume of sales from the two existing My Market shops was already multiplying at a far faster rate than the sales from the traditional outlets which sold Benetton merely as one of a range of brands.

The Scarpas designed the new shop in exactly the same way as they had done in Cortina. There was no counter and the walls were lined with shelves of jumpers in all colours which the customer was encouraged to pick up and handle with no overt pressure to buy.

There was the same bright lighting and loud music. In the spring of that year, My Market opened in Padua. The latest opening saw the same phenomenal response; the queues of students and other young people this time, inside the shop and round the block. Luciano and the traditional shopkeepers could not both be right; yet, in the event, the two men whose shops were nearest the new store, and who had stood in his office and threatened first to withdraw their business and then begged him not to ruin them, saw their own sales of Benetton double. Between them, instead of losing business, they accounted for as much as half as many sales as the new shop.

This was a strange phenomenon. Privately, Luciano had conceded that the two traditional shopkeepers might be right and that the competition from My Market would put them out of business. Instead, in the months that followed the opening, the competition seemed to be stimulating sales of Benetton clothes in both the old and the new kinds of shop. But how long would this last, and how long would it be before someone else came along, as was always the case, and began to compete with Benetton in the market they currently had to themselves? Once this happened, the market would become fragmented and unstable. Luciano did not want this to happen. His clarity of thinking would be cluttered with consideration for others with whom he had no community of interest and over whom he had no control. By these criteria, if there had to be competition, as there must, it would be better for them to compete with themselves than with others. Moreover, the number of suitable people wanting to become My Market shop owners in cities, towns and villages around the country suggested that there was plenty of room for this to happen. But how long would the opportunity be there? And, if Benetton could compete with themselves, should they not also compete with those traditional shopkeepers on the latter's territory, with shops and clothes for a wider range of customers, and not just the bored schoolkids of Belluno, the two smallest sizes of affluent young person in Cortina and the student population of Padua?

Ponzano, the Veneto, 1968

Luciano talked about this to Giuliana.

'I told you,' she said, 'you always say, "If only you could make more!"'

Then he put the question to Tobia Scarpa.

'This is what I want,' he told him. 'Do you think you can do it?'

A short while later, Scarpa came back to him with a series of drawings. Each of these depicted a shop that would sell Benetton, but each one was an entirely new variation on the theme that had begun with My Market.

'Merceria' was for the mothers of their existing young customers. This shop had softer lighting and gentler music, with more classical colours in clothes to match and just enough of the feel of the traditional shop to make the customer relaxed and yet intrigued by the choice that lay before them. 'Tomato' was ultra-modern for teenagers, with bright lights and a chrome and glass interior. 'Fantomax' was an Art Nouveau creation, redolent of Swinging London and the hippy fashion for billowing clothes and mood music. Like My Market, all these shops exclusively carried the Benetton range and none of them carried the Benetton name. None of them had a counter.

My Market was part of a jigsaw and Scarpa had factored in the commercial and social components to come up with the rest of the pieces. The result was a brilliant extrapolation from Luciano's flash of reasoning; a mechanism that could be set in motion across the country, which would function as a single entity and yet compete with itself, and the total yield of which would exceed the sum of its parts.

This at least was the theory, and while Luciano and Scarpa worked on the details, the number of My Market shops and shop owners spread faster and faster, from Belluno, Cortina and Padua, to Florence, Rome, Naples and Trieste. All these new shops were started and operated by friends, and friends of friends – young people with what Luciano and Gilberto regarded as the right spirit and in whom a lack of previous experience was construed as a positive asset.

They included young men and women bored with their jobs in the law and other professions, as well as proven entrepreneurs like Marchiorello. Some had been into the shops in Belluno, Cortina and Padua, and had come away realising that shop owning could be fun and that they too could become part of this retail revolution. Others heard about the shops through friends or in the press; at this stage, although Giuliana would never be at ease with the media, Luciano still gave interviews, a situation which would change over the next decade. Meanwhile, all these new shop owners undertook to buy exclusively from Benetton and sell the same, and on the same terms; no American-style franchise contract, no premium on the use of the name of the shop, no royalties on sales or profits, and no return of unsold stock. All of them agreed to construct their shops in a location approved by Luciano and according to the design laid down by Scarpa. Luciano also reserved the right to intervene if he thought they were running the shop in a way that would harm the name of Benetton.

Initially, as with Marchiorello, these were partnerships, the new shop owners being able to split the opening costs with Benetton. As their numbers multiplied, however, Gilberto decided that direct investment by the company in so many start-ups was neither desirable nor necessary, and would-be shop owners had to raise the money themselves, albeit with advice and referrals from the company to likely lenders. The decision was made to allow them to continue alone, and they were happy to do so. During this period,

Benetton also ended its relationships with the independent retailers that had begun with the Dellasiegas and others.

Whatever their individual backgrounds and circumstances, My Market owners across the country were also soon opening examples of Merceria, Tomato and Fantomax in the same city, town, village and even street. This made sense when they knew the tastes and potential of the neighbourhood. Sales individually fed each other and collectively soared, and the theory that it was better to compete with themselves than with others was proven correct. Yet, while many people who went into these shops had no idea how closely related they were to each other, would-be competitors still held back in the belief that the market would collapse under the combined weight. When the combined numbers of My Market, Merceria, Tomato and Fantomax reached 300 in a single year, these would-be competitors reached a different conclusion. The market was not going to collapse after all, but it would do if they now tried to break into it. The result was that competition between these four kinds of shop was the dominant market force across the country for the next decade.

Riding this whirlwind would be the man who had first come to Luciano with the idea for a shop and who would open many more over the years. Thirty years on, Belluno, where the first shop had opened, would still be a small town where the railway carriages still had wooden seats and were known as the 'Wild West' trains. Piero Marchiorello would still be managing Benetton shops in the town where he now lived, by this time a rich man, in Monte Carlo.

The Villa Minelli, Ponzano, the Veneto, 1969

The country itself was entering turbulent times. Many institutions and businesses at the interface of political and industrial life were in ferment; this culminated in *l'autunno caldo* – the hot autumn – of unrest, strikes and violent demonstrations. There were bombings and killings in major cities. Later, they coined a phrase for these years of bombs and bullets; they called them 'the years of lead'.

In the village of Ponzano, the deteriorating political and economic situation seemed far away. The factory was running at full stretch all the time in order to supply the growing number of shops. The first non-woollen range of clothes, shirts, trousers and skirts was launched to co-ordinate with the woollen jumpers with which they had made their name. The number of people employed on site was already far outstripped by the number working for the many small local sub-contractors who assembled garments exclusively for Benetton. Labour relations were good within the factory and the trade unions were yet to target the company in the way that they were targeting others. Benetton was the major local employer, run by a family who themselves had grown up in the area and who prided themselves on their relationship with their direct employees; the rest of the labour force was indirect. These factors protected the company and its finely tuned production processes for the time being from the strikes and collective bargaining that were causing havoc across industry up and down the country.

All four members of the family were by this time married with children. Giuliana, Gilberto and Carlo commuted into work from large houses on the outskirts of Treviso. Rosa insisted on staying in the house in Santa Bona where they grew up and where the business started; the children agreed, but insisted that she at least allow Scarpa to refurbish and decorate it. Their own ideas of personal luxury were far from flamboyant. Giuliana's priorities would always be work and family, and her principal indulgence was her swimming pool. Even Gilberto, the sports fanatic with the movie star looks, agonised before buying himself a Porsche, although he could afford one many times over. Carlo, meanwhile, spent much of his free time skiing and wandering in the great outdoors.

Luciano and Teresa, and their three children, Mauro, Alessandro and Rossella, had moved the previous year from their house near Rosa to a new house designed by Scarpa, close to the factory itself. Their fourth and last child, Rocco, would be born in 1971. As he had done with the factory, Luciano had given Scarpa complete autonomy over the design of the house. The result was what Scarpa described as a house 'fit for a modern merchant prince', built around a pair of courtyards landscaped with trees, plants and fountains and constructed in the ultra-modern style. The villagers had become used to the 'spaceship' factory, but Luciano's 'princely' house baffled some of them, who could not understand why, when he could obviously afford better materials, he wanted to live in a house made of concrete.

Even Luciano, the most sophisticated and outgoing of the four children, had an ambivalent attitude towards his newfound wealth. The new house was always open to the Scarpas, Marchiorello, Montana and others close to him from the earliest days. They were always welcome for dinner, but dinner itself only began after Carlo had telephoned him from the factory with the countrywide sales figures for the day. Even as an impoverished young man, Luciano had dressed as a breadwinner, and in the early years of the business he had often worn a sober suit and tie. By this time, however, he was affecting a more casual look.

He was also collecting classic cars in his basement garage. He often drove the 1952 Rolls–Royce Silver Shadow, the Jaguar, the Bentley, the Alfa Romeo Giulietta and the Porsche, but invariably did so in a pair of jeans and an open-necked shirt. He and Marchiorello would drive to a business appointment in the Bentley with one of them in the back and the other in the front, wearing a chauffeur's cap. One of them would park the car and open the door for the other. On one such occasion, when they appeared in the office of a lawyer in charge of the sale of a vacant shop site in a stuffy provincial town, the secretary mistook them for gypsies and offered them money to go away. When they explained that they had come about the sale of the building, the lawyer laughed at them and named a steep price. Only when Marchiorello replied with a figure close enough to be real, and added 'What do you think, Luciano?' did the lawyer realise the 'gypsy' to whom he was talking was the rising retail phenomenon, Luciano Benetton.

Later, the other parties to these negotiations would wonder whether or not this disconcerting mixture of informality and commercial muscle had been a deliberate ploy. Some might have interpreted this as a smack in the face to the kind of authority represented by the bank manager who had refused to lend them the money to build the factory. In fact, Luciano was still intensely conservative in many ways and fundamentally too shy to be comfortable with conspicuous consumption; intellectually, he also disdained the pomposity that often went with this. For all his passion for cars, he knew you could only drive one car at a time, whatever it was, and they all went at more or less the same speed; only a few years earlier, he and Teresa had been to Spain and back in a tiny Fiat 500. The popular culture of the time was dedicated to deflating traditional establishment figures and proving that a relaxed approach could go hand in hand with hard-headed commerciality.

There was undoubtedly unfinished business in Luciano's soul from the long years of privation and self-discipline to which he had subjugated his adolescence, but this would not find an outlet in the fancy cars he had in the garage. Instead, he looked to the one source of inspiration that he and his family had known since the earliest days of their childhood, now many years ago, and yet still only a couple of hundred yards away: the Villa Minelli.

In the three boom years since they had opened the new factory, the Villa Minelli's decline had accelerated. The roof was falling in and windows were bricked up; the gardens were overgrown to the point of impenetrability. Peasants kept rabbits and chicken in the chapel and a local butcher set up shop from time to time in one of the once grand reception rooms. Teenagers from the village held trysts in the drier parts of the building. The owner, a private lay institution which ran an orphanage and survived on charity, was only too pleased when Benetton offered to buy the villa.

In addition to being the fulfilment of a childhood family dream, the purchase made business sense. The vendor wished to sell and the company needed more office space. It would have been difficult and controversial for anyone who might have wanted to do so to demolish the Villa Minelli in order to make way for a modern building. The Benettons had ambitious plans to preserve and restore the villa. As an established landmark, it dominated the flat fields and vineyards and was visible on all sides from a considerable distance. The time and money the Benettons intended to spend on restoration would be justified by the statement the renovated villa would make about how far they had come, the family's sense of heritage and their commitment to putting something back into the community. The Minellis had been merchant princes; now it was their turn.

Luciano knew better than anyone else that these different but complementary considerations could all be factored into a single, compelling image: that of a small boy on his bicycle under a wartime sky, gazing intently at the ruined villa and swearing that, one day, he would make it his own.

While Tobia Scarpa and internal finance manager Elio Aluffi scoured the libraries of Venice and Treviso for information about the Villa Minelli and its history, the garden was cleared, the rabbits, chickens and lovers evicted, and elderly craftsmen were tracked down and persuaded to come out of retirement. Meanwhile, the retail revolution that was funding the restoration showed no signs of slowing down. My Market, Merceria, Tomato and Fantomax shops continued to multiply across the country. There were 500 by this time and in all of them the name of Benetton, on a green label with the knot of yarn logo, had long displaced Très Jolie in the brand consciousness of the customer. But although they had left behind the fake French imagery of Très Jolie, they could not ignore the reality of French influence on fashion. Luciano and Marchiorello made numerous research visits by Rolls–Royce across the border into France, to St Tropez. Here they observed the appearance of the latest and shortest mini skirts, the smallest bikinis, the monokini and other phenomena which they duly noted and brought back to Giuliana and her team of designers. These designers included several French stylists by this time, among them a former model for Christian Dior called Lison Bonfils.

Luciano had spotted Lison Bonfils four years earlier when she was working as a designer for a textile manufacturer. He had invited her to dinner and persuaded her to come to Ponzano to work with Giuliana. She was sparky and direct, without a hint of deference to his intelligence and position of power within the company. In a different way from the Scarpas and Montana, she stretched him. When she went back to Paris, she carried on designing for Giuliana from there. She was convinced that Paris was ready for Benetton.

'There are thousands of French kids out there desperate for something decent to wear with blue jeans,' she told them. 'English jumpers are too expensive and the French ones with mohair are horrible. I tell you, the market is just sitting there, waiting for you.'

Luciano and Marchiorello visited Paris, looking for a site for what would be their first shop outside Italy. One day in the spring of 1969, they found what they believed was the perfect place. When he returned to the factory, Luciano decided to call Lison with the good news.

Paris, France, 1969

'What?' she said. 'Near the Champs Elysées? You must be joking!'

Luciano was taken aback.

'It's a great site,' he told her. 'It's in a new shopping arcade right in the middle of the central business district. It's a good investment.'

'Bah!' she retorted. 'You don't want to be there. You want to be on the Left Bank in the Boulevard Saint-Germain. That's where the action is. That's where you'll find your customers.'

'But we've already bought it,' said Luciano.

'Too bad,' she laughed. 'You'll see.'

During the following months, they shipped out to Paris the fixtures and fittings according to Scarpa's specifications, and a comprehensive range of stock. The new shop, once again to be called My Market, was scheduled to open in September. They arrived in Paris in plenty of time for the opening, only to discover that the owners of the shopping arcade were nowhere near ready themselves to open any of the shops.

'Good,' said Lison Bonfils, when Luciano told her the bad news. 'I never liked it. Why don't you look somewhere else?'

Luciano looked at her suspiciously. 'Where?' he said.

'Oh, I don't know. Come on, let's get in the car and go and have a look.'

Later, she swore it was a coincidence that they pulled over on the Boulevard Saint-Germain, opposite an empty shop with a 'For Sale' sign in the window. Luciano rolled down the car window and took the telephone number. A few hours later, he was the new owner. A week later, there in the Latin Quarter on the Boulevard Saint-Germain, the latest My Market opened for business, the first in Paris and the first outside Italy.

This time, there were no immediate queues of young people around the block, but there was a steady stream of students. There was also a fulsome welcome for Benetton from the members of the fashion media. One of these was Sandy Obervitz, an American friend of Lison Bonfils and writer for *Mademoiselle*. As Bonfils had done for her own home country, France, Obervitz now lost no time in telling Luciano that he should take the clothes to the United States.

New York City, United States of America, 1970

Luciano had already visited America in reality since his boyhood dreams of the country with his friend Nico Luciani. He had gone for the first time with Teresa on holiday to New York City a few years after they were married, when their first three children were still very young and the factory and first shop were newly opened. They had walked up Fifth Avenue and other streets and gaped at the buildings laid out like mountain ranges, at the shops so tall they were like cathedrals of commerce. They had stared at the names, for so long part of mythology that the reality was almost impossible to take in: Bergdorf Goodman, Bloomingdale's, Macy's, Saks. As he had been in Rome, Paris and London, and now in New York City, Luciano was part tourist, part researcher, and wholly intent on absorbing as much as he possibly could on this first, precious short visit. The suggestion that he now return there, coming from an American fashion writer, convinced him that the time was right to mount the first assault on the United States.

A few weeks later, repacking the samples in his suitcase before checking out of his hotel and heading back to Kennedy Airport, Luciano was reflecting on how wrong even he had been to think it could be this simple. The buyers for the big department stores had welcomed him cordially enough, as he discovered Americans habitually did, but they made no secret of the fact that the clothes left them cold. Luciano, who liked to think he was so in touch with the young, fashion-conscious public at home, discovered he was completely out of touch with the older, less fashion-conscious, more cost-conscious American public to whom these retailers were experts in selling. These were the most European-minded buyers and retailers in America; yet a jumper that might have been rejected as too staid in Belluno, Cortina and Padua, let alone Rome and Paris, was rejected by them as too fashionable for the American mass market. Furthermore, the Benettons, for all their networks of shops criss-crossing their home country and their solitary My Market in Paris, did not yet have the kind of European reputation essential to hook the brief attention span of the American consumer.

'That first experience of America was an eye-opener,' he would recall. 'I realised that the world was not the same everywhere. The rules were different in America. Human behaviour was different. It was a shock.'

Luciano checked out of his New York City hotel and into the airport a wiser man. One of his first calls when he got home, after Giuliana, was to Lison Bonfils in Paris.

'Tell your friend thanks,' he told her, 'but we're not ready to attack America yet. We need another six or seven years at least – maybe ten.' In the event, nine more years would elapse before they attacked again, and thirteen would pass before Benetton would really take off in America; and even then, this would still be in the first instance in New York City, the north-east and California where the customers – and the buyers – were most 'European'.

Ponzano, the Veneto, 1972

Even at full capacity, the factory was less and less able to meet the rising demand for manufacturing brought about by the wider range of clothing they were making and the explosion in the number of shops. In spite of this, Gilberto insisted that they should not make the mistake of investing in the kind of monster industrial plant that was becoming the focus of discontent for thousands of employees of Fiat and Pirelli in the industrial cities. Luciano also disliked these vast dehumanised working environments, which he saw as time-bombs ticking away until they exploded, as they were now doing, with consequences that would all but overwhelm even the biggest company and would have spelled certain doom for Benetton. Instead, they bought and refitted two more small factories in the nearby villages of Villorba and Monzabano and ensured that the proportion of people employed by Benetton at Ponzano, Villorba and Monzabano was still only 30 per cent of the total number of people working directly for the company; the rest were employees of the many local sub-contractors with whom they were forming closer and closer partnerships.

In the increasingly confrontational climate of the times, the big trade unions were looking more and more closely at Benetton and liking less and less what they saw. The decentralised sub-contractor system was perfectly legal and had honourable precedents in generations of family businesses in the Veneto, but the trade unions saw this system as a threat to their strategy of building a centralised power base. They dubbed the decentralised workers 'black labour' and tried to persuade the employees of these businesses that they were being exploited. At the same time, they urged Gilberto, Luciano and Carlo, who was in charge of production and in the front line in these 'negotiations', to build more factories with direct labour, in the name of the economic regeneration of the area. They also indicated that they required a greater degree of 'participation' in the setting and carrying out of the manufacturing processes than was currently enjoyed by the in-house workforce.

In this respect they underestimated the ability of Carlo to stand up to their persuasion. Although the youngest of the four children, he had started work earlier in life than many of the union officials with whom he was now having to negotiate, and he could handle their tough stance and see through their carefully phrased rhetoric. Luciano, in this respect, was temperamentally further to the political left than his brothers and sister. He had traditionally regarded trade unions as neither good nor bad, but a fact of life. However, he had also seen the business, and the network of shops on which the business depended, grow and flourish, not just through sheer hard work on their part and the part of their employees, but because of the delicate balance between his personal creative control and the commercial autonomy of the shop owner. The idea that collective bargaining and centralised control exercised by committee over commercial and working practices could somehow succeed in the same way was anathema to what he believed had made Benetton a success to date. Companies like Fiat and Pirelli had antagonised and alienated their workers to the point where they had brought upon themselves their nemesis in the form of lightning strikes, excrement dumped on the directors' desks, picketing and bloody intimidation inside and outside their plants. The trade unions had scented victory in the cases of these troubled giants and were hungry for more high-profile capitalist scalps. For Benetton unreservedly to accept their terms would be fatal. Now, however, this force was heading their way, and while Carlo kept the unions talking, this was the time to keep calm and devise a counter-strategy.

Between them, the four Benetton children by this time had twelve children of their own, the oldest of whom, Giuliana's daughter Paola, was thirteen. Giuliana herself, at thirty-four, combined marriage to her industrialist husband and her three children with her job creating new ranges and supervising her growing team of designers. She had just created the first range of Benetton clothes for babies and pre-adolescent children up to and including the age of twelve to wear at home, at school and at play. It was called '012'. The clothes were to be sold through My Market, Fantomax, Tomato and Merceria, and eventually through dedicated 012 shops.

The company was by this time secretly on the way to becoming the largest single consumer of wool in the world. With the creation and marketing of more new ranges of non-woollen clothes for customers from the age of nought upwards, they were also buying increasing amounts of cotton. A walk through the narrow streets of Treviso, let alone the boulevards of Rome and Paris, revealed that the world was also wearing more and more denim jeans and T-shirts, and the company began to make increasing numbers of both to add to the shelves of My Market, Tomato and Fantomax. Unlike these shops, however, where they were still competing principally with themselves, the market for jeans was already beginning to fill up with competitors. These included the American companies Levi Strauss and Wrangler, which were prestigious but expensive, and cheaper, homegrown hybrids using 'original American fabric'. The Italian brands included Fiorucci and Jesus Jeans, the latter of which would shortly feature its most spectacular advertisement yet. This photograph showed a voluptuous female bottom filling a pair of cut-offs, the bottom in question belonging to the girlfriend of the photographer, Oliviero Toscani.

Luciano himself wore jeans much of the time and had observed their transition from redneck and blue collar wear to youth fashion phenomenon while he was in America. There was no problem over design with such a product; marketing would be the deciding factor. It was while he was in America that he came up with the name 'Jeans West' for Benetton's first homegrown entry into the denim market. In 1974, two years after the 012 range was launched, but before a single shop had opened of that name, the first Jeans West shop, designed by the Scarpas, opened in the university city of Padua. More swiftly followed as existing shop owners and new entrepreneurs joined the network. This made them the first shops of their kind in the network to bear the same name as the brand of clothes they were selling. The Benetton name, meanwhile, still had no visible connection with any of the different kinds of shop, appearing only on the labels of the clothes and with the clothes in magazine and newspaper advertisements.

The denim boom which gave birth to the Jeans West range, and would shortly see the emergence of the shops of the same name, also saw the company make its first acquisition of an existing outside brand. The 'Sisley' brand had been established to manufacture and market denim in Paris in 1968 and had little else in common with Benetton clothes and the shops that sold them. The company bought Sisley in 1974 principally in order to obtain the exclusive rights to this denim range exclusively for male and 'unisex' fashion. Luciano intended that Sisley would one day become a more upmarket, masculine counterbalance to the mass-market, predominantly feminine fashions produced by Benetton at this time. The Sisley range and the eventual shops of the same name, although the latter were designed by the Scarpas, maintained their independent status with their own designers and commercial teams, and the Benetton name did not even appear on the labels or in the advertising. This identity, however, although clearly distinct from Benetton, was far from distinct in itself and the brand sat separately and uneasily from the rest of the clothes and shops. Some years would pass before Luciano's eldest son Mauro, having worked his way up through the family business, would seize the opportunity to make his name by taking charge of the Sisley brand. He would integrate it more closely into the Benetton network and turn it into the hip, outdoor, fashion-conscious outlet, this time for men and women, that his father had envisaged when Mauro was only twelve years old.

Luciano's strategy for dealing with the organised labour was to continue the dialogue with his brother Carlo as the frontman, while the four of them combined to promote the impression of Benetton as a refined manufacturer of clothes to order and not an industrial automaton dedicated to mass production. They stressed that they were only a part, albeit the central part, of a circular chain in which sub-contractors formed many more links than they did, and in which the flexibility to shrink one day and expand the next was all important. They pointed to the paramount role of sudden changes in the taste of the consumer. It became obvious, however, that the major trade unions neither understood, nor cared if they did not understand, these arguments.

In the spring of 1974, in spite of numerous concessions, there were two separate days of working to rule at the factory in Ponzano, in protest against 'decentralised' labour. Matters came to a head when the union representatives demanded the greater 'participation' they had hinted at in the manufacturing processes; among other things, in the number of items being dyed at any particular time. Luciano came back to the house each evening during these days increasingly frustrated and angry as these 'discussions' became, to his mind, more and more petty. This was the point, he realised one evening, at which there would have to be no further concessions and the answer henceforth every time would have to be 'no'. The union officials despised weakness even more than many of them despised capitalism itself; sure enough, they began to lose interest in Benetton from this moment onwards and began to look for other, perhaps easier and more valuable targets. Just as the German battle lines had run up from the south through Treviso during the war, so the forces of the militant left had come from the west and blown through the area and now retreated again to the industrial cities, where the final conflict would eventually be fought out.

Benetton seemed to have escaped, but the company would only continue to escape, Luciano concluded, by being a chameleon. What started out as a defensive instinct to keep a low profile became a personal and professional policy. As the political battle lines polarised between left and right in the big cities, the threat of terrorism and kidnapping increased everywhere, far surpassing the threat of militant organised labour. The result was that the company expanded fast, while appearing not to do so. If anything, as the number of differently named brands and shops multiplied, the company itself appeared to be shrinking and the Benetton thread that ran through everything became all but invisible.

Luciano quietly began selling off the collection of classic cars which for some time now he had not even driven out of the garage. The continuing rise in the number of sub-contractors working for the company – each of whom operated under a different family name – hid the name of Benetton from the name-plates and signboards of hundreds of factories where they had exclusive manufacturing and assembly contracts. There were 800 shops across the country by this time and a further hundred in France, Germany and Belgium, and although in every case the goods supplied and the payment for the same went to and from them and Benetton, not a single one of these shops bore the Benetton name. The family deliberately withheld financial information about the company and even Luciano stopped giving interviews. The only Benettons listed in the Treviso telephone directory – or any other telephone directory, for that matter – were the ones with no connection with the business and nothing to do with the family. Even some of these took their names out of the telephone book for fear a would-be kidnapper targeted them in a case of mistaken identity.

Five years earlier, when rapid growth rather than strikes and terrorism were the biggest threat to the company, they had bought the Villa Minelli. Five years on, the restoration work supervised by the Scarpas and Elio Aluffi was nearly complete. Yet the times were such that, instead of being a statement about how far the family had come and their commitment to putting something back into the community, even the newly restored Villa Minelli could be construed as a dangerous provocation.

One day in October of the year of the strikes, Eugenio Peralli, an elderly craftsman who had come out of retirement to work on the villa, nearly fell off his scaffolding in excitement and shouted towards the factory that he had made a discovery. He had uncovered a series of exquisite frescoes hidden beneath layers of plaster and now visible for the first time in 200 years. Luciano in particular was hypnotised by what he saw; it was as if this was a reward for all the hard work and faith that had brought him here, from the day when he had stared longingly at the Villa Minelli as a small boy from the road under a wartime sky. Yet even he would be forced to acknowledge that these hidden treasures, now revealed in all their splendour, would have to stay revealed only to a select few for the time being. A single act of terror could obliterate once and for all that which had survived 200 years of decline, war, refugees and neglect. Only when a stranger, invited on trust, could walk in here and admire them would the spirit of the frescoes be free and the price truly be paid of the 'years of lead'.

The year after old Peralli uncovered the frescoes, Luciano sold the last of his classic cars as part of his anti-terrorist survival strategy. Teresa gave him a special fortieth birthday present.

'We thought you might be needing this,' she said.

Luciano unwrapped the layers of gift paper as the children shrieked encouragement. Inside was an accordion, identical to the one he had sold twenty years earlier to help pay for Giuliana's first knitting machine. He picked it up and, after a few false starts, managed to play an old popular tune from the 1950s and the days when he had played in a band to earn a little extra money.

'The business seems to be doing all right,' Teresa laughed. 'I thought it was about time you got it back.' She told him later, 'You see, honey, the really important things always come back to you in the end.' Luciano would come to be haunted by her words for the rest of his life. Meanwhile, the family enjoyed the music and the singing and the birthday party.

Teresa and Luciano had first met by chance when he was working in the Dellasiegas' shop; now a chance meeting in another shop was to be fatal to their marriage. Four months later, Luciano went to Varese, a town near Milan, for lunch with a Jeans West owner and his staff. At lunch he was placed next to a girl who worked in the shop. Her name was Marina Salomon. She knew who he was, of course.

'Are you familiar with the novels of William Faulkner?' she asked him.

Luciano admitted he was not. She immediately launched into an explanation, not of why she was talking to him like this, but why he should read the works in question. Luciano was by turns surprised, flattered and fascinated; although barely twenty, she had a face that radiated extraordinary intensity and energy, and pretty long dark hair. At the end of lunch, she told him she was shortly going as a student to London for a year.

'That's funny,' he heard himself say. 'I'm going to London myself on business next week.'

This was not true, although the business had been taking him farther and farther away from home and for longer and longer periods. But during the last hour, Luciano had lost the ability to tell what was true and what was not. All he knew was that he wanted to see her again.

Benetton

For the whole of the following week, he fretted in a way he had never done before. This was ridiculous; she was a twenty-year-old student and he was a forty-year-old businessman married for fourteen years with four children. This was madness; this was dangerous.

He flew to London. At the airport, she burst from the waiting crowd and ran into his arms. They spent the weekend together. He came home in love and in shock. She was one of seven children of a cultivated Jewish family and she spoke four languages. A week later, she wrote him a letter saying she loved him, but she could not bear to be party to the break-up of his marriage and his family. He agreed with her. They went back to work, she in London to her studies and he in Ponzano. They both tried not to think about what would happen when she came home for the vacation.

The recession brought on by the world energy crisis and the oil price hikes had come home, as it had done everywhere. Shops were closing across the country and the most dedicated shopper was tightening his or her belt. At the same time, people allowed fuel shortages and price rises to dictate their spending habits only up to a certain point; beyond this point, they would rebel against the cold by going out and buying a new, colourful woollen jumper, thicker than usual, that was made by Benetton. They particularly refused to allow the recession to impact on the needs of baby; 012 shops already numbered over a hundred across the country. Meanwhile, inflation and recession at home were making exports more profitable; and Luciano had a business philosophy he wanted to take to the world.

Death of a dictator: Mussolini and his mistress, Clara Petacci, as photographed by Toscani senior in 1945.

'La Dolce Vita': the Rome of the 1960s made Luciano realise what a sheltered life he had been leading.
CORBIS

'My father was alive and we were all right.' The young Benetton family. BENETTON

Schumacher and Benetton win their first – and controversial – Drivers' World Championship. ALLSPORT

'Formula 1 is not a sport.' Flavio Briatore, the man who seemingly came from nowhere to take over the Benetton racing team. EMPICS

UNITED COLORS OF BENETTON.

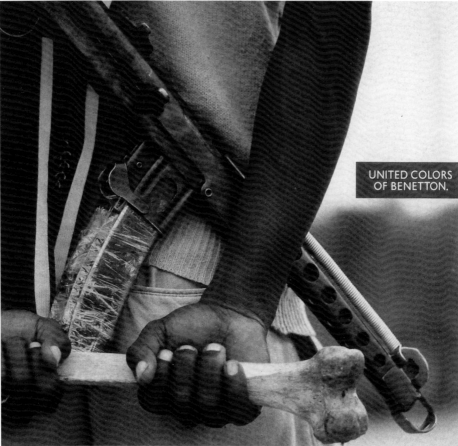

UNITED COLORS OF BENETTON.

'We want damages for loss of business.' The company denied it, but the German revolt was a critical test for Benetton and struck at the heart of Luciano and Toscani's worldwide strategy.
POPPERFOTO/REUTERS

In China, on the other hand, Bentton was at the centre of the biggest consumer boom on earth.
SYGMA

4   Empire Building Without Stress

Ponzano, the Veneto, 1976

The recession deepened, more shops closed across the country and beyond the borders and some contra-cyclically minded entrepreneurs took advantage of the difficult times to increase their stake in the network. This recession, however severe, would pass like all the others, and if Luciano could develop the export business better times would bring a double return at home and abroad.

The first vacation came, meanwhile, and realised Luciano and Marina's worst fears. The moment she returned from London and they met again, they knew they could not, or would not, stay parted from each other. All through the winter and into the spring, while she was there and after she had gone back to London, Luciano lived the double life of the unfaithful partner. He came to know the parallel ecstasy and guilt, the continuous fear of discovery and longing for the same, and the air of unreality that only the next encounter can all too briefly dispel. Luciano also knew that divorce was out of the question and yet his relationship with Teresa had already changed forever. Yet, he had too much respect for Teresa to allow her to find out the truth from other sources; neither was he the kind of man to exorcise his own sense of guilt by allowing the truth to be discovered by accident.

After months of deceit, he told her about the affair with Marina; he wanted a way of life beyond that which he had been living with her and the children, in the house close to the factory. Her response was understandably bitter and miserable; yet he could not stay now, they could both see that, although neither knew what would become of them. There were tears and terrible scenes, all of which had to be kept from the children until they had decided what to do.

Luciano moved out of the family home and bought a house forty minutes away in Venice, into which he moved with Marina. After difficult negotiations, he and Teresa agreed that he should have lunch with the children each day in what had been their family home. The four children were by turns uncomprehending, reproachful, introverted and distraught; yet the strength of the family, which Luciano appeared to have found lacking in himself, or too oppressive for his liking, held them together. Teresa, by the same token, had been one of the Benetton family since the earliest days of their acquaintance when, in spite of the fact that she had not needed to work, she had come to work with Giuliana. She was so close to the family and business that there was none of the awkwardness or veiled suspicion on their part that families tend to project onto the injured partner. This closeness between his wife and his brothers, sister and mother both compounded the initial shock for them and would enable them to adjust. A year after Marina had moved into the house in Venice with Luciano, Rosa would invite Marina and Luciano to dinner.

Others close but less central to the fabric of a family business were not so forgiving. Tobia and Afra Scarpa, for all their intellectual adventurousness and apparent liberalism, were among these. Luciano had made them rich and famous, yet they could not forgive him for what they saw and what he admitted was the irreparable wrong he had done to Teresa. After completing their work on the Villa Minelli, they broke off all contact with Luciano and the Benetton company. Their sense of betrayal was so strong that his behaviour perhaps had touched a nerve somewhere deep within their own uncompromising value system. Their deepest certainties had been shaken and they did not like this.

Marina, too, found her own family supportive but sceptical, and the intense conservatism just beneath the surface of life in Venice and the Veneto made her for a while a social prisoner in their house whenever Luciano was away. Only after a long time would the shock wear off for some of their mutual acquaintances, and Luciano and Marina meanwhile took refuge in the company of each other on journeys to faraway places: the islands off Denmark, the backwoods of New England and the Inca ruins of South America.

How far had Luciano calculated the positive and negative consequences of this upheaval he had wrought on the lives of those nearest to him, and to whom he was first and foremost responsible as a husband and father? Teresa had worked with Giuliana, she had borne him four children and she was a devoted wife and mother. Giuliana herself had found happiness with a man whom she felt no need to reject in order to sense the reality of her own individuality. Gilberto and Carlo were both happily married with children. Was this behaviour on his part merely a mid-life crisis unworthy of such an intelligent and successful man, and a lucky one at that? Was this merely a callous rejection of the values of a world which was now being good to him and yet to which he felt himself superior? Although both these explanations would be voiced by his friends and acquaintances, the truth is that there were uncanny emotional and psychological parallels between Luciano's circumstances and those of his family thirty years earlier. There was little difference in age between the departing Luciano and the age his father had been when he died and left his own family to fend for themselves. Both father and son had four children, who were left without the reassuring presence of a parent. Both sets of children were of similar ages and were left in the care of an incontrovertibly capable mother.

Luciano knew better than anyone the trauma that a sudden departure of a parent inflicted on a child, yet he also knew he had survived this trauma and his children would do so too. All his life, he had done what other people needed him to do. In a sense, his own children were already his second family, having brought up his brothers and sister as a surrogate father. At the same time, where his brothers and sister had struggled from day to day to survive, his own children and their mother already never needed to want for security or material comfort. The effort to ensure this had often taken him far away from them and perhaps engendered a fatal sense of detachment; except that, unlike the case of his father, this detachment would not be fatal, and although his own children did not believe this at the moment he knew he would always be there for them. At the same time, ever since the earliest days of his life as father, son and brother all at once, he had tolerated his responsibilities only by having a parallel freedom which in adulthood could not be achieved simply by membership of a rowing club and co-ownership of a Vespa scooter. Now, did he somehow feel he had discharged a debt, not just to one but two families; his own wife and children, and his father, his mother and his brothers and sister? Was he reaping some kind of emotional payback?

Luciano had a name for the business philosophy he wanted to take to the world. He called this 'empire building without stress'.

At home, this philosophy had seen a single shop, launched with a combination of personal initiative and business instinct, evolve into a network of hundreds of shops founded on the same principles. In France, however, Luciano's initial assumption that Benetton could simply transfer this philosophy to what looked like a socially and culturally receptive fellow European nation of shoppers had been wrong. Only when Luciano, working through the storm raging in his private life, took the French puzzle apart with the help of Lison Bonfils, did he begin to understand why it had not yet worked.

They conferred with Giuliana and concluded that one of their mistakes lay in the colours. These were clean and international, which was part of their youth appeal, but they also had to be French to the French, just as they would have to be American to the Americans if they were to succeed in the United States. Giuliana redesigned the French range of clothes to include softer colours such as lilac and chocolate brown, and the French advertising campaign was researched and geared more exclusively to the local market. The result was that the foreignness of the clothes disappeared and there was suddenly a greater demand where it had previously appeared not to exist in any significant quantity. Buoyed along by the economic recovery after the recession and brought into focus by the new advertising, the clothes – and the shops – took off. The result was that, within two years, by 1978, there would be 200 shops this time trading under the name of 'Benetton' in France, where there had been one My Market. This time, the Benetton name travelled seamlessly across cultural frontiers. By this time, too, Luciano would have a more legitimate excuse to return to London.

London, England, 1977

The location and name of the first shop in London were as crucial as they had been in Paris and this time there was no mistake. South Molton Street is a prestigious, up-market pedestrian street just south of Oxford Street. This is a street to which the shopper has obviously gravitated by design rather than chance and where the presence of adjacent exclusive shops implies the sophistication of the British taste for clothes made in Italy. Only twelve years had passed since the heyday of Swinging London had inspired Piero Marchiorello and Luciano Benetton to call their first shop My Market in homage to Carnaby Street, and in doing so they had unlocked the spending power of the youth of Belluno. Yet, twelve years later, Swinging London was as dead as Belluno had been when My Market arrived and, unlike the French, the British were neither any threat to nor were they consequently threatened by the power of Italian fashion. In fact, there was little in the way of a British fashion industry to compete with France or Italy, at home or abroad, at this time. This made the clean, international style of Benetton clothes all the more welcome and, as yet at least, in no way antagonistic to British tastes.

Shortly after the opening of the first shop in London, which was again called simply Benetton, Luciano and Gilberto were called to Barclays Bank in London to conclude their first ever international loan. Afterwards, they were expected to pose for a photograph. Gilberto had noted with alarm Luciano's casual mode of dress; it was customary on these occasions to wear a suit. He made Luciano go out and buy one especially for the occasion. Luciano posed in his suit and smiled with the rest; his brother and the bankers. As soon as the photograph was taken he left the room and changed back into his preferred clothes.

Frankfurt, West Germany, 1978

The different sensibilities that governed the shopping and dressing habits of the British were even more marked in Germany. This was tricky territory for even the most resourceful Italian salesman, and Luigi Pilota was nothing if not resourceful.

Pilota was Benetton's representative for Germany, as well as central and southern Italy. He knew the Germans were the most conservative of the customers Benetton had met yet in its drive to do business in the international markets. The Germans preferred beige, black, camel, navy blue and red in that order. Even after Udo Jansen had opened the first shop in Germany in Dusseldorf in 1973, it had been difficult for Pilota to find kindred spirits who wanted to become new shop owners – fellow 'Benettonians' as they were known. Even when he had succeeded in doing so, these shop owners had for some years refused to order strong colours. Only when Pilota had at last persuaded one shop owner to display a bright yellow jumper and trouser combination had the other German shop owners followed suit. The following year, for the first time in living memory, yellow became the fashionable colour in Germany.

Ponzano, the Veneto, 1978

In Ponzano, while Giuliana maintained her offices in the design studios at the factory, Luciano, Gilberto and Carlo had moved theirs into the completed Villa Minelli. This time, unlike the opening of the factory eight years earlier, there was little ceremony. The need for security was as great as ever and although the restoration of the Villa was favourably noted in the specialist press, it was hoped that terrorists did not read the architectural reviews. The magnificent surroundings of their own private world, with its high-ceilinged reception rooms and frescoes and windows overlooking the plain of the Veneto, were an extraordinary daily reminder not just of how far they had come, but what they now had to lose. The building made an even more powerful impression on visiting agents, shop owners and sub-contractors. Here, on their own territory that made an unmissable statement, they would never again be patronised by bank managers and lawyers. They and others now came here instead for audiences with the 'modern merchant prince' Luciano, Gilberto, the finance manager, and Carlo, who had shown he could stand up to the intimidating tactics of organised labour.

The Red Brigades themselves by this time had five terror cells oper-ating in Rome, Genoa, Milan, Turin and the Veneto. They were killing policemen, magistrates, academics, editors, journalists and business-men with equal lack of compunction. Their aim was to trigger a mass terrorist movement to overthrow the state, and the reaction of the government and opposition was to form a defensive coalition.

On 16 March 1978, the Prime Minister and Christian Democrat leader, Aldo Moro, was on his way to Parliament in Rome to broker a deal which would bring the communists into government with the Christian Democrats for the first time. Neither the Italian right nor, it later transpired, the American government wanted this deal with the communists to go through. With the connivance of the Italian secret service, the Red Brigades ambushed Moro's car and escort on the way to Parliament. They slaughtered the policemen accompanying him and his chauffeur. Moro himself was bundled away into a waiting car which disappeared into the Roman traffic. Fifty-five days later, they killed him and dumped his body in the boot of a car which they left in the centre of Rome, exactly equidistant between the Christian Democrat and the Communist Party headquarters.

The kidnapping, incarceration and killing of the Prime Minister shocked the nation and whatever the need for reform, the hardening of public opinion towards terrorism would later be dated from this point. The Red Brigades, however, were far from finished and the unanswered questions surrounding the death of Moro were such that they would never be brought to justice on a significant scale. Meanwhile, many of those involved in tracking down the Red Brigades, including at least one journalist and the police general in charge of the investigation, would themselves later be murdered, respectively by unknown agents thought to be working for the far right and by the Sicilian Mafia, the former being fearful that the truth about their role in failing to prevent Moro's death would one day come to light.

The death of the Prime Minister and the apparently deliberate failure by the authorities to expedite the hunt for his killers filled many otherwise influential Italians with despair at the moral vacuum at the centre of power. The fear for the future of the nation was also personal. Giuliana, Gilberto and Carlo and their families all took discreet security precautions and kept low profiles. Luciano himself, the most distinctive and flamboyant of the four, only really felt safe when he was travelling. When he was not flying off in a green and white company Cessna Citation to visit shop owners at home and abroad, he usually drove the forty-minute journey from the house he shared with Marina in Venice to work each day in Ponzano. After the killing of Moro, he still refused to have either a bodyguard or a bullet-proof car in the belief that the rural routes between Venice and Ponzano were an unlikely stamping-ground for urban guerrillas and kidnappers. However, he always greeted the sight of the Villa Minelli across the fields and the house where his wife and children still lived, with relief that another journey had passed safely. The same feeling overcame him whenever he drove back into Venice and the island citadel closed itself behind him and he was back behind his own front door.

The rapid and apparently stress-free growth of the empire continued beyond the borders of their own country into Britain and the countries of mainland Europe. By 1979, the three Benetton factories in and around Ponzano and their ring of satellite sub-contractors were supplying 280 shops in France, 250 in Germany, a hundred in Britain, twenty-five in the Netherlands and twenty-five in Belgium. In each of these countries the lesson learned in France was applied, with dedicated advertising and the colours and textures of the clothes tailored to local tastes within the overall Benetton style. Altogether, there were now 1,700 shops across Europe. Sales had risen by 30 per cent on the previous year alone. The company still withheld information about the size of its operations and profits and kept its name away from the front of the shops, and the family continued to avoid media publicity. In the same year, however, the scale of the Benetton phenomenon began to leak out when the Australian Wool Corporation cited Benetton as the largest consumer of pure virgin wool in the world. The publicity profile of the company was also about to take another leap, with the empire-building move that had begun abortively nine years earlier with Luciano's selling trip to New York City: the first concerted attack on the United States of America.

New York City, United States of America, 1979

This time Gilberto was the advance guard and he did not go alone. Walter Annaratone was the urbane owner, with his wife, of a string of shops in Lombardy, the affluent area around and including Milan in the north of the country. Annaratone wanted to be the partner, with Benetton, in the first shop in the United States of America.

In New York City, Gilberto and Annaratone made contact with the Italian–American Chamber of Commerce. Here, on the recommendation of the latter, they approached a young American businessman of Italian ancestry. Sal Salibello's grandmother had emigrated to America from Sicily and his own Italian sounded to northern Italian ears like the Mafia dialect spoken in movies like *The Godfather*. He hastened to assure his visitors that his resemblance to organised crime stopped there. He had never heard of Benetton but was attracted to the idea of selling Italian casual wear in America.

Salibello, and his equally young accountancy firm, Salibello and Broder, operated out of a tiny office on Thirty-fifth Street and Lexington. Gilberto explained to the young American what he had in mind.

> Benetton is a concept, not just a product. We don't just want to create an Americanised version of our European shops. We want to keep the European flavour, to emphasise it even, but only up to a certain point. We don't want to overplay it. It's this element of newness that will attract the customer; the clothes will do the rest.

Salibello was already sold on the idea, as Gilberto and Annaratone were sold on him. Unknown to him, three other, older accountancy firms had also been recommended to them as possible managers of their affairs in the United States. As had been the case with Roberto Calderoni, Piero Marchiorello, the Scarpas and Annaratone himself, the Benettons backed the man over and above experience and track record. The modest offices of Salibello and Broder became the first bridgehead in the assault by Benetton on the United States.

Back in Ponzano, Luciano, Gilberto, Giuliana, Carlo and Annaratone spent months debating where to open the first American shop. Chicago was one possibility; nobody had ever opened a shop like this there before. Boston was another, with a young, consumer-minded student population on the 'European' coast of America. Washington DC was a third possibility. In time, all these cities and hundreds more would have shops selling Benetton. But in their minds, the European factor was paramount and their eventual first choice was Manhattan, right in the heart of New York City.

At first they tried to secure a site on Fifth Avenue, in the heart of prime retail territory between Fiftieth and Fifty-eighth Streets. This proved impossible; there was nothing available, let alone at the price they were prepared to pay. One day it would be a different story. Meanwhile, they compromised on a site at 601 East Madison Avenue, near the corner with Fifty-seventh Street. This was still a good location with the Plaza, Helmsley Palace and Pierre hotels a few yards away, packed with tourists and visitors, many of whom would know the shop from their travels in Europe. A standard kit for the interior layout, including shelves, changing rooms, carpets, ceilings and lighting, all manufactured near Ponzano, was dispatched to New York with two craftsmen to assemble it.

As they had done in Paris, London and Düsseldorf, they decided to call the first American shop simply 'Benetton', placing a European accent on the interior, which, together with the range of clothing, was identical to that of their new shop in the Champs Elysées in Paris. Annaratone staffed the shop on East Madison with pretty French and Italian sales assistants, each of whom talked to each other in these languages and spoke perfect English to the customer. In the same way, they agreed that the first American advertising, co-ordinated through the Kathy Travis agency in New York, should stress the European origins and international quality of Benetton and the ability to travel across frontiers.

'Last year we made 8,041,753 sweaters . . . sold through 1,573 Benetton stores internationally,' read one. This was also the first advertisement to link the Benetton name not only with the clothes, but with the stores that sold them.

Unlike the first shops in Italy, and like the first one in Paris, however, the New York City opening did not see queues of young people lining the block. The first customers were European visitors and their children, homesick for familiar fashions in the American wilderness. The breakthrough came with the first sale, in January 1980, which brought the first queues, including Americans, and the first coverage in *Women's Wear Daily*.

Annaratone, this time in partnership with Salibello's younger brother John, who had worked for Macy's, took the opportunity to announce that they were going to open two more Benetton shops in the city, this time at 805 Lexington and 853 Third Avenue, on the corner of Fifty-seventh Street. Above the latter, they installed a huge illuminated sign. Soon after the shop opened and the lights came on, there were telephone calls from New York City to Treviso from would-be shop owners wanting to know how they too could become part of the Benetton network.

The opening of the third shop in New York City, and the fact that there was a 'cluster' of shops where there had only been one, meant that the idea of competition with yourself rather than with others was theoretically likely to boost slow sales. Another more tangible advantage was that they could better gauge and anticipate changes in fashion through feedback from three shops rather than one, given that they were several thousand miles away from Manhattan and these shops were the farthest outposts of the Benetton empire. What closed this distance was not just the internationalism of the clothes and the ability to be American to the Americans, but also the global reach of American media in spreading the Benetton name.

Americans were soon reading how Sylvester Stallone, Dustin Hoffman, Sally Field and Jackie Onassis were all habitués of the shop on East Madison Avenue. But the biggest name of all, although as yet a superstar distinguished by her engaging shyness, was photographed for Americans on the other side of the Atlantic coming out of the Benetton shop in South Molton Street in London: the fiancée of the Prince of Wales, Lady Diana Spencer. More than anybody, her endorsement would make the name of Benetton itself, for the first time, headline news: 'Benetton dresses both queens and housewives' proclaimed one newspaper. The newspaper in question was a daily one published in Italy and, unlike the architectural reviews, this one was read by terrorists and kidnappers.

Ponzano, the Veneto, 1980

At home, the tide was at first thought to be turning against the men and women of violence. Events such as the murder of Prime Minister Moro and the 'March of the Forty Thousand' in Turin, when a mass procession of Fiat employees peacefully but forcefully demanded the right to return to work and an end to industrial disputes, were catching the changing mood of the time. At the same time there were few arrests of terrorists and little retribution for those who were apprehended, as if they knew too much to be antagonised by lengthy jail sentences. However many people they had killed, many of them melted back into society, some never to return to crime, others aware that they had acquired criminal skills that were of value in the pursuit of illicit gains for their own sake. The tradition of kidnapping for money, once the preserve of the Sicilian Mafia, spread across the country. In the richer areas, the inhabitants sold their conspicuous cars, as Luciano had done long ago, and maintained what they hoped would be a low and therefore non-provocative profile.

This was easier to achieve in some cases than in others. Luciano and his brothers and sister were now publicly linked by name to a business phenomenon of which, for all to see, they were the prime movers and principal beneficiaries. This linkage was becoming more and more public, abroad and at home. Gilberto was the biggest sports fan in the family and his long-standing support for the Treviso basketball team was financial as well as emotional. When Gilberto suggested that the company should officially sponsor the team, renaming it 'Benetton Basket' and reclothing the players in the green and white colours of the company logo, they did so in the awareness that the public relations benefits would be more tangible than any financial return on the investment. The team was a winner from the start and this success made the link in people's minds between Benetton and sport, an activity with positive connotations and into which Gilberto wanted to take further the manufacturing operations of the company. The fact that the company effectively owned a basketball team also raised still higher the profile of the Benetton name and made it publicly synonymous with business and wealth across an indiscriminate audience.

Benetton was building an empire and, contrary to Luciano's assertion, this could never be a process without stress. Early the following year, Benetton bought the old Scottish knitwear firm of Hogg of Hawick, which Luciano had first visited on his trip to Scotland to learn the 'secret of the itch'. Hogg had been making high-quality, dull clothes in the chilly Scottish borders for over a hundred years. The equipment was elderly and so were many of the staff. But the Benettons had spotted Hogg's expertise and position at the richer end of the market. Giuliana, in a rare interview for this time, smilingly told the business press: 'It was partly a sentimental thing. If it had been a modern plant, we wouldn't have been inter-ested.' In fact, although Hogg's output of 300 garments a day was insignificant beside the 90,000 by this time made by Benetton, Gilberto, Carlo and Luciano knew that, with new equipment, the Scottish factory could make 1,000 garments a day and the market could take this.

The same reasoning rather than sentiment held true the same year when Benetton bought 50 per cent of Fiorucci, the glamorous fashion retailer with a chain of shops across the capitals of Europe and in New York. This time, instead of modern manufacturing methods, Benetton would inject its marketing expertise, taking both Fiorucci and itself to a more prominent position at the higher end of the market – as Luciano had wanted to be the case, but which had not yet happened, with their takeover of Sisley.

The foreign press reported these things and published far more information about the range and profitability of the business than was currently available at home. By this time, few of their fellow country people yet knew that Benetton consumed more than half the wool output of the state textiles concern, Lanerossi. They did not yet know that Benetton had six factories in and around Ponzano, directly employing around 1,600 people, and indirectly employing 10,000 more in over 250 sub-contractors exclusively con-tracted to Benetton, all of which paid wages agreed by union negotiators at the parent company. They did not know that the six factories analysed day-to-day demand by computer and kept in daily contact with 1,500 shops across the country, 200 of which were owned outright by Benetton, and a further 300–400 part-owned by the company. The rest were owned and managed through Benetton's version of the franchise system that had begun with Piero Marchiorello in Belluno, and the public did not know that the company received approximately 50 per cent in value of the turnover of these 1,500 shops. Above all, they did not know the

extent of the profits from all these operations, from the main operating company, Benetton spa, the three main subsidiaries for wool,
cotton and jeans, and the direction of the flow of these profits to
Invep, the family holding company 100 per cent owned by Luciano,
Giuliana, Gilberto and Carlo.

The average person was still unaware of most or all of these
things, and this fact in itself was of little importance. Yet the climate
of the times was such that Luciano and the rest of the family still
preferred to keep a low profile and were as careful as ever about
their own personal security. To be nearer his family and the factory,
Luciano and Marina had moved from Venice to a seventeenth-
century villa in Quarto d'Altino, only twenty minutes' drive from
Ponzano. The villa, 'Il Casone sul Sile' – the Manor on the River
Sile – was covered in vines behind a walled garden that ran down to
the river in question. Its interior, renovated under Marina's supervision, was decorated with oriental hangings and renaissance
tapestries and paintings. Scattered liberally throughout the house
was a flock of model sheep in homage to the family's prodigious
appetite for wool, to which she liked to add on the slightest pretext.
There was a live-in housekeeper, whose husband acted as caretaker
and guard, but Luciano and Marina felt safe here in the countryside
and usually left the house unlocked when they were at home.
Luciano's only other concession to personal security was an armour-
plated Alfa Romeo saloon, which he found similar to driving a tank.
He and Marina often travelled in her car, which lacked armour
plating and was not bullet proof.

Marina had finished her doctorate and published a learned historical study of Ponzano, including the Villa Minelli. She had come
to the conclusion, however, that she did not want to be a historian;
she wanted to go into business. She borrowed money from her
father and bought a shareholding in Conte, a small manufacturer of
silk shirts based in a village near Ponzano, that was indirectly linked

to Benetton. This was her first introduction to business and Luciano stayed back while she threw herself into it with characteristic energy and intensity. Soon, she was making ambitious plans for its future.

Luciano was also making plans for his family business. In May of that year, 1982, he and Gilberto met at one of their favourite secluded dining places near Ponzano with Aldo Palmeri, a thirty-six-year-old director of the Bank of Italy and Masters graduate from the London School of Economics. This was the man they believed could help Benetton evolve from a pure family company into a mature corporate enterprise. Luciano had long considered management education 'a luxury reserved for bureaucrats with nothing better to do', but the rapport between the brothers and Palmeri was immediate and the three of them began to discuss the next step.

The following month, through the Milan stock exchange, Benetton bought the majority stake in Calzaturificio di Varese, a shoe manufacturer, their first ever purchase beyond the garment business. After the purchase, they discovered a raft of hidden debts and concluded that the only solution was to sell off the remaining stock at a loss and start again. This angered the other shareholders, who tried to stop Benetton doing this through the courts. In the midst of all this, and as part of the process of opening up the company with the involvement of a new caste of managers, to be led by Palmeri, the family decided to publish the first ever Benetton annual report. This revealed among other things that sales had multiplied by 600 per cent in the last five years; that these sales totalled US$283 million through 2,000 shops, the latest opening in America and Japan; and that the company was making annual profits of US$19 million. For the first time, these facts were in black and white for all to see and the events that followed almost immediately would prove that the end was not yet in sight of the 'years of lead'.

Empire Building Without Stress

Quarto d'Altino, the Veneto, 10 August 1982

It was a Saturday night after dinner and Luciano and Marina were reading and watching television. The windows were open and the sounds of the hot summer night were coming into the room. Soon it would be time to go to bed. She was twenty-seven, he was forty-seven; seven years had passed since they first met yet, each day, he still marvelled at the closeness between them.

The dogs were barking outside; this was not unusual. In addition to the model sheep, she had assembled a pack of real-life German shepherds; they were probably chasing a rabbit.

Marina yawned and turned the page of her book. Luciano started to speak and then froze. A gloved hand had closed over his mouth and he could feel the cold muzzle of a pistol against his neck.

There were five of them, all wearing grotesque masks. Before he and Marina could register what was happening, he was on his knees being tied up and she was being led from the room. Luciano heard himself saying: 'Take what you want, but don't hurt anyone.' Marina was convinced she was going to be raped as well as robbed. The housekeeper and her husband, meanwhile, having been lured outside by the barking dogs, had been detained downstairs.

Then, although it seemed an eternity, things happened with frightening speed. The five men bundled Marina out of the room, leaving Luciano kneeling and bound. Although he could not hear what was happening to her, she later told him that she threatened to pull the mask off any man who tried to attack her and would memorise his face. They would then have to kill her to stop her describing that face to the police. Nor could Luciano hear her tell them that the villa had a silent security alarm that was already ringing at the police station. Perhaps taken aback by this, they hurriedly rifled the safe, took the money and all her jewellery, left her tied up in the bedroom and fled. There was no such security alarm, but by this time the husband of the housekeeper had managed to free himself sufficiently to call the police. They arrived shortly afterwards. Luciano, Marina, the housekeeper and her husband tried to answer their questions until the hours before dawn. The police left and the four of them remained, exhausted but alive and aware that their lives there could never be the same again. For, as Luciano said, where on earth could you feel safe, if you could not feel safe in your own home?

During the next few days, the press was full of the story of how the 'king of knitwear' had been robbed at gunpoint. Luciano found the details of their ordeal as much of an intrusion as the events of that terrifying Saturday night. He was also alarmed that the press had given precise details as to the location of the villa; were they trying to tip off the Red Brigades? He bought a sophisticated alarm system and had a set of electronic gates installed that could be operated by a handset without getting out of the car. He and Marina then tried to pick up the threads of normal life. Thereafter, however, they locked all the doors even when they were at home, and put down their books and turned down the television whenever the dogs barked in the night. Nearly two months later they had all but recovered from the incident; the robbery, they told themselves and each other, was simply a piece of bad luck.

Quarto d'Altino, the Veneto, 8 October 1982

This time it was a Tuesday night and Luciano and Marina were driving back to the villa from Treviso. They usually met after work in the centre of town, leaving one of the cars there to be picked up in the morning, and coming home together in the other. Tonight, quite by chance, they were in the armour-plated Alfa Romeo.

The approach to the villa lay down a narrow lane, with the electronic gates at the bottom. It was dark and the lane was lined with bushes. Luciano and Marina were approaching the gates when, suddenly, two men leapt from the bushes clutching a hammer and a pickaxe. Immediately, they set about breaking the side windows of the car. Luciano, who had slowed down, sped forward again as the gates opened and pressed the horn furiously to alert the caretaker.

'Call the police!' he shouted to Marina, who reached for the car telephone. The car shot forward through the gates and for a moment it seemed that they were home free. Then they looked back and saw that the two men had jammed the gates open behind them and were approaching for a second attack. Again, they concentrated on the passenger windows, obviously leaving the windscreen intact in order to use the car, probably with Luciano and Marina locked in the boot, for their getaway.

'My God, they're going to get in through the windows!' Marina cried. 'Go back, go back!'

Luciano shifted the gears and stamped on the accelerator, praying that the gates would remain open and that there was no other vehicle behind them in the lane. The Alfa shot backwards at high speed through the gates, past the two men, and back up the lane to the main road. Luciano kept his foot hard down and his hand on the horn for ten miles and more, speechless, while Marina clung to his arm and wept. Eventually, when they were near Venice, he turned off the horn and slowed down.

He drove them first to the house of an industrialist friend of theirs, Max Donadon, who calmed them down. Then they went back to the villa to meet the police who were waiting there. This time too, however, although there were roadblocks and searchlights probing the woods and fields, the attackers got away. Later that night, the police found a fast motor boat moored on the River Sile, which they were able to link to the kidnappers. The River Sile ran east to the lagoon of Venice. With this boat, the kidnappers would have been able to avoid all roadblocks and take Luciano and Marina out to sea, anywhere into the Adriatic and the Mediterranean.

Before they knew any of these things, Luciano had already made up his mind. After he was certain that they were not being pursued and he had turned off the horn and slowed down, he had turned to Marina and taken one look at her tear-stained face.

'That's it,' he said, 'as of now, we don't live at the villa any more. We're going to live in town, near lots of other houses. In a house with real security.'

Shortly afterwards they left for a week's holiday in America. Here, amid the beautiful fall colours in New Hampshire and Vermont, where nobody knew who they were, they walked and talked and regained their composure. They rediscovered how to look forward and not just back to the idyllic life at the villa which they both knew had gone, probably for ever. On their return, they put the villa up for sale and stayed first at the little country hotel where Luciano and Gilberto had met Aldo Palmeri earlier in the year. The villa was empty, for the housekeeper and her husband were too afraid to return. Marina stayed there alone while Luciano went away again on business, but only long enough to exorcise her worst memories of the place and to say goodbye.

In the late autumn, they moved hotels again, still near Ponzano, but wary of staying in any one place too long. Their fears seemed irrational to them, until the police notified all the members of the family that they had uncovered further plots, this time to kidnap Giuliana and Luciano's son, Alessandro. The three brothers and sister, and Teresa, all now acquired armour-plated cars and Luciano hired a chauffeur who doubled as a bodyguard. Marina continued to drive herself in her own car, but henceforth they always travelled together in the bullet-proof Alfa Romeo.

One of the journeys Luciano made on business at this time was to Troyes, in France, where Benetton had decided to buy the long-established Fram knitwear factory. Following the Di Varese lawsuit, the robbery and the attempted kidnapping, anything that any of the Benettons did was deemed newsworthy, and the press made more of the takeover than they would otherwise have done. It was during a journey closer to home, however, before the Fram deal was sealed, that Luciano had another encounter that was not only to change his life, but to change the life of the company. Once again, as had been the case with Teresa, then with Marina, the business would initially bring two people together, then spark a relationship that would prove far greater than the sum of its parts, and the fruits of which would dominate the lives of both parties thereafter. This time, the intermediary was the head of the fashion retailer in which Benetton had recently taken a 50 per cent stake, Elio Fiorucci.

Milan, northern Italy, 1982

Fiorucci had been wanting to introduce Luciano to Oliviero Toscani for a long time. 'He's done some amazing pictures for us,' he told him, 'you've got to meet him.'

Luciano had never heard of him before. At the same time, Fiorucci had been telling Toscani about Benetton. 'You really ought to work for them,' he told Toscani, 'they're an extraordinary company.'

'Extraordinary . . .' Toscani liked the sound of this. Never a man to defer to anyone, he had heard of Benetton and gave Fiorucci the benefit of his opinions.

'Their mistake,' he told Fiorucci, 'is that they behave like an ordinary knitwear company. They should get the message to the world that above and beyond the clothes, they represent a whole new way of living and thinking.'

This was typical Toscani, and it had brought him a long way from the slums of Milan during the war to the latest achievements in a glittering career. As a child, he had carried his father Fedele's tripod and learned the trade of photographer.

'My father's work was real work,' he liked to tell people. 'We all worked, my mother, my sister . . . and it wasn't really such a great job. I grew up thinking photography was a job like any other.'

Toscani, with his studios in New York and Paris and his farmhouse in Tuscany, where he raised Appaloosas, could say these things with the disarming modesty of the world-class ego. After primary school in Milan, his father had scraped enough money to send him to a smart, private, church-run boarding school, where he still liked to describe himself as having been a rebel. It was run by priests, one example of whom would feature prominently in his iconography for Benetton. Toscani had gone from here to the equally exclusive Kunstgewerbe Art College in Zurich. He had taken his first pictures haunting the stage at rock concerts in the 1960s. From there, he had used his connections and gone to New York, hung out with Andy Warhol, and photographed the King's Road set and Swinging London.

He shot pictures for *Elle*, *Harper's* and American, British and Italian *Vogue*. As well as Fiorucci, his clients included Valentino, Club Med, Bata shoes, Prenatal – the trendy French babywear chain – and Esprit, the Californian fashion retailer. He was impossibly hip, and underneath, very, very serious: 'If you love me, follow me,' read the caption beneath his then girlfriend's bottom in the picture he took for Jesus Jeans. Toscani himself loved to be followed, and yet treated with intellectual contempt all those who followed others and anything, except themselves and their own instincts. The Jesus Jeans image had immediately been censored, moving the film director and intellectual Pier Paolo Pasolini to write two articles about the advertisement, arguing that, in this, Toscani had revealed how the Church, capitalism and sex were locked into an impossible relationship. This tribute, from a man of the stature of Pasolini, was also the first time that Toscani could point to evidence for the suggestion that what he was doing was somehow not mere advertising, but image making for a new world, and one in which a new imagery, through the existing channels of the mass media, would supersede the patronising language of consumerism and the mock-reality of 'the news'.

This was the snarling, volatile, hypnotic bear of a man to whom Elio Fiorucci introduced Luciano Benetton at dinner one night, shortly after the robbery and kidnap attempt, when Luciano was still feeling shaken and haunted by the violence that had entered his life. Living out of a suitcase in a series of hotels, a visitor in his own home, he was open to hear anything from anyone at this time and from the first moment of their encounter the flamboyant Milanese photographer made a powerful impression on him. However, vulnerable as he was feeling, Luciano was still not a man to trust his own instincts without some form of corroboration. He observed with interest therefore that Fiorucci, for whom he had considerable respect, and Toscani had a genuine rapport.

If Toscani had become one of the few people to see into Luciano's soul, Luciano had detected the side of Toscani that few people noticed because Toscani hid it behind the hyperbole; his belief in the virtues of hard work, the family and quality in whatever he did. As had been the case with the Scarpas, from whom Luciano was still estranged, Toscani had the intellectual firepower and mental agility to go further than others, not merely for its own sake, but because he passionately believed in what he was doing. Like the Scarpas, and like Luciano himself, Toscani did not suffer fools gladly. He had also had the kind of education Luciano would have liked to have had for himself and wanted for his own children. Toscani challenged him and Luciano paid him the compliment of challenging him in return. At dinner, after they had talked about most other things, they began to talk about working together.

That night in Milan, Toscani became the latest and the most challenging of the select group of challenging figures Luciano allowed to enter his life. This life was dominated at work by the struggle to establish the network and the brand in America and the reorganisation of the business planned with the help of Aldo Palmeri. Palmeri was coming from Rome to Ponzano on a daily basis as a consultant on a short-term contract. Luciano's personal life was also still in flux after the events of the summer and autumn. After meeting Toscani, he returned from Milan to the latest hotel where he lived with Marina, near Ponzano. In Treviso, meanwhile, in the centre of town, a house owned by the business was nearing renovation. Off the Piazza dei Signori, surrounded by other houses, with its steel shutters and high-technology security system, the house was more and more closely resembling that which Luciano had envisaged on the night of the attempted abduction. The merchant prince was about to become a modern-day Doge, a prisoner in his own home, and his freedom would increasingly be defined thereafter by international travel and the Cessna jet parked on permanent stand-by at Treviso Airport. Another eighteen months would pass, and other matters would be settled at home and abroad, before Luciano Benetton would call Toscani with the challenge to produce a worldwide picture strategy.

5   The Fifth Avenue Franchise

New York City, United States of America, 1982

The offices of Salibello and Broder on the corner of Thirty-fifth and Lexington were still the US headquarters of Benetton over three years later, for it had taken them this time to establish even a modest bridgehead in America. Given the vastness of the potential market, Benetton, with only three shops in Manhattan, was still a tiny presence here compared with its profile in Europe. The American market was out there, they knew this, but no amount of advertising on the present modest scale and in the present style and no amount of word-of-mouth publicity, however favourable, would make the breakthrough they wanted. This only came, as Gilberto had inadvertently prophesied to Salibello at the first meeting over three years earlier, when he told him 'the clothes will do the rest'. In this case, it would be the runaway success among American college students of a simple rugby sweater.

This was the item that breached the American market for Benetton, and when it did, it was by the hundreds of thousands. The item came almost unnoticed out of Giuliana's design studio and it was probably the biggest single catalyst for growth since her original yellow jumper nearly thirty years earlier. It was simple, in blue and white with long sleeves and the Benetton name and logo on the front. Ivy League students shopping in New York City while there on summer courses first bought it and took it back to their colleges that autumn. That winter and the following spring, the done thing for these young consumers and future opinion formers was to be seen in nothing but Benetton. Everywhere they studied, in their Ivy League colleges, in towns and cities hitherto starved of shops to meet the needs of a young, increasingly fashion-conscious population, these shops began to spring up. Salibello's office in New York City was deluged with calls from would-be shop owners. Many simply bypassed the official channels of communication and telephoned direct to Ponzano, regardless of the six-hour time difference, and called in the middle of the night.

The runaway success of this single product brought on its shirt-tails the Benetton range, with its two collections, for spring–summer and autumn–winter, and the Benetton name. Increasingly, too, reflecting the partnership between the company and the shop operator, these shops were simply bearing the name Benetton. Sisley, Jeans West and 012 were translatable to America, but the original portfolio of self-competing, ultra-European shops, My Market, Merceria, Fantomax and Tomato, was inadequate to convey the image of the company in America. Many of these shop owners also began to change the name to Benetton to cash in on what was becoming seen as the key word linking family, business and brand.

By 1983, in addition to the three shops on East Madison, Lexington and Third Avenue, shops were opening in Manhattan at South Street Seaport, Eighty-fourth and Madison, Lower Broadway and, at last, on Fifth Avenue itself. The Fifth Avenue franchise was the most prestigious and for Luciano, Annaratone and Salibello this marked the beginning of the coming of age of Benetton in America. The burst of expansion in New York City was accompanied and followed by openings across America; in Boston, Chicago, Cincinnati, Tulsa, Kansas City, Philadelphia, Atlanta, San Francisco and Los Angeles. These shops were opening at a faster rate – four a week – than in any other country and their average size of between 250–300 square metres was larger than their counterparts in Europe. This take-off in sales and shops transformed the Benetton management operation in New York into a countrywide concern with bigger offices in the General Motors building. Here, shop owners and would-be owners from all over the country came to negotiate their terms and see the twice-yearly collections.

Luciano divided America into areas and they set about finding a representative for each one, starting with John Salibello in New York and New Jersey. Luciano himself visited every potential new site and shop owner, criss-crossing America in a display of hands-on management unseen before in the fashion retail industry in that country. He seemed to be able to hold the entire network in his head, crossing different time zones and travelling vast distances, often covering two or three cities in a single day. Sometimes he travelled with Marina, whom he would send in ahead of him to inspect the interiors of the shops. He allowed the kind of media coverage he shunned at home to keep the momentum going: 'Benetton takes on the world,' declared *Fortune* magazine. The New York *Daily News* and the Chicago *Tribune* began to talk of 'the Benetton phenomenon' and the 'colonisation' of America by Benetton, placing the stress on foreignness, in spite of the fact that America was and is a racial melting pot.

Later, Luciano's hands-on approach and the unique nature of the Benetton franchise system would bring trouble here in America and elsewhere between the business and the shop owners. For the time being, however, these were the golden times of empire building without stress in the country of which he had dreamed since he was a boy. The Benetton name was becoming known from coast to coast and further west. In Japan, four shops were opening under the umbrella of the Seibu conglomerate and twenty more were planned.

This was further proof that the name of Benetton could cross frontiers. Marketing, advertising and publicity, however, the means of facilitating this movement around the world, were expensive to buy and erratic in their returns. Many countries where Luciano wanted to see shops open had under-developed or non-existent media resources, in no way comparable with the advanced channels of communication that were giving them such impetus in America and Europe. The most widely spread medium across rich and poor countries was television, but television advertising again was expensive, and there was no guarantee that people would watch it. Luciano had observed that there were very few occasions when you could more or less guarantee that millions of people around the world would sit down and watch television. Sport was one of these occasions.

The Olympic Games was a case in point, but one vastly expensive advertising campaign every four years was not the answer. Sport, however, was the most reliable gatherer of the global audience, just as it was locally, in a country like Italy and a place like Treviso. Gilberto had already proposed and they had accepted that the company should extend its involvement from sponsoring Benetton Basket to sponsoring the Treviso rugby team. The construction was underway of the Palaverde, a 6,000-seater arena for sports and cultural events, for the use of the inhabitants of Treviso. At the global level, however, where advertising might pay back on a corresponding scale, the attraction had to be glamorous and exciting, as well as appealing to the competitive instinct.

There was only one sport that Luciano had observed was capable of satisfying these criteria. This was the most expensive, glamorous and dangerous sport of all: Formula 1 motor racing. Thus it was that Luciano, himself the son of a hire-car company proprietor, and whose own passion for cars had been sublimated since the onset of the years of lead, found himself agreeing with Gilberto that, for US$4 million, they should sponsor the Tyrrell Formula 1 racing team.

This was the era when sponsorship was still dominated by ciga-rette companies such as John Player and Rothmans and oil giants like Agip and Elf. There was an added attraction in becoming the first ever Formula 1 team to bear the legend 'The world's largest knitwear company'. The Formula 1 season ran for seven months of the year and moved around the world from venue to venue; some venues, like Monte Carlo, were more glamorous than others, but all were followed by a vast and still-growing television audience. Luciano, Gilberto and David Paolini, the former journalist who was Benetton's head of public relations, began to attend races and instantly became fans. Marina, however, found the combination of speed, colour, internationalism, excitement, high technology and the human factor, all of which Luciano found irresistible, all too resistible. She took up embroidery to pass the time during races and was unmoved even when the Benetton-sponsored Tyrrell, driven by Michele Alboreto, won the Detroit Grand Prix.

The first season in Formula 1 for Benetton was, in terms of cham-pionship points, otherwise unsuccessful for the Tyrrell team and drivers Alboreto and Danny Sullivan. In seven months, US$4 million had come and gone, but Gilberto and Luciano deemed the invest-ment worthwhile in terms of the television coverage this had

lesser altitude at which he was permitted to operate, Palmeri was still the only non-family link between all the manufacturing and the financial operations of the business.

At every level up to this altitude, Palmeri began to build the necessary structures and systems that would form the complex means to a simple end. This was the ability to be flexible and achieve greater and greater growth. Palmeri put in place a Benetton Group board of directors, an executive committee and a supporting management structure. He hired senior managers with international experience and external consultants as and when they were required. 'When I joined Benetton,' he said later, 'economically the company was doing fine, but the family had the sense enough to realise that growth had become a necessity.'

Palmeri knew that the home market was saturated and that they were at a plateau in their assaults on America and Japan. 'Exports were stuck at 10 per cent,' he said, 'making expansion into foreign markets a must. But this also meant giving priority to a staff of top managers.' Over the next two or three years, he would recruit his trusted friend Carlo Gilardi from the Bank of Italy, as finance director; Giovanni Cantagalli from Minnesota Mining and Manufacturing as director general of operations; Giulio Penzo from the same company as director of legal affairs; Guido Venturini from Alcantara Textiles as director of marketing; Giancarlo Chiodini as head of logistics; and Professor Bruno Zuccaro from Zanussi and Honeywell as head of information systems.

Zuccaro was to oversee the leading edge information technology that would link the shops around the world, in real time, with the revolutionary automated distribution facility that Comau, the subsidiary of Fiat, was building for Benetton nearby at the village of Castrette. If one of the Fifth Avenue Benetton shops, of which there would soon be six, wanted a 'flash' collection of 500 lilac jumpers, they could have them in a short time and at no greater cost than the usual collections. All this amounted, as Luciano liked to put it, to the process of 'raising fashion from the artisanal to the industrial level'.

Palmeri was the key managerial component, but there were significant exceptions to his rule. Gilberto was content with Palmeri as a filter, in the same way that Giuliana and Luciano were satisfied with the new publicity director, Vittorio Rava, and the public relations director, David Paolini. Luciano observed, however, that Lucio Zotta, an experienced retailer hired by Palmeri as commercial director, was having trouble maintaining the delicate balance of relationships between the regional sales directors and product directors, nearly all of whom had been taken on by Luciano himself. The result was that, after only eight months, Zotta departed and Luciano again took on the role of commercial director. Nor did he look for a replacement for the time being. Giuliana, too, preferred to keep her long-standing creative relationship with her design director, Varassi, direct and free from the appointment of an intermediary.

At the same time as these growing pains, there were reconciliations. After the years of estrangement, Afra and Tobia Scarpa were reunited with Luciano and the company for the design of the new distribution centre at Castrette. Teresa and those of the children who were still at home lived in the house the Scarpas had designed near the factory they had also created. Mauro, the eldest child of Teresa and Luciano, had gone from university in Venice to a job in the Benetton shop in Paris. He had started his working life at roughly the same age and in much the same fashion as his father had done; at the age of thirteen, folding jumpers in the Benetton shop in Treviso. Luciano, by this time one of the richest men in the country, had none the less indicated to Mauro that if he wanted money, in this case to buy a motorcycle, he would have to work. Mauro had taken the hint, as did the three other children of Luciano and Teresa, Alessandro, Rossella and Rocco.

Luciano and Marina were by this time living in the house in the centre of Treviso. His most frequent journey from here was the short distance to Treviso Airport, from where he flew to meetings with agents, shop owners and to proposed new shop sites and store-fronts, which he often spent weeks choosing and which were almost always now beyond his home country. These eight storefronts ranged from the classical and understated Benetton, with its dark wood interior, to the other extreme – Tomato – aimed at the teenage clientele.

Palmeri had identified the need to drive up the international mar-kets. Benetton, with its unique version of franchising, could increase the number of shops in this network at almost no investment cost to itself. This left capital free to be invested in more and more advanced communications and production systems and in advertising. The telephones rang twenty-four hours a day in the offices of nearly a hundred Benetton agents around the world, with calls from would-be shop owners wanting to become rich. These agents were entrepreneurs working on commission, themselves owning at least one shop in their designated area and looking for new entrepre-neurs willing to invest between US$10,000 and US$300,000 per shop.

The agents organised the presentations of new collections to retailers and took orders and relayed them to Ponzano. They over-saw the 'flash' collections in addition to the regular ones and the 'reassortment' or reorders of the fastest-selling items. They also co-ordinated the distribution to the shops of the Benetton-financed advertising and marketing campaigns. Luciano, in addition to being the link between all these people, was the key to its continuing growth. Within just over a year, they had driven exports up from 10 per cent to over 30 per cent. He was the travelling salesman, in the role in which he had started life on a bicycle on the roads of the Veneto and which he now played out in the skies over Germany, Scandinavia, the United Kingdom, America and Japan, in the white Benetton Cessna jet – with a green stripe.

The speed at which the business was growing was astonishing. A new example of one of the eight kinds of shop was opening nearly every day. This was in addition to the 2,700 shops already selling the thirty million garments a year that were coming out of the eight factories in northern Italy, France and Scotland. Yet these factories still directly employed only 2,000 people, with a further 6,000 indirectly employed in the 200 or so satellite sub-contractors, all working exclusively for Benetton, and some of which were also owned by Invep, one of the family holding companies. Invep also owned a majority stake in InFactor, a new venture with the country's biggest bank, Banca Nazionale del Lavoro, which was a small business finance operation. InFactor was soon joined by FinLeasing and InLeasing, again controlled by Invep, for leasing deals with sub-contractors to supply them with transport, factory premises and equipment.

In Ponzano, the white interiors of the factory buildings were comparatively calm and sparsely populated. Men in white coats stared at test tubes of coloured liquids, the new dyes that had evolved since the early days of Ado Montana. In the hangar-like cutting room, computer-controlled cutters scythed at high speed through vast sheets of cotton in as many as fifty colours. Another part of the factory was lined with trolleys piled high with ghostly white garments, waiting to be tipped into the vast vats of colour. Giuliana, whose eldest daughter Paola would soon join her in the business, still only employed ten designers, who brought new collections in up to fifty shades here twice a year. A design passed by her was entered onto the computer in the smallest size; the other sizes were worked out automatically. The computer operator then moved around on the screen the various shapes to be cut out to determine the minimum amount of material needed to make the garment. Already, information technology was taking on the process from the people who invented it.

At nearby Villorba, in the basement of the newest part of the factory, Professor Zuccaro's information technology complex was also taking shape. This would soon link the plant with computerised cash tills in shops and stores as far away as Washington DC, where they had once agonised over opening the first American shop, and Tokyo. Nearby again, and as yet little more than a vast shell amid a pile of rubble, the Scarpas' leading edge distribution facility was also taking shape, designed to be capable of emptying and loading a juggernaut truck in under thirty minutes.

Everyone who could pay between US$7 and US$70 seemed to be wearing the stunning range of unconventional colour, the electric blues and dazzling fuchsias and oranges from Benetton: Ivy League college students in New England and California, Left Bank teenagers in Paris and schoolgirls in Rome. In London, the latest Benetton shop on Oxford Circus was the largest anywhere in the world so far, a conglomerate of the eight shops: Benetton, 012, Sisley, My Market, Merceria, Tomato, Fantomax and Jeans West. Jeffrey Wallis, Benetton's largest British franchise holder, was previously owner of the Wallis fashion chain. Had he not successfully reinvented himself, he would have been an example of the kind of old-fashioned shopkeeper who was destined to die. In terms of advertising, the hundreds, and now thousands, of storefronts in eight different designs had collectively acted as the most effective medium.

The second season of Formula 1 sponsorship, although beneficial in terms of television coverage, was proving as expensive and uneventful as the first. This was apart from a delirious third place for Patrese in the Alfa Romeo, albeit behind their rival, Ferrari, in his home Italian Grand Prix at Monza. The low profile of the Benetton name had been necessitated first by the threat to the family during the years of lead and then by the prohibitively high cost of advertising tailored to meet the marketing needs of individual countries. This meant that Benetton's overall advertising budget, the cost of which agents and shop owners did not have to bear, was still only

2 per cent of total turnover. This was doubled to 4 per cent to fund the cost of breaking into America and Japan.

In America, however, the competition was fierce from bigger spenders on splashy advertising like Esprit and Jordache. In search of a competitive edge at low extra cost, and still through the Kathy Travis agency, Benetton advertising there started to stress the international success of the brand: 'Benetton – cotton in all the colors of summer' read the advertisement in *New York* magazine. Below a picture of a couple on a beach, in large letters, were the names of fashionable cities around the world frequented by Americans and with shops selling Benetton.

In America, triggered by the success of the rugby polo, and accompanied by advertising and the Formula 1 coverage, the boom in business and brand awareness was ongoing across the twelve regions delineated on the map on the wall of the Benetton offices in the General Motors Building. In New York City, Luciano realised a long-standing dream when the giant store, Macy's, opened a Benetton section in its sportswear department. Situated between Calvin Klein and Adrienne Vitadini, the Benetton section in Macy's proved a failure, doing only a third of the business done by the nearest dedicated Benetton shop. After six months, the Macy's experiment was ended. Although there would in time be nearly 300 Benetton 'shops in stores' and clothing and sports goods concessions in America, the Macy's experience convinced Luciano and his New York associates that, for the time being, the future lay in the development of the network in its distinctive, established form.

The demand to be part of this network on the part of would-be store owners was heavier than ever. The new American Benetton Services Corporation was turning down twenty licence applications for every one it granted. In spite of the fact that the company was becoming known in America as 'the fast food of fashion', there were and always would be clear differences between Benetton franchisees and those of the McDonald's hamburger chain. Entrepreneurs who failed in their Benetton licence applications – and some who succeeded – would discover this. The differences between Benetton and the likes of McDonald's were clear cut: no written contract, all clothes supplied exclusively by Benetton on a no-return basis, no royalties payable on profits or use of the brand name and preference given to 'our kind of person' over the ability merely to come up with between US$10,000 and US$300,000 to open a shop. Some would later point to this as a means by which the company, and Luciano in particular, could retain a greater degree of control over the shops and their owners than might otherwise have been possible. Others would point out that without this unusual degree of control the Benetton franchises would not have come into existence in the first place and a great many people would not have made an equally great amount of money. Yet in spite of these differences, eleven years later, misconceptions about the nature of the deal would still be promoted by aggrieved Benetton franchisees. Thirteen years later, many areas of the media, including Luciano's local newspaper, would still be calling him 'the McDonald's of the jumper'.

Luciano, meanwhile, installed Francesco della Barba, a tough commercial businessman and fellow native of Treviso, as the first vice-president in charge of the growth and well-being of the Benetton business and brand in the United States. Della Barba's job, in conjunction with Walter Annaratone and the Salibellos, was to drive up levels of business without driving down the standards of the franchise in the United States. Della Barba was the eyes and ears of Luciano, and in many cases he gave precedence to new American franchise holders of Italian extraction. This understandably gave rise to the notion that a glass ceiling existed between non-Italian franchisees and would-be franchisees, and an 'Italian Mafia' as secretive and exclusive as the Sicilian family business of the same name. Although a large number of Benetton agents across America and around the world were either Italian or of Italian extraction, an equally large number of franchisees and shop owners across America were non-Italian Americans, just as they were Britons in Britain, Japanese in Japan, French in France and Germans in Germany. Again, only when hard times and recession came to America, Britain, Germany and the Western world in general would people point to the 'Italian' factor as a contributory and negative one, and would the criticism of Benetton in some of these countries by media and regulatory authorities take on a xenophobic tone.

This impression of favouritism towards friends and friends of friends was perhaps compounded by the fact that people were unaware that secretly even Luciano Benetton could be taken for a ride. It was during this time that Luciano gave a sample collection of Benetton clothing to a potential agent, whom he had met through mutual acquaintances. The man already worked in the clothing industry and professed great admiration for Benetton. He took the sample collection to south-east Asia, had it copied and sold it in America under his own brand name.

Meanwhile, everyone in America, it seemed, wanted to buy and sell Benetton. In the area of competition, however, advertising by big American chains like Esprit and Jordache was already international in its reach and flavour. Benetton could not match this level of spending simply by hiking its advertising budget from 2 per cent to 4 per cent. At the same time, if Benetton was to match and outsell these competitors in America, the advertising had at the very least to make the same impact. In spite of the impression being given in *Life* magazine and others that Benetton was all conquering, the devolved cost strategy on which this expansion depended meant that the company could not directly fund a conventional advertising campaign by one of the big agencies to achieve this impact. The question was, how to achieve the same impact, indeed a greater one, for a fraction of the cost. One night, after dinner with Marina at a place in the hills, Luciano came back to the house in the centre of Treviso with what he thought was the answer.

Toscani could never be caught doing anything so boring as sitting on his terrace with a glass of his homegrown wine enjoying the Tuscan sunset. In any case, it was just before midnight when Luciano called. Nor was he in bed with his third wife. The photographer, in his role as an Appaloosa breeder, was in the stables helping to deliver a foal.

Needless to say, he was never far from a telephone. Tonight was no exception. Eighteen months had passed since they had met at dinner at the house of Fiorucci in Milan. Toscani was surprised to hear directly from Luciano rather than from an agency, but not at all surprised by what Luciano had to say.

'Oliviero, when you have a moment, we need a global image.'

6   United Colors of Benetton

Ponzano, the Veneto, 1984

Toscani arrived in Luciano's office at the Villa Minelli three days later.

'Can you do it?' Luciano asked him.

Toscani replied that he could. He had been galvanised by the resumption of the acquaintance that had begun in Milan eighteen months earlier. Luciano was far more powerful than Fiorucci, and Toscani regarded the collaboration between the avant-garde and big business as his personal terrain. Like Luciano, he had little time for the corporate cowardice and greed of the big advertising agencies. He had come here as an individual with a single, simple idea, as Luciano hoped he would. He called this idea 'All the Colors in the World'.

Benetton

The image was as simple as it was new. Young children and teenagers from different countries and ethnic groups were laughing and smiling together, united in all the colours of Benetton.

Toscani was using the language of racial harmony to transcend the cultural barriers to the same global image that Luciano was seeking for the company. The result was bright and beautiful in its own right, as well as an advance on the nihilism and witless amateurism of the punk era. Toscani disliked using professional models as much as he disliked big advertising agencies. The pictures, like many of his most successful images, would use 'real' children. To co-ordinate the campaign, Toscani suggested to Luciano that he retain the services of Eldorado, the small Parisian advertising agency for which he often worked.

Luciano agreed. The days of the Kathy Travis agency were at an end. Benetton increased its publicity budget to US$12 million, and Eldorado launched the 'All the Colors' campaign in the spring of 1984. The print and billboard campaigns, however, were still distributed in fourteen countries by an advertising giant, in this case, J. Walter Thompson. The combination of 'real' children and Toscani's technical brilliance retains its freshness to this day. Luciano saw the hoarding with the Benetton logo for the first time in Milan. 'I felt a lump in my throat,' he recalled, 'and my heart started to beat faster. It was both strange and wonderful, suddenly to have an image that fitted us like a glove.'

The response around the world was strikingly different to the claustrophobic, self-congratulatory advertising milieu of big business. 'All the Colors' won the *Avenue* magazine award in the Netherlands, but there were hundreds of letters to the company simply from people who liked the message and some from those who did not. In South Africa, the advertisements were banned altogether, except in a few magazines catering to the black community. Some letters from America and Britain reflected the racism to which the images were a response: 'Shame on you!' wrote one correspondent from Manchester, in the north of England. 'You have mixed races that God wants to keep apart!'

The success of 'All the Colors in the World' spurred Toscani on to capitalise on the racial harmony theme. Again, he shot the pictures in his Paris studio with a group of 'real' children ranging in age from four to fourteen and from countries as diverse as Japan, Ireland and the Ivory Coast. This time he added non-Benetton 'accessories' for the children to hold, such as the flags of traditionally antagonistic countries: Germany and Israel, Greece and Turkey, Britain and Argentina, and the United States and the Soviet Union. Toscani and the team at Eldorado also picked up on a chance remark by a visiting UNESCO official. 'My God,' he said, 'it's the united colors we're seeing here!'

Paris, France, 1985

Autumn was mild in Paris, and the temperature of the Cold War was also thawing. The Soviet President Gorbachev and his motorcade were at the beginning of the Champs Elysées, along which the Soviet leader and his entourage would drive to meet President Mitterrand.

Gorbachev and his motorcade set off along the ceremonial route, watched by hundreds of millions of people on television around the world. Halfway along the route the Soviet leader in his Peugeot limousine was observed to look up and gesticulate to one of his aides. Later, they would say this was the perfect moment for Toscani to have tapped into the beginning of the end of the Cold War, and the new zeitgeist of East–West dialogue and perestroika; either way, this was a magical moment and a remarkable piece of luck.

In fact, it had been the idea of Bruno Suter of the Eldorado agency to line the Champs Elysées with billboards showing the poster of the two small black children, one holding the American flag and the other the flag of the Soviet Union, about to kiss each other. Above the two children, the caption read 'United Colors of Benetton'.

Suter would swear he saw Gorbachev register the images. Others closer to the President later confirmed that he said to his aide: 'Who is this Benetton, anyway?' Either way, five years on, Gorbachev and the Soviet Union would be gone and Luciano Benetton would be in Moscow, negotiating to open the first United Colors of Benetton store in the Russian capital. Meanwhile, the images won a clutch of prestigious prizes in France and the Netherlands, including the Grand Prix de la Communication Publicitaire, and the one-million-franc award from the Banque de l'Union Publicitaire. However, in America, the country of the other antagonist in the picture, although Benetton was booming, the image provoked a different reaction.

New York City, United States of America, 1985

The success of 'United Colors' in Europe immediately led Luciano to want to test the campaign in the States. Before this test could take place, however, the company received letters from Americans pointing out that there was a ban in place in the United States on the use of the Stars and Stripes in advertising. After the success of 'All the Colors' in America the previous year, this was deemed to be a risky step. The spring and summer campaign was launched without the contentious picture. The result, at a cost of US$3 million, was an immediate impact across the country and the answer to the question. The key to the success of Benetton on the billboards of

America lay in clean-coloured clothes and brilliantly engineered images of bright, smiling children.

This was the golden period of Toscani's collaboration with Luciano Benetton. For the time being, he could do no wrong. Toscani's global imagery spawned a host of imitators, none of which came close to matching the Benetton style and all of which he held in contempt. He took ideas he had only begun to explore for other clients – 'real' models, real issues and real innovation – and homogenised these with results that would make him rich and famous. This also led to a relationship with Luciano which would far outlive that which the company had with Eldorado and J. Walter Thompson. This relationship would also be quite unlike that between any other creative artist and the commerce that sustained his lifestyle. From the beginning, the flamboyant photographer was determined to hold the territory he had won through Luciano's personal backing. This meant that while Toscani would never be accountable in a conventional fashion, the images he created for the company could never be too predictable for fear of losing his hard-won position.

At the same time, the irony was that, from the beginning, these highly distinctive advertisements, probably the best of his career, were as standardised as Big Macs. There were numerous differences between McDonald's and Benetton, but Benetton never resisted the comparison. The global imagery preached uniformity of social habits and dress, as well as of rights and opportunity, and the common language was American English. The other common features in these images were the Benetton name and knot logo, superimposed on the posters like the stamp of quality control. Within a relatively short time, however, these would also change. 'United Colors' would become the worldwide logo as well as the dominant theme. The Benetton image would be handled exclusively by Toscani and managed by an in-house group of ten people answerable only to Luciano. Toscani would declare this was essential to reflect the 'soul' of the company. In time, however, this preoccupation with reflecting the 'soul' of the company would lead its image, as conveyed in the advertisements, away from the artfully concealed homogeneity that made it work in the first place.

Aldo Palmeri was unlikely to have ventured an opinion on the soul of the company, but the managing director was gratified at the contribution 'United Colors' was making to Benetton's American strategy. Palmeri was driving the company hard across America, where the number of shops would rise from 400 to 500 in 1985, and sales for this year were projected at US$150 million. This leap forward was helped by low transport costs and a strong dollar, which allowed European companies like Benetton and Laura Ashley to export goods more cheaply to the United States. Everyone knew, however, that these conditions could not last and that the advantage would swing back to established homegrown competitors like Gap, who had a stable home currency and manufacturing plants closer to the market-place. In the event of a downturn so severe that government intervention was necessary, the American regulatory authorities would have no hesitation in giving priority to domestic companies over foreign competitors, whom they could penalise with import restrictions and accuse of taking away American jobs. Palmeri insured against this to a certain extent by authorising the US$18 million purchase and refit of a textile plant at Rocky Mount, North Carolina, to make cotton and denim garments and sweatshirts. He was looking to extend the range of Benetton beyond dependence on the fashion market, and not just into related fashion products but also into financial services, increasingly considered an essential accessory to the phenomenon of the 'yuppie' lifestyle. He was also shopping for a major US partner to offer financial packages to the network of shops there.

The key barrier, however, which Palmeri saw to Benetton's achieving the necessary critical mass, was the financial restraint imposed by the family ownership of Benetton Group. Palmeri and Gilberto wanted to create leverage. The solution was to end this 100 per cent family ownership of the core business by floating up to 25 per cent of Benetton Group on the Milan stock exchange. This could be achieved without any weakening of the family ownership at all, for Benetton Group itself was a subsidiary of Invep, soon to be restructured and renamed by Gilberto as Edizione, the 100 per cent family-owned holding company. This ownership structure, and the relationship between the various operating companies under the Edizione umbrella, would shortly give the American Securities and Exchange Commission cause to take a closer look at Benetton when the downturn did indeed come in the United States.

In America, meanwhile, Benetton franchisees and shop owners were making good profits on high margins, which they could afford to cut if the dollar weakened and the government introduced import restrictions. In deference to American tastes, Benetton franchisees and shop owners were adding items like jump suits and oversized cotton tunics to their collections, and opening roomier stores. In New York City, the first American 012 shop for children opened on the corner of Eighty-fifth Street and Madison Avenue. By this time there were six Benetton shops on Fifth Avenue alone. In Los Angeles, California, the Benetton agent was another Italian, Angelo Savardi. The name of Savardi's company, Villa Minelli, hinted at the importance attached to this key American agent and franchisee by the family back in Ponzano. Savardi was having no trouble finding entrepreneurs to open new shops in apparently competing areas of the city. The net effect, as it was on Fifth Avenue and elsewhere, was to drive up sales rather than down across the shops in the area in question.

Luciano himself shuttled to and fro across the United States, attending major openings, checking out new store locations and meeting agents and franchisees from New York City, to Philadelphia and California. 'Nearly all our children had by this time visited the country of which I dreamed when I was behind the counter at the Dellasiegas,' he would recall. These children included his nephew, Carlo's son Stefano, who died in California in a car accident in 1985.

In the same year, Luciano also travelled to and fro across Europe. In France, near Poitiers, he posed with a herd of multi-coloured sheep for an American Express advertisement. In Budapest, he attended the opening of the first Benetton shop behind what was then the Iron Curtain. In Eastern Europe, the political and commercial map was beginning to splinter and reshape itself. Although he would rarely refer to this after the fall of the Berlin Wall, Luciano had been dreaming of setting up manufacturing plants in the Soviet Union to supply the countries of the Eastern Bloc. However rude he and Toscani were publicly about Gianni Agnelli, head of Fiat, in private Agnelli was something of a role model, with his huge factories in Russia and priceless contracts with the Soviet regime. Luciano even had letters of agreement from the authorities in Moscow, confirming that the idea of these Soviet Benetton plants was viable. Now, however, Gorbachev was meeting Mitterrand in Paris, and passing Benetton hoardings on the Champs Elysées, and the whole Eastern European monolith was beginning to crack.

Prague, Czechoslovakia, 1985

Before Luciano and his team left Treviso in the Cessna for the opening of the first Czech shop, he circulated an internal memo. This reminded everyone of the sensitive ground on which they were about to tread: 'Since political authorities will be present, it is advisable to avoid any discussion whatsoever of politics.' In Prague, Luciano and the Benetton party arrived to be welcomed by a delegation of communists in their dark suits. They celebrated the shop opening with the usual clutch of commissars and apparatchiks, but the true networks of the coming power were elsewhere. 'Our real contacts weren't there,' Luciano recalled. 'We knew a German who knew a Hungarian who knew a slightly more relaxed Czech minister. Friends of friends found us a path through the bureaucracy.'

These friends of friends included the future President Vaclav Havel, not long out of prison and working in a brewery, and Frank Zappa, the Los Angeles rock star who was a link between the West and Czech entrepreneurs. Soon, these 'friends' would have opened five more shops in Czechoslovakia. Some of these Eastern European shops were still accessible only to foreigners and highly placed bureaucrats with hard currencies, such as the US dollar and the Deutschmark. Window shopping cost nothing, however, and there were a number of ways in which Czechs and Poles could find hard currency. In Eastern Europe, Luciano would not have to ingratiate himself with the old Soviet authorities and thus only join the likes of Agnelli by emulating them. The 'velvet revolution' of Vaclav Havel and Czechoslovakia would in reality be one in which the dark-suited commissars and their grey citizens surrendered to the vividly coloured woollens that had liberated the youth of Italy two generations earlier.

Rio de Janeiro, Brazil, 1985

This success on the main streets of America and Eastern Europe had yet to be matched by glory for the Benetton name on the race track. The third season in Formula 1, and the second sponsoring Alfa Romeo, was proving more expensive and less successful than the first. The Brazilian Grand Prix was the first of the season. By the end of the race and yet another dismal performance, Luciano and his publicity director David Paolini had seen enough.

'This is no good,' Luciano told Paolini. 'If we're going to stay in Formula 1, I want to have a bigger say in what goes on.'

'The Toleman team's for sale,' Paolini told him. 'Let's go to London and have a look.'

The British-based Toleman–Hart team was in trouble. Ayrton Senna, the most brilliant and mercenary of the new generation of drivers, had wriggled out of a contract with them and was already showing his promise with Lotus. The Toleman team had not participated in the first three Grands Prix of the season. Ted Toleman, the transport tycoon and team owner, had stipulated that he would only continue to race if the team managed to secure a contract with Goodyear tyres. When this failed to materialise, Toleman put the team up for sale.

Luciano agreed with Paolini that it was worth going to London to have a look.

'Negotiate,' he said. 'Make them an offer.'

'Don't you want to come and check it out for yourself?' Paolini asked him.

'No, it's all right. You do it.'

Paolini went to England. Two weeks later, Benetton International NV, an affiliate of Benetton Group based in Amsterdam, became the new owner of the Toleman–Hart Formula 1 team. The price of US$2 million was precisely half the cost of a season's sponsorship in Formula 1.

There was much to recommend the purchase. In addition to giving Luciano and Benetton greater control over their investment, the team had talent. Teo Fabi was a capable driver; John Barnard a talented designer. The team factory was within fifteen miles of London. They engaged Peter Collins, another Briton, as the new manager. Collins put the team back onto the race track for what was left of the season. For Monaco, they entered a single car driven by Fabi. By the time of the last Grand Prix of the season, on the streets of Adelaide in Australia, they had added a second car driven by Giancarlo Ghinzani. At the end of the season, the Benetton-owned-and-sponsored Toleman–Hart team had not scored a single championship point. This did not matter; they now had the control that ownership brought to make all the changes they liked.

They changed the name of the team from Toleman–Hart to Benetton Formula. They exchanged the British Hart engines for the ferociously powerful new turbo-charged BMW unit. The Austrian driver Gerhard Berger was signed to join Fabi. Collins also changed the atmosphere of the team. Benetton was the only sponsor also to own a team and the team showed its roots in the loud rock music that played in the pits, the bright overalls worn by the pit crew and the multi-coloured paintwork of the cars. The cameras would love these manifestations of hip capitalism; they also tricked many other teams, as they had tricked bank managers and solicitors, into thinking that they were dealing with an outfit of gypsies and not with enormously successful professionals. The presence of Luciano at the races – all-powerful yet detached; inscrutable, yet visibly a fan – would give the team an aura that surpassed that of other teams and their sponsors. Luciano's team managers might in time bring in other sponsors such as Camel and Mild Seven cigarettes, but he himself stood out from the dour oil executives, the tobacco barons and the head of Beatrice Foods. Meanwhile, behind all this pizzazz, Peter Collins was quietly building a powerful new force in Formula 1.

There was another, entirely Italian motive for the Benetton purchase of Toleman. The Italian motor racing fans, the *tifosi*, were universally acknowledged to be the most vociferous in the business.

Ferrari, the leading Italian team, was a legend, and the owner of Ferrari was Fiat, itself owned by Gianni Agnelli. Fiat, as Toscani loved to point out, spent as much on advertising in a single day as Benetton spent in a year. For every 100 lire Fiat put in the cash till, it kept only five lire in profits. Benetton kept eleven. Luciano very much wanted to beat Agnelli and Ferrari at their own game and, above all, on their home territory.

The Benetton team nearly achieved this in their first season under their own name in Formula 1. Berger was third in the San Marino Grand Prix at Imola; at the Italian Grand Prix at Monza, Fabi secured pole position, only to fail to start. In the penultimate race of the year, in Mexico City, amid scenes of delirium in the pits, the Benetton of Berger took a triumphant chequered flag. This left Berger at the end of the season seventh in the world championship.

After the triumph in Mexico City, Luciano was so overcome that he embraced Berger and then headed for his own car, leaving the rest to celebrate. 'It may have seemed childlike,' he recalled, 'but I was so excited. As it was at other intense moments in my life, after the moment of triumph, the height of luxury for me was to be on my own.'

In his private life, this was a condition to which Luciano would shortly return. Marina rarely attended the races these days, even with her embroidery. In his capacity as head of the company, however, he had just been joined by several thousand people whom he had never met.

Milan, northern Italy, 1986

The invitations on this occasion had been sent out by Palmeri. These people were outside investors and the occasion was the flotation of Benetton Group on the Milan and Venice stock exchanges.

The size and aim of the flotation were straightforward. Palmeri and the bankers were offering 20 per cent of Benetton Group, hitherto 100 per cent owned by Edizione and the family, for sale to the public. The offer consisted of 15.6 million shares and equity warrants attached to bonds subsequently issued in the Euromarkets in Italy and Frankfurt. This valued Benetton on the market at US$1 billion. The proceeds would be invested among the shareholders, including Edizione Holding.

On the first day of trading at the Milan and Venice stock exchanges, the first ever Benetton stock offer was more than ten times oversubscribed, raising US$270 million in less than fifteen minutes. This was a vote of confidence in Benetton by the markets. Palmeri had achieved this despite the fact that Benetton was outside the so-called 'Noble Wing', the traditional, aristocratic and seemingly all-powerful banking and industrial freemasonry epitomised by Mediobanca, the Agnellis and Fiat. He had driven up the turnover of the company by nearly five times in four years and had proved he could talk the language both of the family and of the bankers. 'The original Benetton formula was based on a brilliant intuition,' he liked to say, 'but now we are applying it scientifically to a sophisticated industrial model.'

Carlo Gilardi, whom he had hired from the Bank of Italy, had a high regard for Palmeri but was strongly opposed to the audacious financial services strategy that was being separately pursued from the Benetton Group by Edizione. 'We were so able and keen and passionate to create fashion, and we had the money, so it seemed to some people the right thing to do,' Gilardi would recall, 'but I thought it was impossible to create this kind of thing without the necessary expertise; it was a dream.' Edizione already had a 20 per cent holding in the private Banco di Trento e Bolzano, two 10 per cent stakes in leasing companies in France and West Germany, and was planning to launch an investment banking business for the textile and clothing sector in partnership with another big Italian manufacturer. This would take the family and the business into the field of currency swaps, corporate finance, underwriting and syndicated loans. Gilardi had major doubts, but would leave Benetton Group for family reasons before he could see them proved correct. Palmeri and Gilberto saw big profits in these areas and regarded it as essential if they were to spread the risks of dependence on clothing and cash in on the opportunities coming with the single European market. Palmeri was in bullish mood: 'Within two years,' he declared, 'we hope to achieve a fifty-fifty mix in group turnover between industrial and financial revenues.'

The other numbers were equally impressive: 3,200 shops in fifty-seven countries; 800 new shops opening during the year with the biggest growth taking place in America, where there would be 161 new shops and a total of 600 by the end of the year; seventy-one new shops in Britain, with a year-end total of 285; and the goal of 7,000 shops within the next five years.

Yet, at the same time, amid the blizzard of information in the share prospectus, the personal factor may not altogether have escaped the notice of these new, outside investors in Benetton. A few months before the share issue, in the spring of the year, Mario Schimberni, the chairman of the Montedison chemicals group had gone on television. Who, asked the interviewer, did he respect most in Italian business? Schimberni quickly disposed of Gianni Agnelli of Fiat, who was a long-standing rival, and was similarly dismissive of Carlo de Benedetti, chairman of Olivetti. The interviewer was beginning to despair by this time. So who, he asked, was the country's most outstanding entrepreneur?

'Luciano Benetton,' came the reply.

Luciano, sitting at his desk in the Villa Minelli, had smiled at this. He had let the distinction between entrepreneurs and managers go unspoken but recognised. 'The share issue is a grain of sand in the stock exchange,' he told an interviewer from the *Financial Times* in London. He talked about how they were going to invest part of the proceeds of the issue in their own suppliers and pieceworkers, giving this the kind of spin which distinguished him from the managers he hired and respected but with whom he had little else in common.

'We like to have the door open from behind and also in front,' he had told the visitor from London at the Villa Minelli. 'Benetton sees its future from an angle of three hundred and sixty degrees.'

The prospect of analysts and institutions threatened to clutter this 360-degree vision. Luciano was aware of the need always to go forward.

We were coming out of the dark period after the years of terrorism and we wanted to become more efficient. We knew we needed modern and skilled collaborators like Palmeri, not only in difficult times, but so that we could grow. We never thought we could be self-sufficient; we knew we had to integrate with people from outside.

Nevertheless, he was restless and ambivalent about the share issue. At the end of the day of the flotation, he walked alone around the automated distribution centre at Castrette. Then he went back to the design centre at the factory.

Giuliana was still there, as she had been all those years ago when he had gone to the little sweatshop where she worked. She was working late, long after most of the others had gone. This time, too, she smiled when she saw him coming.

'Well, we did it,' she said, referring to the events of the day.

This time, however, Luciano only nodded; his mind was still in turmoil. When one of them eventually spoke, it was not the self-assured older brother who always wanted her to make more, the man with 360-degree vision, but the apparently placid, compliant sister of all those years ago. Only now she was showing the steel beneath the flexible façade. 'We did it,' she said. 'So, let's get on with it then, shall we?'

Benetton by this time directly employed more computer operators than it did seamstresses of the kind Giuliana had been. Professor Zuccaro's computer systems were one of the main features of the summer share prospectus and one of the flotation's beneficiaries. A fourth dimension existed to Benetton in the form of a 'virtual' map that linked the operations of the company and its network around the world.

At the centre of this map, two IBM and Siemens mainframes administered a network of 200 Olivetti microprocessors for payroll, billing and stock control. Professor Zuccaro's staff were designing a fourth-generation language to create an 'info-centre' to make this industrial-style system a little more user-friendly. This system was linked to the distribution centre, where a DEC mainframe chattered to the administration centre about stock levels and deliveries. The DEC computer also controlled the automated warehouse. In the design centre, Giuliana's assistants used computer-aided design software on Hewlett–Packard machines, examples of which also controlled the cutting of the cloth.

Every day, in real time, hundreds of shops across Europe uploaded information from their point-of-sale terminals to Ponzano, with data about sales, styles and colours. This virtual map of the business and the brand included the sky beyond the earth's atmosphere; the Benetton service operations in New York and Tokyo were linked into this network by satellite. All this enabled the business to go forward on the basis of more advanced sales information than in probably any other company in the world. 'What interests us most are the orders,' Professor Zuccaro, who also lectured at the nearby University of Udine, liked to say. 'First we sell the clothes, then we make them,' ran a Benetton in-house joke.

This intelligence about the continuous process of fashion changes around the world reassured retailers, whose agreement with the business involved ordering garments several months in advance and did not allow for their return. This also meant that much of the apparent selling power of Toscani's global images had in fact been calculated in advance. All his imagery had to do was not sell the clothes, but give them a new kind of exposure in an already identi-fied market. Toscani himself would claim in time that his images had nothing to do with selling clothes *per se*. He was not being disin-genuous in this. He was merely implying there was some magical quality to his work, and omitting to give credit to the role of soft-ware in the sale of knitwear.

Toscani's spring and summer campaign for the year, again in con-junction with the Eldorado agency in Paris, expanded on the 'United Colors' multi-racial theme. Again he took 'real' models, this time with accentuated ethnic features, the intention being to show that 'although they are dressed in Benetton products, they seem to be wearing national costumes'. This time, the globe itself was the motif running through the pictures. These included a white adolescent dressed as a Hasidic Jew holding a toy globe money box stuffed with dollar bills, standing next to a black teenager dressed as a native American Indian. Although the native American Indian had his hand on the white boy's shoulder in a gesture of fraternal solidarity, the presence of the dollar bills inflamed Jewish sentiments in America, France and Italy. A flood of letters arrived in Ponzano, accusing Benetton of promoting negative stereotypes of the money-grab-bing Jew. The intended humour of the picture was lost on these correspondents, as was the fact that the three directors of the Eldorado agency, and Benetton's publicity man Vittorio Rava, who had to deal with all these letters, were themselves all Jewish. In New York City, meanwhile, Jewish groups threatened to boycott Benetton shops.

This was serious; once upon a time, objectors, for whatever reason, might have threatened to blacken the name of My Market, or Merceria, or Tomato, or Fantomax, or Jeans West, but not all of these and certainly not the name of Benetton. The creation of a single brand, linking the family and the business, meant that all three were a high-profile target, both for genuine protesters and those simply seeking to make political or commercial capital.

The response of the company, first to cover up the banknotes, and then to replace the offending image with one showing a young Palestinian and a Jew holding a toy globe between them only made matters worse. As the New York publicity agent J.J. Gross wrote in *Advertising Age*:

> The Hasidic Jews who wear these kinds of clothes, like the Arabs, are against the State of Israel . . . If the intention of Benetton is to show traditional enemies finding new ways of friendship, this is like showing Hitler with Mussolini.

Luciano's reaction was neither to duck the issue nor to attempt entirely to justify the picture. As well as his many Jewish colleagues and employees, the formative role played in his life by Jewish friends such as the Tagliacozzos and Roberto Calderoni indicated an utter lack of defamatory intent on his part. He recalled:

> I was a bit discouraged, but I had learned a fundamental lesson. We had chosen to promote an image that touched very deep feelings, identities for which millions of people had fought and died. An American critic once wrote that one of the beauties of pure art is its fundamental irresponsibility. We had

reached the limits and felt the responsibilities of commercial art. Everybody was now watching us, and even a small dose of naiveté could hurt us and irritate others. I promised myself I would control our image even more closely in future – this image which was born under a bright star, and which we had nurtured with such good intentions.

Given the innocence of these images compared with what was to come, this seems strangely naïve, however convincing it may have sounded to Luciano at the time.

Meanwhile, Gerhard Berger's first Grand Prix win for Benetton in Mexico City that autumn was all the more of a welcome distraction; and beyond the offices of Jewish protest groups, *Newsweek* magazine was saying 'This is the perfect time to be Italian.'

However, the downside of the single brand strategy, and the high personal profile this brought to the members of the family, was becoming evident to the second generation of Benettons. While newspaper reports were describing the family as 'Italy's Kennedys', they had no intention of emulating the offspring of that dynasty. Of the fourteen children, Giuliana's daughter, Paola, after university and a year at the Fashion Institute of Technology in New York, had been the first to join the business. Luciano and Teresa's son Mauro, was the second. Having started his career as a teenager folding jumpers in his holidays, he had progressed to a Benetton shop in Paris, then become its manager. Although the beneficiary of a relatively secure childhood, he was none the less the eldest son at the time of the break-up of his parents' marriage, and this must have left its scars. Mauro was tough, self-sufficient and acclimatised from an early age to working. When he was given the job of turning round the Sisley brand and shops in the year of the flotation and the first controversy over Benetton advertising, one of the first points he felt impelled to make in a magazine interview was this: 'There is nothing about our family that even vaguely resembles the hatreds and nastiness of *Dallas*.'

Mauro would carve out his own territory with Sisley, appointing a local advertising agency away from Toscani and Benetton to invent a bolder, sexier image, and reinvigorating the business in the United States and Europe to a degree that would surpass the aims of his father. In the process, he also became his own man in a way, perhaps, that even his father would never entirely be. 'I worked hard to get where I am,' Mauro would tell another journalist. 'I wanted to achieve something for myself, and not just to submit to something that was already there.' This was a lesson that all the members of the second generation of the family, if they wanted to be a meaningful part of the business, would have to learn.

Toscani's 'United Colors' images for the 1987 spring and summer collections, again in conjunction with Eldorado, were shot with his customary technical brilliance. They were beautifully bright, clean and conspicuous for their lack of provocation. 'United Fashions of Benetton' showed children wearing the new Benetton clothes in stylised poses reminiscent of high fashion, without the accentuated ethnic touches. Instead of toy globes, with or without dollars stuffed inside, the pictures included accessories that evoked great names like Yves Saint-Laurent, Louis Vuitton and Chanel. This was also all rather cute and tame compared with the preceding year and there were no angry letters to the publicity department in Ponzano.

The Benetton factory at Rocky Mount in North Carolina had turned out 800,000 cotton garments in its first year and this more than doubled to over two million in 1987. The latest and biggest addition to the factory at Castrette, again designed by the Scarpas, opened in January of the same year. The Scarpas were also at work on the restoration of the Palazzo at Corso di Porta Vittoria in Milan, which was being turned into a conference centre and offices. This new addition to the Edizione real estate portfolio was the only survivor of a clutch of historic buildings in the area, the rest of which were demolished in the 1930s to make way for a court house in the monumental style favoured by Mussolini.

The Benetton plants in America, Italy, France and Scotland were expanding in range as well as size, assembling and making a wider variety of clothes and products in new materials. Only 40 per cent of these products were by this time in solid colours, and cotton, denim and woollen garments were made in equal numbers. The two main annual collections contained over a thousand styles, including jackets, coats and blazers. As well as shoes designed by Giuliana's people and made by Di Varese, licensing agreements were in place with Polaroid for Benetton sunglasses and Bulova for Benetton 'world face' watches; plans were also under way for a new 'Colors of Benetton' perfume. With the new, wider range of clothes and accessories came a new and wider range and size of shops. 'Coats and jackets can't be folded on shelves,' Gilberto declared, adding solemnly: 'Benetton underwear is going on sale soon – shops of forty or eighty square metres will simply be inadequate.'

Benetton had already killed the traditional shopkeeper; now, underwear and shoes and watches and sunglasses and perfume were killing the traditional Benetton shop. Some years had already passed since a new My Market, Merceria, Fantomax or Tomato had opened with their small shelves and limited changing space; more and more of the originals had been remodelled and changed their names simply to Benetton. By 1996, My Market would have disappeared altogether and there would only be a few examples remaining of Merceria, Fantomax and Tomato.

Sisley, under the direction of Mauro, was proving such a success that the principle that it was better to compete with yourself than with others was again put into practice. 'Benetton Uomo' (Benetton Man), the competitor to the Sisley shops and brand, opened in main business districts and residential areas, targeting men with purchasing power and selling Benetton lines of clothing, accessories and licensed products. In Britain, the agents and shop owners had discovered that the British male, unlike his Italian or French counterpart, did not like unisex shopping and preferred an all-male retail environment. The vast majority of the new shops that continued to open at the rate of around one a day were now Benetton, Sisley, Benetton Uomo and 012. Of the competition, however, there were also many more examples than there had been only a few years earlier.

London, England, 1987

Giuliana had never claimed to have Luciano's appetite for publicity and gift for the sound bite. 'Of course,' she said, 'we are very well aware of increasing competition. But there is no rival with the same wide range as Benetton. The number of shops is not a problem. Even shops that are situated close together in the same area can have quite a different look in the window.'

Giuliana was speaking on the tenth anniversary of the opening of the first shop in London. The competition was increasing there, this was true. Gap had recently opened there; another American chain, Esprit, was coming that summer. Both these, however, were single-name shops, competitive in niches, but lacking the spread of Benetton and unable to exist as close to each other and as profitably as the shops clustered under the Benetton umbrella. Furthermore, neither Gap, nor Esprit, nor Stefanel had the crucial, unique ingredient that Benetton had and would continue to have for as long as the era of innocence lasted that surrounded its ultimately tragic perpetrator; this was the Diana factor.

Ever since her engagement to the Prince of Wales five years earlier, Diana and Benetton had been synonymous in a way that no attempt at brand power, even with the talent of Toscani, could have achieved. The effect of this association was incalculable in the minds of shoppers. Before the royal wedding, a favourite stake-out for the paparazzi in wait for Diana was the pavement outside the Benetton shop in South Kensington. Two days before the wedding, Diana, one of the richest women in England in her own right, had her cheque rejected by a Benetton shop assistant because she could not find her cheque guarantee card. This made no difference. After Diana married her unfashionable prince, she went on shopping at Benetton. Four years later, Diana took back a pair of trousers and asked for a refund. She was told she could not have one because she had lost the receipt. This did not matter. When Diana had godchildren and children of her own she shopped for them at 012.

Diana was Benetton's not-so-secret weapon in Britain and this advantage would never be enjoyed by the likes of Gap, Esprit and Stefanel. Meanwhile, the British Benetton shop network was undergoing the same metamorphosis as its mainland European counterparts and for the same reason; to avoid saturation and accommodate the new, wider range of products. The original names were dying out and being reborn, as elsewhere, as Benetton, Sisley, Benetton Uomo and 012. The main obstacle with the British was not saturation, but the idiosyncrasies of the British shopper.

In addition to the British male's aversion to unisex shopping, these obstacles included a general lack of sophistication on the part of both sexes when it came to asking for help from the assistant. 'I think window-shopping and browsing are peculiar to the British,' said Christina Lora, the Italian-born manageress of the Benetton shop in Hampstead. 'In Italy, customers wouldn't dream of pulling out handfuls of sweaters and ruining a display. When Italians go shopping they know what they want.' She went on:

> There are people you really have to admire. Jennifer in the Oxford Street shop. Now she could fold. When she'd finished with the classic knitwear, it didn't look like a pile of jumpers any more. It was a moulded shape. A sculpture. Her pinks looked good enough to eat. But customers don't appreciate this. They come in and pull apart beautiful displays. It makes me want to scream. But at Benetton, we are taught control. Always control.

Christina might have been better seeking appreciation of her powers of self-control elsewhere; in a convent, perhaps. Whatever her fate, ten years on where her Benetton shop once stood, a branch of Gap stands today.

Milan, Italy, 1987

The flotation of Benetton Group on the stock exchanges in Milan and Venice still left 80 per cent of the company in the hands of the family, while freeing up large sums of money to spend in the way fast-growing businesses most need to spend: on reducing costs and increasing margins. The new factory at Castrette and the ever-growing use of automation and information technology were two areas in which this money was spent. A third area in which money needed to be spent in order to make savings was the company's colossal consumption of yarn and wool. In January of that year, Lanerossi, one of Benetton's biggest suppliers, had suddenly come up for sale.

Lanerossi had been turned around by investment from the state and the offer for sale was one of the biggest privatisations in the history of the country. The advantages to Benetton were clear. If Edizione could buy Lanerossi, Benetton could exercise a greater degree of control over a key supplier on whom it was dependent.

Gilberto and Palmeri decided to bid in partnership with Inghirami, another textile group with whom they did business. After the first round there were only three bidders left in the ring. These were Benetton and Inghirami, Bertrand Finanziaria, and Marzotto. The latter was the clothing and textile giant whose former boss, Count Gaetano Marzotto, had once lambasted the public sector, which had later turned Lanerossi round, with the words: 'Can the state bureaucrats do something more than he who knows his own business?'

The Benetton–Inghirami axis was favourite to win when ENI, the state-controlled owner of Lanerossi, suddenly announced it was putting up the price and withdrawing the tax breaks previously on offer to the successful bidder. Whether or not this was deliberately intended to put Benetton out of the race, and if so why, would never be known.

Edizione, which would have been the ultimate owner had Benetton won, had just acquired a new managing director in the form of Gianni Mion. Mion had previously been administrative and finance director of Marzotto and made no secret of what he saw as the excessively inflexible structure of his former employer.

Another possible explanation was that Marzotto had used its influence to prevail upon the vendor, citing its longer track record in business; Benetton was an upstart by comparison. Either way, the result was the same. Marzotto was the winner. Later, Luciano would put a new spin on the disappointment. Acquiring a company in an area 'in which we didn't have the right degree of expertise,' he declared, 'would have been a mistake'. Whatever the case, the problem of the wool supply remained. Edizione would eventually only solve this problem by looking about as far away from home as it was possible to go.

Venice, northern Italy, 1987

Nico Luciani had also travelled a long way from the town of his childhood and the scene of his youthful friendship with Luciano Benetton. After qualifying as an architect he had worked in town planning, urban research and on political issues. He had visited many countries before returning to Venice, where he made his home. Although he had not spoken to Luciano for nearly twenty-five years, something had prompted him to write to him about several cultural projects in which he was involved, asking if Luciano would be prepared to help. Luciani had heard nothing until one day the telephone rang at his home: 'Hello, this is Benetton Group in Ponzano. I have Mr Luciano Benetton on the line for you.'

Luciani was astonished; here was Luciano, as if they had spoken only yesterday. 'Nico, how are you? I want to talk to you.' Luciani heard himself agreeing to meet him that weekend in Ponzano.

He drove out there on a Sunday morning still in a daze, not knowing what he was going to find. Luciano was in his office on the top floor of the Villa Minelli. They embraced and he talked as if their friendship had never been interrupted. Luciano took him on a tour of the villa and the factory. Luciani could not help noticing that the two latest buildings were on the site of their favourite canal where they had swum in winter, half a lifetime ago. They drove into town together, just as they had once done on the Vespa across the plain of the Veneto. Luciano showed him the house where he and Marina lived.

Over lunch, he told Luciani about his fledgling Benetton Foundation. 'I understand if you're critical of some of the things I have done,' he said, in an echo of the days when he had been the budding capitalist and Nico the angry young man of the left, 'but do you think if I gave some money for a research centre, you could help?' Luciano was assembling a team with the same precision he brought to bear on the business and he needed someone to co-ordinate it; someone of proven academic and administrative ability; someone he could trust. It dawned on Nico that the passage of so much time meant nothing in itself to Luciano, and that instead of offering to help with his cultural projects, his long-lost friend was offering him a job.

Luciani said he would think about it. They parted as affectionately as they had greeted each other and Luciani drove back, still in a daze, to Venice. After twenty-five years of silence between them, Luciano was asking him to change his life. A few days later, he gave Luciano his reply and stated his terms. 'And so I became director of the Benetton Foundation,' he would recall, 'and it was as if we had been together all those years.'

Ponzano, the Veneto, 1987

Edizione was the key company; it was still 100 per cent family owned and it was fast developing separate interests in parallel with Benetton Group, the sales of which were expected to reach US$1 billion in 1987. These parallel interests already included stakes in many of Benetton's suppliers and sub-contractors, land and property, holdings in banks and in the Jolly chain of hotels. In spite of the failure to buy Lanerossi, the ambition of the company was undiminished. Palmeri's financial services strategy was by far the most diversified and audacious yet.

Edizione already had around US$200 million worth of leasing and other financial business with its agents, contractors and suppliers.

The creation of a new subsidiary, In Holding, was aimed at taking these and other, personal financial services into the lives of Benetton customers. The scenario envisaged a yuppie paradise in which the customer in a one-stop shop in Los Angeles or Tokyo moved around a spacious Benetton store. He or she called at the sweater counter, picked up a purchase, then moved on to buy a pair of jeans. Then came the sunglasses, the watch and the perfume. Last, and by no means least, they checked into a leading edge finance 'counter', where he or she paid a life insurance premium and passworded into a touch-tone screen to bring up the latest movement of prices in their share portfolio. Luciano had coined a name for this scenario; he called it 'socks and stocks'.

The In Holding marketing plan envisaged the same scenario as the shops, whereby agents for its products would be independent entrepreneurs. Palmeri was president. He was aggressively recruiting and had hired Giovanni Franzi, formerly European head of investment banking at Merrill Lynch, as managing director. Franzi was already having talks with his former employers about a joint venture to invest in small private companies. Palmeri had also recruited Gianfranco Cassol, the most aggressive and dynamic financial salesman in the country, to set up the financial services sales network. Cassol expected to have 2,000 agents in place within five years. He himself had bought a 20 per cent stake in In Capital Investment, another new Edizione company which, under the In Holding umbrella, would be responsible for distributing the majority of these financial products. In Holding itself already had a 50 per cent stake in the local operation of Prudential Assurance to sell casualty insurance. By the end of the 1980s, Palmeri was becoming fond of saying that every Benetton jumper, as well as containing wool or cotton, would contain a percentage of leasing, factoring and other financial services. There was no sign, however, that, other than in the off-duty wardrobes of its executives, the Prudential was going into knitwear.

Against these heady ambitions, the failure to buy Lanerossi and the anticipated triumphs of In Holding and the Benetton foray into personal finance, the Formula 1 season passed uneventfully. Benetton were fifth in the constructors' cup, with drivers Thierry Boutsen and Teo Fabi eighth and ninth in the drivers' world championship. At Christmas, shoppers were forced to evacuate the Selfridges department store in Oxford Street, London, when a bomb was discovered in the Benetton outlet in the store. There was speculation that animal rights activists targeting Benetton were behind the incident, although being the world's largest consumer of wool did not in itself constitute a strong case for the prosecution. Two years earlier, when he had posed in France for American Express with a flock of thirty colour-dyed sheep, Luciano had first asked his son Rocco, who accompanied him, if he thought the animals were being exploited. Rocco had replied that they were not. However, after the advertisement had appeared on television, an environmentalist group had unsuccessfully tried to take Luciano to court for alleged cruelty to sheep.

In fact, the Selfridges incident was to be only the first of a series of unsolicited and violent sources of publicity for Benetton. At this time, too, the relationship was beginning to overheat with Eldorado in Paris. Luciano was feeling confident enough to fulfil his long-held dream of controlling the image as an exclusively in-house product of the business. These unsolicited, violent incidents may have prompted first Luciano and then Toscani to consider harnessing images of violent controversy in a controlled fashion to increase publicity for the business and the brand.

The Wiz Nightclub, Paris, France, 1988

Three thousand young Parisians had packed into this hip Montparnasse nightclub for the 'Party of the World', to mark the launch of the new 'Colors de Benetton – Perfume of the World'. The perfume in question was made under licence in France and packaged in a five-sided bottle to represent the five continents.

Luciano was here for the party; at the same time, he was separate, ever observant, different from the rest of the world, whose citizens his corporate philosophy was dedicated to making feel they were all the same. 'My business is a love story with the world,' he told an interviewer after the party, 'founded on a strong will to succeed. Clothes that are bright, amusing and terrific value for money, this is what the world's peoples want.' The interviewer did not necessarily believe this, but she believed he believed it. It was as if there was an uncontrolled, residual innocence beneath the business-like façade, something of which he himself was sufficiently aware to have nostalgia for it. 'Our franchisees have no contracts, no territories, and pay us no percentage royalties,' he told her. 'It is all done by gentleman's agreement, like in the early days.' She thanked him and then they both went their separate ways, she by scheduled flight, he by private jet.

London, England, 1988

'It is always the customer who chooses what sells,' he told the next interviewer. 'Production always follows public demand. Styles are kept simple, the choice of colour is wide, and the price is democratic. This is not a philosophy,' Luciano went on, 'but practical business sense. When we include the season's official fashion colours, dictated by designers, they are invariably the slowest things to sell.'

This time, the visit was to oversee plans to expand the Oxford Circus franchise, check the progress of the 265 Benetton shops in Britain and prepare for the launch of the sexy 'Under Colors' range of underwear. The bra and knickers were dead in the strictest sense, reborn as strongly styled and colourful items that could be worn uncovered and in their own right. The bodystocking was no longer merely a neutral second skin, but a striking, graphically contoured silhouette in black and white dog's tooth checks. 'Benetton may be diversifying, but they have lost none of their flair with colour,' read the newspaper coverage. This was positive stuff of the kind beloved of PR agencies. But the American and British media were hearing other, less positive stories about Benetton from America, which they were biding their time to use to the greatest effect.

Meanwhile, with the boom in sales worldwide, Benetton in all its burgeoning incarnations looked better set than ever for global dominance. The first Benetton shops had opened in Cairo, a new joint venture with a locally owned manufacturing plant, Chourbagi Antaki United Fashions of Cairo. The first Benetton superstore, housing Benetton, Sisley, 012 and Benetton Uomo under one roof, had opened at home. The new 'Zerotondo' range had been introduced to complement the 012 range, with a collection for babies and very young children from nought to two years old.

The 1988 Formula 1 season was progressing satisfactorily and would end with Benetton third in the constructors' cup and Thierry Boutsen and Alessandro Nannini fourth and ninth in the drivers' world championship. In Treviso, the passion of the family for sport, their sense of duty towards the community from which they came, and of course the public relations benefits of this, continued with the establishment of Verde Sport, an umbrella organisation to manage the proliferation of Benetton-sponsored teams, training programmes and sports complexes.

Gilberto, Giuliana and Carlo had all remained faithful to their respective passions for sport, work and family, and outdoor pursuits. Luciano, in spite of the bitter early disappointment of his self-designed suit and homemade bow tie, had travelled further from the aspirations of his youth. He was already making revisionist statements such as: 'I was never interested in fashion for its own sake, but fashion as an industrial product.' Yet, less than two years later, he would write: 'For me, clothes are not just a way to make a living, they are a passion.' Meanwhile, in tune with the new Benetton zeitgeist of clothes and perfume and smart cards, he was making all the right noises. 'Europe must become our domestic market,' he declared. 'We are a service industry, not a fashion business.' As the journalist in Paris had observed, he believed these things because he thought before he said them. However, he also knew where he would find the ultimate frontier at which to put these half statements of truth, half ideals, to the test.

Fifth Avenue, New York City, 1988

Palmeri had wanted to take Benetton Group public on the stock exchange in New York as early as 1987. A year had passed, and he and the company were still sending out all the right signals. Toscani and Eldorado's spring and summer advertising campaign, 'United Superstars of Benetton', took historical figures such as Napoleon, Joan of Arc, Leonardo da Vinci, Julius Caesar and Marilyn Monroe, and showed them alongside each other portrayed by 'real' teenage models. This time, they also included Adam and Eve, with a hint of the denim-clad Eve's breasts peeping from her denim jacket that was just enough to generate the right amount of controversy in America. The children's campaign, 'United Friends of Benetton', featured children wearing toy heads of animals traditionally antipathetic to each other, and won a number of awards.

In North Carolina, the Rocky Mount plant employed ever greater numbers of Americans to make cotton sweatshirts and jeans, ordered through the New York office by 600 Benetton stores across America, and putting the company on the right side of the high US cotton tariff barrier. Edizione had bought the historic Scribner Building on Fifth Avenue and Forty-eighth Street in New York, still the site of a famous bookstore and once home to the publishers of Ernest Hemingway, F. Scott Fitzgerald and Thomas Wolfe. A US$4 million refit of the building was under way and the plan was to restore it to its former architectural and literary glory. Benetton was also importing L.L. Bean shoes from the fabled family factory at Freeport, Maine, and selling them through its Di Varese outlets across Italy. Even Luciano was wearing L.L. Bean and Timberland shoes, and Brooks Brothers shirts and Polo Ralph Lauren ties with his Benetton blue jeans and tailored tweed jackets.

In spite of these positive signals, there was trouble brewing in the American network. America was the home of the franchise as it was traditionally known and the 'no written contract, no royalties' system of agreement was proving inadequate in terms of legal protection required in the minds of some store owners. Already hit by the falling dollar, and perhaps choosing to ignore the fact that America was fundamentally overshopped, American store owners began to complain that Benetton was violating US franchise statutes by allowing new entrepreneurs to open new stores a few blocks or even a few doors away from existing ones. 'They're selling their brand name too often, too easily,' complained one New York store manager, 'and not risking a penny of their own.' Store owners sought legal redress against the company, citing the 'clustering' of shops near each other as being damaging to sales, but found that the Benetton version of franchising was not easily receptive to legal remedy in the courts.

Benetton responded by opening the first American superstores in Manhattan and San Francisco, shifting the emphasis from a larger number of stores in one area to a greater square footage in a single selling space. Existing store owners again protested that the company was trying to drive them out of business. Others complained about the heterogeneous nature of the Benetton shop network, financed and run by individual entrepreneurs. This was the antithesis of the homogenised kind of franchise exemplified by McDonald's, which was more easily understood by litigation lawyers. It also neglected the finer points of American consumer behaviour. American shoppers were perplexed that they could not return a pair of jeans they bought in a Benetton shop in San Francisco to another Benetton store in the same city, let alone one in Cincinnati.

Competitors such as Gap changed their collections every four to six weeks. Benetton, with two collections a year and 'flash' reorders in between, had concentrated too hard on refining this system and neglected the rapidly shifting tastes of the American teenager. Palmeri's filing for the US Securities and Exchange Commission, whose approval he would need for the kind of flotation he had in mind on Wall Street, would have to acknowledge these legal challenges to the Benetton system of doing business in a recessionary United States. The honeymoon period was over for Benetton, and even longer gone was the age of innocence in which the lawyers now acting for Benetton store owners had been the Ivy League students through whom Benetton had first conquered America with a single rugby polo.

In the autumn of 1988, after the launch of the perfume in Paris and the underwear collection in London, Luciano met and listened to store owners and agents across the United States. Many of these had become rich through the Benetton system and their comments on the current climate were more rational than those of their harder-hit counterparts, for whom the only panacea lay in litigation. By the middle of his trip, Luciano already knew what the analysts would also conclude: there was something new, but nothing surprising, about the fact that even Benetton had its faults, especially here in America.

At home, the family management of the business had been made to evolve into a mature corporate entity in a process that inevitably included growing pains. In the same way, the American network had reached the stage where unbridled individualism was becoming counter-productive. A greater degree of oversight and analysis was needed if the network was to be refashioned in readiness for the next economic recovery. The process of maturation had neither diminished the individuality of spirit at the top, nor did this need to dilute the spirit of the pioneers. 'I would hate a situation where we shop owners had to meet regularly and be corporatised,' Lyn Gatti, owner of the two superstores in San Francisco, told Luciano. 'It would be like going back to work in one of the big department stores. I couldn't stand all that corporate bullshit. People who need that don't belong with Benetton. If you introduce so many changes that you lose that sense of freedom, you'll lose the spirit of the whole thing . . . for ever.'

Perhaps she was telling him what he wanted to hear. Whatever the case, Luciano had known her a few years; he trusted her judgement. From elsewhere in America, however, there was news he did not like to hear.

Ever since the bomb in Selfridges in London the previous Christmas, rumours had persisted that animal rights activists were behind the incident. This was less acceptable in public relations terms than a bomb from the IRA, but more acceptable than one from the Mafia. Now, however, came the news that the American animal rights organisation PETA (People for the Ethical Treatment of Animals), had infiltrated the laboratories of the Biosearch Group in Philadelphia. Biosearch had worked for many years for major cosmetics companies, but the animal rights activists had one specific target in their sights. They had gathered damning evidence that animals were being subjected to agonising and fatal tests in order to prove the safety to human customers of the new range of beauty products collectively known as Colors de Benetton.

The story was leaked to the press which gave it massive coverage: 'The Shame of Benetton' read a typical report, 'Exposed! The horrifying secret of Di's favourite firm.' Benetton, with its multi-racial, equal opportunity advertising and people-friendly image, was a far greater catch for animal rights activists and the press than Avon, Procter and Gamble, or any of the other pharmaceutical giants for whom exposure of this nature would have been unwelcome but no surprise. The tests were recounted on the pages of the mass media in appalling detail. Guinea pigs had been cooked alive when a temperature control broke down at the laboratory in what the technicians jokingly referred to as a 'pig roast'. Body lotion had been dripped into the eyes of weeping rabbits. Guinea pigs had had bath gel scratched into their skins. Rats had been force fed scent, bath and shower gels. All the animals had died.

At first, the Benetton Corporation said that it had not known what was going on and was appalled; somehow, however, it did know that such tests were necessary in order to comply with American safety laws. An animal rights spokesman replied that there was no legal requirement for these tests and that around 150 cosmetics companies refused to use them. When big beauty businesses such as L'Oréal, Revlon and Christian Dior came out in defence of animal testing, their endorsement made Benetton look even worse. Two months after the first stories appeared, with the uproar showing no signs of abating, the Benetton Corporation's Leslie Grunberg was forced to make a public statement: 'We have stopped all testing on all animals,' he wrote from his New York office to PETA in America and to the British Union for the Abolition of Vivisection. 'Our company is making a serious commitment to find alternative methods of testing. In the meantime, we will not introduce products that require animal testing.'

Benetton was the first clothing company proven to be using animal tests to make such an undertaking and it had ended its relationship with Biosearch almost as soon as the story had broken. Nonetheless, this was a shameful episode, and the only saving grace was that, if any company could do so, perhaps Benetton could give even a story as damaging as this a positive spin.

Then came further falls in the dollar, and higher purchase costs and further falls in sales. In spite of the cost benefits to shop owners of the American denim and cotton plant, the winds of protest grew as retailers in the most densely clustered streets and cities of the United States felt the deepening recession and consulted their lawyers. However, they had little evidence to link the company directly to their misfortune and so help make a legal case. Although some shop owners and their lawyers looked to the advertising, there was no evidence, for example, that after the notoriety of Toscani's 1986 'globe' campaign Jewish shoppers had boycotted Benetton shops sufficiently to damage sales. Moreover, the cost of all this advertising was borne not by the retailer but by the business. Nor could disaffected retailers and their lawyers find any evidence that the fact that the stories about animal testing for the perfume had originated in the States, was having a negative effect at the cash tills. The perfume, after all, had been made in France, and many people here still believed that it had been necessary to conduct animal tests to comply with US government safety regulations. The company's quick and unprecedented promise to cease testing had indeed given the sorry affair a positive public relations spin.

With growth slowing in the United States, and the number of stores diminishing from a peak of 600, the percentage of Benetton's worldwide business done in America by this time – 14.5 per cent – was still sufficient for these recessionary phenomena to make an impact on the overall Benetton balance sheet. In the short term, prices in the US would have to fall further in order to maintain sales and thereby prevent further shop closures that would damage a company seeking a New York share listing. Many American shops, like others around the world, were already operating with discreet financial assistance of some kind from Ponzano. These closures in themselves hurt sales but did not seriously hurt Benetton, because the shops in question were owned and operated by independent entrepreneurs.

Ten years later, recession in Korea would have exactly the same effect on many Benetton shop owners there, leading to a loss of sales but again without causing significant economic pain to the business. In America, meanwhile, in the longer term, it was becoming evident that the future lay in fewer clusters of shops and greater numbers of single, large, up-market superstores in the right locations. Luciano returned home from his latest tour of the United States reassured that the crisis had passed its worst and with a further conclusion. In order to succeed to the extent to which they were capable, in the United States the Benetton clothes themselves would have to reflect several distinct, but complementary, areas of taste.

These included the traditional WASP colours and conservative pastel tones for customers in New England; more rarefied and sophisticated shades ranging from neon green to nut brown in New York; and light colours for the sunniest states of the Union. In this way, just as they had done in France twelve years earlier, Luciano was convinced that they would at last cross the American cultural frontier.

Palmeri, for his part, meanwhile had found what he believed was the right means to raise cash in the New York markets. The prospect was still real of flotation in the USA in the coming year, but the stress of empire building without stress was beginning to show.

7   Latin Americans

Patagonia, Argentina, 1989

Patagonia is a vast, vertical land at the bottom of the world that runs from north to south, east of the Andes Mountains, in small part belonging to Chile and the greater part belonging to Argentina. Much of this remote and mysterious region is arid, elevated plateau, its rocky coasts lashed by the Atlantic, with Cape Horn at its southernmost tip. Little of economic worth exists in these coastal parts, apart from oil on the eastern seaboard, 1,000 miles south of Buenos Aires. Inland, however, Patagonia has vast tracts of grazing land to match anything in Texas, and by the beginning of this century contained some of the best sheep and other livestock in the world.

The key players in this activity were not the Argentinians but the British; specifically the Welsh, who emigrated there in the nineteenth century, bringing with them the expertise of generations of hill farmers. The British loved the wide open spaces, the solitude and the warm, healthy climate. Many became Argentinian citizens and never returned to the old country. Under their management, Patagonian breeds were perfected and Patagonian wool became big business in the international markets. The British owners and their Argentinian employees together worked the vast estancias, often in an unorthodox alliance against Argentina's city-based, ultra-nationalist governments who covetously eyed the wool trade and its profits.

Argentina shared an appetite for fascist strong men with Italy. Between the First and Second World Wars, just as Leone Benetton had gone to seek his fortune in Ethiopia, many Italians emigrated to Argentina from the famished agricultural regions of Italy such as the Marche in the centre of the country. After the Second World War, rivalry grew between the British and Italians over the ownership and management of the grazing land. Meanwhile, relations between Argentina and Italy had remained close and in more recent times the Benettons had gone there on holiday. 'We shivered when we first saw this huge land,' Carlo would recall. 'We wanted to create a link with it, and not only for business reasons.' Now Carlo Benetton was production director and one of the four owners of the largest consumer of wool in the world. He was also by far the biggest aficionado of the four of the outdoor life. The failure of Edizione to buy Lanerossi had left Carlo and his brothers and sister even more determined to find a way of exercising greater control over the quality of the vast supplies of wool they needed for their growing worldwide empire. Their solution was similar to Luciano's, twenty years earlier, when he had travelled to Scotland in order to learn the 'secret of the itch'. Take your knowledge and your needs and go as far back down the chain as you can go, until you find the source. This was why Carlo Benetton went to Patagonia to buy a sheep ranch.

London, England, 1989

Luciano's second son, Alessandro, was late for his first British publicity appearance for the business. The occasion was the launch of the Colors de Benetton Man range of fragrances at the smart Waterfront restaurant in Chelsea Harbour. He arrived soaking wet from the London drizzle, apologising that it had taken him a long time to park his car.

Alessandro did not drive a conspicuous car, but a modest Ford Fiesta. He lived alone in secure anonymity in a rented apartment in the West London district of Notting Hill. He had taken a degree in management studies at Boston University, which Carlo's son Christian and Gilberto's daughter Sabrina would also attend. Eighteen months earlier he had come to London to work for Goldman Sachs. He was ambitious in a way that was closer to the conventional managerial aspirations of Palmeri than those of his father, and very different in temperament from his older brother Mauro. The only passion in life to which he would freely admit was for the Benetton Formula racing team.

'I try to avoid people who are only interested because of my name,' he told the assembled media. 'I try to be modest and independent, to work hard. I hope eventually to join the family business. But they would only be happy with me if I was good.'

Alessandro sincerely believed every word he said, although these could have been dictated to him by publicity director Vittorio Rava. Either way, it worked. The journalists went away with their free samples of Colors de Benetton Man and wrote gushy pieces about his romantic good looks, his refreshing modesty and his general lack of what the British still persisted in believing was the typical, explosive Italian temperament.

Nobody seemed to have made the connection between the débâcle of the animal testing for the perfume and the image of fresh-faced innocence conveyed by the use of Alessandro to sell it. The result was that he, the business and the latest brand all came out smelling, if not of roses, certainly not of roasting guinea pigs; but of mandarin, lime, sandalwood and patchouli.

New York City, the United States of America, 1989

Aldo Palmeri's solution to the question of raising cash for Benetton Group in the New York financial markets was simple; yet no other Italian company had attempted this before. Instead of going through the onerous and, for a foreign company, intentionally off-putting process of trying to have the stock listed on the New York stock exchange, Palmeri had gone directly to the American retail securities market, offering a stake in Benetton to investors in America, Canada, Japan and Europe. The US$145 million, SEC-registered international issue would be made in American Depository Receipts (ADRs) on the less formal Nasdaq exchange. Palmeri nonetheless saw the issue as necessary in order to broaden the shareholder base of the company. He also wanted to give the business the kind of discipline that came from having to address the strenuous requirements of the American Securities and Exchange Commission and raise enough funds to eliminate Benetton's short-term debt.

Palmeri gave the job of pushing through the ADR programme in America to Carlo Gilardi, the former central banker turned finance director, who would recall:

It was a nightmare because no one here at Benetton knew what a bond warrant was. It was also my first experience of placing shares in the United States. Two months later, with the help of Morgan Stanley and Credit Suisse First Boston, we were successful, and everybody here was talking as if they were experts.

Benetton continued to have the support of business analysts on whose judgement institutional investors and bankers based some of their otherwise impenetrable decision-making processes. The analysts and institutions recognised that Benetton had encountered a credibility problem in America, but also that the company was taking steps to rectify this. The relationships between Benetton Group, the quoted company, and Edizione, the family holding company, particularly confused some people. They pointed out that Benetton Group executives appeared to spend company time (and therefore outside shareholders' money) on other personal Benetton family interests which were of no benefit to outside shareholders. There were other confusing links. In the crucial run up to the New York share issue, two-thirds of Benetton Group's 17 per cent rise in revenues were discovered to have come from the acquisition of shoe, yarn and shirt businesses previously owned by Edizione. There was nothing necessarily illegal about this, but the fact that the buyer and seller were to all intents and purposes one and the same, and that one could therefore tailor the price to achieve the maximum hike in revenues at the optimum time for the other, left industry analysts confused about the true worth of the company.

Palmeri and Gilardi handled these tricky questions as they had done the SEC and the Federal Trade Commission, who were investigating Benetton's retailing practices in America. 'We need to define a new, aggressive strategy,' Palmeri declared, 'we need to strengthen our management in the USA, and we may need some different people.' He also won their approval for his strategy of widening the family of brands beyond the Benetton name, licensing more products and expanding in Japan, South Korea, Singapore, Thailand, Indonesia and India.

Gilberto Benetton was driving Edizione itself – the 'strong box', as he called it – further away from dependence on clothing and Benetton Group. In addition to the new financial service activities of In Holding and the like, on which the jury was still out, they were looking to buy ranches, real estate and businesses in the United States. This strategy would also tie in with the invitation to Americans in particular to invest in a subsidiary of a company that was willing to invest in America. In May 1989, the month of the New York Benetton Group share issue, Edizione also bought a 70 per cent holding in Nordica of Italy, the world's leading ski boot maker. They were shopping for further acquisitions, which had less to do with everyday clothing and more to do with sporting accessories and activities for every season of the year, that would take the business for the first time significantly beyond the Benetton name as it had traditionally become known.

Nordica, and the other new sports subsidiaries, were privately owned by Edizione and run by Gilberto entirely separately from Benetton Group. The independent status of the new sports subsidiaries also meant that the Benetton Group advertising did not cover their activities. Nor, in the short term, were there any plans that it should do so. Within Benetton Group itself, meanwhile, a new communications structure had placed total power for managing the image making of the business and brand in the hands of fewer than ten people.

The relationship with Eldorado was severed, since Toscani had been allowing it to be believed that they were taking too much credit for the Benetton campaigns. This would also shortly be the case with the relationship with J. Walter Thompson. Henceforth, even production and media buying would be done in-house. United Colors Communication became the Benetton body responsible for co-ordinating Toscani's visuals and showing them to Luciano for final approval. The Benetton 'knot' logo also disappeared, replaced with the small green rectangle that has become the company's trademark. There were no more captions, only the words 'United Colors of Benetton' stamped on the green rectangle.

Most conspicuously of all by their absence, the clothes themselves disappeared from the advertisements. Again, while the company liked to promote this as a revolutionary creative step, there was a hard-headed cost-accountancy rationale at work. There were savings to be had in building a single, global brand, rather than trying to tailor a growing range of products to an equally growing and diverse range of countries and markets. A single, global brand, calculated in terms of appropriate imagery, equated to life, death, love, hate, war, peace, religion and the environment. Toscani shopped in this global superstore of issues and his latest images in the cause of the business and brand were the boldest yet. The 1989 campaign delivered an overtly political message championing racial equality. One image showed two men, one black and one white, handcuffed together; a second, a young black man and a young white man in baker outfits, having baked a loaf of bread; and a third, a black woman breastfeeding a white baby.

This last image, to this day, is one of astonishing simplicity and beauty, and is unsurpassed as one of the few by Toscani truly to justify the claims to artistic greatness that he has never discouraged from being made about his work. Yet, while it won prestigious awards in Austria, France, Denmark, Italy and the Netherlands, the picture was pulled from advertising hoardings in the United States after it was seen as a throwback to the era of slavery. In New York, meanwhile, every other bus carried the picture of the black man and the white man handcuffed together splashed across it. In

London, Benetton had already consulted the Commission for Racial Equality and had been warned that the pictures could be misconstrued, although neither the Commission for Racial Equality nor the Advertising Standards Authority found the images in breach of their code of legality, decency and honesty. This misconstruction turned out to be the case. The black woman's breasts, not her colour, were deemed to be too explicit for exposure on posters on the London Underground and the handcuffs picture was withdrawn after black Britons thought it showed a white policeman arresting a black man.

Toscani himself dismissed these complaints as 'Anglo–Saxon neurosis' and pointed to the number of awards the images were winning. He had already finished working on the next phase of the Benetton multi-racial campaign for the coming spring and summer. As part of his hunt for appropriate images to match global themes, he had also been to visit his local maternity hospital. Here, in a delivery room, the man whose own mother had once wanted to abort him had found what he believed was a perfect example of the kind of image he was seeking.

Changes were also taking place within the Benetton Formula racing team. For this season, they had retained the popular Italian Alessandro Nannini as lead driver and signed the Englishman Johnny Herbert as his team-mate. Peter Collins, the team manager, had given Herbert the drive. Luciano, however, had persuaded himself that Flavio Briatore, a Benetton clothing development manager and entrepreneur whom he had met in America, who had an agency that included the Virgin Islands, could do a better job of managing the team.

The installation of Briatore, who freely admitted he knew nothing about motor racing, as commercial manager of Benetton Formula baffled many inside and outside the team. Briatore himself cultivated the image of mystery man, allowing it to be known that he liked the company of beautiful women and displaying photographs of himself in his London apartment with the likes of the disgraced US presidential candidate Gary Hart and the actress Uma Thurman. This glitzy aura did little to recommend Briatore to the petrol-headed racing fraternity, but Luciano was following his policy of matching the person to the job on the basis of instinct, rather than track record. He had observed that morale was flagging in the Benetton team and he was impressed when Briatore made statements such as 'Formula 1 is not a sport, it is an entertainment.'

Peter Collins soon departed from the team as a result. Johnny Herbert, who had badly injured his feet during the preceding season and made one of the most courageous comebacks in Formula 1, was the next to go. Halfway through the season, having failed to qualify the Benetton–Ford at the American Grand Prix in Phoenix, where the heavy braking proved too much for his injuries, Herbert was fired by Briatore. Briatore's choice of replacement was Immanuele Pirro, a touring car driver, who lasted only until the end of the season. Herbert, however, would return six years later to win in Britain and Italy for the Benetton team.

Late in the season, meanwhile, with Briatore in control, Alessandro Nannini won Benetton's second Grand Prix, in Japan. At the end of the season, Nannini was sixth in the drivers' world championship and Benetton Formula were third in the constructors' cup. Under Peter Collins the team had surpassed this overall position the previous year, but this made no difference. By this time Briatore, and not Collins, had Luciano's ear.

Luciano himself had split up with Marina after thirteen years together, and in spite of the many extraordinary and sometimes traumatic experiences they had shared. In time he would move out of town to another villa and hand the house in the centre of Treviso over to his daughter, Rossella. Marina would never speak publicly about the break-up of their relationship, just as she had never spoken about its beginnings. Among other factors, the fact that he travelled more than ever, restlessly criss-crossing the world in search of new territories, must have made the end a self-fulfilling prophecy. Privately, Luciano was disappointed, but he would put his own characteristic gloss on the loss. 'I am convinced,' he would say, 'that we are ultimately alone, whoever we love. Love, for a person, for a family, is the most precious thing . . . but the reality is that the drive is even stronger to follow wherever life leads us as individuals.'

Perhaps this statement itself explains why Marina found the basis of her relationship with a man who could in theory have had anyone, yet preferred to be with her, ultimately wanting. A few years later, Luciano would claim not to remember making this statement. 'Maybe what I meant was that we need to be responsible and committed every day to what we do,' he would say. 'We must reaffirm who we are and what we do. I like this interpretation,' he would add, 'because I don't like people who live in the past, on their memories.'

In fact, the break with Marina was neither the end of their relationship nor the resolution of a long-standing issue between them: whether or not Marina should fulfil her desire to have a child. That year, meanwhile, Luciano took his annual holiday alone in Hungary. On the border between the vast Hungarian plains and the Soviet Union, he contemplated the next new territory he was determined to conquer.

After the unparalleled success of the image of the black woman breastfeeding a white baby, Toscani's 1990 spring and summer campaign again pursued the racial equality theme, albeit in softer tones. This was the continuation of the 'carrot and stick' pattern of confrontation followed by appeasement that had characterised his work since the first 'United Colors of Benetton' campaign and the *coup de théâtre* that had begun with Gorbachev in Paris five years earlier.

This campaign used symbolic, rather than literal images: two hands, one black, one white, passing a baton; a black child sleeping on a blanket of white teddy bears; a white wolf kissing a black sheep; a row of test tubes, allegedly filled with the identically coloured blood of heads of state; and two boys, one black and one white, sitting on a potty together.

This last image none the less aroused controversy in Milan, where Benetton had hired the largest billboard in the world, the 770 square metres in the Piazza Duomo opposite the city's cathedral. The poster was banned by the city authorities and the Roman Catholic Cardinal of Milan on the grounds that it was offensive to the sensitivities of the faithful leaving Sunday mass. Although the company expressed surprise at this, the ten-person communications team would have been even more surprised and disappointed had this opposition not taken place. This was exactly the kind of publicity they would expect to garner from an institution like the Church, and the reaction of the ecclesiastical authorities was noted for future reference. Meanwhile, less controversially and therefore less effective in publicity terms, these latest images of Toscani's would win a string of industry awards, including the International Andy Awards of Excellence in the United States and the Media and Marketing Award in Great Britain for the best print campaign in Europe.

Ponzano, the Veneto, 1990

The vision of In Holding and a yuppie utopia of one-stop shops selling socks and stocks from Los Angeles to Tokyo had turned out to be a mirage. After less than three years in the financial services business, Gilberto decided that Edizione should pull out. 'Although I say it myself,' Gilberto would recall, 'I had an instinctive feeling that turned out to be right. We had got into financial services because they were really fashionable, but we discovered it was a peculiar world, and to me the euphoria could not last.' They began by quietly selling their 50 per cent stake in the local operation of Prudential Assurance; only a year later, the value of this would be zero. They sold the investment plans into which they had bought and these would also soon prove to have been a poor product. Shortly after they sold the last tranche of their financial services holdings, the shares of the latter slumped to only 30 per cent of their previous value. By the end of the year, Gilberto would have disposed of nearly US$300 million worth of financial services interests, all of these to apparently experienced companies within the financial services sector. By this time, too, the effect of the recession on personal spending on investments, life assurance and other savings products would be sending shock waves through an already overcrowded market. 'If we had waited six months longer,' Gilberto would recall, 'we would have had big problems.' Edizione meanwhile retained the investments in factoring and leasing to suppliers and sub-contractors, which had provided the springboard into the personal finance sector.

Disagreement over this strategy and the sale of his financial services brainchild convinced Aldo Palmeri that this was the time to move on from Benetton after seven years as chief executive. Palmeri left to join Benetton's long-standing advisers, Citibank. He remained on good terms with the Benettons, with whom he enjoyed better relations than he did with Toscani, and there was no word as yet of his successor. With Gilardi also gone in order to relieve the strain of commuting from Rome to Ponzano placed on his family and marriage, there was a vacuum in the day-to-day management of the flagship company. In this period of uncertainty, the sudden and dramatic need to exit from financial services was not held against Palmeri; however, the decision to pull out was a reminder of the invisible summit of the Benetton mountain where the ultimate power lay. Laura Pollini, who had worked for IBM, Italtel and media magnate Silvio Berlusconi, had succeeded David Paolini as Benetton communications chief. As Pollini would put it: 'This company appreciates collaborators with an entrepreneurial sense. When they proposed going into the financial services market, they had the agreement of the Benetton family. The decision to pull back was then taken by the family when the time was right.'

Red Square, Moscow, Soviet Union, 1990

The Soviet Union had been Luciano's target as the next new territory he was determined to conquer for some time before his solitary musings on holiday in Hungary. The trouble with the Soviet Union, however, was that a personal introduction was essential in order to penetrate the layers of obfuscatory Soviet bureaucracy. The fact that the communist system of the country was falling apart made it a fertile breeding ground for capitalism, but also made matters more difficult.

As had been the case in Prague five years earlier, official groundwork had to go hand in hand with the identification and cultivation of the movers and shakers. Since the opening of the first shop in Prague, the Eastern European network had grown in 1990 from five to an anticipated thirty-two shops in Czechoslovakia, Poland, East Germany and Hungary. The first shop to open in Warsaw, Poland, sold 3,000 items in the first week and 32,000 items in the first four months. These were mainly jumpers paid for in Polish zlotys and the equivalent in price of a week's pay.

Benetton

Benetton advertising in America and Western Europe was restricted on cost grounds to billboards and newspaper and magazine spreads; in the Soviet Union, Benetton commercials were appearing on the Saatchi-advised Gosteleradio, or Soviet television, which could reach as many as 118 million viewers on a given day. Across the whole of Eastern Europe, people who could afford cable television or satellite receivers were watching Benetton commercials on MTV.

Now, however, the Soviet Union was falling apart and instead of his original plan to supply these countries from giant factories inside Russia, Benetton was supplying them directly from Italy. Luciano was now dealing with the Russian authorities as just another independent, or soon to be independent, Eastern European country, albeit one with 250 million potential consumers. This was why Luciano, his son Alessandro and Benetton general manager Giovanni Cantagalli were sitting in an antechamber in the Kremlin, accompanied by the American businessman Randolph Hearst and Nelson Peltz, waiting for an audience with the Soviet Prime Minister Ryzhkov at a meeting arranged by the legendary oilman and American–Soviet fixer Armand Hammer.

The Hammer connection had initially arisen a year and a half earlier through contact between Benetton Group and the Armand Hammer United World College of the American West, based at Montezuma, New Mexico. Students at the multi-racial college had written to the company, praising the 'United Colors' campaign and invited Luciano himself to attend their fifth graduation ceremony, which coincided with Hammer's ninetieth birthday. Luciano, intrigued and in search of an introduction to the Soviet Union, had accepted.

In New Mexico, the two men had suitably flattered each other before allowing the inevitable conversation to take place. As Luciano recalled, Hammer had then said: 'Luciano, you're one of the great salesmen of all time. Where do you go next?'

'Russia,' Luciano replied.

Hammer did not hesitate. 'That's very simple,' he said. 'All you need is a sponsor. Now,' he added, 'you've got one.'

Hammer was many things he did not want it thought he could be, and he was frequently not what he made himself out to be. This time, however, he was as good as his word. A year and a half later, after a blizzard of faxes and telephone calls, Luciano and his party had arrived at the Kremlin. The meeting was straightforward and businesslike; afterwards they adjourned to Hammer's apartment to celebrate. Hammer had invited them to stay after the other guests had gone and advised them how to endear themselves to the middle-ranking bureaucrats on whose sympathy their enterprise ultimately rested; in this case by showing them the brightly coloured jumpers and other clothes that were friendly manifestations of the alarming new phenomenon of perestroika.

The first Benetton shop opened in Moscow in April 1990. The Moscow shop dealt only in hard currency; others selling in local currency were planned to follow. A joint manufacturing venture was also under way with a state-owned Soviet company at Erevan in Armenia to make T-shirts and sportswear, using local materials and reinvesting the profits locally. This was the first of four such Benetton plants planned in the Soviet Union, and the Eastern European equivalent of the Rocky Mount plant in North Carolina.

Benetton Group celebrated its twenty-fifth birthday at the end of the summer with a party in New York's Central Park, and three days later in Ponzano at the Villa Minelli. At the latter, 600 past and present associates, agents, shop owners, family, friends and employees, some dating back to the first party to mark the opening of the company twenty-five years earlier, were regaled by the music of Cab

Calloway and served with delicacies created by the famous Venetian chef Arrigo Cipriani, served by a hundred waiters who appeared with a flourish from behind specially created sets.

As Edizione progressively disinvested from financial services, the 'strong box' was able to shop for further acquisitions beyond the everyday clothing business of Benetton Group. The next purchase, made through Nordica, was a stake in Rollerblade Inc. of Minneapolis. Rollerblade in-line skates were originally designed as summer training equipment for ice-hockey players and skiers, but were turning into a sporting and leisure phenomenon in their own right. The prospects were sound for Rollerblade, and Gilberto had plans to acquire the remainder of the company in the near future.

After Nordica and ski boots, the next season to add to the year-round sports portfolio was summer, and the purchase of Prince, the American tennis racquet manufacturer. Prince had introduced the first oversize racquet in the history of tennis – it would extend its range into the long-body racquet used by top players like Michael Chang and Jana Novotna – squash and badminton racquets, footwear, sportswear, bags and accessories, golf clubs and other products. Like Nordica and Rollerblade, Prince was separately managed and marketed from the Benetton Group and the influence of Toscani, and would remain so for nearly a decade.

Toscani's autumn and winter campaign for the billboards and magazine spreads of the world continued the use of symbolic images: a young black hand held a multi-coloured bunch of flowers; a young white hand held a palette of vivid colours; a brilliantly coloured parrot perched on the back of a zebra (this image was banned in Saudi Arabia, where religious law prohibited the visual depiction of animals); two pairs of hands, one black, one white, cradled brightly coloured marbles. Again, there were no clothes, and only the rectangular green and white logo. Apart from the potty picture in Milan and the objection to animal depictions in Saudi Arabia, these images for the two collections of the year were uncontroversial. Of the carrot and stick cycle that had come to characterise Toscani's images, this was the latest carrot.

Jerez, Spain, 1990

The first full season for Benetton Formula under Flavio Briatore was marked by triumph and near tragedy. Briatore was consolidating his position by pulling in sponsorship for the team; he had also signed triple world champion Nelson Piquet, then apparently in the twilight of his career, as lead driver while retaining Alessandro Nannini as his team-mate. Piquet and Nannini proved to be a thrilling combination, with the Brazilian finding a new lease of life, outracing the Italian in the first half of the season before Nannini began to move up, finishing second in Germany and third in the Spanish Grand Prix. The aftermath of this race was usually the occasion for an annual party for the team and its supporters, including Luciano and Alessandro. This year, however, it was marred by a freak occurrence in which Nannini, having survived the perils on the track, severed his right hand in a helicopter accident. The hand was reattached by microsurgery, but Nannini was forced to retire from racing for the foreseeable future.

Briatore and Nannini had become close friends and the latter did not know any other drivers to fill the gap. Piquet suggested his childhood friend, Roberto Moreno, take Nannini's place. Piquet went on to win in Japan, ahead of Moreno in second place, and to win in Australia. At the end of the season, Benetton were third in the constructors' cup and Piquet, Nannini and Moreno were respectively third, eighth and joint tenth in the drivers' world championship. With Nannini out of the team, Moreno was retained with Piquet for the coming season, a situation, however, that would shortly change in controversial circumstances that would alter the fortunes of Benetton Formula in a dramatic fashion.

Ponzano, the Veneto, 1990

Apart from the Scribner Building on Fifth Avenue in New York City, Edizione owned outright only the 'walls' as Gilberto put it, of a handful of the 6,000 Benetton shops operated by independent entrepreneurs selected by the seventy-five Benetton agents around the world. Among these, several of the largest shops were linked directly to Ponzano in real time by computer. The function of these flagship stores on prime sites in the central business districts of key territories was reminiscent of the first international My Market shops twenty years earlier. Their purpose was to present a showcase for the business and brand, and gauge the reaction of the shopper in the fastest and most sophisticated manner possible. These new United Colors of Benetton shops were more than double the space of many earlier outlets and of a minimum size of 150 square metres. In addition to the new, bigger stores, the numbers of 012, Benetton Uomo and Sisley, the former directly under the United Colors umbrella and the latter overseen by Mauro, were also growing.

The new growth strategy was to increase the numbers of the right kinds of shop in the right places and concentrate on driving up sales at a time of flattening profits and reduced dividends for shareholders. Emilio Fossati had eventually succeeded Aldo Palmeri as managing director after a period of uncertainty in the wake of the latter's departure, and had already secured the authority to increase the capitalisation of Benetton Group through a new share issue. The family, however, agreed that the share price itself had to rise before a new share issue became attractive to new investors. A key factor in the share price, although it was as yet impossible to quantify exactly how key, was the effect of Toscani's image making on the company's sales around the world. That the growth strategy was linked to the global imagery, however, no one could dispute; and now, after the carrot of the previous autumn and winter, would come the latest stick.

Ponzano, the Veneto, 1991

The deadline for the authority to seek an increase in capitalisation had expired at the end of the previous year, but the current share price was still beneath the level the family and observers considered necessary to be attractive to investors. Meanwhile, the amount of money the company wanted to raise was rising and the moment was not far away when the family and Fossati would have to decide that conditions in the market were as favourable as they were ever going to be.

Edizione, which still owned 81 per cent of Benetton Group, made its latest purchase in the form of Kastle, the Austrian ski maker, and for over sixty years one of the great names in Alpine skiing. The family 'strong box' was also in the process of buying more sheep and cattle ranches in Argentina, spending US$47.5 million on further tracts of Patagonia, including 280,000 Merino sheep, 9,000 head of cattle, including Hereford bulls, and 1,000 horses. Edizione was also investing millions of dollars in artificial insemination and improving breeding processes. Carlo, the outdoorsman of the four siblings, had become an enthusiastic trekker in the Andes.

The role of Edizione, however, still perplexed industry analysts who followed the Benetton Group share price. Dividends from only 19 per cent of these shares went into outside shareholders' pockets, with the rest going into Edizione's coffers. The overlapping ownership relationships between Edizione and Benetton Group occupied the minds of even those analysts who were favourable towards the quoted company: 'I don't think the market is concerned about the cash call *per se*,' noted analyst Paul Dionne, of Pasfin Servizi Finanziari in Milan. 'Benetton will be well into turnaround by 1991. The company is growing fast,' Dionne went on, 'but they also have to make clear where internal funds are going to be invested, and give a more transparent view of the company's dividend policy.' Dionne might have been interested to know that even Rosa, mother of the four owners and directors of Edizione, had taken precautions when they first established Benetton as a company. To coincide with the first day of trading, Rosa had opened a separate bank account in case anything untoward happened to the business. Twenty-five years on, the business had sales worth US$1.6 billion, and Rosa still had her separate bank account.

Other precautionary measures, as depicted in the images produced by Toscani for the new spring and summer campaign, marked the swing back to the 'stick' extreme of the cycle. Toscani's latest images, which were now reaching audiences in more than a hundred countries, were hard-hitting treatments of universal realities, the relevance of which he saw as being in danger of neglect from social indifference. A shoal of brightly coloured condoms swimming across a white background – 'a call for social responsibility in the face of overpopulation and sexually transmitted disease' – was intended to 'demystify condoms by displaying them in a playful and colourful way, like fashion items'. Condoms were distributed in Benetton shops all over the world. In New York City, the company contributed to a programme sponsored by the mayor to distribute condoms and information about AIDS in public schools. Benetton employees also handed out HIV guides in the shanty towns of Rio de Janeiro in Brazil, 'because it was important that even people who could never buy a Benetton sweater should get the basic information'.

The condom campaign caused a great deal of confusion, above all in the United States. The move met with general approval from young customers and disapproval from older people. The image was censored in America on the grounds that it was 'pornographic' and therefore unsuitable for dissemination through traditional press outlets such as supermarkets. A surreal dimension was being added to an already extraordinary business and brand, in which thousands of sheep and cattle were artificially inseminated on Patagonian ranches, while company employees roamed the cities handing out contraceptives. This bizarre juxtaposition was barely apparent before Toscani's second image, by chance, coincided with the beginning of the Gulf War.

The image of a First World War cemetery in Belgium showed long rows of crosses, symmetrically aligned and casting equal shadows, as if a reminder that in wartime, race, creed and age count for nothing and death is the only winner. The image is one of intense, almost unbearable reality, even in peacetime. At the outbreak of the Gulf War it proved too much and was banned in Italy, France, Britain and Germany. Three further images of three children, black, white and Asian, sticking out their identically coloured tongues; of a white boy kissing a black girl; and of a group of Pinocchio puppets in different hues of wood, all marching in the same direction, harkened back to Toscani's softer side and won numerous awards. The image of the tongues, however, was deemed 'pornographic' and withdrawn from display in Arab countries where the religious authorities did not like pictures of internal organs any more than parrots and zebras.

Benetton Group duly announced its plans to recapitalise by selling 12 million shares. The latest dividend to investors had been cut by more than half; the new issue would not be available to existing share-holders. This meant that Edizione, for the first time, was forgoing its slice of the new shares and allowing these to be taken up by new investors. This had the effect of placating those analysts who were critical of certain transactions between the publicly quoted Benetton Group and the private family holding company, and sent out the message that Benetton Group was committed to financing itself. 'We'll use the money,' managing director Fossati commented, 'as soon as the market situation is favourable.'

The aim was to use the money to finance the latest ambitious expansion, this time into Latin America, Africa and the Middle East. The plan was also to prepare Benetton Group for flotation on more international markets, starting in Tokyo and moving on to Paris and possibly Singapore. In addition to the factory in Armenia, other exotic joint ventures were already under way. In China, Benetton had embarked on two manufacturing joint ventures, one of these with a Japanese partner. Twenty-five per cent of the Chinese prod-uct would be exported to Japan, with the rest being sold in China. Luciano declared that they planned to open 300 shops in China over the next few years. He had made his first official visit to Japan as early as 1981; just over a year ago, in 1990, Benetton had signed a manufacturing and retailing venture with the Seibu–Saison con-glomerate; by this time there were 400 Benetton shops in Japan, with a further 200 planned over the coming years.

Other joint ventures had begun life amicably, but turned to acri-mony. The licensing deal between Benetton International NV of the Netherlands and Eco Swiss China Time and Bulova, to manufacture and sell Benetton/Bulova 'Eco' watches, collapsed when Benetton decided to end the agreement three years ahead of its expiry date. The litigation and counter-litigation that followed went through the Netherlands courts to the Supreme Court in The Hague, thence to the European Court of Justice, and continues to this day. Elsewhere, meanwhile, halfway through the Formula 1 motor racing season, the theme of broken contracts and legal acrimony erupted around Benetton in a more reprehensible fashion and on a very public scale.

Monza, Italy, 1991

The motor racing season so far had been satisfactory, if unsensational for Benetton Formula and their two Brazilian drivers. Nelson Piquet had come third in the American Grand Prix; Roberto Moreno had been placed fourth, his best result yet, in Belgium. It was there that a young German, Michael Schumacher, had made his sensational debut for the Jordan team, qualifying seventh ahead of his team leader on a circuit he had never seen.

Flavio Briatore, by the time of the Belgian Grand Prix, had already done a deal with Tom Walkinshaw, the abrasive Scot whom Briatore had just appointed engineering director of the team. Walkinshaw was a formidable operator who had learnt to drive as a child on a tractor in the fields of his family farm in Scotland. He had made his reputation reviving the sports car operation of Jaguar in the late 1980s. To Benetton, Walkinshaw brought in his protégé, Ross Brawn, from Jaguar as technical director and Rory Byrne as head of research and development. Walkinshaw was an ambitious and forceful businessman and Briatore, who enjoyed an extraordinary amount of latitude over the Benetton Formula finances, had invited him to take a 35 per cent stake in the team, due to increase to 50 per cent in the coming year.

Walkinshaw knew of Schumacher and his precocious talent from the latter's sports car experience as a junior with the Mercedes team. At Spa, in the Belgian Grand Prix, after his sensational qualifying position, Schumacher had gone out on the first lap, but Briatore had seen enough. Encouraged by Walkinshaw, Briatore approached

Schumacher after the race and suggested he leave the Jordan team in return for a long-term contract with Benetton Formula. Schumacher agreed, and also agreed that the contract would be effective immediately. Briatore then summarily fired Roberto Moreno from the team and gave Schumacher his place.

Schumacher's first race for Benetton was the very next Grand Prix of the season in Briatore's home country at Monza. Schumacher outpaced Piquet and drove the Benetton to fifth place. By this time, it was clear that Briatore and Walkinshaw, with the financial muscle that was lacking at Jordan, had pulled off a coup in poaching the most promising and mercenary new talent in Formula 1 since the young Ayrton Senna. There were ugly scenes, however, after the race at Monza between Benetton Formula and a bitterly disappointed Jordan team. Jordan had spotted Schumacher and given him his break; they accused Briatore of sharp practice and promised litigation. Many other drivers and motor racing commentators, hardened to the vagaries of Formula 1, were none the less appalled at the way Briatore and Walkinshaw had gone about securing Schumacher's services and said so. However, the new axis at Benetton Formula knew that money ultimately talked and possession was nine-tenths of the law. At the end of the season, with Piquet and Moreno seventh and tenth in the drivers' world championship, Nelson Piquet departed from Benetton and retired from Grand Prix racing. Briatore retained Schumacher and Martin Brundle as drivers for the coming year.

What happened at Monza would be eclipsed first by Schumacher's fulfilment of his promise as a driver and then by his eventual defection, in return for an even greater financial inducement, to Benetton Formula's greatest rival, Ferrari. This was deplorable behaviour as Briatore might later have said, and as many were now saying of him; but Briatore himself, after all, had said that Formula 1 was not a sport.

Ponzano, the Veneto, 1991

The reaction of the Church and city authorities to the image of two children sitting on a potty opposite Milan Cathedral in the spring of the previous year was the underlying inspiration for this year's autumn and winter campaign. Toscani gave this the official theme, however, of 'love, the underlying reason for all life'.

The first image was that of two young models dressed as a priest and a nun, kissing in a fashion that paradoxically conveyed a profound innocence. Their black and white clerical garments, in a touch which few people seemed to acknowledge at the time, reiterated the theme of interracial love.

The image was immediately banned at home by the Italian advertising authority and the Pope himself was reported to be incensed, but it was enormously successful in many countries. In the United States, however, the Anti-Defamation League condemned the picture for 'trivialising, mocking, profaning and offending religious values' and several magazines rejected it. In France, most gratifying for Toscani, the self-regulating Bureau de Vérification de Publicité pompously recommended the removal of the image from billboards and magazine spreads in the interest of 'decency and self-discipline', and in the city of Nantes, a twenty-strong mob rampaged through Benetton shops. In Britain, the image won the Eurobest Award. From Germany, meanwhile, a real-life nun, Sister Barbara Becker Schroeder from Alzy, wrote to Vittorio Rava at Benetton in Ponzano: 'I feel the photo expresses great tenderness, security and peace . . . I would be grateful if you would let me have one or more posters, preferably in different sizes.'

The second image was that of an angelic little white girl and a black girl whose hair was styled to evoke diabolic horns. This proved contentious in the United States and Britain where, like the black man and white man handcuffed together, it was construed as provocative on racial grounds. The image was rejected by *Child*, *Essence* and *YM* magazines, but accepted by *Cosmopolitan*, *Elle*, *Parenting* and *Seventeen*.

Again, the British Advertising Standards Authority had warned Benetton in advance of the likely provocative effect, which of course was exactly what Toscani and Luciano wanted to hear. The negative reaction was subsequently portrayed by Luciano, however, as being contrary to the sense he claimed to have intended. 'One child is blonde and angelic, the other mysterious,' he said. 'They are two sides of the same coin, but which is bad and which is good? It is a bit of irony,' he went on, 'to remind us that stereotyping is useless and that tolerance and love are the supreme values.'

Letters for and against these images poured into Benetton head-quarters at Ponzano; two years later, a selection of a hundred positive and negative responses would be published in a book edited by Laura Pollini and Paolo Landi. The book did not, however, contain the response of Luciano's mother, Rosa. Rosa had not actually seen the images, but she did not like what she heard. 'I don't like these things,' she told an interviewer from her opulent, yet homely apartment in the suburbs of Treviso. She went on:

> My children tell me that those photos are understood by young people and moreover that they cause people to talk about the brand. That means there is more publicity for us, but I feel very badly about it. My children have to stop, or I will get very angry. They have to stop, or else.

All this and more from Rosa, of course, made for more publicity.

Luciano had just returned from Tokyo where there had been a very different response of a kind that did not depend on knee-jerk reactions from interest groups. 'The Japanese advertising industry,' declared the *Mainichi Shimbun* newspaper, which also showed the pictures, 'should welcome such external pressure, if its advertising is confident of being as rich in content and as stimulating as the Benetton campaign.'

The third of Toscani's images, however, generated the most controversy that lingers unresolved to this day. Two years earlier, in the delivery room of his local hospital, he had taken a series of photographs of five newly born babies. He had done so with the consent of the mothers, one of whom had even offered to pay him for his services. Toscani had chosen one of these images, of a baby girl called Giusy, spattered in blood and her umbilical cord still attached, taking her first lusty breaths of life in the world beyond her mother's womb.

The image was and is shocking insofar as it conveys two conflicting realities: the instinctive feeling of intimacy that comes from the first sight of a new life, and the brutal thrusting of this ultimate image of innocence into the cold light of an advertising billboard. The mistake, perhaps, was not so much to have created and used such a powerful and striking image, but not to have restricted its use to the smaller and more approachable format of the magazine spread. Later, even Benetton would admit that the depiction of reality, after all, perhaps could not be larger than life.

As it was, the image of baby Giusy on thousands of billboards across hundreds of countries proved too much for too many people to bear. In America, the picture was blocked by the American Board of Advertising Censors. Even in Japan it was rejected by *Child*, *Cosmopolitan*, *Elle* and *Essence* magazines, while *Vogue*, *Self* and *Partner* accepted it for publication. At home, the protests began in Palermo, where the local authorities asked Benetton to remove all billboards featuring the image. In Milan, too, there was no chance of it appearing on the billboard in the Piazza Duomo, where the authorities declared that the picture 'offended public order and general morality'. Similar criticism at government level forced the removal of the image from hundreds of billboards in Britain, France and Ireland.

Giusy's first moments of life would in time win the Swiss prize from the Société Général d'Affichage and, in Italy, the Policlinic Sant'Orsola in Bologna requested a copy to hang in its labour room. Giusy would also be exhibited in Holland at the Boymans van Beuningen Museum in Rotterdam in a collection dedicated to images of motherhood throughout the centuries. She also occupied pride of place on the cover of issue number 1 of *Colors*, Benetton's new, large format 'news magazine for the global village'. Toscani was editor in chief and the artistic director was the New York graphic designer Tibor Kalman. *Colors* was an expensive production, published in five bilingual editions in over a hundred countries and distributed free through Benetton stores. Issue number 1 began with the theme 'Breakfast in different parts of the world', and also featured a variety of groups living in the melting pot of New York City, including the Gay Police Officers' Action League, and the Black Girls' Coalition, founded by popular models. The magazine was innovative in style and content; if other magazines would not publish some of his images, here, at least, Toscani could and would exercise absolute editorial power.

Meanwhile, the controversy of baby Giusy and United Colors of Benetton was such that blank hoardings and blank double-page spreads replaced the offending image in many places, generating even more publicity. The affair of baby Giusy did not appear to have hurt sales of the business, however, and absolutely could not be allowed to do so. This was why Benetton communications chief Laura Pollini felt impelled to apologise to a British television news interviewer: 'We are very astonished and sorry to have created a problem.' Toscani, meanwhile, reacted publicly with his usual carrot and stick response: 'I'm sad the trouble arose in the UK, which is notable for its tolerance,' he said. 'Maybe,' he went on, 'if we'd used a cat or a dog, they wouldn't have minded so much.' It was pure 'generosity', he added, of Benetton to show 'real' images like a baby's birth; the umbilical cord reinforced Benetton's 'united' message.

Privately, Toscani was seething. 'My way of thinking doesn't conform to normal society,' he raged. 'So what? Shall I be killed, go to prison? I am a photographer, and I have the right to photograph and show whatever I want.' He was equally scathing of regulatory bodies such as the Advertising Standards Authority. 'Who are they?' he said. 'A group of people who sell peanuts and cars. Are they in charge of morality?'

But this was the inner Toscani talking and not the voice he chose at this moment to use in his public capacity as image maker to Luciano Benetton. Meanwhile, privately, he said to Luciano, 'I think we should go further.'

8   The Emperor's New Clothes

Going further, Ponzano, the Veneto, 1992

For the new spring and summer campaign, Toscani had selected seven images conforming to a single theme: 'reality'.

The images included a Mafia killing in Palermo, a flood in Bangladesh, a boat full of refugees from Albania, a burning car in Sicily, a truck overrun by refugees in Liberia, and a Liberian soldier with a kalashnikov, holding a human thigh bone behind his back. The single green and white rectangular logo on each bore the legend 'United Colors of Benetton'. This time, however, none of these images had been taken by Toscani. The supreme egotist, who had first taken all the pictures and then taken all the clothes out of the pictures, had now stopped taking the pictures altogether.

The reaction to these images, used in the context of clothes retailing, was immediate; most of them were banned to various degrees in various countries. Patrick Robert's picture of the Liberian soldier holding the human thigh bone was banned from publication by court injunction in France and by voluntary prohibition in Britain and Japan. Robert, a photographer for the prestigious Sygma agency, who had also taken the picture of the truck overrun by Liberian refugees, commented: 'The absence of an explanatory caption on my photographs does not bother me . . . For me, the objective of the campaign is reached . . . to draw the public's attention to these victims.' Likewise, Gian Luigi Bellini's picture of a burning car in Sicily was deemed by the Irish Advertising Board to be too realistic for a country divided by violent conflict, and was rejected by a French magazine. Franco Zecchi's picture of a Mafia killing in Palermo met with resentment in Italy and was rejected by various publications. The picture of a ship full of Albanian refugees, taken by an unknown photographer, was rejected by magazines in France and Denmark.

But it was the seventh image, however, that unleashed a reaction so strong that, for the first time, the controversy generated by a Benetton advertisement was brought home into the shops on a meaningful scale.

Oxford Circus, London, England, 1992

The art of folding and refolding woollen jumpers, sweatshirts and shirts all day long, perfectly, over and over again, without losing your self-control, was more easily acquired by some than by others, as the manageress of the Hampstead shop and others had discovered. Each garment had to be retrieved from where the customer had discarded it, refolded in exactly the prescribed way and replaced in exactly the same place on the shelves. Two tables stood in the middle of the shop in Oxford Circus expressly for this purpose; they were fully occupied all day, every day. When a discarded garment had to be replaced in a hurry and the two tables were busy, the process was done on the spot instead, in a manner known as 'air folding', which was only for the most advanced and self-controlled shop assistant.

Saturday was the busiest day of the week in this, the busiest of the London shops. This was why the group of gay rights activists from Act-Up, the international AIDS pressure group, had chosen precisely this time to demonstrate against Benetton on the pavement outside the shop. Their plan, however, was not just to target the attention of the passing crowds but also the United Colors of Benetton shop itself and its customers.

After finishing on the pavement, the demonstrators paused for a moment to regroup. Then, in a body, they rushed the entrance and fanned out inside the shop. Here, amid shouts of abuse and glee, muscular, tattooed arms sporting studded leather wrist bands pulled immaculately folded, brightly coloured jumpers by the score from the shelves and flung them high into the air. As the customers and shop assistants scattered, a mountain of disorderly clothes landed on the floor of the shop. All these clothes would have to be picked up, refolded and replaced in the right position. The demonstrators then left as quickly as they had come.

This visitation was just one effect of the seventh image in the series that Toscani had selected on the theme of 'reality' for the new Benetton spring and summer campaign. The image, a picture originally published in *Life* magazine and taken by Thérèse Frare, was that of David Kirby, an American AIDS sufferer, with his family in the moments after his death. Frare, who would win the World Photo Award with this picture, had taken it with the family's consent and their consent had also been given for Benetton to use the image as part of the 'reality' campaign. The monochrome image had been coloured through an electronic process which had heightened the intensity of the composition and given the features of the recently deceased victim a Christ-like aura. Now, however, this carefully devised 'reality' was going out of control. For the first time, the handling of the brand was threatening to damage the image and even the sales of the company.

The Royal College of Art, Kensington, London, 1992

A British tabloid newspaper had shown the image in a scathing issue before its official presentation as part of the campaign. The resulting uproar among charities, politicians and interest groups had quickly been picked up and promulgated by the media around the world. Although many other newspapers also included favourable comment from the public, unfavourable comment, including from Benetton store owners and staff, put the business on the defensive in a way that was harder to shake off than had been the case with the 'little devils' or baby Giusy.

This was why Luciano and Toscani were at the Royal College, to explain and defend the use of the David Kirby picture. 'It is reality,' Luciano told the assembled press corps. 'Our company principally has the function of making people think. You can be more useful than selling a product,' he went on, clearly believing this, although it was equally clear that this belief was not shared by the audience. 'To improve the image of the company,' he said, 'we thought we could do something further. We wanted to have a spirit of sensitivity and care for others, as well as our own product.'

Luciano was speaking, as usual, through an interpreter; this gave him more time to think, but sometimes created an unfavourable impression in the minds of hostile journalists. One questioner, with the current turnover of the business in mind, asked him the US$1.6 billion question: 'Would you abandon the campaign if it ceased to sell jumpers?'

'It's an academic question,' Luciano replied calmly, 'but certainly I would think about it.'

Toscani, for his part, was defiant but careful not to antagonise the questioners, possibly because he sensed that he had lost them from the beginning. 'Why does reality make such a big controversy?' he said wearily. 'Traditional advertising pictures are a bunch of lies. What we show is the truth. If people want to censor it, I am sorry.' He went on, 'We are all in a business, and we all have to survive, we are not a charity.'

'No,' he and Luciano both replied, 'we have no plans to donate money from our profits to AIDS charities.'

This remark, as it was quoted, and the mass-market newspaper coverage in question, belied the fact – unreported – that Benetton was already engaged in a series of initiatives with AIDS groups. In the United States, the company produced a guide to safe sex in conjunction with Gay Men's Health Crisis. Benetton was also starting to advertise in gay magazines, which were generally shunned by the big corporations. In Brazil, the safe sex guide was published in association with the Grupo de Apoio a Pronençao a AIDS, and run in the three biggest daily newspapers. In South Africa, Benetton funded the display of posters showing condoms in front of five hospitals in Cape Town, Durban and Pretoria, in conjunction with the Medical Research Council. In Germany, Benetton participated in a massive fund raiser for AIDS awareness in the country's hundred largest discotheques. The company also donated copies of its posters by request to the International Conference on AIDS in Amsterdam.

In France, meanwhile, the Bureau de Vérification de la Publicité took the unprecedented step before the advertisement was printed of threatening to exclude any publication that dared carry it, or carried the image of the Liberian soldier clutching the human thigh bone. One French magazine, *Max*, for young people, ignored this threat. The editor commented:

> Our readers, those between fifteen and thirty years old, are directly affected by this topic. This campaign is one way of approaching the AIDS problem whilst avoiding the socio-medical aspect. Our readers' letters have shown that we were not wrong.

Elsewhere in Europe, in Switzerland, *Schweizer Illustrierte* also ran the image, saying that it did not offend mass sensibility, but 'wounded only one thing: the rules of the game according to which the message must be dull, even stale'.

New York City, United States of America, 1992

Here in the country where it had been taken, *Vogue* magazine decided to run the AIDS picture. The family of David Kirby himself, meanwhile, reiterated their support for the use of the picture at a press conference, stating that this was a means of illustrating the dangers of AIDS and continuing the struggle against the disease.

'It's what he would have wanted,' said Kirby's father. 'We don't feel used. Benetton is not exploiting our grief to sell sweaters. Rather, it is we who are using Benetton. David is speaking louder now that he is dead than when he was alive.'

Father Tom Cadder was a close friend of the Kirbys. Commenting on the Christ-like aura that some had attributed to the technical manipulation of the original picture, he said: 'Who has really seen a picture of Jesus? I have copies of the original slides and prints, and, untouched, he looks the way many of us picture Jesus.'

Barb Cordle was the Columbus, Ohio hospice nurse who had cared for David Kirby for the last three years of his life. She knew how Kirby had been treated before he had come into her care; how he had been hounded in his small home town; how the contents of the ambulance that had taken him to hospital had been burned afterwards; how Kirby had fought back against the disease and fought for greater education about AIDS and its myths. Ms Cordle could eventually no longer contain her feelings about the criticisms of Benetton's use of the image, and wrote: 'The picture in question has done more to soften people's hearts on the AIDS issue than any other I have ever seen. You can't look at that picture and hate a person with AIDS. You just can't.'

The *New York Times* summed up thus:

> The company estimates that between five hundred million and one billion people have seen the AIDS image, far more than ever saw it when it first came out in *Life* magazine. A public that is reading fewer newspapers and believing fewer broadcasts, might begin to swallow tiny doses of information between the ads for liquor and lingerie.

Elsewhere, meanwhile, there was an unexpected reaction to another of the 'reality' images in the place where the real event depicted took place.

Palermo, Sicily, 1992

They may have liked to kill there, but the 'men of honour' and their offspring did not, apparently, like to see pictures of the consequences. In a bizarre twist, the daughter of Benedetto Grado, the dead Sicilian in the Palermo murder picture, announced she was going to sue Benetton for damages for using the image in its 'reality' campaign. 'How does my father's death enter into publicity for sweaters?' complained Rosalia Grado. 'The picture is pasted up in Palermo for all to see, and it has offended us.'

Perhaps Ms Grado was being a little disingenuous, otherwise her statement would have fitted perfectly into an Italian adaptation of *Through the Looking Glass*. The killing in question had in fact taken place nearly ten years earlier during a gangland war in the city between the Grado and the Corleone families. Benedetto Grado, the dead man, was a seventy-eight-year-old market garden supervisor who belonged to the former family and had served time in prison on the grounds of involvement with the Mafia. He was also related to a Mafia boss who had recently disappeared. The civic authorities who tried to resist the grip of the Mafia on the area lived in fear of their lives and frequently ended up in the same position as the man in the picture, only, in their cases, innocent. Yet they went unmourned by the likes of Ms Grado, her mother and her sister-in-law, who were the three women in the picture shown mourning over the corpse of Mr Grado.

In a further twist, the Magnum photographer who took the picture, Franco Zecchi, was suing the Italian Fascist Party for using it in their election publicity. Meanwhile, it was good for the Catholic Church and other critics of Benetton to know that old-fashioned notions of decency and public morality were still alive and well in Sicily.

Ponzano, the Veneto, 1992

Colors issue number 2 featured as its cover picture the 'reality' image of 4,000 Albanian refugees crammed onto a ship, many of them spilling over the side. Inside, there were striking items on Russian people from all walks of life, with an examination of the phenomenon of fake Western consumer goods and national pride as expressed through the automobile; toys and gadgets made from recycled waste in different parts of the world; clever 'advertisements' showing traditional competitors such as Pirelli and Goodyear united in an embrace; and designer chickens. Toscani's latest brainchild was even bigger and better in style and content than its predecessor. This time, the print run was a million copies, again available free in five bilingual editions in 6,500 Benetton and Benetton-linked shops in a hundred countries. One of these copies had landed on the desk of Aldo Palmeri.

Palmeri had returned after two years at Citibank to his job as chief executive of Benetton Group. 'He was a very clever managing director,' Gilberto would say, 'and our relationship was so good that after he had been gone for some time, we decided to track him down and persuade him to come back.' Palmeri had looked at *Colors* and its contents: the Albanians, the Russians, the designer chickens. Then he looked at the costs.

Palmeri's return to the business had also enabled Luciano to fulfil the ambition he had been harbouring for some time; indeed, it had been a factor in the return of the chief executive. Luciano had decided to go into politics.

Palmeri's return was not the only reason for Luciano's decision, although many outside observers professed themselves surprised that Luciano had chosen to move into political life. The truth was that there were a number of reasons. Toscani was content merely to rail in a libertarian fashion against social injustice and hypocrisies without which his work would ultimately have had no meaning. Luciano, on the other hand, truly believed he could go further. The recent direction of the image of the brand had given it a greater political dimension than ever. The business was well into turnaround as the analysts had predicted, and safe in the hands of Palmeri. Luciano was also an indefatigable, world-class networker, known from the White House to the Kremlin. There were plenty of precedents for businessmen going into politics around the world. The country was undergoing a free-market revolution, in which greater privatisation was seen by Luciano and many others as the key to a stabler and more prosperous future. He feared that the difficult economic situation in Italy, with its spiralling labour costs, might derail this process and bring back the spectre of political and social unrest. 'I am very busy, but I've always wanted to go into politics,' he was misquoted as saying. This was untrue, but here he was offering his services to the nation.

The secretary of the local Republican Party, for whom Luciano had been accepted as a candidate in the coming election, was understandably thrilled to have the support of one of the richest and most powerful businessmen in the world. 'We are delighted to have him on our side,' he declared. At Benetton headquarters, staff in the company's press office fielded calls from journalists and wore Benetton-manufactured T-shirts featuring a blow-up of Luciano's face with the slogan 'Vote Benetton'.

Across the country, candidates included the former pornographic movie star la Cicciolina, and the neo-fascist former model and granddaughter of the dictator, Alessandra Mussolini. The competition was stiff at national and local level. After a recount and by a narrow margin Luciano Benetton was elected to Parliament as republican senator for Treviso.

Luciano had entered a world of terminal individualism, in which politics were seen by the majority merely as a plank to further financial self-interest. Luciano, however, was not entering politics for this reason. As one of the T-shirted press office staff of the time said later: 'He really believed he could make a contribution.'

What made no difference to the voters was the latest twist in his personal life. Although only the briefest and most unexpected of reunions had taken place between Luciano and Marina, as a result of this, at the age of thirty-four, she had become pregnant and given birth to their first child, a son whom she named Brando. The issue of whether or not she should realise her wish to have a child had been resolved to her satisfaction, but not to Luciano's. This time he severed close relations with her once and for all.

Toscani's images for the autumn and winter campaign pursued the 'reality' theme, albeit in a less shocking fashion, and provoked less shocked reactions as a result. The images, again taken by photographers around the world, were of an oil-covered sea bird in the Arabian Gulf; an albino Zulu woman, ostracised by the rest of her South African tribe; a grimy Salvadorean child lovingly clutching a dirty white doll; pigs recycling the contents of a rubbish heap in Peru; child labour at work on a building site in Colombia; Russian police arresting a suspect; and an unoccupied electric chair in an American jail.

These were powerful images, yet they were somehow rendered less so, rather than more, by the presence of the United Colors of Benetton logo. If humankind could only bear so much reality, perhaps the effects of this particular manipulation of it were wearing off.

Aldo Palmeri was looking at the costs of advertising and sponsorship which accounted for nearly 4 per cent of the total revenues of the business and amounted to around US$60 million. The Benetton Formula racing team, in spite of Luciano's fanatical opposition to smoking, enjoyed considerable tobacco sponsorship, but also consumed increasing amounts of money. All these and other areas came under the scrutiny of the chief executive.

Enstone, Oxfordshire, England, 1992

The season had ended with Michael Schumacher, who won in Belgium, and Martin Brundle coming third and sixth in the drivers' world championship, and Benetton third in the constructors' cup. Late in the summer of the year, an expanded staff of nearly 200 people had moved here into a new, leading-edge factory. Luciano's son Alessandro, still based in London, was the family frontman of the team but Flavio Briatore and Tom Walkinshaw were firmly in the driving seat.

Success on the track had less and less to do with sport and more and more to do with multi-million-dollar investments in the technology that defined the difference between success and failure in millionths of a second. Alessandro provided and enjoyed the glamour and the showbusiness side of Formula 1; the 'entertainment' as Briatore called it. Briatore himself and Walkinshaw were meanwhile taking a look at the Williams team, in particular, as an example of just how much difference this technology could make to how fast you went, and just how far you could legally go.

Ponzano, the Veneto, 1993

Toscani was always careful publicly to defer to Luciano, to whom he referred as 'a Renaissance prince, like Lorenzo the Magnificent', albeit, unlike Lorenzo the Magnificent, a patron who gave his protégé a freer rein. 'Luciano once said to me,' Toscani liked to remark, '"Oliviero, don't let anyone ever put their hands on your toy. Not even me."' What Toscani neglected to mention on these occasions was that Luciano had added the words 'Be responsible.'

Toscani had gone on taking the pictures for the United Colors of Benetton catalogues; now, for the new spring and summer campaign, he had also gone back to taking the advertising pictures. This time he had photographed Luciano himself, his 'Renaissance prince', though in a manner that shocked Luciano's stuffier fellow members of the Senate. Several members of the Christian Democrat Party had even approached him with the implausible complaint that his behaviour was lowering the tone of Italian politics. Luciano was defiant. 'I am not stripping for pleasure, but to help people,' he told them.

In the latest publicity image, Toscani had photographed Luciano naked, apart from a discreetly positioned caption that read, in two versions of the picture, 'I Want My Clothes Back' and 'Empty Your Closets'.

This latest Benetton campaign was an invitation to the world to donate surplus clothes of all brands at all 7,047 Benetton stores in all one hundred countries. The deal thereafter was that Benetton would transport the clothes from the shops and subsidise some of the expensive business of sorting them for redistribution worldwide by Caritas, the Red Crescent and the International Red Cross. The campaign ran in a thousand magazines and 150 daily newspapers and was widely welcomed. 'It is a clear break from Benetton's self-serious attitude of the past,' declared the *Wall Street Journal*. 'It also marks the first time the company has engaged in direct action to support a cause.'

In all, 460 tons of clothes were collected in this fashion in 83 countries and then sorted and redistributed to Africa, Asia and former Yugoslavia. The project was particularly successful in Japan, perhaps because people there lacked space for unwanted clothing. Even Moslem countries such as Turkey and Lebanon co-operated, after the size of the print across Luciano's body was enlarged in order to avoid causing offence.

The heightened political flavour of the 'Empty Your Closets' campaign was both a symptom of, and a contributory factor to, Luciano's own political career. However, as he admitted, it was not entirely altruistic. As he liked to explain, the campaign had three objectives: to help the poor who had no clothes, to help the rich who had too many, and to help himself. After they had emptied their closets, the first thing many people would do would be to go out and fill them again.

Venice, northern Italy, 1993

Toscani was on a roll. He had persuaded Luciano to take off all his clothes and he had dreamed up the recycling campaign. He and Luciano had recently visited Cuba, where a Benetton shop had opened. They had met Fidel Castro and invited him to be principal of Fabrica, the globally thinking, locally acting communications academy they were planning a few kilometres from Ponzano. Castro had promised to think about it. Toscani had set up 'Inedito', which he described as 'a fashion pictures production pool' in Paris, the city where he loved to work and at whose Pin Up Studios he shot the Benetton catalogues. Inedito turned out ready-made fashion magazine articles featuring 30 per cent Benetton clothes and accessories, complete with headlines, captions and credits in three languages, available to magazines worldwide.

A new issue of *Colors* had been published, with the contents pursuing the theme of racial and cultural stereotyping through computer-altered images of Queen Elizabeth II and Arnold Schwarzenegger with black skin, Pope John Paul II as an Asian and Ronald Reagan as an AIDS victim. However, this issue of the magazine was smaller and carried advertising for companies other than Benetton such as Philips, Alfa Romeo, Sanyo and Kenwood in space sold by MTV Europe. *Colors* also now cost money to buy – US$3 in America, 400 yen in Japan and 360 roubles in Kazakhstan – as well as to make, and was still sold through Benetton shops. Palmeri had looked at the spiralling budget and decreed that this should be so.

Toscani had been displeased at the arrival of the dark star of cost accountancy in his otherwise bright firmament.

Toscani had been invited to hold an exhibition in Venice as part of the Venice Biennale. He had received and rejected invitations to exhibit before, but never in such an important show and for such a prestigious recognition of the avant-garde. His response was a 400 square metre triptych, hung in a vast room in a specially converted chapel. There were no clothes in this image either, but there were genitals, lots of them, fifty-six sets in fact, male and female, black and white, adult and child, in all shapes and sizes and all photographed by Toscani in loving close-up. The genitals did not include Luciano's, but quite possibly included Toscani's and certainly included those of Toscani's children.

Benetton added its logo and published the picture as an advertisement in the left-wing French newspaper *Libération*. That day, the newspaper sold an extra 40,000 copies and, although there were only ten calls of complaint, the French Bureau de Vérification de la Publicité threatened to sue the paper. Two days later, Eminence, the French men's underwear maker, published a double-page advertisement also in *Libération* showing as many male crotches, this time with the slogan 'We like dressing them'. The result was that visitors flocked to the Biennale, but the exhibition, like the genitals, went largely uncovered in the media while a storm of controversy surrounded the publication of the pictures in the press.

Ponzano, the Veneto, 1993

Toscani's relationship with Luciano was still the principal axis of creative power at the heart of the business and brand. This relationship had never been matched by that between Toscani and Gilberto, Toscani and Palmeri or, for that matter, Toscani and Mauro

Benetton. How much his relationship with Luciano mattered to Toscani was clear from the many statements he made in praise of his 'Renaissance prince'. Just how aware he was of his own power, however, was not so clear. It would shortly become so in a head-to-head confrontation between the creative director and the chief executive.

Luciano attended the Senate once a week; Palmeri steered Benetton Group steadily through this period of Luciano's political career. Sales and profits were both rising and the factory was growing again to meet the increase in demand. The latest addition, designed by the Scarpas, was a vast, automated extension to the plant at Castrette, a pillarless workspace with a suspended roof inspired by the Golden Gate Bridge in San Francisco. It would handle fifteen million garments that year, and would be linked to the wool factory and the distribution centre. Benetton Group was also investing in a joint-venture plant to assemble and cut garments in India, where tariff barriers made imports prohibitively expensive. The business was widening the network of distributors in Latin America and entering into an agreement with one of Mexico's biggest textile groups. More exports and more shops safeguarded jobs at home, and the total number of Benetton shops and points of sale would rise to 8,154 during the year. The number of shops in the Far East alone had quadrupled to nearly 1,500 in five years.

Complementary to but growing fast and still separate from Benetton Group were the sportswear and equipment subsidiaries belonging to Edizione. Gilberto had masterminded the acquisition and development of a clutch of companies: Nordica, Prince, Kastle and, most recently, the Asolo outdoor footwear company and Killer Loop snowboards and sunglasses. These subsidiaries were given the collective identity, chaired by Gilberto, of Benetton Sportsystem. The younger brother, who preferred 'real' sport such as rugby to 'entertainment' such as Formula 1, had long been the member of the family to whom all the others entrusted their money; they knew

it was safe with him. The same sober approach characterised
Benetton Sportsystem. Gilberto was building an empire in parallel
to Benetton Group, but this one was still wholly privately owned.
The image making of Benetton Sportsystem, as yet, was also
beyond the remit of his elder brother's talented but mercurial creative director. Toscani's latest campaign again was a reminder of
just how mercurial this talent could be.

Toscani's autumn and winter United Colors of Benetton campaign
consisted of three stark colour photographs showing an arm, but-
tock and upper crotch. Each image was stamped with the words
'HIV positive'. The declared aim was to highlight the three main
avenues of infection, as well as to condemn the stereotyping of
AIDS sufferers. Benetton had already contacted 200 associations for
HIV positive people and the campaign was customised for different
countries, with the addition of national AIDS helpline telephone
numbers directly below the United Colors of Benetton logo.

The reactions this time included reasoned disapproval from AIDS
groups in the USA and elsewhere who felt that the images wrongly
implied that HIV positive people should somehow be 'branded' for
being so. Other gay and HIV groups were ambivalent about the
images, but decided to use them in their own campaigns. Toscani
was his usual self. 'I don't think I have to justify the adverts,' he said.
'I've got children, and they keep asking me what's going on.' Toscani
had, however, already photographed his children's genitals; other
less colourful parents and their children were more easily bemused,
shocked and disapproving. In France, a government-sponsored AIDS
group sued Benetton for 'hijacking a humanitarian cause for commercial ends'. In February 1995, a Paris court would rule against
Benetton and award damages of US$32,000. Five months later, a
German court would rule in a similar fashion. Arcat Sida, another
French AIDS group headed by Pierre Berge, chief executive of the

Saint Laurent fashion house, sponsored a poster showing a condom stuffed with banknotes next to a 'United Boycott' logo in Benetton's typeface and trademark colour. A French AIDS sufferer, Olivier Besnard-Rousseau, placed an advertisement in *Libération* with his ravaged face and the words 'HIV positive' followed by 'During the agony, sales continue. For the attention of Luciano Benetton'. French Benetton stores were vandalised again and this time sprayed with graffiti.

Luciano was taken aback by these reactions. He and Toscani had devised the imagery and yet they had failed to communicate the message. No amount of investment and commitment by the company in the cause of AIDS awareness seemed able to reverse these reactions. Meanwhile, Benetton store owners in countries of strong religious tradition like France and Germany were becoming more and more nervous. They did not care about World AIDS Day on 1 December 1993 when Benetton and the militant gay group Act Up Paris placed a huge pink condom over the twenty-two-metre high obelisk in the Place de la Concorde. In spite of Benetton's booming sales worldwide, these were difficult times for many traders, with much of the Western world in recession. Yet they had no control over the advertising for the brand. If AIDS activists could take direct action, they were beginning to reason that so could they.

Elsewhere, other more sinister forces were coming to the same conclusion.

Knightsbridge, London, England, 1993

Benetton Formula had finished the season third in the constructors' cup, with Schumacher and Brundle fourth and seventh in the drivers' world championship. Schumacher had come second in France, Canada, Britain, Germany and Belgium, and won in Portugal.

However, Benetton was still not gaining on Williams, who had won both the constructors' cup and the drivers' world championship. This was in spite of the investment by the team in the latest semi-automatic gearbox, active suspension and, in common with other teams, and most crucially, in traction control. In this, electronic driver aids and computer software managed the traction of the car to a degree beyond the reaction time of even the fastest driver, leaving him comparable in status to an airline pilot.

Benetton Engineering Limited, like Benetton Formula, was autonomously run but owned by Benetton International NV, the company registered in the Netherlands. Benetton Engineering had a 50 per cent investment in Tom Walkinshaw's TWR organisation which customised Jaguar cars. This investment was rumoured to be rather bigger than Walkinshaw's stake – if he actually had one, which many doubted – in the Benetton team. Some motor racing observers had difficulty seeing the commercial logic of this from Benetton's point of view. Gilberto and Luciano, however, continued to allow Briatore a free hand for the time being, and the team manager revelled in the social side of motor racing while divulging nothing of his business activities to the press.

In the closed season that followed the end of the racing year, the Formula 1 authorities announced that traction control would be banned for the coming year. Briatore and the other team managers would have to find other, legal ways of making the cars go faster. J.J. Lehto, the Benetton team's new Finnish second driver, broke his neck in testing and, while Lehto would eventually recover, the Dutchman Jos Verstappen took his place.

Meanwhile, a bomb deposited on the doorstep of Briatore's Knightsbridge apartment did little to improve the publicity image of the team boss. The bomb did not explode and was variously said to be a random attack by the IRA on a random address or case of mistaken identity. There were dark whisperings, however, of a 'warning' to Briatore and Benetton by person or persons unknown. Elsewhere, bombs and bullets were reaching their targets and would impact far more disastrously on the image of the business and the brand.

Hum, Mostar, Bosnia–Herzegovina, 1993

Marinko Gagro, the thirty-year-old Bosnian Croat killed in the latest battle, was just one of many who made up the rising death toll in this pitiless conflict in the Balkans. Gagro had been shot through the head and had died in hospital, where his bloodstained clothes had been burnt. His father, Gojko, distraught and overcome by feelings of powerlessness, heard from a Red Cross worker that someone was launching an anti-war poster campaign.

Mr Gagro senior gave the Red Cross worker all that he had left of his son: some photographs. He told the worker to use them in the cause of peace. He also gave the worker a statement in Serbo–Croat: 'I, Gojko Gagro, father of the deceased Marinko Gagro, born in 1963 in the province of Citluk, would like that my son's name and all that remains of him be used in the name of peace against war.' The Red Cross worker thanked him and promised to pass on the photographs and the statement.

Luciano had been wanting to go to Bosnia for some time. The 'Empty Your Closets' campaign had donated tons of much-needed clothing to former Yugoslavia. Luciano felt he could go further. To his intense displeasure, however, the board of Benetton Group, in particular the outside shareholders, would not allow him, as the director of a publicly quoted company, to risk his life in a war zone. Luciano, who liked to get what he wanted, and usually did, had to abide by their decision. However, he still had a profound and possibly naïve desire to do something more, something hard-hitting about the war in Bosnia.

What happened next would be coloured by the confusion of this war. The photographs of Marinko Gagro and the statement by his father came via the Red Cross into the possession of Chem Co, the Trieste-based company that acted as Benetton's agent for Sarajevo. At the same time, a grisly relic of the conflict in the shape of a bloodsoaked T-shirt and a pair of combat fatigues also came into the possession of Chem Co through the agency of the Red Cross. These three components – the photographs, the statement and the blood-soaked clothes – all eventually found their way to Ponzano and thence into the hands of Toscani.

Birmingham, England, 1993

Toscani and Luciano had ambitious plans for Fabrica, the alternative communications centre undergoing conversion from farmhouse and outbuildings, a few kilometres from Ponzano at Catena di Vollorba. The Japanese architect, Tadeo Ando, was a friend of Toscani. The name Fabrica, taken from *fabbrica* (factory), was redolent of Andy Warhol's New York City Factory of the 1960s, which were Toscani's formative years. Fabrica, however, had a healthier ideology. The aim was to select young people from around the world who would be sponsored by Benetton to come to the centre to pursue projects of their choice. There would be no rules, only deadlines for finishing work. As with Warhol's Factory, Fabrica would be noted for its emphasis on freedom of expression and the voluntary cohabitation of diverse agendas.

The marketing of Fabrica was easily achieved through Benetton's worldwide network of contacts in design, communications and the visual arts, and through *Colors* magazine. Four years on, *Colors* would have its headquarters next door to Fabrica and the young South African editor, Adam Broomberg, would be a Fabrica 'graduate'. The question of who would front Fabrica, however, was still open. In Cuba, Luciano had seen himself in the tradition of Armand Hammer, the entrepreneur as iconoclast, forging links with a traditional adversary; in this case, the last communist in the West.

Luciano and Toscani had invited Castro to leave the island for the good of the school, as well as for the good of Cuba. Castro, however, was showing no signs of agreeing to become principal of their latest creation. This was in spite of the fact that Luciano was broadcasting compliments to the Cuban leader at every opportunity: 'He is the perfect figurehead for a cosmopolitan, multi-racial research centre like Fabrica,' Luciano was quoted as saying. 'A charismatic and revolutionary leader who will provide inspiration for a new anti-conformist school which is intended to be an experimental laboratory for creating a better society.' In truth, Luciano spoke of Castro in far more cautious terms and made no such grandiose claims for his latest brainchild, but the press sensed an exotic story and printed what they wanted to hear. The formerly naked republican senator and world's biggest consumer of wool was speaking on this occasion thousands of miles away from the exotic atmosphere of Cuba. He had flown to Birmingham from Treviso for the opening of a new United Colors of Benetton store.

The new, two-storey store was the first of its kind to sell the full range of Benetton accessories from shoes to luggage, including multi-coloured condoms. The atmosphere was festive and in contrast to the concrete and motorway intersections of this grimy midland city. Alessandro, who was with him, was the only person wearing a suit. A Benetton Formula 1 car had been transported there from Oxfordshire for the occasion and parked outside the shop.

Luciano sat in the middle of all this, talking through an interpreter about Fidel Castro. To some journalists, even his most circumspect remarks were preposterous to the point of derangement. Castro had, after all, driven his country into poverty and nearly precipitated a Third World War. Luciano, however, appeared to be perfectly sane; he also knew what the coming United Colors of Benetton campaign would be.

Ponzano, the Veneto, 1994

Toscani had planted a clue.

In 'Global Vision: The United Colors of Benetton', a vast new kaleidoscopic collection of images of the business and the brand, he had declared:

I take pictures, I don't sell clothes.

Advertising is the richest and most powerful form of communication in the world. We need to have images that will make people think and discuss . . . You can see a news photo of the fighting in Sarajevo, and it's in context; it conforms to your expectations. Shocking violence in the news is normal. But when you take the same photo out of the news and put a Benetton logo on it, people pause and reflect on their position on the problem. When they can't come to terms with it, they get mad at us.

His spring and summer campaign showed the bloodied clothes of the dead Bosnian war victim, with the statement of Gojko Gagro, the bereaved father, in Serbo–Croat across the top of the picture. At the bottom left of the picture was the United Colors of Benetton logo. The shocking image appeared on billboards and in newspapers across 110 countries. A special edition of *Oslobodenje*, the Sarajevo free daily newspaper run by a collective of Serbs, Croats and

Moslems, was printed and delivered to the world's eighty leading heads of state.

Leading dailies such as the *Los Angeles Times*, *Le Monde* and *Frankfurter Allgemeine Zeitung* refused to carry this. The Vatican declared that Benetton was engaging in 'image terrorism'. In Britain, Wally Olins, chairman of Wolff Olins, a leading corporate identity consultancy, said, 'Personally, I loathe the ads. But the day is past when a corporation's sole role is just to make money. Companies have become too powerful. The next, inevitable step is that they have to make their point of view known.'

In France, the advertising weekly *Strategies* declared that it would not write about Benetton as long as its advertising continued in this vein: 'Besides the disgust it causes, this ad raises the issue of the responsibility of advertisers. Can one do anything, use anything, to attract attention?' The French minister for human rights and humanitarian action urged people to stop buying Benetton clothes and 'rip them off the backs of those who wear them'. In former Yugoslavia itself, reactions varied according to whether the dead man was seen as victim or aggressor and which faction the image was perceived as helping.

Benetton's press office chief, Marina Galanti, responded, 'If we were trying to sell T-shirts there would probably not be a worse way of doing it. We are not that naïve. It's meant to question the notion of institutionalised violence and the role of advertising. The Art Directors' Club of New York awarded Benetton its 1994 medal for 'raising social awareness through its advertising campaigns'. Benetton also won the Art Directors' Club of Tokyo's award for the best campaign of the year.

Either way, the dead man's clothes were universally assumed to belong to Marinko Gagro. This had been a young man like many others who would have wanted to go on living; to finish his studies, find a job, marry and have children. He was the contemporary counterpart to the unknown victim of the First World War who lay beneath the stones of Westminster Abbey in London. Benetton called the new image 'the known soldier'.

The problem was that this was not the known soldier after all. In Bosnia–Herzegovina, Gojko Gagro saw the image in the newspaper and contacted the German newspaper *Die Woche*. Gagro confirmed that he had supplied photographs of his dead son, which were not used, and a statement, which was. Most emphatically he said that he had not supplied the bloodstained clothing which appeared in the image. He repeated that his son's clothes had been burned at the hospital where he died, adding that if they had not been burned, he would never have given them away: 'It would have been like selling the legs of my son.' Furthermore, he pointed out that his son had died from a shot to the head and not to the chest, as suggested by the bullet hole in Benetton's picture.

So had Luciano and Toscani simply instructed Chem Co, their agent for Sarajevo, to 'find' some clothing for the 'known soldier' campaign? Had they then knowingly added a statement from a different source? And had they really assumed that the man who made the statement would either not notice the image, or notice it but think nothing of the fact that his words had been placed in a different context? This was hard to believe, and, according to Luciano, untrue. According to him, Benetton had indeed asked Chem Co, its agent for Sarajevo, to contact the Red Cross. The Red Cross had sent the clothing to Benetton with the name of the victim. Benetton had contacted the victim's father, who had released the statement that appeared on the image. Gojko Gagro's own assumptions about how his statement might or might not be used were unknown to Luciano and Toscani, who had simply seen his words and the bloodsoaked clothes as the ingredients for the image they were seeking. Toscani was no ballistics expert, but claimed of the hole suggesting a chest wound in the T-shirt, that 'no one could say for sure that that is a bullet hole', and repeated his belief that the clothes were those of Marinko Gagro. This, however, was to ignore the claim to the contrary of Gagro's father, who had no incentive to tell anything other than the truth. Both sides stuck to their story. Either way, the result, ironically, was that even the 'known soldier' was probably unknown after all.

Meanwhile, the 'known soldier' polarised opinion to an even greater degree than had been the case with the AIDS image of David Kirby. In France, several Benetton stores were again vandalised, and trouble was brewing in Germany. This time, however, unlike the embittered victims of the recession across America, where over 300 Benetton stores had closed as a result, discontented European Benetton retailers were coming to the conclusion that they had at last found the grounds to mount a legal attack on the company.

Luciano had decided to send his elder son Mauro, who was marketing manager of Benetton Group, to America to continue the turnaround of the business there. In addition to concentrating on fewer, larger, higher-quality stores in more carefully selected locations, Benetton in America was targeting more affluent customers in their twenties and thirties, people who shopped at United Colors of Benetton and Sisley, instead of teenagers. Teenagers were more cost conscious and would go elsewhere to buy clothes at only a dollar cheaper at Limited's Express and Gap.

Luciano had also decided to quit politics. The self-interest of politicians, exemplified by the media baron Silvio Berlusconi, was proving too much even for Luciano who had truly and perhaps naïvely believed that he could 'make a contribution'. Luciano announced that he would not be standing in the next general election. 'The two roles of politician and businessman are so important,' he said, 'that today for me they are irreconcilable. I believe it is impossible to do both.'

Luciano had reasons for concentrating his energies on the business; he also had the time. He had broken with politics, and he had broken with Marina. She began a relationship with another man, Marco Benatti, with whom she had two more children, both sons, and subsequently concentrated most of her energies on running her childrenswear business. She also harboured ambitions to enter politics.

In addition to the matter of concluding the turnaround of Benetton in America, there were obstacles to be overcome to the growth of the business and brand in Australia and in South Africa, where Benetton sponsored a number of cultural events as part of the celebrations to mark the first free elections in the country. A new Benetton Group share issue was about to be launched to increase the number of international shareholders in the business. In France and Germany, where Benetton retailers were united in their preference for more muted colours, some of these were also uniting to take legal action against the company, citing the 'known soldier' campaign in evidence for loss of income.

At home, Toscani was quarrelling more violently and more publicly with Aldo Palmeri, whom he accused of having a 'rigid and old-fashioned' attitude. Although their differences were over ideals rather than management and budgets, the latter being beyond Toscani's remit, at the heart of their dispute was the direction of Benetton's US$60 million advertising budget. 'Since you returned to the company,' Toscani wrote to Palmeri, 'I am no longer able to work as before. Everything has slowed down, bureaucracy and uncertainty reign supreme.' Toscani concluded with the words: 'Have I ever dared give you advice on finance or running the company?' and said he was resigning.

Palmeri would dismiss these claims as 'utter nonsense', saying correctly that Toscani was merely an external consultant to the group. There was no need to consult Luciano about the clash:

'There is full agreement between us on this.' However, the chief executive was no match in his timing for the photographer and creative director. Toscani made sure his 'private' letter found its way to the press, and at a time when both Palmeri and Luciano were out of the country. This gave him several days in which to make the most of the ensuing publicity, and left Palmeri looking uncharacteristically flat-footed. Toscani meanwhile proceeded to supply the public with what they wanted to hear. The chief executive's imposition of budgetary constraints on *Colors* magazine was the catalyst for their falling out. 'It's not Benetton I'm angry with, it's Palmeri,' Toscani declared. 'He's landed me with a small-time publisher who can't even get the office toilets to work.'

This was a crucial battle for Toscani. He had just lost image-making control over Sisley which, as Palmeri had approvingly noted, was booming under Mauro's management and without Toscani's help. Toscani was seen as taking a huge risk, even by his standards, but he was also taking his 'Renaissance prince' Luciano at his word – 'Don't ever let anyone put their hands on your toy. Not even me' – even if he chose to omit the caveat 'Be responsible' from his version. On this occasion, nevertheless, people were predicting Toscani's demise.

Palmeri too was seen as putting his position on the line. 'Either Palmeri's crazy, or he has the support of the boss,' said one well-placed observer. However, when Toscani's threat to quit became known on the Milan stock exchange, this was allegedly followed by a fall of nearly 8 per cent in the share price of Benetton Group. Toscani was 'a pillar of Benetton's success' declared analyst Ciro Tomagnini of Merrill Lynch in London. There is no evidence that any such fall took place, or that there was such a tangible link between the share price and the mercurial photographer. Had Toscani himself allowed such a story to circulate and gain credibility? Whatever the case, Toscani stayed, and stays to this day. Within a year, however, Palmeri would be gone again.

Benetton

Aida, Japan, 1994

Benetton Formula, meanwhile, had enjoyed a flying start to the racing season. Even after the outlawing of traction control, Schumacher was proving to be the fastest driver onto and off the grid. He had won the first Grand Prix of the season in Brazil in convincing style, and now he had won the second at the Pacific Grand Prix at Aida. In addition to the fastest starts, Benetton also had the fastest pit stops. No one seemingly, not even Williams, could match Briatore's men for the speed with which they refuelled their cars and sent them and their drivers, Schumacher and Verstappen, flying back up the pit lane and onto the track.

This season was fast becoming a triumph for the team in a year when Benetton needed one. However, one man who knew he was faster than Schumacher also believed he had discovered the secret of the real formula for the success of the Benetton racing team.

9   The Burning Brand

Death of an expert witness, Imola, Italy, 1994

The San Marino Grand Prix is too big an event for its country of origin. Instead, the race is held at Imola, making it Italy's second Formula 1 race. The circuit stands in beautiful parkland and is distinguished by its rapid upward and downward sweeps, punctuated by chicanes, and by the formidably fast Tamburello left-hand corner. What happened here at Imola overshadowed the race and Formula 1 racing in general for years to come. This race was not only to see the loss of two men but also, in the words of an insider, the loss 'of the chance to clean up the sport'.

One man in particular had observed Schumacher's incredible start in São Paulo. He had observed Schumacher win there and then again in Aida. Ayrton Senna was a shy, deeply religious man, triple world champion and unquestionably the greatest driver of the modern era. Senna frequently divided opinion, but at a sportsman he enjoyed universal respect. He was convinced that there was 'no way' Schumacher and the Benetton car could have made such a perfect start in Brazil without technical assistance of some kind. He believed 'something sinister' was going on in the Benetton camp.

Some other leading teams shared his suspicions. They too did not believe that the combination of the Benetton chassis and the inferior Ford engine could have made the kind of difference between Benetton and themselves that they were seeing this season. The other drivers urged Senna to continue his researches and he needed little encouragement. He began secretly monitoring Benetton's computers and Schumacher's lap times. He recorded which Benetton engineers were close to Schumacher's car before and after the races. He was compiling a dossier which he intended to submit to the Formula 1 authorities at the end of the season. He intended to go public.

The race at Imola was already preceded by tragedy when the young Austrian driver Roland Ratzenberger crashed into a wall during qualifying and died of his injuries. This was the first fatality in Formula 1 for twelve years. Senna, the most safety-conscious of drivers, led the others in checking the site of the crash before deciding to go ahead with the race.

The race started; Senna took the lead from Schumacher and was determined to stay ahead at all costs. On only the second lap it already seemed that this was a battle between Senna, the man, and Schumacher, apparently half man, half computer. Senna was driving at the outer limit of his prodigious powers when he turned his Williams at 200 miles per hour into Tamburello. The car failed to complete the turn. He hit the wall and came to rest at the side of the track. He moved for a moment; then he was still for ever.

★

The aftermath of Senna's death, which was caused by a breakage due to faulty welding in the steering gear, conveniently obscured the questions about the Benetton team. Schumacher had gone on to win at Imola and subsequently at Monaco. He came second in Spain and won in Canada. In France, Schumacher made one of the most 'perfect' starts ever seen in Formula 1 racing. By this time the other teams were voicing Senna's suspicions.

The FIA, the international motor sport federation, asked Liverpool Data Research Associates, a British software company, to examine the computer programmes used by McLaren, Ferrari and Benetton. Ferrari immediately agreed to hand over the 'source codes' which would enable LDRA to make the check. McLaren and Benetton initially refused on the grounds that to do so would be a 'breach of confidentiality'. Ferrari would be found to be clean, and the pressure on McLaren and Benetton mounted to the point where they too were forced to hand over their computer programmes.

By the time of the British Grand Prix at Silverstone, Schumacher and Benetton had six wins and one second place from seven races. Before the race, Schumacher, who was in second place on the grid, twice overtook the Williams driver Damon Hill, who was in pole position, on the parade lap. At the time, this unprecedented manoeuvre was interpreted as a piece of gamesmanship by Schumacher to psych out the Briton in front of his home crowd. Schumacher was black-flagged by race officials and ordered to return to the pits. The German driver initially stayed on the track and later claimed not to have seen the flag. Eventually he returned to the pits and suffered a ten-second time penalty before joining the race and coming second behind Hill.

The incident at Silverstone made the other teams even more suspicious about Benetton. An attempt to psych out a rival driver seemed an implausible explanation for the bizarre movements of the Benetton car on the parade lap. It appeared almost as if the car had been driving Schumacher, rather than vice versa. After the British Grand Prix, Schumacher was given a two-race suspension for ignoring the black flag. The FIA deferred this suspension at Schumacher's request, so that he could race in front of his own home crowd at the next race in Germany. The FIA, however, had fined Benetton for not immediately handing over the software in compliance with their request. LDRA, meanwhile, were trying to crack the secret of the Benetton software.

Fire in the pit lane, Hockenheim, Germany, 1994

Schumacher had his wish to drive in front of his home crowd. The German was running second and threatening to take the lead when his team-mate, Jos Verstappen, came into the pits for what was supposed to be a routine refuelling.

With the banning of computer-assisted traction control, refuelling stops had become a greater focus of competition between the teams as each tried to send the car and driver back out onto the track in the shortest possible time. The system of refuelling, however, was regarded in some quarters as little more than a stunt to satisfy the desire of the organisers of Formula 1 for televisual drama of the kind that was often lacking on the track. Meanwhile, in addition to being the fastest starters, Benetton were also acknowledged to be the fastest exponents of the refuelling stop.

What happened next at Hockenheim was to linger in the minds of many who witnessed it, not so much for its immediacy, but for the even greater catastrophe that might have taken place. Verstappen was in his car, surrounded by Benetton mechanics and crew, attempting to pump in eighty litres of fuel in seven and a half seconds, when the fuel ignited in a massive fireball. For four seconds, car, driver and mechanics were engulfed in flames, a spectacle of horror seen by hundreds of millions of people on television.

Verstappen and the Benetton crew had an amazing escape. The driver and five mechanics suffered only superficial burns, saved by their protective clothing and their quick reactions with the fire extinguishers. After they had extinguished the fire, however, the minds of many present turned elsewhere, to the image of rivers of burning fuel around a total of twenty-two mechanics, and under a nearby hospitality unit where the laughter of more than a hundred guests had turned to screams of fright.

The initial explanation by the team for the inferno in the pit at Hockenheim was to exonerate human error and attribute it to the accidental introduction of a foreign body, or a faulty link in the pressurised refuelling system. All the equipment, meanwhile, was taken away for inspection. This led to the discovery that the mesh was missing from a filter in the refuelling system, thereby fractionally increasing the speed at which the fuel was pumped into the car. This increase in pressure was thought to have led to the fuel spillage onto the hot exhaust of the car and to the fireball. In an atmosphere in which a fraction of a second could make a difference to winning and losing, it was also calculated that the absence of the filter might have saved the Benetton team up to a second during refuelling stops in the course of a race.

When the missing filter was made public by FIA, the initial reaction of Briatore and the Benetton team was to claim that it had been removed with the permission of the motor racing authorities. The FIA flatly contradicted this statement. Permission for all technical changes had to be requested in writing, and no such request or permission had been made or given. Briatore was told to appear at a disciplinary hearing of the World Council of the FIA in Paris. He continued to protest that the team had done nothing wrong. Tom Walkinshaw, on the other hand, appeared in a television interview and bluntly declared that they had removed the fuel filter mesh in order to gain time at pit stops.

In Britain, meanwhile, LDRA, the company commissioned to examine the Benetton software programme, had at last succeeded in cracking the secret of the Benetton B194 computer, and communicated their findings to the FIA.

What LDRA had found was surprising. The Benetton car driven by Schumacher did indeed appear to have access to a software programme, known within the team as 'launch control', which Benetton claimed had not been used at the critical time. This would have allowed Schumacher to make a perfect start, simply by flooring the accelerator and holding it there. As the LDRA report put it, this system 'could control the clutch, gear shift and engine speed fully automatically to a predetermined pattern'. In lay terms, this meant that, if the system was used, as soon as Schumacher had floored the accelerator and held it there, the computer would take over and manage the traction of the car, determining the correct gear changes and engine speed and ensuring that the car reached the crucial first corner of the circuit in the least possible time with no loss of traction. Such a computer-controlled feat of driving was impossible to match in purely human terms, even by a driver as talented as Senna. This was precisely why the FIA had banned it the previous season and why Senna had launched his own enquiries.

LDRA initially called up the software's menu programme and found nothing untoward. There were only ten items on the menu and none of these were controversial. The key item could only be found by scrolling down to the bottom line of the programme, placing the cursor on an apparently blank line and pressing a particular key. The Benetton software designer had given what happened next the name 'Option 13'.

Option 13 was not itself present in the computer hardware of the car before or after the race. Senna had suspected that it was downloaded from a laptop plugged into the car by a Benetton engineer on the starting grid. At the end of the race, when Schumacher switched off the engine and the power source, the programme was automatically deleted, leaving no trace of its existence. This could explain some of the 'perfect' starts and also the bizarre manoeuvres at the British Grand Prix. On that occasion, something could have gone wrong with Option 13, or with Schumacher's handling of it, causing the car to go into launch control twice on the parade lap and making it surge forward in an unexpected fashion.

If illegal use of the launch control was proved, the position would be serious – comparable to allegations of drug abuse by an Olympic athlete and the prospect of stripping that athlete of his or her medal. In athletics, the authorities had shown themselves to be capable of imposing such penalties in the interests of the sport. For a driver of Schumacher's status, and for the Benetton team, the implications were equally appalling. With this evidence, the FIA confronted Benetton technical director Ross Brawn, who was responsible for the legality of the cars, and Flavio Briatore, with whom they already had an appointment over the fuel filter incident at Hockenheim.

Briatore and Brawn's explanation in response to the allegations was simple. They claimed that they had not used Option 13 after the ban or during the season. They had merely left it on the computer software because it was too complicated to remove it. Briatore also said that the device was hidden behind a range of masking procedures in order to prevent Schumacher 'accidentally' activating it.

This explanation was immediately rejected by LDRA. 'What Briatore was basically saying, is that they weren't cheating,' said one source, 'but that they were doing everything to make sure that they couldn't possibly cheat. But if that was the case, all they had to do was wipe out the programme, which only takes a day.'

A computer specialist with another Formula 1 team which had abided by the ban, agreed. 'Look, we purged our own software of all the illegal systems during the winter,' he said. 'I did it myself. It took two days. That's all. Perfectly straightforward.'

The FIA took the unusual step of making their suspicions public. However, they took no further action against the Benetton team. With Briatore and Brawn's explanation and the deletion of Option 13 immediately after each race, the FIA did not know whether or not it had been used in the crucial races. A finding against Benetton and/or Schumacher would have brought disastrous publicity which might have lost motor racing even more ratings and revenue than it had already lost following the death of Senna. Was there simply too much money at stake in the business that masqueraded as a sport? Briatore, Brawn and Schumacher now only had to fear the lesser ordeal of the hearings in Paris over the missing fuel filter.

However, the suspicions about the Benetton team would linger in many minds for as long as the same team were still in charge. 'When you build a car on the threshold of legality,' former world champion Niki Lauda, a consultant to Ferrari, who themselves had passed FIA scrutiny, would say, 'which Benetton has apparently done all year, and you get caught out again and again, it's simply not right.' Or, as one commentator said, 'The way it was set up, you could have had Mr Bean sitting in the Benetton car, and it would still have beaten Damon Hill off the starting grid.'

Schumacher won first place in the next race in Hungary with or without launch control, but with the indifferent Ford engine. Benetton Formula, however, had lobbied hard and succeeded in persuading Renault to supply an unprecedented three teams at once – themselves, in addition to Williams and Ligier – with the same world-beating engine for the coming season.

In Belgium, Schumacher again took first place, but this time he was disqualified after the race. This was because he had apparently worn down a section of the wooden 'skidblock', or plank of wood, bolted to the bottom of the car as a result of FIA regulations introduced in the middle of the season. The aim of the plank was to increase ground clearance and thereby slow down the cars by reducing the aerodynamic effect.

So low was Benetton's credibility among other teams by this time that doubts were raised about the wear caused during the race. Briatore's explanation was that the plank had been ground down when Schumacher had spun over a kerb. This was challenged by some videotape evidence. The Benetton team by this time was sponsored not only by Mild Seven cigarettes, but also Benetton Sportsystem. The sight of the Benetton Sportsystem logo emblazoned on the side of a car being very publicly examined by race officials on suspicion of breaking the rules, and then being disqualified, did nothing to endear Briatore to the chairman of Sportsystem, Gilberto Benetton.

In Paris shortly afterwards, the World Council of the FIA upheld Schumacher's two-race ban as a result of his behaviour at the British Grand Prix. A few days later, the FIA maintained Schumacher's disqualification in Belgium. However, at the same meeting, they cleared the Benetton team of a deliberate attempt to cheat before the German Grand Prix by removing the missing fuel filter. Nor was there a word from the FIA about launch control.

Briatore was exultant. 'Finally, the truth has come out,' he declared, 'and we're delighted to clear our good name of any allegations of cheating.' This although Schumacher had just been disqualified after one race and banned from taking part in two more, in this case in Italy and Portugal. Both these races were won by Damon Hill, leaving him just one point behind Schumacher in the world drivers' championship. Schumacher won in Jerez and Hill in

Japan. With one race left of the season, Schumacher was still one point ahead of Hill.

The final race of the season was in Adelaide, Australia. Nearly halfway through, Schumacher ran wide and grazed a wall – a mistake he might not have made with traction control – and damaged his car. When Hill made to pass him at the next corner on his way to winning the drivers' world championship, Schumacher's car, too badly damaged to continue, slewed into him. This took both men out of the race and made Schumacher world champion. Benetton came second to Williams in the constructors' trophy.

This was the unedifying if appropriate end to an unedifying season. Briatore and Benetton had been cross-questioned about a banned software programme, escaped from a fireball, been fined, disqualified from one race and banned from two more. Yet they were fortunate that this was the extent of their embarrassment. Had Ayrton Senna lived, the FIA and even Formula 1 power broker Bernie Ecclestone, a close friend of Briatore, might well have been forced to go further. They would surely have yielded to the evidence of the one man whom they could not afford to ignore.

As it was, Senna had taken the rest of his secrets to his grave and Schumacher was champion. Two years later, however, a senior figure in Formula 1 would still be willing for it to be known, albeit anonymously, that he believed Schumacher should be stripped of his 1994 World Championship.

Ponzano, the Veneto, 1994

Gilberto, meanwhile, was continuing to drive the growth of the Benetton team's sponsor, Benetton Sportsystem. Nordica, Prince, Kastle, Asolo and Killer Loop were linked through common ownership and brand power; however, although they appeared to be a seamless, year-round sports line, they were fragmented in a way that was at odds with their closeness to the Benetton name, as Luciano would be quick to point out. These businesses were disparate in size, scattered in location and lacking in the commercial and technical synergies espoused by Gilberto.

Luciano's withdrawal from politics coincided with the political debut of Silvio Berlusconi, who was currently trying to reduce the indebtedness of his empire. This was why Edizione was also spending US$600 million on a majority stake in Berlusconi's Euromercato chain of supermarkets to add to the 450 roadside restaurants trading under the Autogrill and Ciao names, which already belonged to Edizione. Like the brands in Benetton Sportsystem, these names were still outside the range of Luciano and Toscani's United Colors communications strategy.

Toscani had emerged the winner from the disagreement over *Colors* with Palmeri, but was taking no chances after the furore over the 'known soldier'. His autumn and winter imagery for the print media and billboards, approved by Luciano, was a mosaic of a thousand faces, electronically treated to highlight the word 'AIDS' across the centre of the picture. The campaign solicited and attracted little displeasure. Toscani, however, had not entirely suppressed his appetite for bizarre juxtaposition; he had just shot the latest United Colors of Benetton catalogue in the Gaza Strip.

'You have to be courageous, and ready to fall,' he told an audience of students in a rare and electrifying visit to Britain. 'You shouldn't have a hobby. Creativity is your hobby.' He showed a slide presentation of his favourite images, with a running commentary on his pet hates. These inevitably included managers – 'They got no courage' – supermodels, especially Claudia Schiffer, creative directors, although he himself was one – 'Not even God was a creative director. He did everything himself' – and the 'monoculture' of global advertising, of which he and Luciano were the world's supreme exponents. There was no boundary between editorial and advertising. 'Editorial,' he told them, was merely 'the advertising of the advertising.' At this time, Fabrica was soliciting applications from people under the age of twenty-five who were 'not polluted by conventionality', as Elisabetta Prando of Benetton and Fabrica would put it; this sounded like a remarkably cynical statement. But then, as F. Scott Fitzgerald – whose publishers had occupied the Scribner Building in New York City, now owned by Edizione – put it, an artist was a person who could function perfectly while holding two opposing points of view at the same time.

'I am not a salesman,' Toscani had told his student audience in Britain, 'I don't know how to sell.' In Switzerland, Toscani and Luciano stood side by side at the opening of an exhibition of his images at the Museum of Contemporary Art in Lausanne. A similar show would open in the summer at the Museum of Modern Art in Mexico. In Germany, however, United Colors of Benetton and 012 retailers were turning Toscani's words back against the business and brand. They were complaining that by 'I don't know how to sell' he meant exactly that. They were pointing to the timing of the David Kirby and HIV images and the 'known soldier' in tandem with the timing of their falling sales. They were hiring lawyers. They were not interested in Luciano's talk of handshakes and gentleman's agreements, or in the fact that some people considered Toscani's images to be significant works of art. This was strictly business. They wanted compensation – US$3.5 million between five of them alone – because they were convinced that the brand was stopping people from buying the clothes.

There was, and is, no love lost between Germany and Italy. This situation dates back to the reprisals and atrocities carried out by the

Germans at the end of the Second World War. Toscani himself mocked the British for their alleged preference for pets over children, for example, but he also paid tribute to the Royal Air Force for saving his life by preventing his mother from going to the abortionist. He had little time for Germans, however, as was well known to those who worked with him. This was in spite of the fact that his images hung on permanent display in the Frankfurt Museum of Modern Art. There was, however, no consciously anti-German message to his work; he simply could not find a way to bridge the traditional antipathy between the two countries. The only relationships that really mattered to him were those with his wife, his six children (from three different mothers), his three grandchildren and his Appaloosa horses, and with Luciano. Toscani not only knew Luciano better than anyone else, he also knew the bottom line. As one high-ranking, non-family member of the business put it, 'If Mr Benetton suspected for a second that the recent campaigns were causing losses, he would have fired Toscani immediately, even though he is a close friend.'

Luciano, however, was not only convinced that the discontented German retailers were wrong, he was determined to prove them so. Intellectually, he could easily understand why they might have believed they were right, but in his mind he believed they were wrong and in his heart, too, he could not accept a proposition that would strike so devastatingly at the core of his communications strategy. Germany was a major international market for Benetton, with around 400 shops and outlets across the country. Further to provoke even a relatively small proportion of discontented shop owners would only provide them with more ammunition and at his own expense. This reasoning was also a factor in Luciano's ensuring that, this autumn and winter, Toscani came up with a softer United Colors of Benetton campaign.

Benetton

Kassel, Germany, 1995

The first hearing saw Benetton as the plaintiff and not the defendant. Heinz Hartwich was a Kassel shop owner whom Benetton was suing for non-payment of US$590,000 worth of clothes he had ordered and of which he had taken delivery. Hartwich was arguing that he should not have to pay because this sum corresponded in value to the amount he had lost in sales through Benetton's advertising campaigns. As his lawyer, Ulfert Engels, put it, 'We want damages for loss of business. If Benetton forgets the bill, then we will be quits.' He declared:

> Just look at the changing revenues of the textile industry in general, and look at Benetton. Benetton had five or ten years of much higher than average turnover. Then they went down to 15 or 20 per cent below the general level. It's very clear. The campaign caused 95 per cent of the problems. The additional pressures accounted for just 5 per cent.

Benetton retorted that although some German retailers claimed their turnover was down the previous year, the market share was stable, in spite of a crisis in the textile sector. A few German shops had closed, but others had doubled their turnover. Hartwich was merely using the advertising images as a scapegoat. 'He failed to pay for goods in 1986 and 1989, when our advertising campaigns were less hard-hitting,' a spokesperson said, 'so how can he blame our advertising for loss of turnover?' Marina Galanti of Benetton went further:

> It is a normal situation – an unpleasant situation, if you like – where we sometimes have to take retailers to court to pay debts. Hartwich has had payment problems since a time when our advertising images were of smiley happiness. By making a fracas about this, he and others have found a good excuse not to pay.

238

Hartwich, meanwhile, was carrying other brands in his shop, breaching the exclusivity agreement between the company and its outlets. He was also displaying a placard advising people not to buy Benetton. He claimed to have German mothers on his side, telling reporters that some of these had said their children were being ostracised by friends for wearing Benetton clothes. The hearing here was adjourned for seven weeks. Courts in Dusseldorf, Braunschweig, Mannheim and Cologne were also due to begin hearing similar cases.

Hartwich was only one of ten retailers from Germany who had gathered recently in Mainz under the banner of the Benetton Retailers' Interest Group. The group claimed, however, to have the support of 150 retailers operating 250 Benetton shops. 'The main aim,' said a spokesman, 'is to take away the feeling of powerlessness.' Other retailers, meanwhile, had formed the 'Pro-Benetton' group in Germany to 'fight the discredit done to Benetton by the disgruntled retailers'. Both sides were outwardly confident they would win. The Germans, however, had won the initial advantage, as their lawyer Ulfert Engels was quick to point out. 'Our tactic was to get Benetton to sue,' he said, 'otherwise we would have had to fight in an Italian court; and we prefer to fight in Germany.'

Ponzano, the Veneto, 1995

Toscani announced that the United Colors of Benetton spring and summer campaign would feature old and new forms of alienation and isolation. 'The images will be typically hard-hitting and strong,' he declared.

The first showed horizontal strands of barbed wire from different and troubled parts of the world, including Bosnia, Lebanon, Israel and South Africa, as well as from private gardens. The second showed a haunting collection of TV antennae against a grey sky,

symbolising the 'invisible barriers erected by the overcrowding of video images, which not only affect interpersonal relationships, but also people's perception of reality', as the press statement put it. The alienation campaign was billed as 'an invitation to an open discussion on real and virtual prisons, on the mental and televisual dictatorships which restrict freedom'.

Again, whatever the company said, these were more conciliatory images than dead AIDS sufferers, HIV positive buttocks and blood-soaked clothing. But there was also an integrity to these images on their own terms, which emanated from Toscani's own beliefs and lifestyle. The latter, by this time, was one of luxuriant self-sufficiency, albeit of the kind made possible by the presence of cooks and au pairs. Toscani woke up in his farmhouse in the Campigallo, the Golden Valley, near the Tuscan coast an hour south of Pisa, without the help of an alarm clock. He breakfasted off his own bread and olive oil. He drove his daughter the six miles every morning to primary school. He worked as well as lived here, on his own land, in the region from which he took his own name. He drank his own wine, ate his own vegetables, delivered his own Appaloosa foals and resoled his own shoes. He consumed newspapers from all over the world, but did not possess a television. Toscani hated television:

> A man can watch half an hour of television and think that he's seen a civil war in Africa, the disappearing rain forests in the Amazon and genocide in Bosnia. In truth, he hasn't seen a thing. In truth, he was seated in his armchair and saw images that were presented, accelerated, slowed down and mediated by someone else.

A photograph, on the other hand, 'permits a first viewing, and then an individual reflection. It solicits participation, and encourages individuality in interpretation.'

In the evenings, he and Kirsti played games with the children, some of which they invented themselves, and he helped out with the homework. He and Kirsti had been married for eighteen years, and if visiting journalists sometimes came here, took their hospitality and then went away and sniped at their 'perfect' lifestyle in the Golden Valley, it clearly worked for them.

Toscani had no office or even a desk at Ponzano, and when he came to Benetton he stayed with Luciano. Luciano, by contrast, lived in luxurious isolation rather than self-sufficiency. He had moved back out of Treviso and into a villa, this time with professional body-guards. His idea of a perfect evening was to relax over dinner with the small group of friends he had known for many years. Above all, he liked to travel – three weeks out of every four – around the world-wide network of agents and shops and to new shops in Japan, Korea, Thailand and South America. The previous year had been a difficult one for the business with bad trading conditions, rising wool and cotton prices, and stagnating profits. Luciano travelled, listened and observed, noting the comments of agents and shop owners, and con-sumer trends. They had developed a phrase, 'cleaning the network', for the process by which these agents and shops were regularly observed and, where necessary, their performance adjusted; and they did this with a ruthless clarity of vision that was at odds with the image of the 'gentleman's agreement' that Luciano still liked to imply was unchanged since the early days of the business.

Cleaning the network number 1, New York City, United States of America, 1995

Luciano had sent Mauro to New York to conclude the turnaround that had begun here under Francesco della Barba. There was no change in the agreement between Benetton and its store operators but a greater degree of consultation and customer feedback. Benetton had 150 stores across the United States, far fewer than the peak of 700 at the height of the yuppie years, but these served a more upmarket range of customers than Gap, which had grown on narrower margins to 1,400 stores by this time. The selling square footage of United Colors of Benetton, Sisley and 012 had also doubled in five years, mainly due to the opening of the megastores in the north-east and California. There were also 271 further 'shops in stores' and concessions across America. In addition to the softer, more conciliatory 'United Colors of Benetton' campaign of this spring and summer, American Benetton retailers launched an advertising campaign developed by Chiat/Day in New York City, aimed at a more conservative audience. This focused on the clothes and not the issues and included TV spots as well as eight-page magazine spreads.

The results of these changes were beginning to seep through into the balance sheet. America and Benetton, it seemed, were through turnaround and financial analysts in the USA were optimistic about Benetton's prospects. The markets here discounted any changes in consumer behaviour at the expense of the business that might have arisen as a result of the perception of the brand. This autumn, Salomon Brothers would issue a 'buy' recommendation on Benetton stock. By this time, too, another set of shops would have been subjected to close, and in this case, public scrutiny.

Cleaning the network number 2, Kassel, Germany, 1995

After the initial hearing, the press here had been strongly on the side of the German shop owners, casting Heinz Hartwich as the hometown David against the foreign Goliath. Given the state of German–Italian relations, and of Germany itself, the failure to win over the local press depressed but did not surprise Laura Pollini and the Benetton media communications team.

Benetton's lawyers, meanwhile, were suddenly making a favourable impact on the mind of the judge. As had been the case in America at the height of the discontent among Benetton retailers there, so Germany was in deep recession. The judge told the defendants they would have to discount this and convince him that there was a link between the fall in sales and the advertising. While the German press continued to drive home the message that this time Benetton had gone too far, the retailers were unable to prove conclusively that this was the case. The judge decided that they were using the advertising issue as an excuse for not paying for the clothes already ordered but unsold, and returned a verdict in favour of Benetton. In France, the courts would reach a similar conclusion.

Although the company would always deny this, these were not just local victories but also test cases for the Benetton global brand strategy. The truth was that ultra-shocking imagery is only acceptable in times of guilt-inducing affluence. If Toscani had possessed a television, he might have noticed that much of the Western world was still experiencing the effects of deep recession. In a recession, this kind of imagery only made people who already felt bad feel worse. Toscani had been walking the tightrope, as usual, and in neglecting to take this into account he had fallen off it. The brand image had got away from the business and alienated the people who both sold and bought the product.

The dissidents in Germany and in France had had little or nothing to lose. A precedent in their favour, however, would have resulted in the immediate firing of Toscani and left a sword hanging over the head of Benetton for ever. The bottom line was that if the dissidents had won, both Luciano and Toscani would have been discredited in their implicit claims to be not merely advertisers, but communicators. The *schadenfreude* would have been immense, not only in

Germany but also in advertising agencies around the world, hitherto jealous of Benetton's in-house success and long the butt of Toscani's jibes at their expense. After the relief of the victory, the lesson of the experience was clear. The network would have to be regularly 'cleaned' in future. Hartwich and his fellow dissidents were unlikely to have seen the humorous side of this expression; however, even they might have admitted that it had a suitably Germanic ring.

Sarajevo, Bosnia–Herzegovina, 1995

'Anyone can open a shop after the war,' said Vesna Kapidzic. 'We think it is nice to open this store during the war.'

Kapidzic worked in the new United Colors of Benetton store in Sarajevo. In spite of her words, the opening of the first shop in the heart of this shattered city was meant to signal the return of some sort of 'normality' and tolerance to the region. Benetton's agent for Sarajevo was still Chem Co, the Trieste-based company through which Toscani had received the bloodsoaked clothes and the testimony of Gojko Gagro. *Oslobodenje*, the collectively run free newspaper which had carried the 'known soldier', and carried on publishing throughout the war, was also one of the business ventures of Zlatko Dizdarevic, one of the two partners who owned the shop. Dizdarevic had taken the opportunity afforded by the Benetton link to become a Benetton retailer.

Vesna Kapidzic was excited about the commercial prospects for the opening. She was not to be disappointed; however, unlike the reaction of the youth of Belluno to the opening of the first My Market thirty years earlier, she knew that demanding teenage tastes could survive and flourish, even in a war zone. As she would ask Benetton's media relations manager, Federico Sartor, 'We will be getting the same collection as the rest of Europe, won't we?'

Ponzano, the Veneto, 1995

Benetton Group was returning to growth this half year, with a 7 per cent rise in sales and a 6 per cent rise in profits. The company had cut costs and prices, and the victories in court had also helped to silence the critics. The previous year, the business had successfully issued ten million new shares. The once-murky relationship with the family holding company had taken on a greater degree of transparency. Salomon Brothers had issued its 'buy' recommendation. Carlo Gilardi had returned to the company, this time as managing director.

The shares were traded on the Milan, Frankfurt, New York, Toronto and SEAQ exchanges in London. This still left 71 per cent of Benetton Group in the hands of the four members of the family. The company was also forming new 100 per cent-owned subsidiaries to manufacture and distribute Benetton products in Portugal and Tunisia, and strengthening its stake in and control over the business in Brazil. Luciano was shortly to pay another visit to Japan, where Benetton was selling its interest in four local marketing companies and increasing its stake in and control over the Japanese business. Benetton was also opening in Pakistan.

At home, the second half of the Scarpas' new two-part automated plant had opened at Castrette di Villorba. These unique plants were and are the only ones of their kind in the world, designed and built with no internal columns and with a suspension structure that feeds the strain of supporting the roof back into a central reinforced concrete frame. The cost was US$130 million; although Gilberto had calculated Benetton could have saved 20 per cent of its labour costs simply by moving to Spain, the commercial rationale was simple. It was impossible to automate clothes assembly, which was still done by the army of sub-contractors scattered across the Veneto. It was, however, possible to automate design, cutting, dyeing, packing and dispatching. This would reduce dependence on high local labour costs and avoid both moving to France and the commercially uncertain – and politically unsound – practice of American clothing giants. Like global nomads, they migrated from one bloc of cheap, often child labour to the next, in politically dubious countries such as Bangladesh, Malaysia, the Philippines and Indonesia.

The two new plants at Castrette di Villorba only employed 640 people, yet turned out 80 million pairs of jeans, skirts, shirts and cotton garments per year. Luciano said the decision to build them was 'both philosophical and practical. It was a calculated risk, but in our view it still makes sense to manufacture in Europe if you use the most advanced technology. I like the idea,' he added, 'of keeping a European manufacturing centre, because it keeps the technology going. I see it as an act of faith in the future.'

Edizione was again growing in size and diversity. The family 'strong box' by this time owned 130 companies, of which only 29 per cent of the biggest, Benetton Group, with a turnover of US$1.6 billion, was publicly quoted. In addition to 71 per cent of Benetton Group, in order of size, these holdings included 100 per cent of Benetton Sportsystem and, within this, again in order of size, Nordica; the American brands Rollerblade and Prince; Kastle, Asolo and Killer Loop. They included 50 per cent of GS–Euromercato supermarkets and 60 per cent of the newly privatised Autogrill highway restaurants and the Ciao chain. Edizione was at the forefront of the tendering process for investment in the privatisations that were transforming Italy. Gilberto and the family holding company were also in talks with the state authorities about bringing the expertise they had acquired in Autogrill, Ciao and GS–Euromercato to the running of retail services at airports, on more highways and on the railways.

'What would have happened if my father was still alive? I am convinced that things would have been very different.' Luciano, Gilberto, Giuliana and Carlo Benetton. REX FEATURES

The Villa Minelli: a childhood dream come true. BENETTON

The early images were striking, but they contained little hint of what was to come. BENETTON

Toscani and his circus come to town: the first peaceful shooting in living memory in Corleone.

EUGENIO BARBERA

Giuliana in her design studio. 'You always say, "If you could make more."' And she always did.

REX FEATURES

*The 'Sunflowers' campaign. The
critics cried exploitation, but
something in the wild man reached
out to these children of a lesser god.*
BENETTON

Man versus half-man, half-computer? Ayrton Senna takes the lead from Schumacher at Imola. Shortly afterwards he was dead, and his secrets died with him. CORBIS

For the sake of a fraction of a second's advantage. Near-tragedy in the pit lane at Hockenheim. POPPERFOTO

The 'known soldier' – or was he?
Either way, the image-making was
running away from the business, and
the brand was going out of control.
BENETTON

Luciano and the Benetton family in
the straitjacket of creative 'madness',
by Toscani. BENETTON

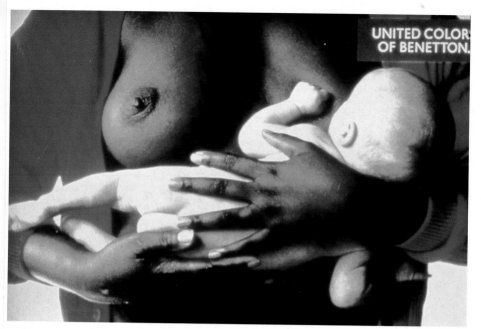

Perhaps Toscani's finest hour – yet while this image won awards across Europe, it was pulled from billboards in the United States. BENETTON

United in shadows and silence. In wartime, race, creed and age count for nothing and death is the only winner. ADVERTISING ARCHIVES

UNITED COLORS OF BENETTON.

'Love, the underlying reason for all life.' This image of tenderness prompted condemnation in the United States and riots in Europe; it also won prizes – and real-life nuns wrote asking for copies. SYGMA

Baby Giusy's first moments of life. Her mother had even offered to pay Toscani for his services, but the immediate results were blank hoardings and empty double-page spreads. BENETTON

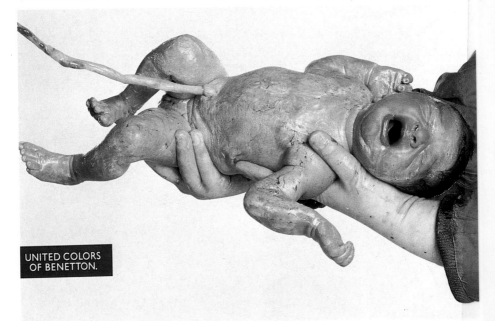

UNITED COLORS OF BENETTON.

Edizione Holding by this time also included 75 per cent of 21 Investimenti, the investment company headed by Alessandro with interests in companies making olive oil, coffee, ice cream and hydromassage baths, and 100 per cent of United Optical spectacle frames. They included 85 per cent of Di Varese shoes; 100 per cent of Verde Sport; 100 per cent of Edizione property, which owned commercial and non-industrial properties, including the ranches in Patagonia, the Buffalo Ranch in Somerville, Texas; and 1 per cent of Banca Commerciale Italiana and others.

Benetton Group may have been the public flagship business but it was only the ninetieth largest company in Italy; Edizione, the private, all-powerful holding company, was the sixteenth largest in the country. The aggregate sales of the 130 Edizione companies, led by Benetton Group, were worth no less than US$6.4 billion. Edizione, moreover, was still 100 per cent owned by four people. Luciano, Giuliana, Gilberto and Carlo were dollar and sterling billionaires. Of the four high-ceilinged offices in the wings of the Villa Minelli, all of them decorated with magnificent frescoes, Gilberto's was the only one with giants painted on the wall.

Edizione, through Nordica, was about to increase its stake in Rollerblade to 90 per cent in a leveraged deal that would leave Goldman Sachs with the remaining 10 per cent. In parallel with the development of United Colors of Benetton, Sisley and 012, Gilberto saw Sportsystem as the way forward to growth in America. Gilberto planned to float Rollerblade on the New York stock exchange, a move he intended as a prelude to the flotation in New York and possibly London of Benetton Sportsystem. In a gesture of confidence in Toscani, his images were to be extended beyond Benetton Group and used for the first global advertising campaign for Sportsystem. Aldo Palmeri, meanwhile, with whom Toscani had clashed the previous year, again left the company in an amicable parting. Palmeri was succeeded as managing director of Benetton Group – the only non-family member to bear the title, which was simultaneously held by Luciano and Gilberto – by his protégé and long-time colleague, Carlo Gilardi.

The four billionaires on the board of Edizione would soon be joined by Alessandro in his capacity as head of the family's private venture capital arm, 21 Investimenti. Alessandro had started up the company with his friend and fellow London resident and scion of an Italian business dynasty, Andrea Bonomi. In addition to their investments in olive oil, coffee, ice cream and hydromassage, Alessandro had come close to buying Lotus, the struggling sports car maker. Negotiations had collapsed, although there was still talk of taking a minority stake. Alessandro went shopping closer to home instead and bought into a local TV station, which he renamed Milan 6.

Alessandro's cousin, Stefano, who had died in the car accident in California ten years earlier, was commemorated in the latest addition to the La Ghirada and Palaverde sports complexes that Gilberto had established as a very public private gift from the family to their home town. This was the La Ghirada Centre for Sports Documentation, a library and resource centre dedicated to the memory of Stefano Benetton, complete with a vividly coloured cyber-room called Net Surfer Land, where young visitors could enter the world of sporting information via the La Ghirada website. As many as 3,000 children and young people came here to these sports complexes every day in summer. Entrance was free, but there was sponsorship from businesses as well as Benetton, and a shop selling products made by Benetton Sportsystem. The atmosphere here was youthful and idealistic, light years away from the cynicism and greed that masqueraded as the 'entertainment' that was Formula 1. Nevertheless, a hard truth was here for those who chose to look, perhaps one that recalled the fact that sport had been one of the few forms of relaxation available to the family's own teenage years. The motto of the Chicago Bulls hung over the door of the volleyball complex: 'Only the strong survive'.

Catena di Villorba, the Veneto, 1995

Luciano pulled a folding chair into the garden and set it up by the shallow, reflecting water. He sat here in the sunlight for a moment in silence and then said, 'It's beautiful, isn't it? You've got to admit it . . . it really is beautiful.'

Toscani's friend, the Japanese architect Tadeo Ando, had transformed this L-shaped farmhouse with a simplicity of style that recalled and exceeded that of the house the Scarpas had designed for Luciano and Teresa. The courtyard was squared off by a concrete path lined with concrete columns that ended without a horizontal and seemed to hold up the sky. The lake was only three inches deep, yet in its stillness it gave off a perfect reflection of the roofs and colonnades. The purity and innocence of this place were compounded by the silence, by the plain pine doors and oval windows and hallways, and by the lack of people.

This was Fabrica, the 'electronic Bauhaus' as Toscani had christened it, conceived by him and Luciano. Toscani had devised the first Fabrica image of a black man with differently coloured eyes, and saw the school as 'a challenge, a school like any other', a place 'capable of seeing the future through those eyes'. Now, Luciano was unveiling Fabrica to select members of the press.

There had been commotions behind this tranquil scene, worthy of any grove of academe; about the role desired by Toscani, about who was to administer this place, and about the cost. Members of the media and *culturati* professed not to understand why Benetton should want to spend a rumoured US$20 million on a turnkey arts school, far from New York City or London or Paris, here between the vineyards and the cornfields of the Veneto, and yet apparently expect nothing in return. Fabrica provoked and unsettled these graduates of straighter schools in the media and so they offered nothing in return, dismissing it variously as a rich man's whimsy, a plaything of a bored businessman and a manifestation of Toscani at his most hubristic. All these things may have been true, but were not the whole story. Behind Fabrica was also a shrewd business intention and the fact that this was the school this thinking billionaire never had.

Luciano was a youthful sixty years old and his casual clothes, mass of grey hair and gold, round-rimmed glasses gave him the air of a professor for the new millennium. He had no plans to retire, but he had plans for this place, just as he had for the Benetton Foundation. He would later say:

These places are not just a cost, there are economic and practical things at work here. When you have wealth, it is good to pay some attention to creating research facilities like these. They can be a stimulus to us here in the business. They can offer objective judgements on the less successful aspects of what we are doing.

At the time the latest carefully selected journalist had sat on a chair next to him amid the Zen-like calm of the colonnades and Ando's lake. She herself was multi-lingual and well educated. She had listened politely and gone away to write yet another article rubbishing a rich man's fancy.

Luciano had sat by the lake and politely answered her questions. She asked him what would be left of Benetton thirty years hence. As she chose to report their conversation, his reply was surprising. 'The school,' this ambitious, ultra-pragmatic businessman is implausibly claimed to have told her. 'There will always be the school.'

Enstone, Oxfordshire, England, 1995

Luciano's son Alessandro had retained his passion for motor racing, tried and failed to buy Lotus, and taken his father's place as the family frontman for the Benetton racing team. The previous season had ended with Schumacher's first world championship amid circumstances of controversy of precisely the kind that the team's sponsor, Benetton Sportsystem, did not want. Briatore, nevertheless, had kept his position and survived to fight another season, with the help of Schumacher, the courageous Johnny Herbert as his teammate and the new Renault engine.

The results had been spectacular for the team and both drivers. Schumacher had won in Brazil and Spain, where Herbert had come second; he had won in Monaco and France; and Herbert had won in Britain. Schumacher had won in Germany and Belgium, but had been given a one-race ban for rough tactics after the latter race. In spite of the Renault engine, he was having to drive more closely, it seemed, to the edge. Herbert had scored a delirious win in Italy. Schumacher had won the Grand Prix of Europe in Germany and again at Aida and Suzuka. The world championship double, for driver and constructor, had gone to Schumacher and Benetton, with Herbert fourth in the drivers' world championship. These twin victories had done much to expunge the shame of the previous season.

However, in a manner reminiscent of the way Briatore and Walkinshaw had poached Schumacher from the Jordan team, the German driver now accepted an even bigger inducement of US$38 million to leave Benetton for their arch rival, Ferrari. Tom Walkinshaw had also gone elsewhere, in his case to the Arrows team.

Briatore responded promptly by signing Jean Alesi from Ferrari. Alesi had come fifth in the drivers' world championship in the preceding two seasons and was an enormously popular figure among the drivers. Although a French resident, he was the son of Sicilian parents. Briatore was not entertained, however, when Alesi soon showed his true colours. After having signed with Benetton, Alesi made it clear that he was not in any circumstances prepared to drive except by the rule book. This may have partly been a desire on his part not to be tarnished with the suspicions that lingered about Schumacher; this was also a mark of Alesi the sportsman. Gilberto, who was by this time taking a closer look at the investment by Benetton Engineering that remained in the TWR group, would doubtless have nodded his approval.

Catena di Villorba, the Veneto, 1995

Toscani may have dreamed up Fabrica in an idealistic moment, and the school may have appeared in a haze of PR-speak about 'learning by doing'. The hidden agenda, however, was that Fabrica would eventually take on from Toscani the image-making role for the business and brand. Although he had more collaborators than he liked it to be known, even Toscani could not go on for ever, although he would have been the first to dispute this. However, as he would have been the first to point out, there was no one person who could step into his shoes.

The selection process for Fabrica initially discouraged direct applications and included recommendations from a network of top art schools, consultants and other informal, but informed sources. The emergence of an effective caste of alumni to take on Benetton's in-house communications strategy would eventually offset the cost of starting up here by bringing, as Luciano repeated, some kind of measurable commercial return.

Beyond Fabrica, and its first tentative short films and videos,

Benetton was undertaking a cultural and educational offensive. In Treviso, the Benetton Foundation was accumulating significant assets that would in time include scholarly publications about landscape, gardens and the history of the Veneto, the first social history of games, and a 50,000 book collection donated by Fernanda Pivano, the Italian translator of American 'beat' literature and poetry, to be housed in Milan. In France, a fundraising campaign was launched in conjunction with the anti-racist group SOS Racisme. In Italy, a similar campaign was launched in collaboration with the Association for Peace. In India, DCM Benetton India Limited launched an AIDS awareness campaign on public hoardings, in schools and in the media.

The most ambitious project, however, was still at the planning stage. 'The Colors of Peace' was a programme aimed at teachers and pupils in elementary schools in Italy, Germany, France, Belgium and Spain to promote better relations between different cultures. This programme would supply 130,000 schoolchildren and 16,000 teachers with inspirational books, exercise books and posters, on the Jesuitic principle that children of different nations, caught this young, might grow up to avoid the kind of prejudice and received opinions about each other that, fifty years after the end of the war, still characterised relations between Germany and Italy.

This was also a charm offensive, there was little doubt, but yet again there was a commercial underside to the idealistic gesture. India was and is one of the most protectionist of developing countries. DCM Benetton India was a joint venture with a local concern and had to pay attention to the local and national government, for whom the privately funded AIDS awareness campaign could also be a source of political capital. Again, it was no coincidence that France and Germany were the two countries in which Toscani's advertising had provoked the most violent reactions against Benetton, and, in this same year, had resulted in French and

German court judgements against Benetton for offending the sensibilities of HIV-infected people.

There was no rest for the family in the cause of the business and brand. Thirty minutes from Fabrica, in Ponzano, Toscani and Luciano had produced their spring and summer image. Luciano had been through the experiences of bereavement, parenthood twice over, first to his brothers and sister, then to his own children, and of divorce. He had been through romantic attraction and companionship and luxurious isolation. Now it was time to do madness. It was time to take the family, which had once hidden in fear of its life from the gaze of its own fellow citizens, to the main streets of the world.

10   A Town Called Corleone

Ponzano, the Veneto, 1996

This time Toscani had photographed the family, fifteen of them altogether, in a smiling group. The difference between this and other family groups was that everyone in this picture was also wearing a straitjacket.

The picture was intended to convey an image of 'offbeat, original entrepreneurial creativity', as the company put it, for dissemination through leading European daily newspapers. Europe was the part of the world in which the brand strategy had gone too far away from the brand and threatened to backfire. The implication of the picture was that this could not be anything other than a wholesome, hard-working family, whose last intention was to offend or shock. As

Luciano put it, 'The idea was to show a united family, and a family which, though it is not eccentric, is also not all that serious . . . and how a certain type of madness can produce great things.'

Although there were fifteen members of the immediate family in the picture, Luciano also took pains to emphasise that the strait-jackets did not imply a binding obligation for the family to join the business. 'The future of the firm does not depend on the presence of our children within it eternally,' he declared. 'If they want to prove themselves, and enter the firm, then they are welcome to make their career on their own merits. If they want to do something else, there is absolutely no pressure on them to enter Benetton.'

In addition to Luciano, Giuliana, Gilberto and Carlo, the picture showed eleven Benetton children. Luciano's sons Mauro and Alessandro worked in the business; his daughter, Rossella, worked with the Benetton Foundation. Giuliana's daughters Paola and Daniella worked in the business; her son, Carlo, was a financial con-sultant elsewhere. Gilberto's daughters, Sabrina and Barbara, were students, the former in Boston. Carlo's sons Massimo, Andrea and Christian were respectively studying in Venice, Urbino and Boston. Of the eleven children, five worked in or near the business. Three were in Benetton Group, one in 21 Investimenti, and one in the Foundation. Three people were missing from the picture: Giuliana's daughter Franca, Carlo's son Leone and Luciano's youngest son Rocco, who was working in the United States.

Toscani's *Colors* magazine had moved its editorial offices from New York to Paris and was edited by a twenty-five-year-old American based in Fresno, California, Alex Marashian. Marashian had com-plete editorial freedom and in the latest issue he had chosen to exercise this on the theme of 'war'. The pictures included a dead African with the top of his head blown off and a close-up of the mangled legs of a landmine victim. The cover bore the strapline

'Shopping, fashion, travel and genocide'. The anti-war message was conveyed with unprecedented ferocity in the graphic form in which *Colors* had distinguished itself as unique from other publications. *Colors* cost £2 and 350,000 copies were published through news stands around the world. The fact that the magazine, with these images of other people's suffering, was also on sale in Benetton shops led some aid agencies and war photographers to question whether or not this use of the horrors of war was compatible with the act of shopping in United Colors of Benetton or Sisley.

Toscani's spring and summer billboard campaign for United Colors of Benetton pursued a similarly visceral theme. An image of three human hearts, identical in colour but labelled differently according to race, loomed out of the billboards of the world. This image was also timed to coincide with the international 'SOS Racisme' congress, to mark the United Nations organisation's world anti-racism day, held with forty delegates from around the world at Fabrica.

Fabrica and *Colors* were still the wild elements in the Benetton image-making process and, in terms of their quality and originality, it was desirable that they should be so. For, unlike the carefully contrived publicity image of the family in straitjackets, this was where the true creative 'madness' lay. At the same time, however, these two elements were slowly and surely being pulled together under the same roof.

Benetton Sportsystem had already adopted Toscani's anti-racist imagery in its advertising. A new headquarters for Sportsystem was planned in a villa undergoing conversion near Ponzano. Gilberto was chairman of a group that had grown in only three years to employ 2,000 people and sell into over a hundred countries, with a turnover that was rapidly reaching half that of Benetton Group. In addition to the common advertising style, there were further links between the two companies. They operated as separate subsidiaries of Edizione, but following the purchase Sportsystem would use Benetton factories to make the knitwear for its Sportsystem Active range. The managing director of Benetton Sportsystem, Silvano Storer, estimated that the business was already seventh among the top sportswear firms in the world, after the likes of Nike, Adidas and Reebok. Unlike some of these businesses, however, Benetton Sportsystem was not excessively dependent on cheap labour in poor countries to keep down its manufacturing costs.

With Sportsystem sales about to hit the US$1 billion mark, Gilberto and Storer formally announced plans to float 30 per cent of Rollerblade on the New York and London stock exchanges. Rollerblade already accounted for 45 per cent of the world sales of in-line skates and sales were still rocketing. The flotation would recoup some of the investment that had taken them to a 90 per cent stake in the company and free up funds for further growth, particularly into 'soft' products such as sports clothing and shoes (skis, boots and racquets counted as 'hard' products). The ultimate aim, however, was to float not just part of Rollerblade but the entire Benetton Sportsystem group in New York and London the following summer.

In the event, this would not happen; a single, cash-rich buyer would buy Sportsystem from the family holding company and amalgamate it with a business and brand with which it was already closely linked. This time, the more transparent relationship between buyer and seller, and the monitoring of the deal by independent intermediaries, would satisfy even the fussiest of outside shareholders that the price was a fair one and not simply calculated to improve the buyer's balance sheet. Yet, in the months that led up to the deal, stories would again circulate in some quarters speculating as to where the buyer's money came from and, even, whether or not this buyer actually had any money at all.

London, England, 1996

The first, the golden age of innocence was over for Benetton in Britain's capital and in cities across the country. It was as if the passing of the Diana factor and the crisis for Benetton were two sides of the same coin. The Princess, who was once synonymous with Benetton, was estranged, hounded and haywire. Gap stood where Benetton had been in Hampstead High Street and on a string of similar sites across the country. Two of Benetton's biggest licensees had gone into liquidation within two weeks of each other. One had run some of the most prestigious stores in London and had collapsed with losses of £400,000. The other owed creditors, including Benetton, £200,000. Refurbishments had pushed up costs and delays had left the shop to open with the wrong season's stock. There had also been disputes between the agent and the licensees. On this occasion, however, there was no excessive advertising campaign at which to point the finger of blame, and other British store owners were increasing their orders by between 20 and 30 per cent. As Professor Zuccaro was also discovering at home in Italy, the difference between those who succeeded and those who did not was that the winners knew when the time had come to clean the network.

Ponzano, the Veneto, 1996

Professor Zuccaro was grappling with the phenomenon of the 'millennium bug', whereby the coming of the year 2000 would bring a digital apocalypse to the world's computer programmes. These were currently unable to handle the date beyond that point and they would simply cease to function. A meltdown of this kind would spell disaster for a business like Benetton, which relied on information technology across its operations and had long since employed more computer operators than seamstresses.

Professor Zuccaro wanted everyone to know that they should keep calm; he was on the case. 'Adjusting to the year 2000,' he declared, 'is a large-scale exercise in project management. In our case, it means converting six thousand programmes, corresponding to six million lines of code.'

The software already existed that would enable Benetton to beat the millennium bug and the business had accepted tenders from which it had chosen as partners Gruppo Engineering, with its 'Change Now 2000' solution. Gruppo Engineering already had an agreement with the Canadian company, Informission Group, to use their RECY2000 system, which was the choice of other large European companies. Professor Zuccaro had his own teams of his software engineers working overtime to tailor these solutions to the Benetton systems. He said:

Our basic choice is clear – a system for each company. All companies associated with Benetton Group must have a strong degree of independence to be able to respond in real time to the needs of a very fast-moving market. The progress over these past months has been rapid, both the tools and the contractual plans for the suppliers are now running smoothly, as are the occupational and inter-personnel contacts.

Professor Zuccaro and his colleague Giancarlo Chiodini had a little more than three and a half years in which to make it work. He and his teams had already finished, tested and installed the most immediately crucial systems, those dedicated to the sales and shipment of clothing. The next to be finished were the systems which linked the business with the agency network around the world. At the latest estimate, he was on course to finish this within eighteen months of the millennium. All this was strangely difficult to translate into the language of brand power; information technology might be the most critical element in the survival of a business, and yet even a company as skilled in communications as Benetton could not find a way to give this battle against a potentially apocalyptic scenario a public relations edge.

Patagonia, Argentina, 1996

Benetton was not merely the world's largest consumer of wool; by this time, through Edizione, the business also raised more sheep than anyone else in the world. The latest addition was a 165,000 hectare ranch, with 45,000 Merino crossbreeds. With the other ranches in Patagonia and Texas, the ranch and farm portfolio extended to nearly a million hectares. With 280,000 Benetton sheep and 7,000 shops around the world, this approximated to forty sheep per shop. Yet, in terms of wool, the million kilograms the Benetton sheep supplied each year were still only enough to supply the business with 10 per cent of its needs. Aldo Palmeri had once prophesied that every Benetton jumper would also contain a proportion of factoring, leasing and financial services. In the event, this had not come to pass; however, every sheep in Patagonia could count itself as part of a unique real estate portfolio that reached beyond the ranches there and in Texas to include the buildings housing flagship United Colors of Benetton stores in the United States, Germany and the Czech Republic. This real estate portfolio included the Scribner Building in New York City and, in Italy, the Hotel Monaco e Grand Canal in Venice and the Asolo Golf Club. In addition to these 280,000 sheep, two horses also found themselves on the receiving end of the reaction to the autumn and winter campaign.

Bnei Barak, Tel Aviv, Israel, 1996

In small towns, people tend to take the law into their own hands, and this was a small settlement where orthodox militants had appointed themselves the guardians of public decency. The posters had hardly gone up before the word went round and the white paint was brought to the offending site. Here, in a perverted version of the do-it-yourself spirit of the Zionist pioneers, the orthodox militants proceeded literally to obliterate the image of a black stallion from the United Colors of Benetton billboard. The stallion in question was in the act of mounting a white mare, the image of which the settlers left intact. This striking and surprisingly humorous picture of the two horses, with the undertones of racial harmony reminiscent of the image of the kissing priest and nun, was Toscani's autumn and winter campaign image for United Colors of Benetton. Toscani had not had to look far afield for his subject; he was the owner of the two horses in question.

Toscani's Gaza Strip catalogue had already inflamed local sensibilities and affronted Zionists in America. Elsewhere the conservative mayor of Nice in France also banned the black and white horses image, stating, bizarrely, 'The shocking and provocative presentation of coupling black and white horses is attempting to incite either racism, or human behaviour that is contrary to our republican values.' Toscani, meanwhile, decided to go to Israel to shoot more images. As long as people with reactionary agendas continued to behave in this manner, he reasoned, he had every justification in continuing to provoke them with images that 'speak to us of the spontaneity of nature, which is becoming more and more difficult to grasp in our artificial world, where nothing is what it appears to be.'

Toscani had been delivering a foal when Luciano Benetton had first called to tell him that they needed a global image. His next image would also be precisely what it appeared to be: a wooden spoon against a white background, which he devised as the official logo of the first World Food Summit of the United Nations Food and Agricultural Organisation.

Cleaning the network number 3, London, England, 1996

The first two sheep were yellow and blue and arrived by taxi. They were followed by a third, this time pink, which emerged from a pink convertible Cadillac. Luciano himself arrived shortly afterwards in a green taxi. He was wearing a brown jacket and dark trousers, with a green tie decorated with lambs jumping over stiles. It was raining.

This was the scene at the opening of the new Oxford Circus megastore, the largest Benetton shop in the world. The three-storey, 1,600 square metre store stocked a comprehensive range of United Colors of Benetton and Sisley men's and women's wear, the Undercolors underwear range, children's wear from the 012 and Zerotondo ranges, and a new line called 'Mamma of Benetton'. The elegant, curved, grade 2 listed building had been revamped by a team of British architects and interior designers co-ordinated by Tobia Scarpa. There were marble floors and moulded ceilings and Venetian chandeliers and a steel and maple staircase. There were video screens and DJ consoles and exhibition spaces. There were the sheep. There was Luciano with Magda, his interpreter, who gave him time to think. He was patient, he was courteous and he was exhausted. He kept glancing at the closed circuit TV screen that monitored the sales of clothes and accessories on the floor below. Then he flew on again, having satisfied himself that the network had been cleaned, the business reinvented, and the brand safely moved on from the days when leather-clad gay activists trashed the shops and the staff stayed up half the night folding the garments and putting them back on the shelves.

Cleaning the network number 4, New York City, United States of America, 1996

The megastore which opened in the Scribner Building on Fifth Avenue and Forty-eighth Street was marginally smaller than the one in London at 1,200 square metres. Again, there was a comprehensive range of United Colors of Benetton, Sisley, Undercolors, 012, Zerotondo and Mamma of Benetton plus a café and a bookshop. The Mayor of New York City himself had written to Luciano expressing his appreciation of the job Benetton, or rather Edizione, had made of restoring this fine building.

Again, too, the aim here was to go forward with smaller clusters of larger shops, catering for a more fashion-conscious and sophisticated clientele. Soon, Luciano reasoned, this new network of fewer, larger and more profitable shops would become a self-fulfilling prophecy. Countries anxious for Western-style consumer credentials, like Saudi Arabia, Brazil and Romania, would be able to award themselves accreditation in this respect simply by pointing to the presence of a Benetton megastore in their principal cities. This was why similar megastores were also under way in Jeddah, São Paulo and Bucharest.

The new issue of *Colors* magazine was entitled 'Get a job'. The images and texts included a stonebreaker in Bangladesh, a slaughterhouse worker in Germany, a sex educator in Ghana, a bodyguard in Palestine, a windshield washer in Italy and, in France, a worker at the Ludix erotic accessories factory in Saint-Denis, spraying the genitalia of a blow-up doll, using non-toxic, hypoallergenic paint.

In true *Colors* fashion, there were shocking jobs, humorous jobs, dangerous jobs, underpaid jobs that were essential and futile jobs that were overpaid. All the jobs shown here were legal, however, and when Toscani received a telephone call from a place synonymous with employment of a violent and illegal nature, at first even he thought it was a joke.

Corleone, Sicily, 1996

Giuseppe Cipriani was the new mayor of the town and the first to be elected specifically on an anti-corruption ticket. Cipriani was thirty-four years old, a lapsed communist, bespectacled and slightly built, with a shyness that endeared him to many people, but not to the Mafia.

Cipriani had received a message shortly after his election. A severed calf's head had been placed on the doorstep of his twenty-five-year-old girlfriend, Marinella Miceli. Anonymous, guttural voices had telephoned him and warned that his own head would be next.

The Corleonesi were the dominant force in the Sicilian Mafia. Luciano Liggio, head of the Corleone clan in the 1960s, had been a man who, in the words of one Mafioso, 'liked to kill. He had a way of looking at people that could frighten anyone, even us.' Salvatore 'Toto' Riina took over from Liggio, became the 'capo di tutti capi' or 'boss of bosses', and was currently on trial in Palermo, accused of ordering more than 150 killings, many of them committed by his own hands. These and other 'men of honour' had made billions of dollars out of narcotics and their power enabled them and their families to live openly in the area. Of the 181 known Mafia 'families', comprising 5,000 members living in Sicily, the Corleonesi were the most feared, and as many as 500 of their members were believed still to be living in Corleone.

Things had begun to change, however, after two killings that had shocked even Sicily and resounded around the country. These were the murders of two popular magistrates engaged in the anti-Mafia campaign. Giovanni Falcone and Paolo Borsellino were murdered in car bomb attacks allegedly at Riina's bidding and, in Corleone, the local population decided they had had enough. In a town where the Mafia had traditionally hired and fired the mayor, they backed Cipriani and his anti-Mafia ticket and elected him with 69 per cent of the vote.

The new mayor knew about Toscani and Benetton. He had seen the United Colors of Benetton 'reality' picture of the aftermath of the murder of Benedetto Grado. Cipriani eschewed bodyguards, walked around the town, sat on park benches talking to people and worked to restore a sense of post-Mafia ordinariness in the hearts and minds of his constituents. Cipriani may have been a local boy, one of five children of an agricultural worker, but he was a child of the global age. 'What we need,' he liked to say, 'is cultural change, a change of mentality. We need to be more dynamic. We need to be proud.' He had come to the conclusion that Corleone needed a new global image to replace that which had been created by movies like *The Godfather*. As Luciano Benetton had done, Cipriani had called Oliviero Toscani.

Toscani and his assistants had come here on a reconnaissance visit. This in itself would have been impossible a few years earlier, before the election of the new mayor, for it would have required the permission of the Mafia. The mayor, however, was not about to give Toscani carte blanche to add Corleone to the litany of shocking images in the cause of Benetton. On his first visit, Toscani had made a promise in return, 'not to sell a product, but to prevent people buying another, the Cosa Nostra'. The Cosa Nostra themselves had not been amused when one of Toscani's assistants had approached a pretty, blue-eyed girl in the street. They had proposed that she model for them, only to discover that she was the daughter of Salvatore Riina.

Toscani and his entourage had returned to Corleone and their project was to shoot the new spring and summer United Colors of Benetton catalogue with real models on the streets of the town. They had hired forty-eight young people for a day's work and a fee of £70 each. Dark-haired Sicilian beauties, of the kind Francis Ford Coppola would have kept cloistered behind the shutters, posed for Toscani in the clothes against a backdrop of peeling walls and balconies hung with washing. The people of Corleone peered at Toscani and his travelling circus of stylists, make-up artists and dressers as if they were from another world; which was what they were.

The town's tiny tourist office was requisitioned as a changing room. 'Just look at my daughter,' gasped one mother, as her fifteen-year-old was made over by a French hairdresser. 'I've never seen her look at herself in a mirror before. She's always such a wreck. It's wonderful to see her doing this, wonderful.' Toscani himself darted through the narrow streets, pursued by his entourage and by press photographers, at whom he fired periodic barrages of abuse and glanced from time to time to make sure they were still there. This was no mere fashion shoot, after all, but the testimony of 'symbolic witness to the cultural, moral and economic rebirth of Italy's Deep South'.

Later, after Toscani and the circus had left town, there would be questions about the value of the exercise. Benetton, after all, would not have ridden with such alacrity to the rescue of a town in the grip of halitosis or Alzheimer's disease. Yet, if the Mafia image was the hook on which the latest collection was to hang, was this not merely perpetuating the picture the mayor wanted to expunge in his post-Mafia world?

In short term the answer was, probably, yes. The media coverage of the event inevitably concentrated on the atmosphere of the hot, shabby, claustrophobic little town, with its impassive older citizens and its invisible but omnipresent 'men of honour'. The antics of a fashion shoot, however professional, were also an easy target for the cynical journalist. In the longer term, however, a precedent had been set insofar as a commercial venture had been undertaken of a legitimate nature, and in a very public fashion, over which the men of violence had equally conspicuously been unable to exercise any influence. By the time the two million copies of the sixty-eight-page spring and summer catalogue appeared in seven languages, the images it contained were of a shocking normality, preceded only by the briefest statement acknowledging a town and its young people 'refusing to bow to the weight of history, tradition and discrimination'. By this time, too, the mayor had been sufficiently encouraged to contact Fiat, the giant car maker, and Barilla, the pasta maker, with similar requests to include Corleone in their locations and offer entrepreneurial opportunities to its young people. 'How do you think it feels,' said one sixteen-year-old model for a day, 'when you go outside Sicily and you say to someone "I come from Corleone". They just sneer at you: "Son of a Mafia boss, are you?" You're branded from the start.'

Meanwhile, the mayor, Toscani and Benetton were all satisfied. 'They want publicity for their products,' Cipriani said, during a break in the shooting, 'and we want publicity for our cause. And the fact that he's here, and they're here,' he went on, gesturing at Toscani and the press who were pursuing him, 'means that we are getting what we wanted.'

This first peaceful shooting in living memory in Corleone also raised another question about the business and brand. This was the question that no one asked out loud and yet a tiny number asked in their minds. Were Benetton not just a family, but *the* Family?

This question was not only difficult to ask openly, but objectively impossible to answer. If it was true, no one, by definition, would admit this. What mattered was that the perception resurfaced from time to time, and this perception was used to explain other questions about the business that the people who espoused it could not otherwise be bothered to answer.

These questions included how Benetton Group had grown to be so successful, whether or not Luciano was party to the fraudulent bankruptcy of the Fiorucci clothing company, and who had put the bomb on Flavio Briatore's doorstep. The further away from the business, the more likely this perception was to be offered as an explanation for these things. It was occasionally to be found in the press: 'For starters,' commented one unsubstantiated piece, 'no one knows how Luciano Benetton came from nowhere to build up a global clothing empire . . . When the offices belong in a spaghetti western, you don't expect everything to add up.' Nor indeed did this statement, which belonged in a movie of the mythical Italy of spaghetti, bad red wine and mandolins.

The closer you came to the business, however, the faster this perception of Benetton as a manifestation of the mob evaporated like early-morning mist. Benetton Group, although the biggest, was only one of the 130 companies owned by Edizione. Edizione, not Benetton Group, was the yardstick by which the true worth of the family could and should be measured. Edizione and Benetton Group both published accounts, which were audited by experts and believed by analysts and shareholders. The fact that the majority of the companies were in private hands was not an indication of illicit private funding, but an example of a characteristically Italian desire to return control instead of surrendering it, first in part to institutional shareholders, and then altogether to another buyer, in the way so beloved of businessmen who dreamed ultimately of nothing more than retiring to Florida.

The mayor of Corleone, for his part, would hardly have called in

Benetton

Toscani and Benetton to help him if he had thought that they were part of the criminal organisation of which he was trying to rid the town and its people. Beyond Italy, all Italians were and are unfairly bracketed with the Mafia at some time or another. Yet inside Italy there are a hundred different countries lacking in effective central government, plagued by corruption, and in which the family and business are the only coherent social units. This is why Luciano himself had entered politics. 'I thought I could do something about the waste in public spending,' he had said. 'If you become a member of Parliament, you soon realise there's no ceiling to the amount of money they can spend – and people would be voted in to squander money in their voters' interests. It was a vicious circle.' He had neither gone into politics in order to further the interests of Benetton, nor left because Benetton was in trouble. 'It wasn't the business that suffered,' he said. 'I suffered.'

One Anglo–Italian businessman, close but not beholden to the Benetton family, said:

My family are from Naples, and I don't see a connection between Benetton and the Mafia. Why should there be? The carabinieri have broken the Mafia in Italy with changes in the law and the use of the gun. Yes, there was a 'dark' period when the business seemed to be growing very fast, without many visible assets, and that is the kind of vacuum into which the Mafia have often liked to step. But I am absolutely sure that they didn't.

The same source offered another explanation:

There is a culture which goes very deep in Italy, and which the likes of American investment banks don't always understand. It is a culture of who you know, and of using this knowledge. It may appear crooked, in the sense that it depends on who you

270

know, but it is also a defence against far greater crookedness. My family has been close to the Benettons for twenty years, via Citibank, which helped them to float, and which is one of the very few foreign investment banks to succeed in Italy. It is who you know, and how you use it.

If the reader still chooses to believe that Benetton are linked to – or are – the Mafia, there is nothing that this book can do to persuade them otherwise. They do not need to read further. But before they literally close the book on Benetton, they might consider one point. The families who practise organised crime in Italy have done so down the generations, having started from beginnings in an introverted, rural, southern atmosphere of poverty, violence and fear. The Benettons were the children of a small businessman in the politically independent and outward-looking industrial north. They had their own background of poverty, violence and fear in the years during and immediately after the Second World War. They had nothing else in common with the other, far poorer, more violent and more fearful equivalent many hundreds of miles away in the south.

Ponzano, the Veneto, 1996

The strategy of opening fewer, larger, new stores was beginning to pay off, both in terms of the growth in shipments to customers and sales reported back to Ponzano. Forty-five per cent of these sales were from autumn and winter collections, 35 per cent from spring and summer collections, and 20 per cent from 'flash' collections. In the new factory at Castrette, the overhead lines were carrying clothes made from Fabric 206, a new material that did not wrinkle and was suitable for the traveller. The new Robostore 2000 system was picking out and shipping up to ten million of these and other garments in a single month. There were fewer end-of-season stocks and more reorders. Benetton was also carrying out more detailed research into customer trends and paying higher agents' commissions as part of the process of cleaning the network; 350 new stores were scheduled to open in the coming year alone. There were also changes in the financial strategy of the business. The Cosmetics Group, with its short and turbulent history, had been reorganised and was in the process of being sold. The Japanese sales and distribution companies had been sold as part of the reorganisation of Benetton Group in Japan. At the end of the year, Benetton Group would be left with a substantial cash surplus for the first time in its history, and it would be time to go shopping.

The new issue of *Colors* explored the theme of 'Shopping for the Body'. The cover featured a pubic wig manufactured and sold in Japan, known as the 'Night Flower'.

'My grandfather made the first Night Flower fifty years ago, after the adolescent daughter of family friends committed suicide,' Takashi Iwasaki, President of Komachi Hair Company, told *Colors*. 'She had no body hair, and when she reached marriageable age, knowing she could no longer conceal this, she killed herself.' Komachi sold Night Flower mainly to schoolgirls and brides. 'Our best month is June, and the bridal season,' he told *Colors*, 'but we also sell a lot in spring and early fall, when the students go on class trips and the girls have to bathe together.' Komachi explained that, for many customers, the Night Flower was a means of passing through a difficult stage in their psychological development. 'Eventually, they're able to do without the wig altogether,' he concluded. The latest issue of *Colors* also included features on bionic arms, silicone ears and personal hygiene at home and on the road.

*

Alessandro Benetton and his 21 Investimenti group were also shopping. After the near-purchase of Lotus cars, and the stake in the Milan TV station, Alessandro and his fellow venture capitalist, Andrea Bonomi, were using their 21 Investimenti vehicle to buy into businesses in Europe. These already included the British company Johnson Radley, the country's largest producer of moulds for the glass industry; Karrimor International, which made outdoor clothing and equipment, and for whose traditionally staid shops they planned a radical make over; and the Spanish carton maker, Picking Pack. 21 Investimenti's latest purchase was a stake in Basic Group, which manufactured and marketed sports and casual wear for Europe and Japan, and which was looking to grow and penetrate the United States, South America, Africa and China. Alessandro was currently looking to buy into the eyewear business in Italy and America.

One of Alessandro's indirect business activities, however, had been curtailed after his uncle Gilberto had run his eye over the figures. This was Benetton Engineering Limited, which owned a 50 per cent stake in Tom Walkinshaw's TWR group. Gilberto was unimpressed by this investment. As he tersely put it in the Benetton Group annual report:

> The inclusion of this company within the scope of the consolidation would have distorted the consolidated financial statements to the point where they would not have provided a true and fair view of the financial and operating position of the Group.

Benetton International was selling Benetton Engineering with its 50 per cent stake in TWR back to Tom Walkinshaw; this was an investment which had gone out of the Benetton coffers and into a company that was too far away from the core business. The sale price of £16 million suggested just how large this investment had been, and how long it had remained in TWR after Walkinshaw had withdrawn any investment he might have made from the Benetton team. As Gilberto would recall: 'We thought it would be of use to us in Formula 1; but it wasn't.'

Enstone, Oxfordshire, England, 1996

This was a trying season for Flavio Briatore and Benetton Formula. Walkinshaw had bought into the Arrows team. He was still making lofty statements about his former partnership with Briatore. 'When I took over Benetton, it was a shambles,' he declared, 'but we made it a good and competitive team.' Walkinshaw's protégé, technical director Ross Brawn, had followed Schumacher to Ferrari. Jean Alesi and Benetton had failed to win a single race this season and the team had therefore failed to win the performance-related bonuses from their main sponsor, Mild Seven, with whom their contract was to expire in eighteen months' time. Alesi was rumoured to be talking to the Jordan team from whom Benetton had poached Schumacher five years earlier. Alessandro Nannini, whose arm had been successfully reattached after his helicopter accident, had been promised a test drive with Benetton, but this would not lead to a place in the team. Alesi and Briatore agreed that the Frenchman of Sicilian parentage would remain as lead driver for the coming season, partnered by the former Benetton driver, Gerhard Berger.

Alessandro Benetton remained as family frontman for the time being in the role first filled by his father. Gilberto Benetton, however, had not stopped with the sale of Benetton Engineering and its stake in TWR; he was taking a long, hard look at the future of Benetton in Formula 1.

Ponzano, the Veneto, 1997

Toscani had also been motoring; he had been involved on the way to Ponzano in a hundred-car motorway pile-up. He had climbed out of his Mercedes, which was undamaged, helped some young people out of their crumpled hatchback and then, unfazed, taken several rolls of film before driving on again.

Toscani was looking at the processed pictures on the lawn of the Villa Minelli. The afternoon light was beginning to fade. The roofs of the nearby office buildings, which were designed to change colour with the weather, were turning pink and mauve in the afternoon sun. 'There were four young people in there,' he said, pointing to the crashed car. 'The girls started to scream. It was a Francis Bacon kind of thing, you know? There you are, in the middle of an artistic happening. Incredible. It looks like a Greek tragedy. A modern Greek tragedy. A modern tragedy.' He paused for a moment. 'Okay,' he shouted, 'let's do the streakers!'

If an artist was one who could hold two opposing points of view at the same time and still function perfectly, Toscani was the artist supreme. He had come here to shoot the autumn and winter United Colors of Benetton catalogue, again, as he had done in Corleone six months earlier, using 'real' models. This was why Toscani's casting director, Brice Compagnon, had selected the models from Benetton's headquarters staff. This was why Toscani was photographing the kitchen staff in woollen hats. This was why three members of the design team were strutting towards him down a corridor with their jackets and jeans undone to reveal lacy underwear, while Toscani backed down the corridor firing his motorised Nikon at them and singing 'Hey, Big Spender'. This was why Gilberto, the most conventionally good looking but also the most reticent of the three brothers, was wearing a giant pair of denim trousers. This was why Luciano was standing against the outside wall of his office in the Villa Minelli wearing a red jumper, his hair coloured with green vegetable dye. And this was why – although he later feared it made him look ridiculous – Luciano was apparently happy to pose like this. 'People are taking notice of what is happening,' he said, 'and that is good.'

Melbourne, Australia, 1997

In the first Grand Prix of the new season, the refuelling controversy again erupted, albeit at the opposite extreme. Alesi, in spite of repeated warnings from Briatore that his contract would otherwise be terminated, ignored six attempts by the Benetton team to persuade him to come into the pits to refuel, even when Briatore had the two largest members of the team lean over the wall and gesticulate at him to do so. Alesi had carried on driving and run out of petrol. Berger had finished fourth. Former Benetton driver Martin Brundle, a commentator for British television, advised Alesi on air to go straight from his car to the airport.

Alesi and Berger fared better in the next race in Brazil, where Berger came second and Alesi sixth, but less well in Argentina, where Alesi was seventh and Berger sixth. In the San Marino Grand Prix at Imola, Alesi was fifth and Berger spun out. In Monaco, Alesi had been the one to spin out and Berger had finished a lowly ninth.

Briatore was becoming rattled. Alesi and Berger were cornering him in the Benetton motor home after races and demanding better cars. Alesi was still in talks with Jordan, to whom he would offer his services for just US$1 million, a lowly figure by the bloated standards of Formula 1, but an indication of his love of driving. Briatore, meanwhile, was trying to negotiate the purchase of the new US$20 million Mecachrome engine before Renault withdrew their engines from Formula 1 at the end of this season. 'When you have a good result, everyone is easy to talk to,' he said, wearily. 'All winter the car was good in testing. We never had a problem until we came racing.' Unknown as yet to Luciano and Gilberto, he was also trying to sell the team itself, in spite of the fact that in the strictest sense the team was not his to sell.

'This is not a job for ever,' he went on quietly. 'There is a lot of pressure, testing, racing, with no time for yourself.' The glamour seemed to be wearing off for the man who liked to be photographed in dark glasses with celebrities and surround himself with pretty girls. 'You find out inside yourself whether or not you have the motivation. Normally, to go on in this business, you need a championship. I already have that, and a constructor's championship'. He concluded, 'The moment I feel the motivation go I will give the job to somebody else. This business always causes pressure, but, at this moment, it is still fun. We are working on these things. In Canada, we will have a much better set-up for the car.'

Mild Seven had already removed their logo from the cars in Britain, France and Germany in line with the ban on tobacco advertising there. David Mills, a millionaire London solicitor and offshore tax specialist who was consultant to the Benetton racing team, had resigned his job a few days after the British government announced the ban. Mills cited as his reason a conflict of interest; his wife, Tessa Jowell, was Minister for Health. The motor racing authorities subsequently successfully lobbied the British government into a U-turn over the ban.

Briatore himself had not been a chain smoker, but he was becoming one. In Canada, Alesi raced hard to come second, while Berger retired. By the time of the Italian Grand Prix, Benetton would be locked in another legal battle with Jordan, this time over who would secure the services in the coming season of the brilliant and diminutive new talent, Giancarlo Fisichella. By this time, too, Briatore would no longer be in the driving seat.

Cleaning the network number 5, Enstone, England, 1997

Alesi and Berger drove the rest of the season knowing that they were going to be succeeded by Fisichella and Alexander Wurz. Briatore did not last this long. By the time of the Luxembourg Grand Prix he was gone. He had already bought the Ligier team while he was still manager of Benetton Formula and sold this after a couple of seasons; he was also known to be setting up a leisure club in Sardinia. Nevertheless, only a year later he would be sighted back at Benetton headquarters in Ponzano, this time in his capacity as salesman for the Mecachrome engine.

The new manager of Benetton Formula was David Richards, a trained accountant and head of the Prodrive engineering company. Richards had hoped to persuade Gilberto that Benetton Formula and Prodrive should merge, a deal which would have made him millions. He had set off for Ponzano confident that he would succeed, only to be charmed out of this by the Benettons and persuaded to content himself with a salary of US$1 million a year. Richards had made a conspicuous success of the Subaru rally team and had a sponsorship agreement with BAT, the tobacco giant, which he was well positioned to bring to Benetton after the expiry of their deal with Mild Seven. BAT and Richards were also talking about the tobacco company taking a stake in the Benetton team.

Alessandro had officially handled the negotiations with Richards and Prodrive, but, in addition to his professional advisers, he had done so under the eye of his Uncle Gilberto. Gilberto had decreed that they should dispose of Benetton Engineering and its stake in TWR; he had subjected Briatore and his business affairs to closer scrutiny; he had cleaned the network.

Alessandro, for his part, had acted with integrity and dignity throughout the storm surrounding the Benetton team. For all his charm and hard-working mentality, and his years with Goldman

Sachs, Alessandro perhaps lacked education in the school of hard knocks, which was hardly surprising and not to be held against him. He was joined in his capacity as president of Benetton Formula – and as Luciano's eyes and ears – not by a seasoned street fighter, but by a person who has hitherto barely featured in this story. This was the person who did not work in the business and had been among those missing from the 'straitjacket' picture of the family the previous year. The new commercial director of Benetton Formula was Alessandro's younger brother, Luciano's youngest son, twenty-seven-year-old Rocco Benetton.

With the team in the safe hands of Richards and under the ultimate control of Benetton Group, this time they could afford to instal a relative innocent as family front man. 'You need someone like Richards to run a team in Formula 1,' commented one source close to the team, 'someone who will keep the engineers from spending too much money, make the PR people work and keep the drivers happy. It's an impossible job, on the surface of it.' Within a year, it seemed Richards was in agreement with the latter point. In 1998, he would resign to pursue his Formula 1 ambitions elsewhere. This left the youthful Rocco not merely as family front man, but *de facto* manager of the Benetton Formula 1 team.

11　The Main Streets of the World

Yangon, Myanmar, 1997

Luciano and his party flew in on one of the three private jets that belonged to the business and checked into the Inya Lake Hotel. From here, they took a cruise up the Irawaddy aboard the former Rhine river steamer, *Road to Mandalay*.

The Benetton agent for Myanmar (formerly Burma) came here every two or three months from Italy. He had local contacts, but he was something of an unknown quantity to the Burmese expatriate business community, who liked to regard themselves as being at the cutting edge of business practice. Luciano had come to see for himself.

Aung San Suu Kyi, the Nobel peace prize-winning campaigner for democracy in this country, had called for developed countries to boycott the military government with economic sanctions. Two Burmese comedians had been arrested after a show in which they made irreverent remarks about the military, charged with offences against public order and sentenced to seven years in a labour camp. Luciano's own politics were pragmatic and slightly left of centre, and he still had hopes that one day Fidel Castro might at least pay a visit to Fabrica. However, he saw no contradiction between the multi-racial, egalitarian image of United Colors of Benetton and the idea of doing business here in a country ruled by force. 'It would be impossible,' he said later, of the suggestion that there should be an economic boycott. 'Our relationship is with a local businessman who wants to do business with us and import our products. It is independent of everything else.' He might have said the same of Saudi Arabia and Syria, two more countries of doubtful political hue, where United Colors of Benetton could also be found on the main streets of the principal cities. A few weeks later, meanwhile, he would at last fly to Sarajevo where the war was over and the board had given its consent for him to observe the extent of the peace dividend for the business there.

Fifth Avenue, New York City, United States of America, 1997

Eighty-five years after Scribner's had opened up here as one of the country's most genteel publishers, and eight years after Edizione had bought the Beaux Arts building it was back in the literary business. This was the launch of 'The Salon', a bimonthly series of literary readings and arts discussions that would take place in the new basement café. Carlos Tunioli was Benetton's director of US operations. 'We wanted to configure it to sell clothes,' he declared, 'but also to retain the feel of an early 1900s bookstore.'

The combined megastore, cafeteria, bookstore and arts and cultural centre was kicking off a season of 'cutting-edge artistic and literary salons with major writers and opinion-makers'. There were readings by Mercury recording artist Maggie Estep, author of the upcoming *Diary of an Emotional Idiot*; Joel Rose, author of *Kill Kill Faster Faster*, and Daphne Merkin, author of *Dreaming of Hitler*. Many of these were authors of the 'youthful, provocative and edgy' series of books published by Crown, who were also co-organisers of The Salon. There was a panel discussion on the Whitney Museum's Biennal. In the café, Benetton and the Rizzoli bookselling chain were engaged in an experimental venture to sell books on fashion, exercise, grooming, health and fiction: 'In other words, books that appeal to young women with active lifestyles,' said Rizzoli's John Brancati.

This was a long way from the days when consumer trends were measured by whether or not a dollar difference in price was the difference between Benetton and Gap, for customers in search of a sweater. Many people were deceived, however, by the fact that Gap had nearly doubled the number of its shops across the USA during the same period that the number of Benetton shops had fallen by more than half. Benetton's turnover in the States was bigger now than it had been when it had twice the number of shops across the country. The Salon was not just a manifestation of this turnaround, but its beneficiary, and Benetton benefited in return from the public relations value of this association. There was nothing, on the other hand, to link Gap with heavyweights of the calibre of F. Scott Fitzgerald, Hemingway and Thomas Wolfe.

Elsewhere, on the main streets of the world, Benetton formed an alliance with Inditex, one of Spain's largest garment manufacturers and distributors, with a network of directly operated stores in Spain and other parts of Europe. The aim was to form a joint-venture company to market clothes bearing the 'Zara' label in a new network of stores in Italy. In Moscow, a wholly owned subsidiary called 'Benest' was formed to promote the Benetton image in Russia. In Paris, the latest issue of *Colors* was published; this was entitled 'Marriage'.

Rue des Archives, Paris, France, 1997

Colors had reached its twentieth issue and was distinguished by a vitality and originality that might even have impressed Aldo Palmeri. The editorial staff, designers and contributors were drawn from dozens of countries scattered around the world, with the editorial offices in Paris. 'Marriage' was, as ever, informative to a comprehensive degree, with items on legal gay weddings, shopping for a bride, underwater ceremonies, hymen restoration, murdering your partner, divorce and the consequences of remaining unmarried on life expectancy.

Even the editorial staff were unsure as to how many copies of *Colors* were printed, but this exceeded 350,000 in seven bilingual editions (English paired with French, German, Spanish, Italian, Croatian, Slovenian and Korean) in over sixty countries. Now, after twenty issues and five years of peripatetic existence, the editorial offices were leaving Paris and coming home. Like Fabrica, Toscani called the shots but the family controlled the purse strings. *Colors*, too, was being pulled closer into the centre of the business and brand.

Florence, northern Italy, 1997

In a vast railway shed on the edge of the city, a crowd of journalists were staring up at the cavernous ceiling space in which were hanging

hundreds of images of the faces of teenagers. Toscani had photographed these over the preceding two or three years, recruiting
them from the streets of Paris. The faces were identically shot in full
face and in close up against a white background, and enlarged to
bleed out to the edges of the picture. This had the disconcerting
effect of reducing the presence of the photographer and the viewer
virtually to nothing. There were boys, girls, rich kids, street rats,
black and white. This was 'Faces', the new autumn and winter campaign for United Colors of Benetton.

Luciano and Toscani sat side by side in the railway shed and
answered questions. 'Do you ever think about giving up making
clothes, and just making images?' one member of the press asked
Luciano.

According to the press reports, Luciano seemed startled by this,
and replied quickly: 'No. The conditions of the market, the difficul-
ties of our competitors; this is what makes me feel alive.' Later, he
would insist that no one had ever asked him such a question, and
that his 'answer' was equally fictitious. 'What I would say,' he added,
'is that when the market is difficult, it's a challenge. Moments of
crisis are moments of opportunity.' Either way, his responses, true or
false, reflected the unspoken but unquestionable linkage between
the business and the brand that existed in his own mind; a linkage
that he was determined should continue to operate subliminally in
the minds of the public.

Toscani, for his part, seemed to be feeling the pressure that came
from having to keep ahead of the competition. 'Other companies
have been catching up,' he said. 'We want to underline that we were
doing all this from the start.'

Luciano and Toscani were deliberately launching this campaign in
a building that was anathema to the traditional Renaissance image of
Florence. They were talking in a developed market to people who
knew what Toscani meant when he said things like 'The editorial is

the advertising of the advertising'. Elsewhere, however, there were new markets that had no free media and no free media coverage to be provoked through the calculated use of controversial advertising imagery. Like the first My Market shops thirty years earlier, the new megastores in Saudi Arabia and the twenty-eight new stores in Syria were shop windows for the business and brand in a medialess part of the world. This was one of the reasons why Benetton had recreated the main streets of this world beneath the lawns in Ponzano.

The Shopping Street, Ponzano, the Veneto, 1997

Here, beneath the lawns, is an underground street, lit by artificial light and lined with the range of shops. All the shops are Benetton shops and they run the length of both sides of the street. The Shopping Street, as they call it, is the ultimate statement of ambition for the business and brand.

This main street of a town undergoes changes of lighting that alter its appearance throughout the 'day'. At 'night', although it may be midday above ground and the height of summer, the street is dark and the windows of United Colors of Benetton, of Mega Benetton, Blue Family, Benetton Man, Benetton Woman, Sisley and 012 shine out under a black sky studded with stars.

Six times a year, plus a number of 'flash' collections throughout the year, these shops are screened from general view, and the street is raised into a stage for the presentation of new collections to eighty agents and area managers from around the world. These include long-standing agents from the United States, Europe and Japan, such as the extraordinary seventy-year-old Mrs Suzuki – who personally prepared Luciano's meals when he visited her in Japan, only after testing them on her friends first – as well as agents from new territories such as Mr Merchant from Pakistan. One agent alone may cover more than one country – Sweden and Finland, for example. Another may be one of several agents for a single, large country such as Germany. They have come here for a presentation which is in most cases taking place nine months in advance of the actual selling season, and for the thousands of foreign shop owners the wholesale prices of the collections are set at fixed exchange rates covered by Benetton's bankers. The 'real' models are from the American military bases of Aviano and Vicenza, from Paris, and from around Ponzano and Treviso.

The presentation starts, the models appear, disappear and reappear in the clothes and the agents go home again to the United States, Canada, Japan, Germany, Britain, France, Syria, India, Brazil, to hire venues and present the collection to their store owners. The store owners make their orders through the agents and the clothes are sold; only then will they actually be made and dispatched to the stores.

The marketing and promotions catalogue will also be dispatched to the stores, with photographs by Toscani and an introduction by Mauro Benetton. The catalogue contains examples of the merchandising material and confidential hints to store owners about sales techniques: how to prevent regular customers from waiting until the end of the season to buy at reduced prices; how to sell slow-moving stock without waiting for the end-of-season sale; and how to entice customers looking for sale items to visit the store more frequently and so buy more clothes at the full price.

The company recommends the retail prices, but the store owners are free to adjust them. The clothes will go on sale and the store owners will report back their sales. Luciano and his team will analyse the results and convey these to Giuliana and her 200 computer-aided designers who create 8,000 styles a year and are working on the next collection. Others are working on the next presentation, and so the cycle goes on. It is thirty years, and a long way, from the time when Pierro Marchiorello called Luciano with an urgent request for more stock and Luciano and Carlo drove up to Cortina with a car full of jumpers.

Ponzano, the Veneto, 1997

Benetton Group had also been shopping; this time, it had bought Benetton Sportsystem. The former had bought just under 60 per cent of the latter, with the opportunity to purchase the remainder by the spring of the coming year. Gilardi would recall:

> The sporting image suited us and it also suited the casual wear and leisure manufacturing sector which we are in. Furthermore, it would have been ridiculous for Sportsystem to go ahead without any synergy from us. it had been nice to have a sister company with effective Chinese walls between us, but stupid in practical terms . . . like two ships sailing to the same destination in different directions.

Negotiations were tough between Gilardi, managing director of Benetton Group, the buyer, and the seller, the managing director of Edizione, Gianni Mion. Gilardi would explain:

> One part of the group was buying from another, so we had to be seen to ensure fair play. This was a really crucial element. We had to be very public about this transaction. In fact it was an awful deal to begin with, and the battle was on between me and Mr Mion. We get along fine; this was business.

Both sides appointed merchant banks to handle the valuation and fix what was thought to be a fair price. Gilardi eventually persuaded

Mion to accept a lower price for the second tranche of the shares than originally agreed. His strategy was to pay a lot for the advice, but less than he might have done for the business. 'Mr Mion was a little disappointed,' he recalled, 'when only a month later Adidas purchased a similar company for a lot more money.'

The plan to float first Rollerblade, then the entire Sportsystem division, on the New York and London stock exchanges had been rendered unnecessary by the cash-rich status of Benetton Group and the desire of the business to invest in an acquisition that was close to home and not a foreign company that would depend for its success on local managers. Flotation would have raised the cash to recoup the purchase costs of Nordica, Rollerblade, et al., fund future growth and handsomely reward the family shareholders in Edizione, but this would have been at the price of surrendering control to more outside shareholders. The purchase by Benetton Group of Sportsystem raised the cash, kept control within the family and made Benetton Group bigger and better able to grow, particularly in the United States.

Benetton Group also made a bond issue on the Luxembourg stock exchange and appointed a German banker, Ulrich Weiss of Deutsche Bank, to the board of directors. Weiss was an English speaker, which Gilardi felt was important, and a respected figure in the field of corporate governance towards which Benetton Group, like all European companies, was being pulled slowly but surely by European Union directives. Gilardi was looking for more directors with international experience to join the Benetton Group board.

Benetton Sportsystem had become part of the Benetton business and the plan was to develop the existing brands and new sportswear lines in parallel with United Colors of Benetton, Sisley and 012. These stores, however, were generally considered too small to carry the sportswear collections and these would be sold through traditional sports retailers, with 'corners' in larger sports stores and a new, dedicated chain of sportswear megastores, initially to open in Italy. The renovation of the Villa Loredan, which would be the new head-quarters of the sports equipment and clothing brands, was nearing completion nearby. Another local building, in this case a former Relais et Château restaurant, was also undergoing conversion into an eighty-room guest house for visitors to the new and expanded Benetton Group, complete with helicopter pad; part of this guest house, however, was also expected to recoup its investment by running on a profit-making basis.

Sportsystem was currently making a loss as a result of the down-turn in business in the United States, Japan and the Far East, a factor which had helped Carlo Gilardi negotiate the reduction on the agreed price of the second tranche. As a result, new management was carrying out sweeping changes. Rollerblade's operations were moved to Prince's facilities in New Jersey; the ski boots and in-line skates would henceforth be made at the Nordica plant in northern Italy; the manufacturing of Kastle skis was almost entirely sub-contracted to third parties in Italy, with the remainder sub-contracted to manufacturers in Eastern Europe and the Far East. The smaller brands, such as Asolo and Kastle, were considered for possible disposal or inclusion into different distribution networks.

The analysts and institutions, always a mixed blessing to a 'public family company' as Gilardi liked to call Benetton, watched these moves and made approving noises; after all, the share price of Benetton Group had risen by as much as 300 per cent at times in the last few years. The family had also concluded that the name of Benetton Sportsystem should disappear on the grounds that it diluted the brand power of the business that was closest to Luciano's heart. As Luciano would put it: 'The old name was too much linked to the name of Benetton.' They would keep the existing brand names such as Nordica, Prince, Killer Loop and Rollerblade, and had devised a new name for a new range of Benetton sportswear that would be linked to all these brands. They called this simply 'Playlife'.

Benetton

Hebron, the West Bank, Israel, 1997

The family had appointed a German to the board of Benetton Group, but Toscani was sending out discordant messages to the German TV crew who had been following him around Israel and the occupied territories, asking awkward questions, quite possibly deliberately, at times when he was least disposed to answer.

'Mr Toscani,' the German camera operator yelled, just as Toscani was setting up his next shot, 'two years ago you went to Gaza and took pictures of young Palestinians looking happy and well-dressed in their Benetton outfits. Anyone who has been to Gaza knows that in reality the people are poor and miserable. Aren't your pictures a very cynical way of selling T-shirts?'

Toscani turned on the camera operator with a look of unstinting hatred. 'I think you should stop sitting in your armchairs and watching TV,' he spat, 'and complaining how cynical other people are. You should look at the mirror, not the TV. Then you'd realise how disgusting you are,' he concluded, with a loud guffaw of laughter and went back to setting up his shot.

Toscani had come back to the Middle East to shoot 'Enemies', the coming spring and summer catalogue for United Colors of Benetton. His catch-phrase themes of equal rights and inter-racial harmony were running into trouble here, which may have exacerbated his short temper towards the camera crew, who in this case simply happened to be German. Towards the Italian crew, however, who were following him in an official capacity, he was endlessly considerate and went so far as to help them capture the best angle of him at work.

The work itself was to compile an inspiring story of ordinary Jews and Palestinians overcoming their religious and political differences through everyday contact. In Tel Aviv, Toscani had shot three students, two Jews and an Arab, sharing an apartment. He had shot a Jewish man who bought his newspaper every week at a Palestinian news stand. He had shot several Arabs willingly submitting to a close shave with an open razor from a Jewish barber. So far, so good. Here in Hebron, however, the place bristled with heavily armed Israeli 'settlers' who hated Palestinians. Toscani had had to fake the shot he was setting up of two women friends, one Israeli and one Palestinian, bringing in an Israeli–American news photographer and a Palestinian colleague working for an American news agency.

Now the Germans were giving him grief. Toscani decided to shoot them, too, casting them in the role of the gutter press. 'Hey, you, get in the picture!' he yelled, manhandling them into the shot. 'You've been breaking my balls all day, now get in the picture. No, not the woman over there, you're too pretty. The press is ugly, UGLY!'

Then Toscani and his circus were gone, moving on, back to Jerusalem in a cloud of dust from their convoy of four-wheel drives. They left behind them two communities still divided by the high, barbed-wire fence that stood between the old Arab town and the new Israeli settlement. In the old souk, the shopkeepers complained that this band of visitors had taken their pictures without giving so much as a cent in return in the form of a purchase. Toscani himself was unrepentant and probably dreaming of his home and horses back in Golden Valley. 'I came here to capture an image of two friends,' he said. 'I'm not interested in the rest. That's for journalists. I'm not a journalist. I see the world in a different way.'

A few minutes earlier, however, he had taken a different line. Then he might have been Luciano, answering uncomfortable questions about doing business in a country like Myanmar. 'Companies are the new churches,' he had declared. 'It is only through their input that problems can be solved. Most of them prefer to remain detached. But the economy is the key to progress in the modern world.'

The economy was certainly providing global citizenry opportunities for Toscani and his entourage. After Jerusalem, they flew out of the Middle East and back to Paris, Venice and Ponzano. The spring and summer catalogue would come and go and the circus would move on to the location for autumn and winter. Even the morally elastic Toscani, however, might have felt a twinge of discomfort at the fact that this one would present a comforting and entirely specious image of peaceful co-existence to shoppers in more fortunate parts of the Arab world whose governments paid lip service to the plight of the Palestinians, but privately did nothing to ease their misery. This catalogue would go down well in the stores in Syria and the megastores in Saudi Arabia.

London, England, 1997

Benetton condoms had been manufactured by Okamoto Industries Inc. and sold for some years in Japan, one of the world's most densely crowded and expensive countries, and hence one of the biggest markets for prophylactics. In Europe, too, safe sex would henceforth bear the name of the family, the business and the brand. These were the new United Condoms of Benetton.

The new Benetton condoms would be available in four varieties: Colours, Exotica, Skin Thin and XL in packets of six, designed, after a market survey, to minimise embarrassment at points of sale. They would also be on sale in Benetton stores. They were manufactured under licence by the Australian multinational, Ansell International, which was to latex products what Benetton was to knitwear. Ansell, in addition to several brands of condom, made latex gloves for householders, industrial, medical and dental use. After the launch here, the plan was to introduce the United Condoms of Benetton into France, Denmark, Greece, Russia and Turkey.

La Ghirada, Treviso, the Veneto, 1997

Playlife was devised as the brand and slogan to convey the new clothes for the Benetton Group sports and leisure philosophy. This brought it within the image-making influence of Toscani, who had returned from the heat and dust of Palestine and come to the local sports complex to shoot the pictures for the first Playlife calendar.

Toscani would select twenty-four images from the four-day shoot, two of which would feature on each month of the calendar. This time, real models played themselves, as well as modelling the clothes. Fisichella and Wurz, the two new Benetton Formula 1 drivers, posed with models wearing mechanics' overalls. The Benetton and Sisley rugby and volleyball teams, both of which were frequent national champions, featured in the pictures. Each month was dedicated to a sport in which Benetton marketed the clothes, the equipment and the brand, from Formula 1 to motorcycling, skiing, rollerblading, tennis and snowboarding.

The calendar was big and glossy, but there was nothing new about a big, glossy calendar, so this one would be even bigger than usual. It would be printed in a limited, numbered edition, and billed not merely as a calendar but as a 'global communications vehicle'. This was an expensive free corporate gift for the walls of executive offices, for rarefied rooms, hushed except for the murmur of fax machines and lit by computer screens; a far cry from the heaving mass of the rugby scrum and the shouts of the volleyball court.

Catena di Villorba, the Veneto, 1997

The tranquil, depopulated place where Luciano had sat amid the Zen-like calm of the lake and the pillars that held up the sky had changed; this was a place where things were happening. Fabrica had students, twenty-two of them, a scruffy, affectedly unshaven and crop-headed crew, in contrast to Gilberto's clean-cut basketball and rugby players a few kilometres away. They came from many countries, from the United States, Argentina, Germany, Spain, Wales, Ireland, England, recruited by Fabrica's Chantal Prod'Hom, and given ten days' probation followed by three months to a year's free housing, food and transport.

This generosity was also a dangerous temptation. Carlo Spoldi, a painter and former employee of Saatchi & Saatchi, was the head of graphics here. Spoldi was thinking of introducing compulsory morning karate lessons for the students to combat their innate tendency to indolence, a tendency that was compounded by the dreamy atmosphere of this place and the soporific summer heat of the Veneto. Spoldi was also wondering whether or not the students, although they were all under twenty-five years old, were already 'polluted by conventionality'; perhaps they should lower the maximum age to twenty.

The students, meanwhile, were demonstrating their ability to produce in a fashion worthy of the industrial phenomenon that was responsible for bringing them here in the first place. They had made sixteen videos about drink-driving, which had been broadcast on the local TV station, Channel 5; five videos about racism for MTV Europe, which also sold the advertising space for *Colors*; and designed a new logo and campaign for the Food and Agriculture Organisation of the United Nations. One student from Milan was working on images for Playlife. In the music department, another, from New England, had composed a tune for Bic razors. There were plans for Fabrica books and a Fabrica band.

Fabrica was a contemporary version of the further education Luciano had never had. Journalists who had had the advantage of a greater education than him came to inspect the set-up and went away so often to write it off as a rich man's fantasy. Yet there was an underlying commercial edge to this place, with its probationary period and threat of karate lessons; an awareness of the bottom line, which journalists so often chose to ignore. Although, as Laura Pollini said: 'The idea of Fabrica is a laboratory for the communication of the future,' there was a hard-nosed component in its potential to take on from where Toscani and his team would one day have to leave off.

Elisabetta Prando had been with the communications side of Benetton for a long time. She had edited *SOS Racism*, the collected edition of thoughts from the conference held at Fabrica the previous year. 'Fabrica is first and foremost idealistic,' she said, 'but there are deadlines.' *Colors* had just come home here to its first permanent headquarters to be edited by a Fabrica 'graduate'. The forthcoming issue was entitled, simply, 'Death'. 'I am looking forward to that,' said Elisabetta Prando.

The word 'franchise' is derived from the French, meaning 'freedom from servitude'. McDonald's and Coca-Cola were the biggest and best-known global franchises, yet neither had a leading-edge communications school, with a hard-edged commercial agenda below an idealistic façade. This alone was Luciano's creation, and this distinguished the school from a rich man's fantasy, in the same way that the brand power of Benetton distinguished the business from these traditional franchisers. Yet, long after this place had opened, even Luciano's local newspaper was still calling him 'the McDonald's of knitwear'.

12   The Family

London, England, 1998

oscani was here to talk about 'Death', the new edition of
Colors which had just hit the news stands of the world. The
contents included nuggets of information about the cause, definition, meaning and implications of death around the world, and
advice on how to prepare for death, according to the country in
which you might be killed accidentally, murdered, commit suicide or
expire from natural causes. The magazine also contained the familiar, product-free advertisements for Sisley and United Colors of
Benetton, and one for Diesel: 'Over ten styles of legwear, eight
weights of cloth, twenty-four different washes. Everything from
streaky to sandblasted. They're not your first jeans, but they could
be your last. At least you'll leave a beautiful corpse.'

Toscani was enthusing about how no one else was prepared to advertise in this latest issue: 'Death is probably the last pornographic issue,' he declared. 'We talk about sex. But death has a kind of pornographic mystery.

'This is not advertising,' he insisted. 'A company like Benetton has to invest in research. Sony has to invest in technical research, but, at Benetton, technical research as such is not a big investment.' Luciano, when he became aware of this last remark, would privately 'clarify' this point with Toscani, pointing out that Benetton did in fact make a significant investment in technical research. Meanwhile, Toscani ploughed blissfully on.

A sweater has two sleeves, wool is wool. A company like this must be intelligent enough to invest in communications research, because it is the communications that will make the added value to the product in the future. The product is more or less the same. The difference is the communications. I hope we sell a lot of sweaters so that we can make the magazine. Luciano hopes so too. Benetton is doing advertising for *Colors*, not vice versa.

He was talking about Luciano. 'Historically, a lot of art was publicity. In the Church, for example, Renaissance artists worked for the Pope. We all work for the Pope,' he mused. 'There is always a Pope somewhere.'

Toscani liked to mock Luciano whenever he caught the latter wearing a tie; this time, however, he was wearing one himself. Then he was off again to the next interview and the next flight back to Milan, and from there to Paris and home again. The spring and summer 'Enemies' campaign was soon to be launched. Toscani would shortly shoot the images for the autumn and winter catalogue, amid conditions of great secrecy, at the St Valentin Institute for disabled children at Ruhpolding in the Bavarian Alps in Germany. He may have been a wild man, but the untamed part of him would break through to these children and they would recognise in Toscani, the monster of unconsidered articulacy, something in return. The results would be a set of pictures which communicated happiness through the obstacle of 'handicap' which even Carlo Gilardi and the men in suits would acknowledge was a work of art. The next issue of *Colors* meanwhile was also in preparation. This time the theme would be 'Fat'. However pornographic they tried to make this, however, the advertisers did not seem to mind; the magazine had already sold space to Caterpillar, Hugo Boss, Benelli, the Body Shop and to Fabrica.

Jeddah, Saudi Arabia, 1998

Alexander Wurz, one of the two new drivers for the Benetton racing team, was here to open the newest megastore on Tahlia Street, one of the main shopping streets of the city. The new store carried the full range of United Colors of Benetton, Sisley, 012, Zerotondo, Undercolors and Mamma at Benetton, in addition to accessories and footwear. At 1,300 square metres, this was the second largest Benetton shop in the world after London.

The agent for the Middle East was Francesco della Barba, who had been the first vice-president of Benetton in America. The Benetton network in the Gulf was approaching 200 stores, all of these shop windows for the business and brand in a traditionally medialess part of the world. Although the public relations strategy tactfully stressed the sophistication of the Gulf and Middle Eastern consumer, the most sophisticated of these had been accustomed for more than two decades to spending their oil wealth in the high fashion houses of New York City, London and Paris. The growth of Benetton on this side of the Gulf was in reality a response to the emergence of a

Middle Eastern middle class. Things were changing here, albeit slowly, with the first sporting competitions openly held for women about to take place in Qatar. To be the first and the biggest on the main streets of this part of the world was to ensure in the short term at least a lead on the competition that would inevitably follow for the attention of a new, sophisticated, middle-class consumer. However, on the other side of the Gulf, Francesco della Barba and a resourceful – some might say foolhardy – partner were taking Benetton on to the main streets of the world's 'pariah' nations.

Baghdad, Iraq, 1998

Ahmad Samha was a survivor in a region of oppressors and victims, and as such perhaps the most entrepreneurial yet of the long line of 'collaborators with an entrepreneurial sense' as Laura Pollini called them, that had begun with Piero Marchiorello in the 1960s. Samha was a quiet, slightly built man, and lacked obvious political connections in a part of the world where these were regarded as essential to success in business; and yet he was successful. A native of Syria, like Luciano he had worked out of school hours from an early age; at fifteen, he had left school altogether to work full-time on the four sewing machines he had bought with his savings. By the time Francesco della Barba and Benetton came to Syria in search of a franchisee in the mid-1990s, Samha owned a factory exporting clothes to Europe. He knew how to work the system. He knew the local shopkeepers and facilitated Benetton's expansion into Syria by signing up sub-franchises for individual stores. Samha and his company, Amal – Arabic for 'hope' – had built up a chain of thirty-two Benetton stores in Syria, all of which he supplied in a joint venture with Benetton from his own factory. The rich minority desperate for Western fashions unavailable in the dimly lit bazaars had flooded to the bright, clean Benetton shops advertised by posters featuring happy foreign faces in Aleppo and Damascus. This was a limited market, however, and with around 400,000 items sold a year, Samha believed it had reached saturation point.

Now Samha and Benetton were bringing the same shops and happy foreign faces to the mean, miserable streets of the capital of one of the vilest and most hated regimes on earth. Here, amid the peanut hawkers and chicken vendors, another rich minority stepped out of their Mercedes and headed for the opening of the latest Benetton megastore. This was the so-called Iraqi élite, united like their Syrian counterparts by their familial and political closeness to the Iraqi regime, and by their desire for linen suits, plaid shirts and designer jeans. As they flooded into the new store, one of only two in the country, Ahmad Samha had the opportunity to examine at close quarters the exclusive customer base which he hoped would provide the solution to the saturation of his home market.

Samha already had plans to take Benetton into further 'pariah' nations, including Algeria and Iran. Meanwhile, he was gratified to see here at the opening that one customer alone was purchasing over 150 articles from the United Colors of Benetton range. Her ability to so do, however, did not signal the onset of the liberation of the Iraqi people through Western consumer goods; it may even have carried a hint of the emperor's new clothes. Her survival was dependent more than that of almost anyone else upon the survival of the monstrous regime in question, for she was none other than the wife of Saddam Hussein.

New York City, United States of America, 1998

The opening in Jeddah made the superstore on Fifth Avenue the third largest in the world. At the lower end of Manhattan Island, in another landmark building, a new kind of spokesman was launching the newest spring and summer campaign for United Colors of Benetton. This was a continuation of the series of faces, this time of children from all around the world, and this time launched by a UN spokesman as part of the collaboration between Benetton and the United Nations.

This was the fiftieth anniversary year of the Declaration of Human Rights, approved by the United Nations General Assembly on 10 December 1948. The rationale for both parties was clear cut: both the UN and Benetton needed greater brand awareness, and the UN had acknowledged that Benetton was one of the few companies in the world with the inclination, the budget and the credibility to make an investment in communications on this scale and of this kind. Benetton was also unique in its connection with the UN, which went back to the visit by the UNESCO official to Toscani's Paris studio and the first 'United Colors' campaign thirteen years earlier in 1985.

The United Colors of Benetton/United Nations campaign, in addition to the billboards, buses and bus shelters of the United States and Canada, also featured in the superstores, stores and newspapers in the United States, Canada, Britain, Japan, Germany, Australia, Austria, Korea, Denmark, Finland, France, Hong Kong, Ireland, Italy, Norway, Portugal, Spain and Sweden. In addition to the imagery, the spring and summer catalogue went out to shops around the world, featuring the clothes as modelled by the Arab and Israeli inhabitants of Jerusalem and the West Bank. The eighty-page *Colors* magazine 'Enemies', published in association with *Newsweek*, carried the collection with an introduction by Luciano.

Luciano, in spite of, or perhaps because of, the difficult circumstances of its making, described the catalogue as a 'testimony to peace'. He went on to reprise the sentiments behind the 'known soldier' campaign that had misfired so badly four years earlier.

'Conflicts aside,' he wrote, 'people want to live, buy and sell, fall in love . . . there's a world where bombs scatter death among ordinary people; sometimes when they're out running one of the most ordinary errands, like shopping.' This statement, although true insofar as it reflected Benetton's presence in Sarajevo and Baghdad, pragmatically ignored the fact that Baghdad was subject to a United Nations trade embargo. As such, this statement would be interpreted in some quarters as a manifestation of a profound cynicism that used the language of humanitarian sentiment to disguise a venality of purpose, even though the wording was in keeping with the sentiments of Benetton's partner in the preceding joint exercise, the United Nations.

On the main streets of experimental and controversial markets like Jeddah, Damascus and Baghdad, Benetton and its agents and local partners had targeted an exclusive and relatively affluent minority in order to carry the business into the new places on which it depended for its growth, and ultimately its survival. These new markets were by definition volatile, and although the immediate business risk lay with the shop owners, the risk also existed in a potential decline of demand for the clothes and products manufactured in and exported from Italy. In Korea, the Far Eastern recession continued to decimate Benetton shop revenues, but the effect on Ponzano was minimal. In Russia, panic buying at the plunging rouble emptied the shelves of the twenty Benetton shops there, but Luciano's response again reflected the calculated risk, hedged by Benetton's much-vaunted flexible manufacturing capability, that he knew they ran by being there in the first place. 'Now we have to see if the Russian stores can keep paying for their supplies,' he said.

Nevertheless, the business still had to keep on growing. In the United States, this meant continuing to open fewer but larger stores across the country, and at the same time extending the target from the affluent minority to the cost-conscious mass market. Benetton needed a partner in the latter enterprise, and found one in Sears, the nationwide chain of department stores. As of July 1999, in 450 Sears stores across America, there would be 1,800 'Benetton USA' corners selling a new, basic clothing brand designed for the American market.

This was the latest twist in the story that had begun with Luciano's first, eye-opening one-man visit to America nearly three decades earlier and had continued through the first cluster of shops in New York City and the unexpected runaway success of a single rugby polo. It had continued with the first 'All the Colors' campaign and its successors, the phenomenal growth of the late 1980s, the recession that followed and the rethink that led to the cleaning of the network. It was nearly two decades since a single Benetton corner in Macy's had opened and closed after only six months. Since that time, and in addition to the network of individual shops and stores, nearly 300 Benetton 'shops in stores' and sports goods concessions had opened across America. Benetton had the prestigious Scribner Building on Fifth Avenue, and Luciano himself had been awarded a Laurea Honoris Causa in law from Boston University. Benetton Basket even had two former players, Vinny del Negro of the San Antonio Spurs and Toni Kukoc of the Chicago Bulls, in the NBA. Yet middle America was a mountain still to be conquered, and they were only on the middle slopes. Sears was the base for the final assault. This time, Luciano was hoping he had found the partner to take them to the top.

Rome, Italy, 1998

Giancarlo Fisichella, a Roman and the other new driver for the Benetton team, was here to open the newest megastore. Like the others in New York City, Jeddah, Leipzig and London, and the mega-stores that would shortly open in Milan, Berlin and Tokyo, this one carried the full range from United Colors of Benetton to Mamma of Benetton. Fisichella, Wurz and the new Benetton–Playlife team were coming good this season. Fisichella was a tiny man, more like a jockey than a racing driver; the cars, for their part, had grown bigger and bigger over the fifteen years since Benetton had first entered Formula 1. A few kilometres away from the factory at Ponzano, an anonymous garage housed the entire collection of Benetton Formula 1 cars, from Michele Alboreto's Tyrrell to Fisichella's Benetton.

This newest megastore was laid out on three floors of a distin-guished piece of real estate in the Piazza Venezia, an area of historical, commercial and cultural importance. There were lead-ing-edge consumer essentials; a hair salon for the under-twelves and a large aquarium visible from the ground floor. The megastore was open all day, seven days a week. The site was between the Via del Corso, the Quirinale, the Corso Vittorio Emmanuele, the Capitol and the Roman Forum, and was packed with people. Many of these were visiting the capital for the first time, just as Luciano had done thirty-eight years earlier. Thirty-eight years on, and just a few blocks away, near the old Jewish ghetto, there still stood a hand-ful of shops that were owned and operated by the Tagliacozzos, two of whom were now dead, where Luciano had once stood in wonder at a future he knew he had to take to the main streets of the world.

Ponzano, the Veneto, 1998

Benetton remained the key to the public perception of the family, the business and the brand, but Edizione was ever the strong-box. Gilberto had steadily and unobtrusively diversified the family-owned holding company to the point where sales of Benetton Group, although booming, accounted for less than half the overall revenues. Benetton Group had probably the biggest and most advanced manufacturing capacity of any clothing company in the world, but it did not own the 8,000 Benetton stores in 120 countries. Edizione, on the other hand, already owned hundreds of millions of dollars of real estate in New York City, Tokyo, Rome, Venice, Milan and Patagonia; the real estate, increasingly Italian government property destined for privatisation, and the service sectors in which this was located, was the way of the future.

Gilberto intended this future for the family holding company to include customer services not only on highways and at train stations, but also at airports, of which the biggest privatisation, Rome Airport, was scheduled to take place later in the year. Edizione had just taken a stake in Pirelli, one of the country's largest real estate groups, with whom Gilberto intended to bid for the Rome Airport privatisation. They were also targeting others, including the state-owned company that managed the country's main train stations. 'We decided to use our experience in retail as the basis for diversification,' Gilberto said. 'We realised that the service sector was lacking. And working with clients and consumers is our daily bread.'

Luciano, the architect of much of this retail experience, was fielding questions from reporters about the timing of the launch of the new Playlife range of sports clothing. The first dedicated Playlife store would open shortly, in Bologna; fifty more would follow soon across Europe. The immaculately renovated villa that served as the new Playlife headquarters featured a 4,000 square-metre subterranean workspace, including two life-size Playlife stores reminiscent of the Shopping Street at Ponzano. Like Benetton franchisees, Playlife agents and franchisees could come here to inspect the latest Playlife sports clothing, along with Rollerblade skates, Nordica ski boots and Killer Loop snowboards. But with another economic downturn underway, was this really the best time to enter a market already crowded with the likes of Ralph Lauren Polo and Tommy Hilfiger?

'In moments of confusion, good projects get even more attention,' Luciano told them. These words might, and perhaps should, have been inscribed above the front door of Fabrica. 'We know world markets,' he added. 'We know young taste, and young people who practise sports. It will be more than a product' – he was warming to his theme in the way he had done in the earliest days – 'it will be a way of seeing things. Beyond the product, we need to give a sensation of something different. We will create something around the brand.'

So, with all this diversification, did he still see himself as a clothing manufacturer?

'Yes,' he said, 'but maybe the next generation of Benettons won't.'

Treviso, the Veneto, 1998

The former Dellasiega shop in the town was no longer there, but there were still Dellasiegas in the local telephone listings. This was still a town of traditional shopkeepers, and of traditional shoppers. There were still plenty of women in fur coats of the kind who once came into the shop to be served by the young Luciano Benetton. There were also the discreet offices of Edizione Holding and 21 Investimenti, and the shops, United Colors of Benetton, Sisley and 012. On the opposite side of the Piazza Crispi from the United Colors of Benetton store, were the headquarters of the Benetton Foundation, with its burgeoning research facilities and associates. The director was still Luciano's boyhood friend, Nico

Luciani, curator of all this and much more, including the memories for which Luciano professed such little interest and yet which were so fundamental to his very being.

Luciano landed at Treviso Airport. He spent most of his time in the air, and when he was not aloft, he was shy and seemingly aloof with strangers. He was alone; alone in his life. He never seemed tired and he was always on the move. His face often seemed expressionless, but his eyes were moving all the time.

Luciano was driven by car from the airport to the Villa Minelli, from where the questions in the fax he had dictated in the sky over California had long since been answered. His office was in the right-hand wing of the buildings, adjacent to the main villa, next to that of the joint managing director, Carlo Gilardi, and opposite those of Gilberto and Carlo. He went home from here to the villa where he lived between Ponzano and Treviso, and he would soon be going back to the airport.

Less than a mile from the original factory, which was now Giuliana's design centre, still stood the futuristic concrete house which the Scarpas had designed and built for Luciano and Teresa. Their four children had lived there with their mother after Luciano had left. Then, one by one, they too had left home. Now Teresa lived on here alone, happily enough by all accounts, in the now modest-looking house 'fit for a modern merchant prince' in which her merchant prince had not lived for over twenty years. Many people who worked in the business did not even know that the house still existed or that she was still there.

In adulthood, the business for which Luciano had sacrificed his childhood had also taken the place of family, lovers and all but the smallest, closest circle of long-standing friends. To be alone was, to him, the ultimate in luxury, and also the ultimate price of success for Luciano Benetton.

Benetton

Ponzano, the Veneto, 1998

Benetton, owned and run by Luciano, Giuliana, Gilberto and Carlo, was the most successful and controversial family business and brand in the world. The Benettons also operated the world's most advanced clothing plant nearby at Castrette di Villorba. They had built the 190,000-square metre plant instead of closing down and going overseas in search of cheap labour at a time when they were competing with factories that paid only 10 per cent of the wages Benetton was paying. Many people had questioned the wisdom of this investment, as they always questioned everything about Benetton. Now, however, the other global clothing companies were being forced to move on again in search of new sources of cheap labour, and Benetton was still here. The automated distribution plant a few hundred yards away from here could dispatch 30,000 boxes of clothes a day, every day, to shops at the four corners of the earth. This distribution plant, with its whirring elevators and towering gantries, was and is unique in the industrialised world. They called this place the 'Big Charley'.

The imagery of United Colors was emblazoned on the walls of the Villa Minelli, the offices, the design centre, and the hoardings around the manufacturing plants and the perimeter of the site. Yet, beyond the United Colors, there were the black and white shadows of control, for only a handful of people actually worked there. Here, in Big Charley, the nucleus of the operation was a group of computer-controlled robots. There were three kinds of robot; three of the first kind, eleven of the second, and three of the third. The first kind of robot gave the second kind of robot a cardboard box, and the third kind showed the second where to put it in the stacking system. The second kind of robot put the boxes in the right place and then they pulled them off again, and the boxes were loaded for transport by train, truck, ship and air to Los Angeles, London, Crete,

Dublin and Sarajevo. Together, in action, the robots made an awesome sight.

These were the latterday children. These robots were willing to toil all hours, driven by hard work and self sacrifice in the cause of the onward progress and prosperity of the name of Benetton. The first kind was the father, the second was the child and the third was the mother. The real children called them 'the family'.

Source Notes

Prologue: The Family

Author conversations and visits to Ponzano, December 1997 and June 1998; Luciano Benetton and Andrea Lee, *Io e Miei Fratelli*, Sperling e Kupfer Editori, Milan, 1990.

1   Birth of A Salesman

Author conversations and visits to Badoere, Treviso and Ponzano, December 1997 and June 1998; *Treviso Lungo Il Sile*, Viarello, 1995; Guido Vergani, *The Sala Bianca: The Birth of Italian Fashion*, Electa, Milan, 1992; *Vogue USA*, 15.9.46; *Life*, 24.11.47; *The Nation*, 31.1.48;

Fortune, 1.1.54; Oliviero Toscani in the *European*, London, 3.2.95; *Independent*, London, 31.7.93; Luciano Benetton and Andrea Lee, *Io e Miei Fratelli* op. cit.; Paul Ginsborg, *A History of Contemporary Italy: Society and Politics 1943–1988*, Penguin, London, 1990; *Independent on Sunday*, London, 22.9.96; *Independent*, London, 28.9.96; *Telegraph Magazine*, London, 2.12.95; Norman Lewis, *The Honoured Society*, Penguin, London, 1967; *United Colors of Benetton*, INSEAD-CEDEP, Fontainebleau, 1996; Daniel Yergin, *The Prize*, Simon & Schuster, New York, 1990.

2   A Woman of Substance

Author conversations and visits to Ponzano and Treviso, December 1997 and June 1998; Luciano Benetton and Andrea Lee, *Io e Miei Fratelli*, op. cit.; *Sunday Express*, London, 23.11.86; *United Colors of Benetton*, INSEAD-CEDEP, op. cit.; *Sunday Express*, London, 20.9.87; *Independent*, London, 4.4.92; *Daily Mail*, London, 23.4.88; *Sunday Times*, London, 20.5.90; *Newsweek*, Washington, 22.8.83; *Time* magazine, Washington, 13.1.86; *Financial Times*, London, 24.5.86; *Business*, London, 11.87; *Independent on Sunday*, London, 22.9.96.

3   The Secret of the Itch

Author conversations and visits to Ponzano and Treviso, December 1997 and June 1998; *Sunday Express*, London, 23.11.86; *Daily Mail*, London, 20.9.91 and 23.4.88; Luciano Benetton and Andrea Lee, *Io e Miei Fratelli*, op. cit.; *United Colors of Benetton*, INSEAD-CEDEP, op. cit.; *Independent on Sunday*, London, 22.9.96; *Financial Times*, London, 16.12.81 and 24.10.83; *Sunday Times*, London, 20.5.90 and 12.6.94; *Newsweek*, Washington, 22.8.83; *Times*, London, 24.8.84;

European, London, 18–24.4.96; Luciano Benetton in *Brand Power*, New York University Press, New York, 1994.

4   Empire Building Without Stress

Author conversations and visits to Ponzano and Treviso, December 1997 and June 1998; Luciano Benetton and Andrea Lee, *Io e Miei Fratelli*, op. cit.; *Times*, London, 7.12.96; *Financial Times*, London, 16.12.81; *Sunday Times*, London, 17.5.87; Ginsborg, *A History of Contemporary Italy: Society and Politics 1943–1988*, op. cit.; *Verde Sport*, Benetton Group, Ponzano; *Newsweek*, Washington, 22.8.83; *United Colors of Benetton*, INSEAD-CEDEP, op. cit.; *Vanity Fair*, New York, 1.95.

5   The Fifth Avenue Franchise

Author conversations and visits to Ponzano and Treviso, December 1997 and June 1998; *Verde Sport*, Benetton Group, Ponzano; *United Colors of Benetton*, INSEAD-CEDEP, op. cit.; *Financial Times*, London, 24.10.83 and 9.5.89; Luciano Benetton and Andrea Lee, *Io e Miei Fratelli*, op. cit.; *Business*, London, 11.87; *Newsweek*, Washington, 22.8.83; *Global Vision: United Colors of Benetton*, Robundo Publishing Group, Japan/Benetton Group, Ponzano, 1993; *Independent*, London, 4.4.92 and 16.12.92.

6   United Colors of Benetton

Author conversations and visits to Ponzano, Treviso and Milan, December 1997 and June 1998; *United Colors of Benetton*, INSEAD-

CEDEP, op. cit.; *Global Vision*, 1993; *Independent*, London, 25.1.92; *Time* magazine, Washington, 13.1.86 and 27.7.87; *Financial Times*, London, 6.6.85; *Newsweek*, Washington, 26.8.86; Luciano Benetton and Andrea Lee, *Io e Miei Fratelli*, op. cit.; *Sunday Times*, London, 20.5.90; *Independent*, London, 13.6.92; *Business*, London, 11.87; *Daily Mail*, London, 27.4.87 and 2.3.92; *Publishers' Weekly*, New York, 31.3.97; *Verde Sport*, Benetton Group, Ponzano.

7   Latin Americans

Author conversations and visits to Ponzano and Treviso, December 1997 and June 1998; *Times*, London, 25.5.96; *Financial Times*, London, 9.5.89 and 7–8.7.90; *United Colors of Benetton*, INSEAD-CEDEP, op. cit.; *Sunday Times*, London, 12.1.89 and 20.5.90 and 26.1.92 and 25.5.97; *Today*, London, 22.3.89 and 27.3.93; *European*, London, 7–9.9.90 and 5–7.4.91; *Independent*, London, 13.6.92 and 4.9.94; Luciano Benetton and Andrea Lee, *Io e Miei Fratelli*, op. cit.; *Sky*, London, 5.91; *Global Vision*; Oliviero Toscani, Channel 4, 3.97.

8   The Emperor's New Clothes

Author conversations and visits to Ponzano and Treviso, December 1997 and June 1998; *Global Vision*; *United Colors of Benetton*, INSEAD-CEDEP, op. cit.; Marina Galanti in *PR Week*, London, 25.4.97; *Colors* Magazine issue number 1; *Verde Sport*, Benetton Group, Ponzano; *Independent*, London, 13.6.92; Benetton Group Annual Report 1996, Ponzano, 1996; *Financial Times*, London, 7.4.96; *Colors* magazine issues number 2 and 3; *Elle* magazine, Paris, 3.93; *Independent*, London, 20.6.93 and 31.7.93 and 15.9.93; *European*, London, 24–30.12.93 and 4.2.94; *Business Age*, London, 1.94; *Times*, London,

16.2.94; *Guardian*, London, 26.2.94; *Cosa C'Entra L'AIDS con i maglione?* ('What does AIDS have to do with knitwear?'), Mondadori, Milan, 1993; *Wall Street Journal Europe*, 20.4.94.

9 The Burning Brand

Author conversations and visits to Ponzano and Treviso, December 1997 and June 1998; *Sunday Business*, London, 30.6.96; *Independent*, London, 1.8.94 and 22.1.95; *Daily Telegraph*, London, 11.8.94; *Sunday Times*, London, 24.4.94 and 26.11.95; Edizione Holding Annual Report, 1996, Edizione, Treviso, 1996; *Business Age*, London, 1.94; *European*, London, 22.4.94 and 20.1.95; *Vanity Fair*, New York, 1.95; *Benetton par Toscani*, Musee D'Art Contemporain, Lausanne, Switzerland, 1995; *Toscani Al Muro: 10 anos de imagenes para United Colors of Benetton*, Museo de Arte Moderno, Mexico City, Mexico, 1995; *United Colors of Benetton*, INSEAD-CEDEP, op. cit.; *Guardian*, London, 11.2.95 and 21.9.96; *Marketing Week*, London, 3.2.95; Benetton Group Annual Report 1996, Benetton Group, Ponzano; *Verde Sport*, Benetton Group, Ponzano; *Independent on Sunday*, London, 3.11.96; *Telegraph Magazine*, London, 2.12.95; *Observer*, London, 16.3.97; *Los Angeles Times*, Los Angeles, 13.9.95.

10 A Town Called Corleone

Author conversations and visits to Ponzano and Treviso, December 1997 and June 1998; *Colors* magazine issue number 14; *Observer*, London, 18.2.96; *Vogue*, London, 4.96; Benetton Group Annual Report 1996; *Sunday Business*, London, 30.6.96; *Financial Times*, London, 7.4.96; *Sunday Times*, London, 29.9.96; Edizione Annual Report 1996; *Telegraph Magazine, London*, 2.12.95; *Times*, London

25.5.96; *United Colors of Benetton*, INSEAD-CEDEP, op. cit.; *Colors* issue number 17; *Elle*, Paris, 10.96; *Independent on Sunday*, London, 15.9.96; *Publishers' Weekly*, New York, 31.3.97; *Sunday Telegraph Magazine*, London, 10.11.96; *Financial Times*, London, 2–3.8.97; *European*, London, 14.11.96; *Colors* magazine issues number 18 and 19; *Sunday Business*, London, 15.12.96.

11   The Main Streets of the World

Author conversations and visits to Ponzano and Treviso, December 1997 and June 1998; Benetton Group Annual Report 1996 and Half-Year Report 1997, Benetton Group, Ponzano; *Colors* magazine issue number 20; *Sunday Times*, London, 25.5.97; *Independent*, London, 9.9.97; *Observer*, London, 16.3.97; *Guardian*, London, 28.7.97; *Independent on Sunday*, London, 12.10.97; *SOS Razzismo*, Fabrica/Feltrinelli, Milan, 1997; *La Reppublica*, Milan, 17.12.97; Credit Lyonnais Securities Europe, *Textiles: Italy*, London, May 1998; Giuberga Warburg, London and Milan, Italy, *Benetton Group*, May 1998.

12   The Family

Author conversations and visits to Ponzano and Treviso, December 1997 and June 1998; *Guardian*, London, 2.2.98; *The Economist*, London, 15.8.98; Reuters, Milan, 17.9.98; *Colors* magazine issue numbers 24, 25, 26, 27 and 28.

Index

NB: *Numbers are filed as though spelled out, e.g. 012 is filed under Z for zero. Italian surnames containing prefixes are filed under the prefix, e.g. della Barba, Francesco.*

Index

Index

Index

Index

Index

Index

Index